The Ghosts of Eden won the 2010 Waverton Good Read Award, given to the best first novel published in the previous twelve months by a British author. It was shortlisted for the 2011 International Rubery Book Award.

Also by Andrew JH Sharp: *Fortunate*, a novel set in Zimbabwe.

THE GHOSTS OF EDEN

Andrew JH Sharp

Matador
9 Priory Business Park
Kibworth Beauchamp
Leicestershire LE8 0RX, UK
Tel: (+44) 116 279 2299
Fax: (+44) 116 279 2277
Email: books@troubador.co.uk
Web: www.troubador.co.uk/matador

First published by Picnic Publishing Ltd, 2009

ISBN 978 1783065 530

British Library Cataloguing in Publication Data.
A catalogue record for this book is available from the British Library.

Typeset by Troubador Publishing Ltd, Leicester, UK
Printed and bound in the UK by TJ International, Padstow, Cornwall

Matador is an imprint of Troubador Publishing Ltd

1983

No man can know where he is going unless he knows exactly where he has been and exactly how he arrived at his present place.

Maya Angelou

The shadow of the British Airways jet scythed over the ruched earth, making easy passage across the jagged desert terrain, never slowing for ravines, craggy outcrops or dried up rivers. Without a sound it ghosted landscapes of splintered rock, brecciated granite, bouldered river beds. It traced cities and waters and snows that elicit mystical resonances through time: Alexandria, the Valley of the Kings, Khartoum, the White Nile, the Mountains of the Moon.

In the first class cabin of the jet Michael Lacey controlled his breathing, trained his gaze on a speck on the aircraft cabin window and remembered a child. A child long dead. For years, recalling the child had been taboo but, as the hours passed in the confined space of the cabin, he hunted for an effective distraction. The more troubling the thought the greater the relief of his symptoms, as if his mind had room for only one ordeal at a time. He believed, until today, that he had banished his claustrophobia by holding fast to his staunch faith in the power of rational thought. Now he had his suspicions that its return had been triggered by an increasing proximity, as the aircraft travelled south, to the child's resting place; that it was not the tight tube in which he was trapped that was to blame for the sensation of an immovable weight on his chest, but the notion of the child, buried in his destination.

'Do you believe a native curse can kill?'

It took a few moments for Michael to register that the question was for him. The fleshy man in the adjacent seat was leaning across, his breath wheezy and musty with combusted tobacco.

Michael gave an almost imperceptible shake of his head.

'That's what I think,' said the man, his voice bursting with relief. 'It's a good thing I do, because they say if you believe it then it comes true.'

Michael felt a small but unyielding increase in the suffocating constriction around his torso, as if he was in the muscular coils of a fat serpent. A point would soon be reached when his ribcage would crumple and the valves of his gut would blow. Sweat patches spread out from under his arms.

'A native paid a witch doctor to put a curse on me, said I'd cut him up on a business deal. As I pointed out, it was only a verbal, nothing on paper.'

The businessman shifted closer. His heat pressed against Michael like a wall. 'It's the guy's revenge. It's just below the surface, my friend. They're all the same: Sunday they're crooning to Jesus in church; Monday to Saturday they're consulting their God-awful mediums, their …' he paused to pant a little, 'revolting ghouls. They don't know which religion to settle on. Not like us; we got no time for that stuff.' He thrust himself closer, depleting the air of oxygen with his sucking inhalations. 'Not until our funerals, huh?'

Oh God. He was going to have to lunge for the exit door and yank the red handle. Ah, the sweet relief when he exploded out into the boundless air.

'D'you play golf?'

A swimming feeling came and went. Even when not fighting for breath, Michael found small-talk as appealing as mutually chewing gum. He held on, determined not to black out.

The man tried again, in an eager, you're-my-buddy voice, 'Any hobbies?'

The pressure was building to an agonising climax. Think. Hobbies? A martial art would have been immediately useful but no, he had no hobby. His job was his hobby, mistress, wife. He pursued excellence in his surgical practice as a holy man seeks the divine, felt a brotherhood with men who understood the incisive, rigorous life necessary to make some small betterment to the world.

The man could not be dissuaded; he started rolling about, trying to get something out of his pocket. 'You'll be interested to know I'm a member of the Magic Circle. Got a trick I can show you.'

Turning, Michael surprised himself by forcing out a few words, 'Look, I'm sorry. I have to work something out in my head. Can't talk at present.'

The man sank back, releasing a slug of belly air. 'I'm easy, friend. I'll show you later. You won't be disappointed; it's a classic.' With that he shut up.

Michael put his face to the window. The glass looked a foot thick as if he was locked in a bathysphere, but he tried to project himself outside. His eye was drawn to the heated landscape below but his mind returned to paleoanthropology lectures at medical school, hunting out the subterranean – bones in the sands from a time of profound amnesia: *Homo habilis, Ardipithecus ramidus, Ardipithecus anamensis*; ancestors from deep time where no names of place and event exist because none could articulate a name. It seemed pitiful: each generation had to learn anew their own little world. But then came Homo sapiens. At this genesis, as was revealed to Michael when he was very young, God asked man to name the animals. After the naming of the animals, man gave names to the happenings of his life, creating a remembered history for his children. They became acquainted with the history of their tribe. Michael's run of thought ran into the ground. In the same African soil lay the bones of his recent forebears: his parents, his grandparents, his great-grandfather. Their bones lay amongst those ancient bones. He turned his attention to the aircraft's wing and studied the rivets.

In the periphery of his vision he became aware of a blue shadow.

'Excuse me, sir. I do hope you're comfortable. May I ask if you'd like a drink?'

Michael threw a glance at the stewardess. Comfortable? As comfortable as Jonah in the whale. She was smiling at him, although her eyes betrayed a hint of concern: a can-I-help-in-any-other-way look.

He made himself smile back at her fleetingly. 'Could do with … a Bloody Mary …'

His voice died away in a deflated hiss, but he saw the suggested tension in her expression dissipate as if she was relieved to offer practical help – a balm for whatever troubled him, like a nurse administering a tonic from a drug trolley.

'Certainly, sir. Ice as well?'

'As well as what?'

She extended her smile and quashed an elevation of her pert stewardess eyebrows.

'Oh! Yes. Thank you.'

'Sir, if there's anything else you'd like, any way I can help at any time,' that empathetic smile again, 'do use the call button. I'll be with you straight away.'

Help? Is it true there's always one parachute on board? Is it true that one can get oneself sucked outside through the toilet bowl?

She acted as if pouring his drink was a delight: a levity in her movements, a quick tilt of her head when she dropped in the Worcester sauce, her blonde ponytail whipping back and forth like the tail of an eager puppy, a happy giddiness about her. Michael guessed he had bought her inflated jollity with his first class ticket. She opened a drawer in her trolley and lifted out a petite silver tray. She arranged the Bloody Mary and its stick of skewered olives and red peppers, swung out his tray for him and placed his drink. She turned to the businessman but he was asleep, his head resting on the pillow of his double chin.

Picking up his glass and finding a minor relief in its chill on his finger tips, Michael turned his attention to the blue-black of the sky. They were nearing the equator, giant thunder clouds towered about him; an intimidating extra-terrestrial landscape of gravity-defying forms.

'Ladies and gentlemen, will you please fasten your seatbelts. We're starting our descent.'

Whether because of the announcement, or the success of his mental strategies, the claustrophobia relaxed its hold to be replaced by a new but curiously delicious fear. Fear because of an apprehension of landings, but delicious because his fear was charged with the excitement and extravagance of dropping from the sky to an exotic place. He had asked for a window seat – for fresh air, he had told the rather easily amused Naomi at Heathrow. He sighed silently, recalling their parting words.

They were standing near the departure gate, facing each other, in those pre-departure moments which seem for lovers both not long enough and dragging.

'You OK, Michael?' she said, suddenly serious.

Her tall wispy body stiffened. She pursed her lips so that they drained of colour; a sign that he was about to be interrogated. She could be perspicacious, could Naomi, as fitted her occupation as a prosecution lawyer.

'Why? Do I look ill?'

'You seem, I don't know, distracted.' A faint vertical line appeared between her eyebrows. 'Sometimes I can't tell what you're thinking. Often, actually. You've been tense since you accepted the invitation.'

'Have I?'

'Like you don't want to go. You weren't like this for Miami or Chicago.'

'Really?'

He could not tell her why: she would want to probe, to dig it all up. Some things were best left unspoken, buried deep. It disturbed him, though, that she had detected unease. True, when the invitation came from the secretary of the Lake Regions Surgical Association to speak at their conference he had immediately written a polite refusal, aghast at the prospect of returning to Africa. But then he had torn up his letter, knowing that if he had successfully decoupled himself from the past then he must accept. The act of going back would confirm that an accident of birth and a run of bad luck – to be plain: being orphaned at twelve and murdering a best friend, all on the same day – need not haunt a man for the rest of his life; need not keep a hold over him. It was possible to resurrect oneself; to overcome. But that should be a private matter. Confession was for the religious.

Naomi was starting to look cross; the tuck in her forehead had deepened.

There was no honest answer that would not unearth old bones. 'I'd better go through – the gate's open.'

She did not move. 'Michael, it's not us is it – you know – you and me?' She searched his eyes.

He tried to smile, to reassure her, desperate not to hurt her, and was arrested by the pull of those vivid blue eyes he loved to look into when they made love, but were now willing something more from him. 'You and me? I don't …'

She interrupted him. 'I want to understand you, Michael. It's important we don't hide things from each other.' She had moved a little closer, an uncertain small step.

'Hide?'

She drew back and her face flushed; he was not sure whether out of anger, or because she was going to cry. A sadness came over him; a resignation: all his relationships foundered eventually. He always put it down to his work-centred life, although others managed to combine an exacting career and a contented coupling. There seemed little pattern, or logic, to the timings of these break-ups – after all, he was the same person that he had been in the first flush of affection. It pained him.

He summoned a compromise. 'Naomi, I give in, you're very perceptive. You know I like things to be ordered and predictable. Well, they say Uganda's still chaotic – dangerous even – after what happened there. Idi Amin, President for Life, Conqueror of the British Empire and all that, has bolted, but there're still thugs off the leash with guns. I hate putting myself into situations I can't control. Makes me jumpy.'

She looked amused, if a little incredulous. 'Oh Michael, that's so silly – not like you at all. It's just a conference. Everything'll go like clockwork.'

Now that he had shared a fear she appeared satisfied, her movements becoming fluid and light again and the crease melting away; so when they kissed goodbye he was surprised to find her lips unyielding.

The aircraft had pierced the cloud mantle. The land was a vivid rainy-season green, nothing pastel. An arterial network of blood-red tracks fed the voracious foliage. He reminded himself: just a conference.

He risked a glance at his companion. The man had not moved since his abortive attempt at conversation, but what sparked Michael's professional interest was that the wet exhalations marking his less than welcome proximity had also ceased. He watched the man's chest, looking for a rise and a fall, wondering how long he could hold his breath and waiting for the hungry intake of air that would follow a period of sleep apnoea.

With a growing unease Michael leant across and said, 'Excuse me.' There was no response. He pressed a finger into the man's podgy hand and released it. The thready capillaries failed to refill. He slipped his fingers around the wrist to feel for a radial pulse. Not a flicker. The ruddiness had drained from the man's face. His eyes were not completely closed – drying slits.

Then he remembered the man's last attempt at conversation and hastily withdrew his hand. Was this his magic trick? If so, it was impressive. Michael undid his seatbelt and turned towards his patient, noticing as he did so how his own breaths came more easily now that he had a pressing clinical problem to solve. He gently lifted an eyelid. The pupil was dilated, as if the essence of the man had left through its wide aperture. He pressed two fingers into the neck below the angle of the jaw. No carotid pulse.

I'll be damned, he thought, shaken; the man had quietly expired. No fuss. And if a magic trick, whose? The sweat patches under his arms turned icy. Michael sat there for a moment taking control of himself and considering what to do. Stand up and shout for help? Stretch him out in the aisle and start resuscitation? He knew it would be futile. The man had been motionless for well over ten minutes. The pupils were fixed. He pressed the call button above his head.

The stewardess sprung from behind the cabin curtain, all smiles, and tripped towards Michael. He could see she had been waiting for him to call, had rehearsed soothing words. She started to ask how she could help but Michael interrupted. 'Excuse me, this gentleman's dead.'

She looked from Michael to the man and back again. He met her eye but she seemed temporarily stumped, unable to decide between smiling warily at their practical joke or running down into economy to fetch a colleague. Her hand hovered, trembling, over the back of the seat.

'Very peacefully,' Michael added, to soften the shock, suddenly aware that his professional calm might appear inappropriate.

The stewardess shook the man's shoulder.

'Sir! Sir! We'll be landing soon.'

The man's arm dropped and hung dead in the aisle. The stewardess's hand went to her mouth. Michael saw he had to take charge.

'I'm a doctor, a surgeon. He must've had a massive heart attack.'

Massive heart attack always seemed a reassuring thing to say, combining no-one-could-do-anything-about-it with must-have-gone-in-a-painless-instant. Other possibilities, such as *pulmonary embolism* or *cerebrovascular haemorrhage*, seemed less consoling, too coldly technical.

The stewardess straightened up uncertainly, then leant towards Michael, a quivering of her lips and cheeks threatening to fracture her finely set facial features, and whispered, 'Shouldn't we do something? Umm … confirm he's actually … this is my first time …'

A necessary familiarity with death enabling him to fast track past the surprise, coupled with a certain weariness at the emotional incontinence of others, prompted Michael to run an alternative script. What about making an announcement? One of the passengers has died of witchcraft. Please check your neighbour for signs of life in case it's not an isolated case.

But he said, 'It's OK. He's definitely gone. Just leave him as he is. Let your colleagues know, of course. I'm sure the captain will alert the authorities. No need to worry the other passengers.'

'I'll tell the captain.' She hesitated, looking at the dead man again.

'No rush. He's not going anywhere,' Michael said, and smiled faintly.

She shot him a censorious look, turned abruptly and disappeared through the curtain. He regretted his flippant remark – an empty-headed, and therefore uncharacteristic, *faux pas* – and put it down to the rush of euphoric relief at the easing of his claustrophobia.

Michael leant across and replaced the man's arm in his lap, now washed by a sense of unreality, and a little guilt that he had not engaged him in conversation. He hoped that the man had no one who loved him too much. There was peril in excessive love. He was relieved that he would not be breaking the news himself to a wife or a daughter. When it fell to him at work (in some hastily vacated side room with chairs that were too low to sit in with any decorum), he felt that a sluice gate retaining a torrent of tears was about to burst. That puzzled him: it was not as if he let himself get too emotionally involved. After all, he had many other patients to attend and it was expected of him that he kept a reasonable detachment, remained composed.

He tidied the dead man's hands one over the other, creating some dignity. Something dark lay on the man's knee: a black feather, a cockerel's, he guessed, with a bronze sheen along its vanes, its barbs unbroken. The man's curse came to mind. But the feather must have been a prop in his trick; it had probably fallen out of his sleeve. He slipped the feather into his pocket as a small act of defiance against superstition.

Kaaro Karungi – The Beautiful Land, Rift Valley
1958

Alas! This spear lies cold
O Aligo! O hunter!
This spear that I once trusted
Now lies cold
Acholi Dance Song

ONE

In the regions of the Great Rift Valley, a thousand years and more before Europeans in stout khaki had found their fever-punctuated way into the interior, the illustrious Arab explorers and geographers (in robes of rippling silk, and of such fame as Abu Abdallah Muhammad bin Muhammad Abdallah) reported tales of Africa's bright heart: great foaming fountains lying between mountains whose snowy peaks were as luminescent as the moon. Those who looked on them were unable to look away and so, fixated, they stood there until they died. Beyond the mountains, reported the survivors, spread a limitless sea that evoked a deep yearning, a joy, an abandonment, so that men would throw themselves into the waters from the steep slopes.

Below the highest peak Am Kaam, King of Egypt, built a palace, and fashioned eighty-five statues of gleaming copper from whose mouths the waters of the Nile gushed, making their way by cataract, ravine, swamp, quicksand and flood down to thirsting Alexandria. In the deep forests of the region pygmy peoples lived all their lives amongst blades of light from the leaf-fragmented sun, while on the sun-blasted and thorny plains warrior peoples lived by spear and ritual, their goats and children periodically devoured, even in the brightness of the day, by the hideous brute called Nundu which roamed where it pleased.

When darkness fell some men changed into beasts of prey. To ward off these terrors the priestesses of the female spirit Nyabingi beat their drums to gather the people from every direction out of their conical grass dwellings, to dance in unison and so create the sound of a ceaseless stamping of feet that became even louder than the pounding of the drums, and so to drive away the evil of the night. Such were the stories of the fear and darkness in the native's soul that the Bazungu children overheard.

The *Bazungu*, a tribe from far away, shocked the inhabitants of these parts into acquiescence, for they appeared as if they had been skinned – all raw and red – and, what is more, the native children overheard that they had been known to feed on human flesh. The *Bazungu* mapped the valleys, hills and rivers; cut roads from outpost to outpost; created gardened hill stations with fired-brick buildings set by rule and plumb line in a land that had never, in all the ages, seen a perfect perpendicular; and erected English church steeples with metal sheeting that glinted as signals of a new order under the equatorial sun.

In those days the Bahima, who roamed the rich grasslands of Kaaro Karungi, did not measure the passing of time by dates but by the passage of events. By the same paradigm the passage of each day was marked entirely by happenings, not clocks. In such a world a young boy like Stanley Katura had no need for haste, but there was a rhythm of duties, matching the requirements of that world, which he and his older brother, Zachye, adhered to from their earliest years. It was a rhythm they would have continued to keep until they died on the calf skin rugs in their dwelling, and were buried with a terrible but storm-short grief in the dung heap at the edge of the kraal, were it not for the timing of their births – occurring as they did in an age when the meaning of time itself changed for ever.

Their day divided into fourteen occasions. First came *enkoko yashubirira*, when the cock had crowed – the cock that had been placed for this purpose on a shelf in the hut. This was shortly followed by *akashesheshe*, the arrival of a thin dawn light that washed the sky of its blackness. Then came in dependable succession *ente zakomoroka* – cattle go out of the kraal; *ente zazagira* – cattle stand outside the kraal in the open space; *ente zasetuka* – cattle move off to pasture; *abasetuzi bagaruka* – the herdsmen return; *abantu baza omu birago* – men go to their mats; *abeshezi baza aha maziba* – waterers go to the wells; *amasio gatsyoro* – herds run down to water; *amasio gakuka* – herds finish watering; *amasio gairira ebibanga byamaka* – herds come close to the vicinity of the kraals; *enyana zataha* – calves enter; *amasio gahaga* – herds are finished milking; and, at the end of the day, *abantu batarama* – when men visited each other; when neighbours would sit together under the darkened sky to tell in conversation and in formal recitation of the magnificence of their cattle and the greatness of the deeds of their ancestors.

At *ente zazagira* the hot beery breath of Bejuura Kagunga, chief herdsman, and the cud-steamed exhalations of the cattle formed warm pockets through which Stanley and Zachye moved in the cool morning air as they prepared to leave the kraal for herding.

'Take them to Kwayana hill,' said Bejuura as he prodded Stanley hard with his staff. He swung the staff to point west. 'And don't disgrace your father again.'

Bejuura jutted his jaw towards Stanley and jabbed at him repeatedly. His left eye was set rigidly on the boy while his right eye, damaged at birth by the same malevolent spirit that gripped his mood, wandered and rolled uncontrollably in its socket. The incident Bejuura referred to involved Stanley, who was short-sighted, confusing a harmless jackal for a threatening hyena while tending his father's calves, taking fright, climbing a tree, the herd running off, so that a party of men had to be out all night in dangerous country rounding them up. The next day his father, Kaapa Katura, had told him the story of Runuza, the young warrior who had protected thirty cattle on his own against three famished lions in a hard drought. Stanley had heard his father recount the story before but still his father told it, and then dismissed him with no embroidering admonishment. Kaapa Katura spoke little but always in parable, as did all the elders of the clan.

The cattle guided the two boys out into the wide plain of red oat, star and lemon grasses, now aflame in the radiant light of the morning. The boys had no need to shout or curse, for the cattle were wise and knew their destination, the boys merely their guardians. The older boy was strong, and firm in his tread for one who was not yet a man. Stanley, following closely behind, had to lengthen his stride to step in the faint impression of his brother's footprints in the thin dust, his legs like slender saplings on which his knees formed bulbous tumours, his oversized head wobbling awkwardly on lean shoulders, out of rhythm with his gait.

'Keep moving, The One With The Blaze On Her Forehead,' Zachye coaxed.

'You're the laziest calf of the whole clan,' Stanley said, light-heartedly, and then added, 'I think She Who Lifts Up Her Horns Brown As The Enkurigo Tree is the toughest.'

This was the calf given to him when he cut his first teeth, for he cut his lower teeth before his upper and so, as was the custom, he had been placed ceremonially on the back of the calf and gifted her to nurture and cherish. He had heard of those ancient warrior-herders who had grieved three days for their deceased wife but five days at the death of their gifted cow.

Zachye shook his head and said, with the confidence of an older brother, 'She Whose Horns are Like Polished Reeds will be the strongest when she's fully grown.'

'But mine had The Strawberry One as a mother,' Stanley said. A calf mooed knowingly.

'If her mother had been She Whose Horns Are For No Mere Display, I might agree,' Zachye replied.

Stanley looked at his favourite and thought that her already magnificent horns, firm flanks and black, tufted tail were more than a match for Zachye's favourite, but he said, 'She's finer than any cow of the Abasita clan.'

Zachye spun his spear above his head so that it buzzed like a wasp. 'Today, I have two secrets to tell you.'

Stanley's heart skipped. The days when Zachye had secrets to tell were the best. Zachye had told him many hidden things: who killed old Rutaaba on his bed, where the diviner found his herbs, how to build a beehive, the colour of a red woman's nipples. Their mother often said, 'Zachye, you know too much for one who still drinks only blood and milk.'

Zachye spoke again. 'But one of those secrets is no little secret. It concerns my youngest brother.'

'Your youngest brother?' Stanley asked, and then, after a few paces, 'Is that not me?'

'Yes, of course. Who else? The ghost of the dead one?'

Stanley risked treading on a snake concealed in the grass beside the track in order to draw alongside Zachye. He did not understand. How was it possible for there to be a secret about himself? He knew everything about himself, unless it related to an occurrence of the night when a boy's spirit might fly elsewhere. He felt afraid.

'What is this secret?'

'I said that there were two. Which do you wish me to tell first?'

Stanley hesitated. 'Do not tell me any if it will make me frightened.'

Zachye said quietly, as if he spoke to himself, 'It is I who fears.'

'Do not tell me then.' Stanley dropped back behind Zachye again. He had never heard Zachye say such a thing before.

The cattle spread out to graze on Kwayana Hill, a low hump on the plain, while the boys played beside a granite boulder, collecting twigs and dry grass to make a small bed of kindling in the overhang of the rock. Stanley took a leaf-wrapped package from his cowhide sling and peeled back the leaf layers to expose a blackened metal pot. He spat on his fingers before lifting out three small lumps of charcoal, and placed them in the hollowed centre of the kindling. He blew smoothly into the brittle wood. A thin stream of smoke curled up the side of the boulder between breaths; soon a faint red glow appeared. He held the kindling against the glow until it flared into a tiny flame that spread in a crackle of heat and light. Dizzy, he lay back and watched as Zachye added more twigs. Fire could be created from the laborious spinning of a fire stick, but far better to carry the fire concealed as a dusky spirit in the heart of the blackened wood; to entice out the flame with the persuasive ghost in their breath.

'I'll tell you something you don't know,' Zachye said, as he squatted by the fire. 'There's a clan that's kept fire alive in one coal since the days of their fathers' fathers.'

'How do they do that?' Stanley asked, wide-eyed.

'No one knows. It's a clan secret.'

'Is this one of those two secrets you have for me?'

Zachye smiled slowly. 'I'm ready now for one secret.'

Zachye motioned to Stanley to come near. Stanley understood; they could not risk the spirits in the boulder behind overhearing.

'The clan's medicine man takes the coal to a certain big rock at midday when it's too hot to touch. He places the coal on the rock. The hot spirit in the rock enters the coal. They say that when the spirit leaves the stone it turns cold – as cold as the springs in the forest.' Stanley shivered. 'And I'll tell you something else. If anyone touches the rock after its spirit has gone into the coal, their blood runs like a cold stream.'

Stanley hugged his knees and leant a little towards his older brother, staying close, watching his fingers move amongst the flames, expertly turning the grass and wood to nurture the heat in the coal, as sure in this delicate task as he was in guiding a spear to its soft target.

Soon they turned to play, building a miniature kraal, breaking off thorns from an acacia to make a fence to enclose the huts. The stems of dry reeds served as walls while the roofs they thatched with grass. Zachye found a wafer-thin cowpat to carpet the floors and sweeten the air of the huts. They carefully smoothed the kraal's compound with the side of their palms. Zachye pinched an ant that was heading for his hut and flicked it away.

'Die cursed rat! You shall never enter the house of King Zachye.'

They leant back against the boulder, twisting grass and twigs into cow shapes and placing each in the stockade, until their wealth grew and they became the richest of the Bahima, and all the clans spoke highly of them and praised the splendour of their cattle.

Whilst they continued to play Zachye said, 'Now I'm going to tell you the other secret.' Stanley held his breath. 'Our father is sending you to school. He says you must have the Bazungu's Education.'

Stanley stared at the model kraal. He tried, but failed, to picture how this other future would look constructed in grass, stick and stone. 'Why me?'

Zachye popped a little air through his lips as if to indicate it was a trifling question. 'Perhaps because you're the crafty one and were born in a waning moon, so you'll have luck.' He became busy, pushing his hut towards the centre of the kraal and placing a bull beside it.

Stanley sensed that Zachye regretted telling what he knew, but a pressing bafflement made him bold. 'I don't understand. You're the older brother.'

'Well, it's nothing,' Zachye replied forcefully, stabbing a finger through the bull. 'It's because you're puny so can't look after the cattle on your own.'

The insult stung Stanley, not because it was not true but because Zachye had never spoken harshly to him before. He let the hand that held his model cow drop to his side and was about to turn away when Zachye said, less unkindly, 'You'll learn to read.'

Stanley had seen a book when he was a little younger. It belonged to Felice, a distant cousin who had visited the kraal with her father. Felice stood apart on the edge of the compound in her unsoiled skirt of a burnished blue and oh-so-white blouse, her face deep-lustred with oil, lips subtly sheened, eyebrows symmetrical arcs under a high forehead from which arose her shaped hair like a headpiece of their far ancestors from Abyssinia.

It was the first time Stanley had studied at close proximity what happened to a Bahima when they had the *Bazungu*'s Education. Looking at Felice he became aware, but without shame, that he was naked apart from a scanty wrap of red barkcloth below his protruding belly. His skin was matt grey from ingrained dust, except for the shiny scars on his legs. Felice's ankles were like the buffed neck of the queen's best gourd. Flies settled frequently on Stanley's face but veered dizzily away from the scented Felice.

He, Zachye and all the other children blended naturally with the kraal and the land, just like the cattle; as if they were merely different shapes of the same stuff. The soil-impregnated soles of their feet joined them to the earth. Dust to dust.

Felice appeared to be made of something else; something synthesised by the supernatural, her parts generated from magical smeltings in the fires of distant and strange smiths.

Stanley had been too shy to speak, but Zachye asked, 'What is that?' pointing to the glossy object which Felice clasped to her waist.

Felice spoke with a coy confidence, like a woman much older than her years. 'It's a book called *David and Mary*. It tells a story.'

'How can it tell without a mouth? Show me how it speaks,' Zachye replied scornfully.

Felice lifted the object in front of her unnaturally pointy chest, peeled it apart and said, 'It tells of the courtship between a man and a woman in a big city.'

She started reading in a tongue that Stanley did not understand, but learnt later was the *Bazungu*'s language. Her lips moved through absurd contortions, her voice becoming shrill.

'Let it speak in Runyankore,' Zachye said impatiently.

Felice hesitated, and then, peering intently at the page, spoke in Runyankore, pausing before words that she could not easily translate – and some she perhaps believed should remain reserved for the *Bazungu*'s world – speaking those words in their language.

'Mary left the … *office* at *eleven o'clock*. She waved goodbye to her friends and caught a *taxi* to the *coffee shop*. She was excited to see that the handsome young man in the smart *suit* was sitting at the same table on his own again. His *sunglasses* were next to his cup and *saucer*. He looked up and met her eye. She turned away, but not before she saw him beckoning to her to come over. Mary pretended she had not noticed and ordered a *coffee* with *sugar*, but without milk.'

Zachye interrupted again. 'Let it speak of cattle.'

Felice looked up, and although she did not look directly at Zachye her smile held a hint of condescension. This shocked Stanley but Zachye didn't seem to notice.

'Books do not speak of cattle,' Felice said.

Zachye pondered this. 'Then what are they for?'

'They tell stories from other lands where they have no cattle.' She closed the book. 'They want no cattle and they need no cattle.'

Zachye shrugged and lost interest. He turned away and walked out of the kraal shouting, 'Those people living far away are not Bahima.'

Stanley wanted Felice to read further, but she was looking down at her shoe-clad feet as if embarrassed that she had been discourteous. Stanley agreed with her in silence but his curiosity soon got the better of him. 'Why did the woman not want to speak to the man?'

Felice continued to stare at her shoes.

On Kwayana hill, Stanley stopped playing. He threw the model of She

Who Lifts Up Her Horns Brown As The Enkurigo Tree into the fire, and watched the straw twist in an agony of heat and disappear.

'I'll be going away. I'll not be able to come with you to look after our cattle.'

Zachye was lining up all the cattle outside his own hut. 'I'll tell you what. Our cows won't know you any more, but you'll have a big car and you'll work for the *gavumenti*. You should be very happy.'

Stanley looked to the far hills that marked the edge of the only life he had needed. Through a thin watering of his eyes he saw a billow of dust moving along beneath the hills. He thought it might be from a vehicle making its way down the road that had been cut just a year before. Then, as he looked, the dust rose high into the air, becoming a pillar of cloud. It seemed to Stanley to signify some omen, but for what he could not tell. Zachye came beside him and stood silent, also staring at the dust. When Zachye spoke his voice sounded like that of an adult: solemn and fearful.

'I don't like it, Stanley – it foretells fire.'

Two

After the pillar of dust had dispersed in the heat haze Stanley and Zachye rested, lying on top of the rock in the inadequate shade of a stunted tree. Today they would not return to rest on their mats in the kraal at *abantu baza omu birago*, to avoid having to retrace their steps for *abeshezi baza aha maziba*, the occasion for taking the cattle to the watering places. Wispy clouds formed in the dry-season sky, tried to puff themselves up, failed and disappeared. The cattle stood motionless between occasional twitches of their flanks and flicks of their tails; futile spasms of will, trying to free themselves of the tireless flies. Stanley felt the hardness of the rock beneath and the passivity of the sky above. Even the ghosts of the dead, ever present in the wind, were still. His world seemed inert and had forever been. Until today.

He put his arms out and tried to grip the rock beneath with his fingertips, as if he could hang on to what he knew. He thought that the vulture hanging high above him, wings outstretched on a column of sultry air, had twisted its head to look at him.

He became desperate to speak to his brother. 'Zachye?'

'What?'

'What will happen at the school? How is the Education given?'

Zachye was silent. Eventually he said, 'How would I know?' and got up and walked away.

Zachye's ignorance disturbed Stanley. His brother had always known everything: how to treat sickness in the cattle, where to find good grazing, the ways of the hyena and the jackal, which snakes were poisonous, all the stories of the clan, how to captivate the other children with heroic recitations. Now he saw that the Education was so alien that even Zachye knew nothing of it. He could not think of anyone who lived nearby who had gone to school, for on the plain they were all late in taking the Education. The closest relatives at school were his cousins Felice and Kabutiiti, but they lived far away and had fathers who worked in the towns. How could a herdsman like his own father, who was still suffering from the effects of the rinderpest outbreak that had decimated the family's herd a generation ago, find enough shillings to pay the school fees?

Stanley saw that Zachye was standing watching the cattle, perfectly still, resting on his spear. He was looking intently at three of the youngest calves, as if memorising the details of their colouring, the form of their growing horns; as if gaining an understanding, by the calves' interest in him, of their intelligence. He heard Zachye murmuring their names. Later the calves would know their own names and would wait patiently to be called each morning for milking.

Stanley fell back again, knocked down by the realisation that no one he had heard of had returned from the Education to tending cattle, drinking blood and milk, and living in a thatched dwelling on skins. They left forever for the town. They forgot the names of the cattle. It was unimaginable. He tried to picture himself pleading with his father to let him stay, leave him be. That was just as unthinkable.

Soon he heard Zachye saying, 'Lift yourself, Stanley. Get moving, you dreamer.'

Stanley scattered the embers of the fire and the remains of the model kraal with his foot. He understood Zachye's haste for he could see that other cattle were already approaching the gully where the tepid waters from an underground spring formed pools that, in a good year, sustained herds of five hundred. Space was limited, and herders fought to secure drinking for their charges.

At Zachye's word the cattle needed no further encouragement to start out. As they neared the gully they quickened their pace so that Stanley had to trot to keep up. Zachye ran on ahead. Stanley heard a grunt behind him and something stung his ear. He turned to find a boy, about his age but broad in body and skull, flicking him with his switch. He recognised him as one of the Abaitenya clan, whose totem was a house burnt down and a yellow cow.

'Shift your cattle out of the way or you'll feel my spear,' the boy said with a snarl. Dried trails of spittle on his chin struck Stanley as particularly threatening.

Zachye was well ahead now with the leading cattle. The Abaitenya boy's cattle were already passing Stanley, pushing up against and overtaking his own cows: a disturbing mixing and dilution of his precious herd. The boy shoved him aside and lashed at She Who Lifts Up Her Horns Brown As The Enkurigo Tree. Stanley attempted to grasp the switch but the boy was quick and kicked him in the thigh, overbalancing him. He fell heavily, bruising himself on the pot for charcoal that hung off his shoulder as the boy set himself on him. The hooves of the cattle thundered around them like drums, drowning the noise of the boy's fists pounding at his head and chest.

'You Who Is Puny, face the wrath of The One Who Is A Breaker Of Bones,' panted the boy in a parody of the recitations of the tribe.

Stanley tasted blood. Panic swelled in his gullet like stuck meat. Spittle flew. He twisted and flailed his arms but the boy was strong, spitting words at him, one for each blow, 'When … ever … you … see … me,' more pounding about his head, 'and my cattle, step … out … of … my … way.'

Then out of the dust familiar feet appeared, the flaying fists were gone and the boy was crying out, face in the dirt. Zachye's foot pressed with firm precision against the boy's neck as he twisted his arm behind him.

'I Who Heap Up The Dead repulsed them at Kwayana with The One Who Seeks No Help,' Zachye boomed.

Stanley loved Zachye for that recitation: even as he picked himself up he planned to expand the line into a full poem that evening and insist the younger boys learn it to ensure the mini-triumph lived on. Zachye pulled the boy's arm back further, making him cry out. Stanley found himself anxious that Zachye was going to dislocate the boy's shoulder. When Zachye became angry he could lose control of his actions; there had been the incident when he threw a spear at a group of boys who were leering at his cousin. Luck prevented the spear finding flesh.

'I'm not hurt. Let's leave,' Stanley said.

Zachye released the boy, after giving his shoulder one last pull, and said, 'Now go, fly eater! And if we see your pocked cattle take water first we'll drown you in the milk of a yellow cow.'

As the boy ran on ahead, his arm cradled, Stanley walked again with Zachye. Who would come to his aid at school? There might be hundreds of Abaitenya boys. His whole class might be Abaitenya.

When they caught up with their cows at the pools they found the boy frantically separating his bewildered cattle from theirs.

Thirst quenched, the cattle and brothers dawdled back to the kraal, leaving a frenzy of flies on fresh cowpats in the gully and parties of pale-cream butterflies sipping delicately from the hoof-print hollows.

As they approached the kraal Stanley saw their father waiting on the track to inspect his cattle. Looking at his father standing tall, his kumzu of brightly coloured cloth in vertical bands of red ochre, black and green hanging in straight folds from his shoulders, Stanley knew he could no more ask his father to change his mind about sending him for the Education than he could ask the diviner to retract a revelation. He prepared himself to show respect, averting his eyes as they drew close.

When they were within three cattle lengths the boys stopped and knelt. Their father asked them to rise, examined Stanley and said, 'I see the cattle are good but you are scuffed. You must give me explanation for this.'

'I was beaten by another boy coming to water,' Stanley said, still looking down.

'How was the matter finished?' his father asked.

'Zachye came and beat the boy.'

His father said, 'Zachye, continue with the cattle into the kraal. I wish to speak to Stanley.'

Zachye, head still bowed, obeyed. Kaapa Katura walked out along the track, Stanley following.

'That another boy struck you is no great matter. If it becomes your teacher, and you learn that it's our kinsmen that give you help, you have learnt well.' His father continued walking. 'In matters more serious we've had the council of the clans, or the King himself, who take into account the tradition of our ancestors. But now there are new ways. Disputes are taken to the courts in the town where a man who has no knowledge of our families and clans, and the ways of our fathers, makes judgement on the basis of books of rules from the British, or even the Baganda.' Their father had always been suspicious of their tribal neighbours the Baganda – agriculturalists with powerful kings. 'Then there are those who call themselves the Twice Born. These people say that retribution is not for this life and that a man must turn the other cheek if he is struck.'

Stanley found his father hard to understand when he spoke in riddles and without regard to his young age but he listened carefully. His father stopped walking and turned to look out over the plain.

'I do not say these words to condemn the passing of our own courts. I tell you because I know that our clan will not go back to the old ways. Those who do not learn the new ways will grow old with bitterness. They will depart without peace.'

Stanley risked glancing up. His father looked out into the far distance as if watching for the arrival of someone; or perhaps for some portent. He spoke again. 'Many seasons ago our people walked here from the North. They left what they knew and travelled through dangerous lands until they found the place that gave them, and their cattle, comfort again.' He was gently nodding his head as if he had seen what he was looking for and it confirmed his expectations. 'We have to walk again. That is why I'm sending you to school. This is your walk.'

When Stanley had been told earlier that he was going to school, he had been shocked that he would no longer be able to tend the cattle with Zachye. Now his father had added immeasurably to the enormity of what was to come. His walk was to be of the same importance as that of those far ancestors. Would his great-grandchildren tell of it in recitation around the fire? But where he was walking, would there still be fires in the evening and recitations under the night sky? His father's decision to give him preference over his older brother was in itself a break with tradition. The old customs were being trampled.

His father was waiting for him to speak. All Stanley could say was, 'What is Zachye to do?'

'I don't have the fees for both of you to go to school and I need Zachye to tend the cattle.' He spoke with finality. Stanley waited. 'You may return now.'

As he approached the kraal Stanley saw that Bejuura, who as head herdsman had responsibility for inspecting all the cattle on return in the evening, was flailing his spear about in front of Zachye. Zachye was listening in sullen silence to his agitated questions.

'You goat-minder, you should have returned at *abantu baza omu birago*. Did you sleep while the cattle wandered? Are you to join your crippled dog-brother in disgrace? Ah, here comes the little runt now.'

Bejuura stabbed his spear into the ground to indicate where Stanley should stand to receive his admonition. Then he noticed the brothers' father walking back to the kraal. For a moment his wandering eye stopped revolving as if trying to focus on their father and judge his distance.

Then he said, 'Just go – both of you!'

As they hurried away, Stanley said, in a surprised voice, 'You didn't answer Bejuura.'

'If I had answered Bejuura he would have struck me and then I would have struck him back. No! I would have driven my spear into his eye. The eye that can see us.'

Stanley nodded enthusiastically and said, 'He would have deserved it.' He always expressed agreement with Zachye, although he was nervous of violence, to defuse Zachye's anger and to be a good brother.

Zachye swung around on him. Stanley stepped back for he could see how the sinews in the arm that held Zachye's spear were tight and how his chest swelled.

'Are you stupid? Do you think I wouldn't do such a thing? And don't you know what calamity would come on us if I did? Listen to me, my innocent brother!' Stanley watched Zachye's arm. 'I'm going to tell you something you'd better believe. One day I'll kill a man. Yes, I feel it. I won't be able to stop myself.' Zachye's sinews still strained. 'In our grandfather's days I would have brought great wealth to the clan. I would've raided and brought back cattle. Men would've made recitation about me. Now I can't let my spear leave my hand for fear of the *gyoogi*, in case they come and take me away, put me in a prison with hard walls.' Zachye turned away. 'I should have been born my great grandfather.'

Stanley could not think of anything to say that would not blow on the fire in Zachye's heart, for he himself would soon be joining the world of the *gyoogi*. He would soon be going to houses with hard walls, the cattle would no longer determine the occasions of his day, he would be walking a new walk. But most of all he feared that he would no longer be able to protect Zachye from himself. Although he was small and not strong, Stanley found that he could cool Zachye's heart – smother flames that might light the very thatch of their dwellings.

They saw their mother come out of the hut to fill the milk pots and Stanley was glad of a reason to walk on; he was thirsty and hungry, and he needed comfort. As he approached he thought with some pride that his mother resembled the milk pots in form. Her slender neck and narrow head emerged smoothly from a truly bulbous body, the whole, including her head, covered in a white robe, for it was the custom for those women still following the traditional ways to cover themselves from the men. Her proportions made moving around the kraal an effort; she appeared to propel herself by swaying, with difficulty, backwards and forward, as a pot might were it alive. All the girls in the clan, as soon as their bodies started to lengthen and a long time before their womanhood became apparent, were filled with milk and kept from expending energy by seclusion in their huts, forbidden all activity. By the time they had their first menstruation they had become softly plump Bahima beauties, and none more so than his mother who had been a highly desirable bride to Stanley's father, fetching a high bride price considering the relative poverty and low status of her family. If she had been of royal lineage she would have been carried on a pallet from place to place. The passage of many rains had not diminished her proportions and charm. Stanley considered her a fine dancer, sitting on the floor with the other women, her arms and head weaving a complex pattern while a mesmerising sound, between hissing and buzzing, came from her lips, evoking the cattle moving through tall grasses.

She filled the returning herdsmen's gourds in turn from the largest pot, which she rested on her forearm, skilfully directing the silky white ribbon into each gourd without spilling, her upper limbs as lithe and skilful as her lower limbs were squat and slow. A pipe hung limply from her mouth, the stem slotting comfortably into a permanent depression in her lower lip formed from years of pressure.

Without removing her pipe she gave the boys the greeting to keep harm away. 'How have you spent the day?'

Stanley waited for Zachye to answer with the reply to keep harm away: 'We've spent it well.'

'I've smoked the pots today. Eh! Your milk will taste as good as the King's.' Nearby were the black traces of a fire of scented grasses, where she had smoked the pots.

Stanley and Zachye squatted on the floor of the compound with their backs against their family hut. The kraal smelt homely and sweet, of dried cow-dung and fermenting millet. They filled their stomachs with the scented milk.

As Stanley let the last drips fall on his tongue, panic bubbled up again like the hot spring of Kitagata. 'Will they give me milk at school?' he cried.

'Eh! So, your father has decided.' His mother was frowning. She sat down on a low wooden stool, enveloping it, and started vigorously rotating a milk gourd back and forth to make butter.

'You'll eat potatoes, bananas and sorghum. They're not so bad; I've tried them,' Zachye said. 'But you'll have to eat eggs. Those are bad,' he added, with hardly disguised pleasure.

Stanley felt nauseous; chicken eggs were an excrement.

'They clean themselves with water instead of clay or cow's urine,' his mother said, confirming how filthy were the practices of the outside world.

'But that will offend the spirits.' Stanley felt aghast at the thought of being thrown into a place where he was to be made to break every taboo.

His mother said, 'The spirits have some respect for a man with the Education, but never think that you can ignore them completely like the Twice Born. Remember how Nyabutyari died after failing to make offerings in the ghost huts.'

Nyabutyari was a clan member who had converted to Christianity. Still, Stanley found it curious when he was told that the red people, who did not leave offerings in ghost huts, or follow rituals as precautions against the spirits, were little troubled by the ghosts. He had heard it said that the red people's curious appearance made the spirits leave them alone. Perhaps the cruelly thin lips, maize-yellow teeth, pinched nose, pallid eyes and limp hair were repellent to the spirits. Or maybe it was their sickly-sweet odour. Or could it be true what an old man had told him: that the *Bazungu* were themselves the embodied spirits of his own ancestors, the Bachwezi, who had been prophesied to return from the North?

'But why aren't the *Bazungu* troubled by the spirits?' Stanley asked.

'The ghosts of our own dead have no business with them; but they have their own spirits. They're afraid of a spirit of the sun for they wear hats on their heads. Eh! I have heard that not to do so curses them with death. And they have their own taboos; such as a married woman may not lie with her husband's brother or his friends.' She smiled to herself.

Stanley burned with a desire to talk to his mother about the Education; she would likely give him some notion as to what to expect (he knew how she loved to talk, although just to the children and the other women, never to the men lest they beat her for her forward opinions). She knew everything about appeasing the spirits and how to avoid curses and spells whatever the circumstance. She despised the new ways but that did not mean she was not quick to see advantage where it might be gained.

She stopped her churning to rest.

'You'll learn the wisdom of the *Bazungu*, but their wisdom is for living in their own lands and in the towns amongst their own people. In other matters the *Bazungu* are not as wise as us. In the lands of our fathers the wisdom of our elders exceeds the wisdom of the *Bazungu*.'

She took her pipe from her mouth and put it down, as she always did if she was to tell a story. 'There was the burning of the skins before I was given by my father to your father. The British said that the skins the people wore were full of lice that caused itching and disease, and that these lice were contaminating the hospitals and schools that they were building. The skins must all be burnt and the people must wear cloth. The chiefs took counsel among themselves and asked the augurs what the ancestral spirits desired. It was agreed, although the people did not itch much, that the British were scratching terribly and firmly believed that their suffering was due to the people wearing skins, and because cloth was not difficult to obtain, and skins were not of ceremonial importance, and the auguries were favourable, and this matter was of great concern to the British, the wisdom lay in agreeing to burn the skins. Eh, we're a shrewd people and our understanding is deep. We'll one day have herds that cross the horizon.'

She looked askance at Zachye. 'Zachye, what's the matter?' He was rubbing his little toe hard in the dirt.

'I have a jigger.'

'Let me get it out,' Stanley said, anxious to please Zachye. He ran into the hut to find the stick splinter kept for removing jiggers.

While Stanley was absent his mother looked sharply at Zachye.

'Are you going to let him? He cannot hold a steady hand.'

'Let him cause me further pain. It doesn't matter,' Zachye answered, and spat at an ant. He missed it. He smeared it with his heel.

'What troubles you?' his mother asked.

'My father has forgotten his eldest son. He's sending my young brother for the Education before me.'

'Eh! Don't you see that your father has trusted you with the wealth of our family? Hasn't he given you his own spear to defend our cattle? Aren't you the one to bring us an increase of our herd? So isn't your father favouring you over the younger boy?'

'My mother, I don't wish to leave our cattle. They are my brothers and my sisters but, even so, my father shouldn't be sending Stanley away.

If there's merit in the *Bazungu*'s Education he should've instructed his eldest son to go. If Stanley goes he'll become like one from a foreign tribe. He's like milk – he'll be easily soured. He'll come back and speak ill of us and look down on us like my cousins Felice and Kabutiiti.'

His mother sighed. 'When you go and live with fly eaters you eat flies.'

Stanley returned with the sharp stick. He knelt at Zachye's feet and lifted his brother's foot onto his lap. He could see the white swelling under Zachye's little toe, tense with eggs. He started picking at the overlying skin. Zachye sat impassive, letting the weight of his leg rest on Stanley. Stanley drew blood but Zachye did not flinch.

Stanley was filled with a hunger to hear old stories, stories he had heard before, to be certain that they had not changed; that the new walk could not change the old walks. 'Mother, please tell me again why I'm called Stanley.'

His mother never tired of repeating the tales of the clan and so she spoke without hesitation, rocking the churn back and forward in a rhythmic accompaniment to her words.

'Your father's father lived in the days of a great king.' She did not speak his name for, like all the kings of the Bahima, his name had been erased from the language after his death. 'Your father's father remembered the seasons before the coming of the *Bazungu*. At that time there came a certain *Muzungu*, the first red man to make passage through these lands, these very lands that you see when you look out from this very place.'

She pointed out from the kraal with her chin.

'That *Muzungu*'s name was Stanley. He was powerful for he had fought our enemy Kabarega and prevailed. The King sent Buchunku, a prince of the royal clan, to make blood brotherhood with this Stanley, for a brother cannot fight a brother. That *Muzungu*, the one whom they called Stanley, feared our spears and wished to make passage in peace. So he also wished to become a brother to our clans. In this way blood was mixed and from that time on, to this very day, the clans of the

Bazungu do not fight with the clans of the Bahima and neither do the clans of the Bahima fight with the clans of the *Bazungu*. In this way your father gave you the name of Stanley to make remembrance of the mixing of our blood with the *Bazungu*.'

She stopped to bend her ear to the churn that she rotated and rocked in her supple hands, listening for the slap of the whey as it thinned.

'And your father remembers the passing of the *Bazungu* by his father's kraal when he was a small boy and thought them most strange, but wonderful. When your brother Musa and your sister died, he named you after a *Muzungu* because he believes the ghosts of the *Bazungu* will protect you.'

Stanley had not seen a red person. The kraal was far from a road and although Stanley, the first *Muzungu*, had walked through their lands, the *Bazungu* now stayed in their cars. Stanley wanted to meet a *Muzungu* and say to him, 'Greetings! I'm your blood brother.' He became excited to think that there might be *Bazungu* children at school.

His mother shook the butter from the churn into a wooden bowl. Stanley slid Zachye's foot off his lap. He had de-roofed the nest of jiggers and squeezed out the eggs. Blood trickled down the sole of Zachye's foot. 'I've done it,' Stanley said proudly, and looked up at Zachye hoping for an approving nod, but Zachye was looking crossly at his mother.

'Stanley will need shoes. He'll need cotton clothing. What are we going to do? Sell a calf? Diminish our herd for the sake of the youngest son? We'll reduce our wealth to be thanked by his pity? That's what'll happen. I know it.'

'Eh!' his mother agreed. 'He'll need more than the *Bazungu*'s clothes – he'll need school fees and books.'

'Then let's sell his own calf, She Who Lifts Up Her Horns Brown As The Enkurigo Tree. He'll not be in need of her where he's going.'

With that Zachye picked up his spear and left, walking with no limp despite the pit in his toe. Stanley looked after him, still kneeling in the dirt. He felt alone – as if he was at school already.

He heard his mother say sharply, 'What are you sitting idle for? The herds are all entered. Go and do your duties.' And then to emphasise that nothing had changed in the lands of their fathers, she added, 'You'll soon have to wait to drink your milk until the herds are finished milking, in the same manner as the men.'

With that she got up and went to sit by the door of her hut, in readiness to receive each milker. They came to her and spoke the name of the cow they were to milk. She handed each man the pot belonging to that cow.

Stanley picked himself up and moved off through the milling cattle and men. Smoke from the small fires burning around the kraal drifted into the dimming sky as if it was the smoke that darkened it. Soon the milking commenced, with each milker shouting 'Shi!' and then the name of a cow. Each cow answered her call, jostling her way forward between the other cows, and stood still before the milkers to be relieved of her pressure. Stanley led each calf to stand in front of its mother as she was milked. In this way the mother's milk flowed rich and free. If a cow lowed for her calf then all the men shouted the name of their clan and their King, so the cow knew that she was not alone in her yearning but was one with the clan, and that the men stood with her, shoulder to shoulder. Before the udders of the cow were empty the calf was permitted to drink; then the teats were smeared with ash, and the men shouted 'Shi!' and the name of the next cow.

As Stanley led his calf to its mother he thought of how he would be forgetting her name, of how Zachye would become a stranger to him. It was too much to bear. He would rather meet a *Muzhwago* – one who went out at night to transform himself into a beast of prey – than be estranged from his brother. He made a vow on all his ancestors that he would find a way to make it impossible for his father to send him away.

That night he dreamt that his calf had fallen into an ant-bear hole and that he could not lift her out on his own. She was lowing pitiably. He called to Zachye for help, but as Zachye approached hairs sprung from his neck and he turned into a lion (as some men are said to do) and came at him. He woke just as he smelt the animal's fetid breath, hot on his face. He sought comfort in listening to his mother's soft snoring, and then turned to confirm that his brother slept peacefully by his side.

But Zachye's bed was empty. Stanley's skin moved. His thoughts flew to the moon-shadowed plain beyond. Did his brother roam at night? Was he a *Muzhwago*? He lay thinking that it was going to be impossible to get back to sleep, but when the cock crowed for the second time he found Zachye beside him. He reeked of beer.

THREE

On the morning of the second day of Stanley's refusal to leave his calfskin bed his father came to speak to him.

'It's time to rise and help your brother with the cattle.'

Stanley felt ill from deceiving his father by feigning sickness, but he said, 'Father! I can't rise. I'm sick. I've pains in my stomach.' And in case that would not be enough, he added, 'And in my back.'

His father walked about the hut, restless. 'My head as well.'

His father continued to pace. Stanley knew what was on his mind: children died so readily – running about the kraal today, buried in the dung heap tomorrow.

'If you cannot rise you may have offended the ghosts by an omission; or broken a taboo. Have you any wilful matter to divulge, or must I fetch the diviner to find the cause?'

'Eh, he's far too young to have offended the ghosts himself,' said his mother. 'We'd better look to ourselves for the cause of his illness.'

There was no ailment that was not derived from the supernatural. Indeed, if it were not for the interference of the ghosts a man might live forever, excepting perhaps that he might die of a great age having lived his allotted time.

'I don't think I've done anything to offend the spirits, Father,' Stanley said, and then groaned quietly because he lied. He became fearful that the ghosts of his ancestors would find him out and strike him down. He had heard that sometimes the spirits caused the issue of putrid fluids from the nostrils of those who caused them offence, so they were driven mad by a stench that they could never escape.

His father turned to his mother. 'We'll prepare him blood today that he may regain his strength. Perhaps his beating hangs heavily on him.'

He took the metal tipped *ekirasho* to lance the cow, the wooden *eichuba* for collecting the flow and the leather thong to aid the filling of the vein, and went outside. Stanley heard him gathering men to help hold the cow's horns while he pierced a vein in her neck. The cow lowed and stamped. His father returned with the wooden pail of blood and gave it to his mother.

'If he's not regained his strength by the evening we'll seek out the diviner,' he said as he left.

Stanley's mother heated the blood on the fire in the hut and added milk. 'Drink it, my son.'

Stanley sat up eagerly and sucked it up; not quite as good as dried blood cakes with butter and salt, but good enough to want to run his finger around the bottom of the gourd to wipe it clean. He stopped himself, for to show such eagerness would hardly befit his sickened state.

'Cho! You've strength for drinking, certainly,' his mother said, a little coldly.

Stanley did not know how long he would have to lie on his bed before his father concluded that he was not only a weakling but was also too sickly to send to school; that he would be risking scarce cash on a frail child; a child who might not stay the course to complete the Education. Just as unpredictable was the attention of the diviner. Would the diviner have the power to smell his deception or detect it in the auguries? But without another means to frustrate his father's plans he would have to see this through.

All day Stanley lay on his bed, stubbornly determined, but feeling as reckless as the flies that traced crazed tracks around the hut, and as daring as the lizards that darted in and out of the thatch above his head. He lulled his mind listening to the soft flow of milk from churn to churn, the small snappings of brushwood to stoke the fires and the familiar voices of the women as they went about their duties. He closed his eyes, as if sleeping, when his mother came in to check on him and when Zachye looked in after herding.

In the evening he smelt the smoke from the men's pipes and listened to the trading of riddles around the fire: '*Shakushaku!*' cried the challenger, '*Shamba igira*,' cried the contestant. The stakes were high, for a calf was wanted of the loser. Later he heard an uncle make recitation, and could picture him standing with his spear held horizontal in his right hand. He spoke each verse with speed and without drawing breath, making quick stabbings with his spear for emphasis, the gradually falling pitch of his voice punctuated with the regular beat of high-toned syllables, while his words made play with meaning and rhyme. As each verse ended he snapped his fingers and the men chorused 'Eee!' Stanley heard of the sufferings of their ancestors, the Marvellous Ones; of scorching drought when hoes replaced cows as bride price; of those who fought all night until the cock crowed; of Bagyendanwa, the royal drum and its wives and cattle; of the days when the king would drink poison on finding his first white hair; of when the cattle played with antelopes; of night-grazing under a full moon when the heat of the season made day-grazing hard on the cattle; of recent events such as the risible advice given by the vet from the *gavumenti*, and of the ignorance of those hangers-on of the Europeans. At this the men laughed, some nervously for they had been tempted to go and seek employment: slashing grass or moving stones in the service of the gavumenti in order to pay the hut tax; or had kin in distant kraals that had sent their children to school, or been appointed to positions of influence in offices, churches and schools. But tonight all the clansmen and their cattle were united and strong. Stanley heard a child ask Zachye to recite, for he had a rare ability for one so young. Zachye matched his uncle in speed and rhythm, and the men, the children and the women all made appreciative 'Eees' when he had finished. A calf lowed loudly. Everyone laughed.

At first Stanley did not notice that the light from the fires outside had dimmed as a dark shape filled the doorway, but he startled when he heard the rustle of a gourd rattle, serpentine in its smooth hissing. The diviner stood over him, but turned around as if sniffing the air and did not look down at him. An amber glow from the doorway half lit the diviner as Stanley found his eyes drawn from the figure's beaded anklets to his tunic of fine skins, right up to his tall leather hat studded with polished cowry shells and the claws of beasts that preyed at night. He gasped at such finery.

Stanley's mother stoked up the fire while his father watched from the other side of the room. The diviner lowered his bag to the floor. Stanley recognised it as the skin of a young jackal without a seam, for its bones and innards had been removed through its rectum which now formed the mouth of the bag. The diviner took herbs from inside his tunic and circled the walls of the hut, making sweeping motions, gathering up evil influence. He bent over Stanley and, to Stanley's alarm, firmly rubbed his torso, arms and legs with a wad of herbs held tightly in his hand. Stanley started giggling, even though he was afraid, for he was ticklish. The diviner ignored him but his mother spat, 'Enough!' With a sudden movement the diviner cast the polluted herbs outside and Stanley heard the alarm cry of a crow, even though it was night.

Reaching into his bag, the diviner pulled out hooked metal implements for scarifying, for blistering and for bleeding, a small horn for cupping, blackened gourd cups for mixing medicines, twisted roots and strings of skin of indeterminate origin. But these would not be required until after the divination, for which the diviner's hand came out of the jackal's hind parts filled with millet seeds. He squatted down and spat several times into his hand, murmured something inaudible and scattered the grain across the floor. Stanley stared at the strewn seed, their tiny shadows alive as the fire flared and danced, his fright mollified by fascination. What if he tried to read the augury himself? With a secret thrill he imagined that he might become a diviner when he grew up: become schooled in their secrets, interpret the hand of the dead on the living, have a hat that rose tall and commanding, be called to the sick to bring hope or foretell doom with solemn compassion. But he wouldn't charge much, for when people were sick it would be unkind to further their distress.

The diviner's wise eyes continued to scan the augury while an intonation stirred low in his chest and passed his softly moving lips. He turned to look at Stanley as if unbelieving of some information that had been given him.

He stood up before he spoke. Stanley's mother and father straightened themselves.

'The ghost of a great ancestor, a god no less, none other than one of the Bachwezi, none other than Mugenyi, yes, it is he who has been offended. He, the one who loved cattle, who shared their resting places and in whose care no cattle ever died.'

There was no hesitation; no intimation of uncertainty. If there was doubt, Stanley thought with fear, it lay in whether the great ghost would accept an appeasement and lift the sickness from him.

'You must sacrifice the cow that is dedicated to Mugenyi.'

Stanley's mother gasped.

'She must be sacrificed,' the diviner repeated.

His father stepped forward, his brow furrowed. 'The boy is to be sent away to school. Does that offend Mugenyi?'

'I cannot know what offends Mugenyi, but your suggestion does not find favour with me for then it would have been the father that lay ill, not the child. The ghost of Mugenyi would not punish the child for his father's offence.'

Stanley found the diviner's voice had become distant; a terrible dread gripped his heart. He was thinking of the calf that was dedicated to Mugenyi, the calf that must be sacrificed: She Whose Horns are Like Polished Reeds. Zachye's favoured calf. He looked towards the diviner but could not meet his eyes. He feared the discovery of his deception; he feared Zachye's spear-happy wrath if he ever found out that his favoured cow was sacrificed under a false precept. And how, in the whole pantheon of their gods, could he have offended the kindest one? His chest heaved; he feared the pricking sensations creeping up his fingers and the spasms of his wrists, as if the evil that had been cast out with the herbs had found its way back to him.

His mother was looking at him, fright in her eyes, as if she had gravely underestimated the severity of her son's condition and been nonchalant to the point of negligence in assuming this was some minor curse, easily appeased. Stanley saw that she looked at him as she had looked at his dying brother and his dying sister in the last season of the rain, on this very bed.

His father, a man of action and not given to hasty eruption of emotion, said, 'It'll be done tomorrow,' and moved to see the diviner away. But the diviner was looking hard at Stanley in puzzlement.

'He's only a child; an innocent. It's an intriguing circumstance.'

Emboldened by the diviner's hesitation, his father said cautiously, 'There are those who say that the ghosts can be appeased by the medicine of the *Bazungu*.'

Stanley's mother uttered a cynical chuckle and was about to speak, but his father lifted his hand to quash her.

The diviner said emphatically, 'In this case the medicine of the *Bazungu* cannot help.'

No medicine can help, Stanley thought. He had brought calamity on himself. There was no way out. He wished that he could appeal to Ruhanga – the supreme God who had created Rugabe and Nyamate, the first man and woman – over the interfering ghosts, shadowy spirits and complicating *Bazungu*. But Ruhanga did not concern himself with the affairs of men.

Later, sweating into the congealing night, Stanley came to his own conclusion about the displeasure of the ghost: Mugenyi had foreseen that his deception would lead to the unnecessary sacrifice of a cow. This had surely pierced Mugenyi's heart – he who loved cattle the most. Then Stanley became confused, for if Mugenyi had not become angry in the first place then the diviner would not have augured Mugenyi's displeasure and ordered the sacrifice of the cow.

He startled to a loud and abrupt movement in the thatch above him, as if some creature, or embodied spirit, had spasmed. The tingling in his fingers returned. He strained his ears so hard that he heard a cry far out on the plain, far out beyond the fences of the kraal. It might have been an owl's call or it might have been a man's scream. It might have been one and the same, for at night certain of the living and certain of the dead transformed into beasts; the boundaries between them dissolved to take on strange and terrifying forms. When he saw a shadow cross the embers of the fire in the hut he tried to scream, but all he could manage was a wheezy exhalation as if he had been winded. Zachye stepped over him. He stank of beer again.

Stanley wanted to pour out his relief, but Zachye would not have appreciated him drawing attention to his late entry. Their mother slept lightly. Our father will beat him for stealing the men's beer, Stanley thought. But he gained comfort when he heard Zachye's noisy breathing and the close proximity of his strong limbs.

On the third day of Stanley's sickness Zachye came to the door, having groomed the cattle at *abasetuzi bagaruka*. He touched the end of his spear and said, 'Today I'm going to bring our clan's justice to an Abaitenya boy.'

Stanley sat up abruptly. 'Don't do anything to him or you'll be taken away.'

'Don't you tell me what I may or may not do, little brother. The boy injured you. He ruptured your spleen and I'll pierce his. Don't worry – I'll do the deed surely and quickly. A man does not spear a lion slowly.'

'No! He didn't injure me. I've hardly any bruising. He was the one with the bruises,' Stanley pleaded.

'*Taata egi*! Your heart is too soft, little brother. Why do you defend those who've harmed you? Are you one of the Twice Born already? You fell sick after he'd attacked you – for that I'll avenge you.'

Zachye's face was set and he turned to leave.

Stanley cried out, 'Zachye! My sickness is in my heart. I'm sick because I'm going to school. I'm sick because my father chose me for this over you. And now I see that another boy is to be punished for the sickness in my heart.' Then he remembered more and blurted it out. 'And your favoured calf is to be sacrificed to appease the ghost of Mugenyi.'

Zachye came in from the doorway. Stanley closed his eyes, waiting for Zachye's fury to burst, but Zachye's voice when it came was quiet and menacing.

'Then what's the remedy for this sickness of your heart? What ghost are we to appease for that? What other cattle are we to sacrifice?'

'The remedy is for our father to let me stay – to let me carry on looking after our cattle.'

Zachye raised his voice, 'Our father cannot take back the words he's already spoken. And anyway, I wouldn't accept my father's change of heart; an insult cannot be so easily forgotten. Don't you know that the diviner also demanded payment of a calf? So, with that and the sacrifice of my calf, our wealth is greatly diminished at your own stupid hand. Whether you go to school or stay on your bed you'll make us poor.'

Stanley felt the hut shrink. He wanted to run out and away into the plains; to take the calves and roam distant and secret valleys where no one could find him. He started weeping silently. Zachye stood looking at him, then turned his face away and stared out at the lands. Then his shoulders slumped and he turned back.

'Little brother, you've behaved like a coward but, since I see it was on my account, I'll not tell it abroad. You're not accountable for our father's actions.'

There was a grudging tenderness in his voice that Stanley had never heard before, but now Zachye buried it, stamping his spear down on the ground, saying firmly, 'Now get up and let's go out with the cattle. You're to tell our father that you're fully recovered. He'll have to negotiate with the diviner.'

Stanley put his feet on the floor, wiped his nose with his fingers and went to collect his spear from the doorframe.

As they left the kraal they found their father watching the cattle leave. Their mother was returning from ablutions.

'Father, excuse me, this morning I'm well,' Stanley said.

His father looked surprised, and then relieved.

'Ah! You seem strong. The diviner was mistaken then. So we'll not need to sacrifice the calf to Mugenyi.' He pressed his finger into the bowl of his pipe to compress the tobacco, and then said unhurriedly, 'I'm minded not to pay the diviner – he failed to divine the illness correctly.'

Stanley's mother dropped her pot and lifted her hands as if she had seen a calamity. 'Cho! Madness has entered you to speak like that. Such a thing would offend Mugenyi's ghost further. He may strike you down – and the boy.'

'It's not Mugenyi that I speak against. It's the diviner. Just look at Stanley. Does it look as if he's cursed by a ghost – the ghost of a god?'

Stanley drew himself straight and held his spear firm and vertical.

His mother glanced at him through screwed-up eyes as if unwilling to look at what should not be, then said, 'The diviner will seek vengeance if you don't pay his fee. He's powerful.'

Stanley's father sucked on his pipe nonchalantly. 'These days there are other powers. He can bring a case against me in the court in the town. Let him do that.'

His mother had drawn her cloak tightly around her. Some of the men and women had come close to listen: such vexatious matters had touched them all. 'He may not be able to lay his hand on you in this life but when he dies his ghost will return to harm you, or the boy. Think of the boy.'

'The ghosts have less influence than they used to. When Stanley has grown they may be further diminished.'

She shook her head vigorously. 'You're bringing us shame. You're putting your hand in the fire. You'll have to look behind you for the rest of your life. And so will the boy.'

Their father took his pipe from his mouth and examined it. 'We're condemned to have to follow two paths – the new and the old. Sometimes they travel together and sometimes apart. We have to choose the path that is suitable for the occasion.' He saw that Stanley and Zachye were still standing listening; rapt and tense. 'Your cattle are wandering – go and see to them.'

As the boys hurried out they heard their mother warn him. 'Even the Twice Born cannot forget the ghosts of our ancestors – they linger about us always. The living and the dead cannot be so easily separated.'

FOUR

Zachye walked fast along the track with Stanley trotting to keep up. The cattle sensed Zachye's irritation and hurried ahead of him, agitated and pushing past each other until they came to a favourite grazing by a hot spring. Here Zachye dug the end of his spear into the ground and stood hanging on it while he looked broodily into the pools of steaming water. Stanley stood a little behind him and did not speak for fear of causing offence.

An increasingly loud rumble drew their attention to the road beyond the spring. A car, as red as a fired pot and with a roof as white as milk, drew up and stopped below them. There was a metallic clicking noise, like the call of the puffback bird, then the doors opened and four *Bazungu* – a man, a woman and two boys – got out. The woman wore clothing of striking colour that Stanley could not equate to any object in their world, although he might have once seen a little flower of the same vibrancy. Both the man and the woman wore small dark disks in front of their eyes so that they could not see, and yet they were as sure in their actions as the sighted.

Two *Bazungu* children ran towards the water shouting, their shoes making flat impressions on the mud at the edge of the pools. It seemed that bees pursued them or that they crawled with ants, for they did not sit still for a moment but darted about, jumping from rock to rock. Stanley had heard that *Bazungu* children never had to work and perhaps this imbued them with much energy. They held miniature cars in their hands and put them down and picked them up many times, and frantically moved stones about as if they were being whipped to play at speed. Then the Bazungu children saw them. One of the boys shouted, 'Come and make play with us,' in Runyankore, although in the dialect of the Bakiga who lived in the faraway hills.

Stanley wanted to run down to play and to say, 'I'm your blood brother,' but no greetings had been exchanged and they had the cattle to mind.

He watched the *Bazungu* closely and saw that the adults had put out chairs and a table. From a large container with a highly polished smooth skin they pulled out glass bottles, square pots unlike any gourd or pottery in the kraal, other small packets – not of bark or skin but shining. The woman opened these, took out white food and placed it on plates of the same red colour as the car. She called the two *Bazungu* children.

Stanley heard their names: Simon, Michael.

Then the *Bazungu* ate their food with their hands, even though Stanley had heard that the *Bazungu* never touched their food with their hands lest they become contaminated. He remarked on this to Zachye, who said, 'Maybe these ones are from a different tribe.'

After they had eaten, the red man took another small object from the car and fixed it with a twisting motion onto the thin legs of a stool without a seat. He placed it a few steps from where they ate and then ran back to his chair. The *Bazungu* all looked at the object and smiled together as if it were commanding them to do so, except one of the boys who stuck out his tongue. Then the man took another object from the car, placed it on the table and pulled out a long spike, longer than the object was deep, which made Stanley gasp. The object made a squealing noise so that Stanley and Zachye jumped and tensed to run away, but then they heard it making music: a jaunty, spangly, danceable song of skilfully plucked strings, playful drums and African voices. Stanley saw his brother relax and lean forward, captivated. His knees moved with the rhythm and he smiled. Stanley could not understand the language but knew that it spoke the voice of Africa. More than that: it had the same speed and driving rhythm of a recitation.

Then the *Muzungu* woman spoke sharply to the man and he spoke sharply back. She spoke sharply again and the man touched the music maker. Now it played new music, this time sorrowful and airy – on an instrument that could not be imagined. Zachye and Stanley stood listening while the *Bazungu* ate their food. Zachye took a step forward as if to hear better.

The *Muzungu* woman looked at them, and then shouted.

'We're not welcome,' Zachye said. They got up, and moved away from the *Bazungu* who had come to their place and made them unwelcome.

On the way back Zachye spoke just once. 'One day I'll get the Education and become like a *Muzungu*, to be able to buy strange things. I'll first buy the thing that makes music but then I'll buy cattle – many cattle. And then, little brother, we'll herd them together in our old age and tell of the things we've done in recitation and we'll listen to the music.'

'I thought you didn't want the Education,' Stanley said. But Zachye failed to reply. Stanley saw that he should not ask again.

When they entered the kraal they saw their mother taking offerings of milk to the spirit hut dedicated to Mugenyi. She was still throwing spears of dissent at their father, the seriousness of the matter making her bold.

'If we cannot attribute our misfortunes to the ghosts, then what can we blame our sufferings on? If there are no spirits to appease, then we're at the mercy of that which does not see us and does not care: the rocks, the forests, the skies. Then we're to be pitied indeed.'

Their father appeared in a less belligerent mood, his head hanging a little as if lashed into submission. He had stopped replying and was fiddling with the tobacco in his pipe.

Their mother said, 'And do not be so sure of the wisdom of sending Stanley to school. Ten cattle in the kraal are better than a hundred prophesied.'

She paused, gathering voice. 'And what if Zachye is laid on his bed while Stanley's at school? You'll have to give our cattle to others to follow them out to pasture, or you'll have to follow them yourself. He who has no dog must bark for himself.'

When she saw the boys she signalled for them to follow her.

In their hut, she said urgently to Stanley, 'Get back on your bed. I'm going to tell your father that you're ill again. It's the only way to remove his madness; to make him give offering to Mugenyi and pay the diviner.'

Stanley looked around for Zachye, but he had slipped away.

He could not disobey his mother, so he climbed onto the skins and lay out stiff with his arms by his side, as if he was ready to be rolled up and taken off for burial. He lay rigid until his mother went to leave the hut, but she met his father coming in.

'Get up, Stanley.'

His mother intervened. 'But he's ill again – he's had to take to his bed again.'

His father was not to be deflected. 'There's a craftiness here. Now get up.'

Stanley arose, with a helpless look at his mother. His father pushed him out of the door. 'Go and groom the cattle.'

He stumbled away, and found Zachye playing mweso in the dirt with his friend Erinesti. 'You must have told our father that I pretended to be sick,' Stanley said.

Zachye made his move, scooping a stone from one of the hollows that they had dug in a grid-pattern in the dirt and placing it in an adjacent hollow.

'Yes, I did,' he said. 'There's been enough of this. Now leave us alone. Go and attend the cattle.'

Stanley persisted. 'Our father won't pay the diviner.'

Erinesti looked up at him and said, 'Take a gift to Mugenyi. He may help you.' He smirked at Zachye.

Zachye said, 'Erinesti is right; you should seek out the diviner – but they say he has a wild spirit. Remember Nuwa, who was never seen again.' Both he and Erinesti shook with laughter.

Stanley wandered away, troubled. Zachye was right; by his own hand he had brought difficulty to his family and by his own hand he must carry it away. He had to seek out the diviner.

FIVE

Stanley sat on the floor inside the hut of Merabu, his father's other wife, casting millet seeds and studying the pattern of their fall, hoping to find out for himself the secrets of the diviners. His father sat on a stool outside the entrance of the hut while Merabu cut his hair – shaved close, except for a few tufts in diamond patterns, as was the fashion in those seasons. Merabu was young and pleasing to look at, although not as full-bodied as their own mother. Their mother tolerated Merabu, despite their father spending more time with Merabu than with herself. Indeed Stanley thought that his mother frequently tired of his father, becoming sullen or argumentative in order to drive him away into the arms of Merabu. Merabu had two living children, one on the breast and the other an infant. The clan held its collective breath, waiting to see if they would survive better than Kaapa Katura's other children.

Stanley heard Zachye's voice outside the hut. 'May I speak with you, Father?'

Zachye waited for permission, which his father, enjoying the attention of Merabu, appeared in no hurry to give.

Eventually his father said, 'Yes, Zachye?'

'Sir, I wish to go to school.'

Stanley looked up from the scattered seed to see his stepmother glance at Zachye in surprise at such a bold request. She stopped shaving her husband's head.

His father, frowning, said to Merabu, 'Carry on,' and then to Zachye, 'I'm sending Stanley to school.'

Zachye sounded peeved as he replied, 'But why didn't you choose your oldest son?'

Stanley feared his father would strike Zachye for his impudence, but instead his father said, 'You're to look after the cattle,' adding, as if not without sympathy for his oldest son's feelings, 'You're wise in their ways and strong. Stanley is small and weak and won't be able to look after the cattle on his own.'

Zachye answered eagerly, 'We'll find someone else to look after our cattle. They could go out with Keesi's herd.'

His father took a long time to reply. 'It's true, alas, that our cattle are few enough in number to join another herd, but I don't have the money to pay two school fees.'

'I'll bring the money, father.'

Kaapa Katura shifted on his stool, waved Merabu's hand off his head and turned towards Zachye. 'Now you're vexing me with your persistence. How will you do such a thing?'

'Erinesti tells me that the *Bazungu* like to pay men to pull up plants in their kraals and make rain for their grass.'

'Enough! Go, boy.'

'Father?'

Their father raised his hand threateningly. 'Go! I have had to accept charity in order to send your brother to school. It's easy for those who dig in the dirt making vegetables, or who trade goats, or who work for the *gavumenti* to find the fees, but for us who follow the ways of our ancestors, who have no need of shillings …' He grunted, tiring of explanation.

Merabu signalled Zachye to leave.

'Thank you for your audience, sir,' Zachye said, and left with what Stanley thought was a light step for such an unsatisfactory outcome to his request.

Excusing himself, Stanley ran past his father and stepmother and caught up with Zachye. 'What shall we do?' he asked, breathless with anxiety.

Zachye turned to Stanley with a satisfied smile. 'My father has not vowed against me going to school. It's just the fees. I'll get what I want. I'm strong – like my ancestors. You'll see.'

'What do you mean?'

'Just wait. Don't ask me any more.'

Stanley was relieved that Zachye seemed to have forgiven him; but his relief was overshadowed by the knowledge that Zachye was plotting something. As Zachye would not discuss it, he could not prevent Zachye hurting himself – or others.

Stanley walked across a shallow valley to reach the diviner's kraal. To avoid detection he took a track less frequented and set out during *abantu baza omu birago*, when the men and boys were resting from the heat of the day. Only those who had a petition came to the diviner's dwelling, and like all other children Stanley had kept away. He did not know how he would be received or whether harm would come from his approach, for there were many restrictions, taboos and rituals that he had not yet learnt. As he drew close he felt an increasing pressure in his stomach. A tight copse of small, twisted trees and overgrown thicket, like the giant hairball of some monstrous hyena, marked the location of the diviner's kraal. The copse emitted a carcass-like odour. Animal horns, and black and bronze feathers, hung from a branch as a warning to passers-by that the air was viscid with ghosts and spirits. Beside the copse a tall conical hut made entirely of grass hissed in the sun. A fence of thorns surrounded the kraal, but this was only a rudimentary barrier as the diviner had charms that gave protection and warned away animals.

Stanley stopped the length of a late afternoon shadow away. But the diviner had prescience, for he emerged from his dwelling and stood looking at Stanley. Today he wore a simple white robe and a single band of leather around his head.

'I see you're well, or do I look on the ghost?' His voice was quiet and low but hinted at suppressed power, like the sound of distant thunder.

'I'm well, sir,' Stanley said, his voice thin and squeaky.

'You may come near.'

Stanley kept his head down and came closer. The diviner motioned him to sit on the earth while he took the stool by the entrance of his dwelling and sat down.

'What is your request?'

Stanley could not answer although he had rehearsed it. He sat silent.

'If you have nothing to say then you must take your leave.'

Stanley spoke, but not the words he had rehearsed. 'Can a diviner teach a boy like me to read the auguries?'

The charms hanging from the tree moved, although there was no breeze. The hem of the diviner's robe rippled.

'These secrets are taught by fathers to their sons.'

'Oh! My father cannot teach me for he's not a diviner.'

'Then you cannot learn to read the auguries.'

That seemed to be the end of the matter, but shortly the diviner spoke again. 'There is another way. Some see visions to receive their secrets.'

'I'd like that,' Stanley said, glancing up at the diviner, who held a thin grey bone in one hand while he ran the fingers of the other up and down its shaft.

The diviner started tapping the bone and Stanley waited eagerly for him to speak again. 'It's not for me to give you visions. But maybe Ruhanga will grant these to you.'

Stanley imagined himself sitting on his bed in the dead of night, with Zachye snoring unaware, as a man in a white kumzu came and whispered the secrets of the spirits to him. But there was another matter.

'Unfortunately, sir, I'm going to school.'

The diviner's bone snapped in two, although it rested in the palm of his hand. Stanley exclaimed 'Oh!' but it seemed a small thing to the diviner, for he ignored the bone and said, 'Some who go to school receive visions, but they are not for reading the auguries. These are visions of new ways, ways of the future: some see how to fly in the sky, or how to fight with guns, or how to send their voice to talk in a box many lands away. At school you'll receive such dreams, but don't forget the arts of your fathers. Do not despise them, or you'll hate your very self.' The diviner's face darkened. 'I have heard that some call the spirits of our ancestors "devils" and pray against them. Those men become cut off from our fathers. They have forgotten where they came from. They don't know where they belong.'

Stanley found the diviner difficult to understand, but he took some courage from the diviner's willingness to speak as if one man to another man and said, 'Do you think that Mugenyi is still angry with me?'

'Your sickness has left you, so his anger is lifted,' said the diviner, without hesitation.

'Excuse me, sir, will our father have to pay you?'

'He'll have to pay. As agreed.'

Stanley struggled to remember his rehearsed words. 'Sir! I fear to tell you something.'

'Tell it, or I'll auger it,' said the diviner. Stanley thought he heard him chuckle to himself.

Stanley spoke so quietly that the diviner had to lean down to hear him. He told how he had deceived his parents because he did not want to go to school. How he had lain on his bed saying he had pain. And now he had come to the diviner because it was unfair that his father should have to pay for his son's deception. His father was a poor man because the rinderpest had destroyed the herds of his father's father. And so he had a request: that the diviner would accept payment from himself. He, Stanley, would pay in full himself when he had finished school and got a job with the *gavumenti*. The words came out quickly, and he did not look at the diviner as he spoke. It was as if he was making recitation in front of the men of his kraal – as he had seen Zachye do. When he had finished he took breath from such hurried words and waited to know the diviner's answer, heart beating like a bird in a net: awaiting freedom, or death. Gruff noises came from the diviner's chest as if the spirits were discussing within him the matter at hand.

'You're bold for one so young in years.'

Stanley feared the diviner was about to refuse the request on account of his impudence. He said faintly, 'I'm not strong. That's why I'm being sent to school.'

The diviner got up, towering above Stanley. Stanley closed his eyes tight.

'I'm a poor man myself, but I'll accept your promise.'

Not many days later Stanley found Zachye absent from his bed when he woke early in the morning. The cockerel on the shelf under the thatch had not yet crowed, so Stanley did not wake his mother but got up quietly and went to Erinesti's hut to see if Zachye was there. Looking in, he saw only the supine shapes of Erinesti and his sisters. He moved around the kraal, between the cattle, along the thick euphorbia fence, whispering 'Zachye!'

He jumped when he felt his shoulder gripped from behind.

'Looking for someone?' It was Bejuura. The men took watches through the night – more for protection of the young calves from leopards than from raiding parties, in these new days.

'I couldn't sleep.'

Bejuura held him there, his grip causing pain. 'Don't crawl around the kraal before the men are up. Next time I may mistake you for a beast and kill you.' Stanley tried to turn around but Bejuura held him. 'Go straight to your bed and wait for the men to rise.' As Stanley tried to look over his shoulder, Bejuura slapped him hard on the ear and hissed, 'Do not turn! Are you deaf? Go back to your hut.' He pushed him away and Stanley fled to his bed.

When the adults found that Zachye was missing, and after his mother and the other women had ceased wailing that this augured calamity, his father called the men together to look for him. Stanley was questioned. Yes, Zachye had gone to bed with him. No, he did not smell of beer. No, he had heard nothing in the night.

The boys were left to milk the cattle but were not to go out for grazing until the men had found Zachye. The men moved in groups of three, in an easy, loping stride to cover distance as efficiently as possible. They returned tired at *abasetuzi bagaruka*, unsuccessful. Stanley's mother asked his father whether he had paid the diviner. When his father was noncommittal, she went again to make offerings in the ghost huts. His father told the men that he was going to walk to the police station. When Stanley asked to walk with him he refused, saying it was too far and that he needed to make haste. It would be nightfall before he got there.

For two days Stanley pastured the cattle with Erinesti. The cattle seemed to miss Zachye; they lowed continuously and wandered restlessly, so that he and Erinesti could not rest at *abantu baza omu birago*, but had to call the cattle's names often to persuade them to stay together. The cattle refused to listen to Erinesti, as they did not know him. Erinesti became irritated when the cattle were better persuaded by Stanley – although Stanley thought that even with him they obeyed with poor grace.

Stanley tried to make friends with Erinesti saying, 'Zachye must have gone a long way away.'

'Not that far,' Erinesti said. He started throwing stones at crows.

'So you know where he is,' Stanley said.

'Maybe.'

'Please tell me.'

'If I knew I wouldn't tell you.'

'I'll not speak to anyone. I'll just go to him and tell him to come back before the *gyoogi* come.'

'He may be dead by now,' Erinesti said, casually, as if it was a small thing.

'Why do you say that?'

'He went with two spears. He'll use them.'

Stanley remembered the boy who had attacked him. Surely Zachye had not continued to bear a grudge.

Erinesti started laughing. 'Bejuura is missing his spear. He accused me of stealing it, but he missed it on the night Zachye went out and he knows Zachye took it. If he's exposed he'll be disgraced. He must have slept on his watch.'

Stanley thought back to the night when he had got up to look for Zachye and remembered how Bejuura had been so reluctant to let him turn around to look at him. What good was a man on watch without his spear?

'I beg you tell me where Zachye's gone,' Stanley pleaded.

'I've already said more than I wanted. Don't speak of this at the kraal.'

Erinesti returned to throwing stones. Stanley wandered among the cattle unable to play, or even chat to the calves. He kept looking out, as if Zachye might appear on the horizon – tall, with two spears. Then he abruptly stopped walking. He was trying to remember what Zachye's face looked like. He could recall Zachye's tall form and the way he carried his spear, but he could not see his face. He became fearful at the meaning of this sudden incapacity. Perhaps it told that Zachye was already a ghost. He turned to press Erinesti again but, as he did so, he saw a flash of light on the road far away – the sun catching the bright metal on a vehicle. The car stopped, and two men got out and started walking along the track towards the kraal. As they got closer Stanley could see that they were *gyoogi*, in their black jerseys. Zachye had told Stanley that *gyoogi* – the word for the dark blue flies that frequented dead animals – sounded like the English word jersey. That was why the police were called *gyoogi*.

'Look, Erinesti!'

Erinesti had already started rounding up the cattle.

The *gyoogi* walked slowly, leaning back a little to balance themselves against their bellies. One of them held a stick, or spear; Stanley could not tell which because it was wrapped in a dark cloth. When the boys arrived back at the kraal, hurrying the cattle, they found the *gyoogi* had entered Merabu's hut with some of the men, while the rest of the clan crowded around the entrance. Stanley went around the back where he could listen more easily. He heard Merabu offering the *gyoogi* milk. They preferred tea, but accepted beer when they learnt that there was no tea. The *gyoogi* said they wished to interview the men of the kraal. Stanley heard the men say that this should be done in the centre of the kraal where the clan members normally gathered, so that everyone could hear what was happening, but the *gyoogi* refused, saying that they must conduct their business in something that could be equated to an office – not outdoors, like primitive people.

The men were to be summoned into the hut, one by one. The *gyoogi* enquired if any man was missing. Stanley's mother shouted from the doorway to say that her son was missing and that her husband was looking for him. He had been gone two days and had not yet returned.

'On that matter I have news for you,' one of the *gyoogi* said.

The crowd quieted.

'Your husband found your son in the town yesterday. He attended the police station to report him missing but returned later to say that he had found him. Pah! The youth of today! He's taken him to see an uncle and will be gone a little while longer.'

His last words were almost drowned by an outpouring of celebratory ululating from the women and a concordant murmuring from the men.

A *gyoogi* spoke above the din, 'Please! Your attention everybody. We're here on a different matter. A very serious matter.'

The noise died instantly. Stanley strained, not to miss a word.

'We're investigating a crime. A terrible crime. That is why your small village has received not one, but two, inspectors. This is Inspector Obonyo and I am Inspector Babumba.'

'But what crime?' someone shouted.

'Please, please, do not hurry the law,' Inspector Babumba said. 'The law cannot be pushed like … er … you people push your cows. However, I can reveal that the crime we're investigating concerns a killing. That's all I can inform you – that's all you're permitted to know – until we're authorised further.'

'That is true,' Inspector Obonyo said. He had a deep voice like the King's drum.

'Yes, of course, the law agrees on this point,' Inspector Babumba said.

The *gyoogi* made it plain that their official business must commence without further interruption. They instructed the men to line up in front of the hut and assigned Bejuura to the door to call each man through at their bidding. Stanley came around the hut to be near the line, hugging the curve of the wall to push his way close.

The first man looked pleased to be first. This would be an event talked of for many seasons to come.

Stanley heard Inspector Babumba say, 'What you're permitted to view here is exhibit number one.'

'Ah!' the first interviewee exclaimed.

'This spear was used in a mortal crime.'

Stanley pictured the spear, black with blood from point to tip.

'Do you know the owner of this spear?'

There was no reply.

The Inspector repeated his question slowly in case the man was an imbecile.

'What of it?' the first interviewee said.

'This spear was used to kill.'

'Ah!'

'Please, please, it is necessary for you to inform us of your answer. Do not keep the law waiting.'

Stanley heard Inspector Obonyo agree, 'That's true. The law's waiting.'

Now the man spoke, but quietly, as if he did not wish to be overheard. 'It's the Head Herdsman's spear.'

Inspector Babumba asked loudly, 'The Head Herdsman's spear? Are you positive in your identification?'

The crowd exclaimed 'Eh!', and all eyes were on Bejuura.

Stanley heard Bejuura's sullen voice, 'I'm the Head Herdsman. This man's right. That's my spear.'

The crowd gasped and shrunk back. Stanley took the opportunity to push a little nearer to the door. The daub pressed rough against his cheek.

'Then where did you go three nights ago?'

'I was in the kraal all night.'

'You have a strong arm to throw this spear eight miles.'

Inspector Babumba chortled to himself. There was a short silence and then Inspector Obonyo laughed. It sounded to Stanley as if a hippo had belched.

Inspector Babumba said, 'This spear, this very spear which is revealed to you by the law, was found at the scene of the crime.'

'It must have been taken by a ghost. I was not there.'

'You're spinning fables for the children,' the Inspector replied, and then added, slowly and pointedly, 'Telling ghost stories.'

Inspector Obonyo's voice vibrated the packed-earth floor again. 'That is exact. Ghosts – they're just for the kids.'

Everyone was quiet.

'The law does not believe in ghosts. We cannot arrest a ghost. The judge cannot sentence a ghost. The law cannot hang a ghost.'

'Hang?' Bejuura's voice sounded thin.

'You're under arrest. You must accompany us to the police station for further questioning.'

Stanley squeezed his head around the entrance but all he could see were the whites of the *gyoogis*' eyes in the dark hut: triumphant and staring. Why doesn't Bejuura tell them that Zachye stole it? Stanley thought, but then considered the shame.

The *gyoogi* handcuffed Bejuura and led him away. The crowd shook their heads. As Bejuura passed, Stanley saw his wandering eye fix on him, and stay on him long past the angle an eye could naturally revolve.

For a long time after the *gyoogi* had gone the men and women discussed Bejuura's crime; at first in terms of disbelief that one with a roving eye could find his target with a spear, and then later agreeing that they had always suspected he could kill, and were thankful that the clan members had escaped falling victim to such a man.

Once again Stanley found himself lying awake at night. When he had asked Erinesti what they should do, Erinesti had said that it was up to Zachye on his return to speak up if he chose.

A quiet Zachye walked into the kraal with his father two days later. When Stanley asked him where he had been he shrugged his shoulders. His father told his mother that he had found Zachye trying to find work in the town. She did not ask more for she was bursting to tell them what had happened to Bejuura.

'Murder?' Stanley's father repeated.

'It was murder. Bejuura killed a man, but he left his spear at the place.'

Stanley's father shook his head slowly. 'Bejuura?'

Zachye had been listening intently. Now he spoke up. 'Father, I have something to tell.'

'Not now.'

'Sir, it concerns this matter with Bejuura.' His parents swivelled around. 'It was a goat.'

'What goat?' his father asked.

'It was not murder. I only killed a goat.'

'Don't speak in riddles. Speak plainly.'

'I wanted to take its skin and sell it in the town. To pay for my school fees.'

'How does this concern Bejuura?'

'I killed the goat with Bejuura's spear. I took his spear.'

'Cho!' his mother cried.

'But who used that spear to carry out the murder?' his father asked.

Zachye shrugged. 'It was not me.'

His father stood motionless for a long time, and then said, 'Tomorrow I'll walk back to the town, to the police station. Zachye, you will come with me.'

They left early, Kaapa Katura and Zachye, and returned, silent, the next evening after dark, with Bejuura. Bejuura went immediately to his hut. Zachye said nothing, and Stanley knew better than to ask. His mother spoke little for days but Stanley waited patiently, knowing that she would tell him when the will to keep any promise of secrecy she had made to his father had weakened with time.

She told Stanley, 'There was no murder. The police wished to frighten Bejuura. The goat belonged to an important man.'

'What will happen to Zachye?' Stanley asked.

'Nothing. Zachye's too young to be arrested but your father,' she put her hands to her head, 'he will have to pay for the goat.'

Their father came into the hut that evening when Stanley and Zachye were about to sleep.

'Zachye, I'll be sending you to school with Stanley. It'll be safer if you're not out on your own on the pastures. Bejuura will not forget you wronged him. My cousin, Felice's father, is to pay your fees.'

Zachye looked triumphantly at Stanley but his father reprimanded him, 'I have shame that I should have begged again. Do not disappoint me at school.'

Stanley slept the sleep of one untroubled by the spirits. To think his protector would be going with him to school! But his mother went out to make offerings in the ghost huts. When she returned she stood for a long time watching over her sons while they slept. Outside in the kraal the cattle moaned, and on the far horizon a grass fire burned.

SIX

Felice's father, Kaapa Katura's cousin, sent shorts and shirts for Stanley and Zachye. At first Kaapa Katura said he was minded to sell them for cash to pay the hut tax but the village headman dissuaded him, saying that the schools did not want people in 'backwards' clothing of skin or bark. The night before their first day at school the boys' mother permitted them to put on their uniform. With the younger children watching they pulled their shorts up as high as they could, but as soon as they let go the shorts dropped to their feet. The little children laughed. Zachye boxed one on the head.

'They are for big *Bazungu*,' Stanley said.

Zachye examined his shorts, turning them around to find an alternative way of wearing them.

He puzzled over the buttons before saying excitedly, 'Look, these are to tighten them.'

They threaded the buttons through the buttonholes and tried again. Zachye's stayed up but Stanley's fell to his ankles again.

'You will have to hold them,' Zachye said. 'You cannot go to school naked like a baby.'

They swaggered around, their legs moving back and forward inside, and independent of, the wide leggings. Then they put on their new shirts (the shoulder seams of Stanley's shirt reached halfway down his arms) and then paraded up and down with their spears. Stanley held tightly onto his shorts with his other hand. The onlooking children drew back to let them pass.

That night, lying inside his shorts, Stanley could not sleep for thinking about holding his shorts all the way to school and all day at school. So he unthreaded a bark strand from the hut wall and tied it around his waist. There were floppy folds above the makeshift belt, but when he stood the shorts stayed up.

They started out before dawn: Stanley, Zachye and their father. He accompanied them in silence to the road, by which time a thickening band of light was spreading across the eastern horizon in the direction of the school. Without a word Kaapa Katura took their spears, turned and left them to walk on down the road. Later, when Stanley had become familiar with measuring distance by the multiples of a fixed yardstick, rather than the passage of the sun across the sky against the speed of walking, he would work out that the distance each way was nine miles. Only nine miles from the old world to the new.

As they looked ahead down the road they saw other children, in twos and threes, walking in the same direction, all quiet as they emerged from the night.

Stanley dated their arrival into the new world not by their stepping into the school compound but by the rude and terrifying appearance of a bus, which came out of nowhere from behind. For a moment it was as if a crested crane was shrieking in his ear, and then he found himself being propelled into the culvert by Zachye. The bus, horn still honking viciously, passed above them: a high wall of rubber, metal and glass. Giant machinery on the rampage. Stanley lay frightened in the ditch while the single rear light gouged an angry red line down the road. He had instinctively tightened his hand as the bus leered over him, but he found no spear to grip.

The tension of the past days of anticipation broke when he picked himself up. He trembled, and made a pretence of wiping dirt off his shorts. A shout caused him to look up. Zachye had jumped into the middle of the road and was screaming 'Bean eater! Egg sucker!' at the disappearing bus, whooping as if he was a raiding warrior. Shouts of agreement, and companionable laughter, answered him from the other children down the highway.

'Come on, let's get there,' Zachye said. 'We'll soon be running down this road in my big car, then the bus will get out of our way.' He held up his arm as if balancing his spear and quoted a favourite recitation, 'He Who Is Of Iron, at Burimbi, called up the Abahandura with The One Who Drives Off The Foe.'

Zachye strode on with new vigour. Stanley followed uncertainly in the wake of Zachye's recharged enthusiasm. It seemed that the bus had so excited Zachye that he expected to pick up his car, and the box that made music, at the school that very day. But Stanley longed to be back in the kraal, leading the calves to their mothers, hearing the milk spraying into the gourds from the stroke of the teats, smelling the sleepy smoke from the dozing fires.

Thirsty, for they had drunk little milk in the haste of leaving, they followed the other children into the school compound past a sign, which they could not read. Six hard-walled buildings, with shining metal roofs and black-framed windows cut in orderly repetition along the white walls, lay in two neat rows along each side of the compound on raised concrete plinths. Standing outside the door of the last building on the left, where the rising sun flashed from a pane of glass, was a squat man with skin of such a deep and non-reflective black that Stanley nudged Zachye to draw his attention to him.

'He must be from far away – further than the hills,' Stanley said, staring.

They could see by the flicks of the whites of his eyes that the man was scanning the compound, although his head remained motionless, stuck well forward on his shoulders, his neck short or possibly absent. His tie looked like a pink belly streak under the shell of his black jacket.

'His mother was a beetle,' Zachye sniggered. 'Let me guess – a dung beetle I think.'

Two other boys nearby overheard him, laughed, and then passed on the man's nickname to the other children.

With a jerk of an upper limb, Dung Beetle crossed his chest with the short knobbed stick he held, and shouted out, in Runyankore but with a rasping foreign accent, 'Attention! Attention! All P1 children this way.'

'Are we P1?' asked Stanley to Zachye, buffeted by the milling children.

'How do I know?'

The youngest children were heading that way so they followed, and were encouraged by the twitching of Dung Beetle's stick to enter the classroom. Stanley looked around to find the *Bazungu* children, but there were none. This surprised him: if this was the *Bazungu* Education, where were the *Bazungu*?

Inside the classroom the children made way for Zachye. He looked tall and muscular compared with everyone else.

'Are you one of the teachers, sir?' a girl asked Zachye.

Zachye looked down at her and then around at the other children, some of whom were looking up at him expectantly.

'Heh? I'm starting at school.'

'Hah! Your father must be poor. He cannot send you to school until you're old,' the girl said. She and her friends turned to each other and giggled.

Zachye pushed his way to the back of the class. He leant against a window and looked out. Stanley stood beside him feeling the cold of the concrete under his bare feet. Two small, upside-down flies buzzed on the window ledge. Zachye silenced them with sticky shots of spit.

Dung Beetle came in and scuttled in a fast-legged action to the front of the class. The children stopped talking immediately and averted their eyes. Dung Beetle spoke in English. 'Good morning, children.'

Stanley did not understand. No one else spoke and no one looked at Dung Beetle. He brought his stick down with a loud crack on his table so that the children jumped.

'When I say "Good morning, children" you must answer "Good morning, teacher."'

He repeated his greeting. A few replied timidly, 'Good morning, teacher.'

Dung Beetle became agitated. 'Attention! P1 children! Look at me! I'm your teacher. I have my school certificate. For too long you have been quiet when your elders have spoken to you. That is respect, which was good, but now you must learn something new.' He hit the table again with his stick, making Stanley jump again, although Stanley could tell from Zachye's slouching stance that he was not intimidated, or impressed. 'This is your first lesson. When I speak to you, then you must look at me and you must answer me loudly. That is the way of the school certificate.'

He greeted them again. More answered him, but he was not satisfied.

'You! Come here.' He pointed at Stanley. Stanley moved forward, looking at the floor. The teacher put his face to Stanley's. 'Good morning, children.'

Stanley was barely audible. 'Goo maw.'

The teacher's arm swung in a wide arc and the stick buried itself in the folds of Stanley's shorts. 'Look at me when I speak to you and speak loud.'

Stanley glanced anxiously at the teacher, whose face was still close to his own. His bulbous cheeks and prominent forehead reminded Stanley of the outer mouthparts of some strange forest animal – or beetle – that might suddenly extend itself, fix onto his face and suck him. A musty odour seemed to be oozing from some pore. But then the teacher withdrew, as if taking pity, and sent Stanley back to his bench. He saw the wide eyes of the other children follow him back. The stick had not hurt but this first lesson had been hard.

'Now we have lesson number two,' Dung Beetle said. 'Stand in front of the benches.'

The children complied urgently, although they stood too many to some benches and too few to others.

'Sit down.'

They started to bend.

'Stand up.'

Some sat down.

'Sit down.'

Some stood up.

The stick fell on the table again. 'No, P1!'

Stanley, mindful of lesson number one, and of the stick, looked fully at his teacher. For a moment Dung Beetle said nothing, as if overwhelmed by the enormity of his task. He said wearily, 'When the headmaster comes in I'll command you to stand up, to sit down, to stand up.' His voice strengthened. 'If anyone does not obey, they will feel the full power of my stick.'

They practised until all knew lesson number two. It was as well, for soon another man came in who could only, by his bearing and the way their teacher backed away a little, like a nervous insect, be the headmaster. Dung Beetle recovered, and jerked himself straight – even his head was higher between his shoulders. He held his stick diagonally across his chest, as if giving a pledge. Then he rasped, 'Stand up.'

Everyone stood.

'Sit down.'

Everyone sat down.

'Stand up.'

Everyone stood up.

'First rate!' the headmaster shouted.

Dung Beetle's head subsided onto the front of his chest again, his grin stretching out, a deep red cleft beneath his nasal spaces.

Then the headmaster turned to the class and yelled at them in short sentences, as if they were sitting far away on the hill behind the school. 'You are fortunate. You have Mr Mbuzi as your teacher. He has passed the school certificate.' Dung Beetle tapped his stick on his chest and dipped his head. 'You are forty in this class. Only two of you will receive your certificate.'

Stanley looked over at Zachye, puzzled. Why was there such a shortage of school certificates? Zachye's return look was steady and reassuring, and he indicated with his finger that the two certificates were for Stanley and himself.

'Do not be sad. You will know geographies and handworks. Also, English and algebras. First rate. Also, rural sciences. All are useful to our new country.'

Dung Beetle's head oscillated up and down a little, whilst his beady black eyes stayed still, fastened on the headmaster. Stanley thought that if his teacher had an extendable tongue he could easily lift a fly off the headmaster's nose.

'The school is shoddy after the holidays. This morning P1 will tidy up. You will pull up the weeds. You will remove the stones from the field where we grow our vegetables. Mr Mbuzi will supervise you after registration.'

A table and chair had been set up in the middle of the compound. A woman in a bright yellow jacket and high hair (just like Felice's, Stanley thought), sat at the table with her elbows resting on a large open book. The headmaster stood behind her. Dung Beetle pushed the children this way and that but they had no idea what he was trying to do. Eventually a queue was achieved with Zachye at the front. Stanley stood behind him. The woman at the table asked Zachye his name, the name of his father, his village, the headman and how old he was.

To this last question, Zachye said, 'It's like this: after I was born my mother weaned me, and then I helped in the kraal, and then I looked after my father's cattle.'

'Yes, that's what has happened to you, but when were you born? What is the date of your birth?' She tapped her pencil on the table.

Zachye turned out his hands in a daring show of exasperation. 'I was born on the day my mother gave me birth.'

Someone tittered in the queue behind.

'This boy's from an ignorant family,' the headmaster hollered, making the woman in the yellow jacket startle forwards. 'Ask him which group of children he belongs to.'

'What's your group?'

'Ntooro dance.'

'He's about twelve,' the headmaster said.

The woman wrote it in the register.

When Stanley was asked the same question he replied that he was the younger brother of Zachye. The headmaster took stock of him, and told the woman to give him the age of eight.

As the children came out of the queue Mr Mbuzi set them to work, pointing out the area to be cleared and where to put the waste. All morning they pulled up weeds and picked out stones. When they thought they had finished Mr Mbuzi pointed out smaller stones that they had not yet removed, and when those had been collected he pointed out still smaller stones, poking them with his stick.

Stanley stuck by Zachye. He longed for some milk, but he worked hard for he did not want the stick. Zachye handled the weeds and stones with reluctance, only picking out stones on the surface – avoiding getting dirt under his fingernails. 'Why are we soiling ourselves working like people who dig in fields and keep goats?' he grumbled. 'We're being taught to become like boys from another tribe. If our father could see us now he'd be provoked.'

'We must listen to the things Dung Beetle says, and then it'll be you and me who get the school certificates,' Stanley replied.

Zachye muttered, 'Listen to the beetle and pick up his dung for him.'

Just when Stanley thought he would faint from thirst, Dung Beetle called, 'Attention P1! Come for food now.'

Again they were corralled into a line, this time in front of a tap standing on its own over a drain at the edge of the compound. Dung Beetle held a metal plate, on which was a large green cube. Zachye took his place at the front of the queue again because the other children lined up naturally behind him. He looked around and pulled Stanley in front of him. Stanley was glad to go first; he had seldom drunk water, but he was thirsty enough to drink whatever was provided. Dung Beetle called him forwards. Stanley cupped his hands under the tap, let them fill and then bent his head to drink.

'What are you doing, boy?' asked Dung Beetle, inserting his stick between Stanley's lips and his hands. He thrust the plate towards him. Stanley looked at Dung Beetle, confused. He could not think what was expected of him, so he took the green lump on the plate, put it to his lips and took a bite. It had the texture of the hardened fat of an animal. Dung Beetle snatched it back.

'Are you so ignorant?'

Stanley started gagging, and spat again and again, although his dry mouth had little to spit. The food was worse than he could ever have imagined. He thought it little wonder that his ancestors had decided to take nothing but milk and blood.

'Ha! He has eaten the soap,' shouted a voice in the queue. The line disintegrated as the children stepped out to see.

Dung Beetle was shaking his head. 'This is soap. Have you never seen soap? You don't eat it. You wash your hands with it. Where have you been living? Does your mother not wash your clothes?'

Even in his distress, Stanley remembered lesson number one. He looked straight into Dung Beetle's black eyes, and said clearly, 'My mother cleans our clothes with butter, sir.'

He gagged again but kept looking Dung Beetle in the eye.

Dung Beetle spoke to himself, wonderingly, shaking his head, 'Butter? Ah! For cleaning skins and bark. So, it's true, I've been posted to a backward place.' Then he addressed Stanley, 'Let me show you.'

Dung Beetle took the soap and created a rich lather all the way down his forearms, and then held up his arms to the line of children. 'In teacher training college I was informed of something that I didn't believe. I was informed of a new idea, a modern idea: that you youngest children would need reading, writing and arithmetic, yes, but also soap! How I doubted this idea; surely spelling and algebra were all that were necessary. Now I stand here and think that my supervisors were progressive educators.'

After the children had all washed their hands, some still giggling and whispering 'Soapy Stanley' to each other, they were summoned to a building full of tables and benches. White enamelled mugs, large jugs of water and pans brimming with creamy, yellow plantains lay ready on the tables. At last Stanley could drink. But first the headmaster gave an address, still shouting, welcoming the newcomers to the school, saying that if they worked hard they would be able to help build the nation, and might even become teachers themselves one day – 'First rate'. Zachye caught Stanley's eye and pulled his neck in to imitate Dung Beetle. The headmaster finished his address with a prayer. Stanley noticed that the teachers mumbled 'Amen' when the headmaster had finished. All except Dung Beetle, who croaked.

The children scooped up dollops of plantain with their hands and ate eagerly, but Stanley hesitated, making an expression of disgust to Zachye.

'You can eat this,' Zachye said, and took a little himself.

Stanley stared at the yellow mountain. The taste of soap came back again. He shivered deep in his chest and tears came to his eyes. Then he became aware that Dung Beetle was standing over him. He could hear his rasping breathing, which quickened in pace like an annoyed cricket. Stanley bent his head and a tear plopped onto the wooden table, making a dark spot.

Dung Beetle was speaking to him, but had bent down and put his face near so that the other children could not hear. 'This food is good. Look at your brother – he likes it. You should try some. Some day, little boy, when you're grown, it'll remind you of the good times you had at school.'

Stanley put the tip of a finger on the food and then touched the tip of his tongue, holding his cup of water at the ready. But he found it quite edible, and he joined Zachye in scooping handfuls with the other children.

Back in the classroom Dung Beetle said that the next day they would be working again to make the school tidy, but before they went home he wished to teach them lesson number three. On his desk was a neat stack of exercise books and pencils.

'These are your writing books. These books belong to you. These are your pencils. These pencils belong to you.'

Stanley was following well. Lesson number three was not difficult. He wondered how many lessons there would be until school certificate. He thought there might be as many as one hundred.

'So, here is lesson number three. If your exercise book or your pencil is lost, you will have to pay many shillings to buy another one.'

Stanley felt cross at the injustice of it and turned to Zachye, who had a quizzical look. Why would they have to suffer for such random events?

Dung Beetle knew their thoughts, for he said, 'When I was a child, I was like you – I believed that ghosts caused such things. I didn't believe that I myself, by my own foolishness, could cause anything to break or become lost. But this is not a progressive belief.' He scratched his back with his stick. 'We must take responsibility for our own actions.'

Stanley needed time to think about lesson number three, but he was excited to receive his book and pencil. He remembered Felice and her book, and believed that when he opened his book he would somehow hear the story of Mary and her friend again. On the cover of the book was a picture of two *Bazungu* children, holding hands, and walking together towards a mountain. Stanley stared at the picture for a long time. They were the only *Bazungu* children he had seen at school. When he opened the book he was surprised. Each page had only lines. He could not make the book speak, although he looked at it hard and moved his lips silently.

Rusoro Town, Uganda, Independence Day
1962

Together we'll always stand.
from the Ugandan National Anthem

The drumbeats faded. A man in a knee-length cape, banded in black, yellow and red, climbed in a dignified manner onto the podium in the centre of Rusoro stadium. Next to the podium the Ugandan flag, in the same colours (black for the people, yellow for the sunshine that gives light and sustenance, and red for the blood brotherhood of man) hung proud on a freshly painted white flagstaff. Two policemen in khaki drill, socks pulled taut to their knees, stood as rigid as their rifles either side of the flagstaff. A British officer had earlier lowered the Union Jack. The ranks of the Boys' Brigade fidgeted in anticipation. Stanley pressed his cymbals into the side of his thighs lest they spontaneously sound but Zachye spun his drumsticks carelessly in his fingers.

The man in the cape lifted a loudhailer (also belted in the national colours). He cleared his throat down the device to prime its mechanism.

'Ladies, gentlemen, chiefs, headmen, workers, children, clerks, officials, Boys' Brigades, youth of today, elders, traders, Girl Guides, clergy of religion.' He paused between each greeting, so that each group could feel their inclusion in, and importance to, the new nation. The European ladies smiled, as if pleased to be addressed first and foremost. Some groups clapped themselves as they were greeted.

'We are here in the stadium to celebrate our Independence Day.'

The dignitaries on the platform, and the Europeans in the crowd, applauded in a stately manner. The rest of the crowd ululated. Songs started spontaneously from different points in the stadium, to just as rapidly die away as the speaker continued.

'On this day we have received our independence.'

More clapping, louder this time, but drowned by a roar from the crowd. Only those closest to the speaker heard him say, 'Our nation is born.'

The man spoke of the coming together of many tribes under one nation: like the Children of Israel, like the followers of Mohammed, like the four tribes of the British, but also like the clans and tribes of these very lands in days past who had accommodated each other in treaties and understandings. So all were bound together, but now irrevocably, as Ugandans. Unity under the wise and forward-thinking leadership of Dr Apollo Milton Obote. More cheering. He introduced each of the other speakers in turn. All pledged themselves and their constituencies to the advancement of Uganda.

As soon as the last speaker had taken his stand the Boys' Brigade leader, Mr Nyaishokye, turned to face his brigade. He held his baton across his upper lip to signal that the moment had come for the band to lead the parade around the stadium. Stanley wore his uniform with pride: they had been chosen because they represented the future. They were young, disciplined, uniformed and loudly exuberant. For months they had practised, and today they had left before daylight in a bus laid on for them by the district administration. Now, pressed from behind by the other groups in the parade and forbidden to step over a ribbon on the ground in front, they were bunched up so tight that they had difficulty finding space to bring their instruments to their lips or chests. Stanley found himself being pushed forward into Zachye. Zachye's head whipped around. He cursed.

'It's not me,' Stanley said.

He looked at Zachye, pleadingly. Zachye scowled and turned his attention back to the bandmaster. Stanley tried to recall the last time that Zachye had been agreeable towards him. At school Zachye always went with a group of older boys nicknamed the *shenzi*. They skulked around in a pack, like stray dogs; sat sullen in class; organised strikes on the least pretext; beat up those they disliked; and made themselves a nuisance to the girls. At home Zachye ignored him, or made remarks about the ignorance of the unschooled peasants in the kraal, including his mother, and, during the holidays, when his father instructed him to go with the cattle (now that it was safe, after Bejuura's death in an incident with hyenas while he was drunk), he grumbled about having to do a herdsman's work. He said that it was not suitable work for the *Wabenzi* – the Mercedes class.

Suddenly they were away, Zachye launching forward, ahead of Stanley, his elbows out as he raised a spectacular drum roll that introduced the bugles. Stanley counted the beat as he marched along, waiting to clash his cymbals. It felt good to be marching with Zachye, and right that Zachye should lead and be playing the more difficult instrument. He was proud of the panache of his brother's playing, and today he listened especially carefully to ensure he kept to Zachye's rhythm. Music was the only school subject that Zachye was better at than himself. It was painful to think of it: how Zachye was so tense in anticipation of his test results, but how he, Stanley, always came first; always received the prizes and was the one to please Dung Beetle. It was not that Zachye did not want to succeed. Once, when he was tending the cattle with Zachye in the holidays, he found Zachye studying his exercise book, but when he had offered to help Zachye had said 'Pee off,' and thrown the book aside.

They carried on marching noisily around the track. Behind them children from schools from as far away as sixty miles followed, in blocks of uniform colour. A *Muzungu* woman led a group of bemused *Bazungu* children from the nearby European boarding school. The ladies of the Mothers' Union, in bright headscarves and bold-patterned dresses, swung in a fluid dance in opposition to the fixed beat of the band. Veterans of the King's African Rifles, in black-tasselled scarlet pillbox hats, leopard-skin coats, and white boots, brought the parade to a startling finale. They were led, it was announced, by a Captain Idi Amin. The ceremony ended with the singing of the National Anthem.

Oh Uganda! May God uphold thee,
We lay our future in thy hand.
United, free,
For liberty,
Together we'll always stand.

Stanley clasped his cymbals to his chest, to hold in his pride. Mr Nyaishokye caught his eye and they sang the verses loudly to each other.

Stanley loved Mr Nyaishokye. At Sunday School Mr Nyaishokye had told him and his friends of the Uganda Martyrs, the first Ugandan Christians, whom the king had put cruelly to death.

'They died singing,' Mr Nyaishokye said.

The brigade enacted the scene one Sunday, and Stanley volunteered to be a martyr burning at the stake. Standing there in the pyre of wood and grass, he imagined his shoes and socks, shorts, shirt and then body melting away in the weightless power of the flames. A spirit entered him, but he felt no fear. From that time on he decided to live as if he, Stanley Katura, was an Uganda Martyr who had not been reduced to spitting fat and black ash but had been preserved from the fire like Shadrach, Meshach and Abednego, in the furnace of King Nebuchadnezzar, in that land in the Bible. What would Shadrach have done with the rest of his life? Stanley found himself nicknamed Saint Stanley after that, but he lost no friends. And, best of all, no one ever called him Soapy Stanley again.

The Boys' Brigade had to walk a long way back to their bus: out of the stadium with the still effervescent crowds, across a wide waste-ground normally frequented by goats nibbling on forlorn stands of grass, and then down the main street towards the bus park on the edge of town. The band mixed with the crowds as they walked towards the road. Stanley felt a tap on his shoulder. It was Kabutiiti, his cousin, with some others, whom he assumed were friends from the capital.

'Oh! We didn't expect ...' Stanley said.

Kabutiiti shook his hand. 'We decided to drive here for the celebrations when we heard that you were both performing in the parade.' He congratulated them on their playing. A smiling city-girl in a shimmering red blouse, black skirt and glassy high-heeled shoes stood by his side. She wore a yellow headband. Stanley waited to be introduced.

'Do you not recognise me?' she asked.

Stanley was sure he would have remembered such a pretty girl, but for a moment his mind was blank.

'You're Felice,' Zachye said, pulling down a fold of shirt that had ridden up above his drum. 'Forgive us,' he added, 'we're just herdsmen.'

Stanley winced with embarrassment. Here was the daughter of the man who had paid for their education, and they had met her before, although over four years ago. How could he have failed to remember her? Had she changed so much? Yes, he decided, she had. All the men passing by were glancing at her.

'It's OK, it's a long time. I was the girl with the book. I think I was arrogant, so let me apologise for that and then it's quits.' She smiled at them, relaxed. They grinned back, intimidated.

Kabutiiti introduced his other friends: Wilberforce, going to Makerere University to study law; Godfrey, starting soon with Barclays Bank in Kampala; Joseph, due to start training as an accounts assistant with East African Airways.

'We're staying in the Pelican Inn, up the hill. Can you come for drinks? You can see the lake from there. We can give you a lift back home in my father's car if you wish.'

Kabutitii's friends nodded cheerily in agreement. Stanley looked at his brother. It should be possible.

'We've got to go back in our bus,' Zachye said. He looked towards the street as if to show that they might already be late.

'Another time then,' Kabutiiti said.

They walked on together, Kabutiiti beside Zachye asking after the family, Stanley noticing how Zachye was a little distant in his replies. Felice came up beside Stanley, saying that her father had told her how well he was doing, and that she hoped they would see him in the capital some time. Perhaps he would get a place at the university. She hoped to go there herself; most girls from her school did. She was now at a boarding school, a school originally set up for the sons of chiefs. Had God not blessed her? She talked to him as if he was a modern boy, someone who belonged to her group, no longer a herd boy who could not read. He started to feel at ease and a little excited. If he went to the capital he would have companions such as Felice and her friends. The future blossomed bright – in yellow, shimmering red and jet black.

They said goodbye on the main street, Zachye remaining reserved; more than that, Stanley thought: shifty. They walked on in silence.

The shops were shut for the national holiday and everyone was on the road: Indian shopkeepers, with and without turbans, and their families, the men in conversation, strolling with their hands clasped behind their backs, the women in glowing saris; dapper young African men in pressed trousers and collared shirts, talking loudly in groups with their well-shoed girlfriends from the offices on the hill above town; large men displaying brightly patterned *kitengi* shirts; village people, bare-footed but in newly washed shorts, woollens and wraps, wandering about, examining the faces of the modern Ugandans to understand what they themselves must become. Down the centre of the street bunting spanned the lampposts. High on each lamppost was a picture of the Prime Minister's benign and young-looking face. Prime Minister Obote also looked down from above the doors of the Indian *dukas*; no one wanted to be seen to be anything but loyal Ugandans. Above one shop Stanley could see fresh paint on the sign. 'Patel, Patel and Patel' was still there, but he could just make out '(All British Subjects)' through the paint.

They walked on past a billboard advertising 'The completely new Anglia – the Belle of the Ball'. The slogan puzzled Stanley, but he noticed that the car was sunshine yellow, like the strip in their new flag. They passed the Caltex petrol station, its uniformed attendants ready for service with their window-cleaning rubbers and flimsy carbon-paper receipt books. Beyond the road that branched off down to the lake the town became less certain of its order. The white-painted kerbstones were gone and in place of the smooth water run-offs down the side of the road the tar ended like a broken biscuit. Erosion gullies ran between bicycle repair sheds, kiosks and small bars with glassless windows and rough wood doors. The buildings bore the names of Ugandan proprietors written on the peeling plaster in uncertain capitals, as if their tenure was provisional. The lampposts did not extend this far, and as the outskirts of the town were reached magnificent eucalyptus trees gave way to common black wattle. Just before the bus park the tar gave out and the roadside trees became grey from a dirty coating of exhaust soot and road dust. The town was frayed at the margins, but Stanley was confident the fine weave of its centre would extend rapidly outwards now that Independence Day had come. One day there would be a tar road to their kraal, so that Zachye could drive right up to the entrance in his Anglia. Stanley blinked hard, cutting the dream. How could Zachye ever have such things? He would never get his school certificate. Stanley resolved again to help him if he could. If Zachye would let him.

At the bus park soldiers were climbing into the back of an army truck. The boys looked on admiringly, for here was the real thing. Boys' Brigade now seemed like a child's game.

Zachye surprised Stanley by saying to him, 'They have big bands in the army.'

The truck drove off and the children cheered at the soldiers sitting facing each other in the back. But the soldiers did not cheer back. Stanley thought it was because of their importance in defending the new nation. It must have weighed heavily upon them.

A group of boys about Zachye's age, but in dirty school uniforms holed at the shoulders, hung around a kiosk signed *G.O.B. Bazanyamaso High Life Beverages*. Others stood leaning against a billboard, which read 'Together we'll always stand', from a line in the National Anthem.

An Indian boy, about their age, walked purposefully past them, carrying a tin of cooking oil. One of the boys leaning against the kiosk, with one knee bent and his foot on the wall, shouted, 'Hey, half-boy. Go back to India.' A pied crow investigated a discarded tin near the kiosk. 'And take your scavenging Indian crows with you.'

Another boy tapped his forehead in the place where the Hindu women painted their red bindi, and shouted, 'Bullet hole.'

The Indian boy did not turn his head, but he quickened his pace. Stanley was about to pass comment on their rudeness on this of all days (were there not two members of parliament named Patel?), but he saw Zachye had put his hands in his pockets and, checking to see that Mr Nyaishokye was looking the other way, was drifting towards the boys. As he did so he shed his military bearing and slumped into a rolling walk, his limbs lolling at his side. Stanley saw Zachye speak to the boys and take the offered draw on a cigarette. He seemed to know them. A barefooted girl in a soiled dress came from behind the kiosk and greeted Zachye in a less than formal manner, offering an outstretched arm to him, which he slapped. Stanley was unsure whether this was a gesture of affection or dismissal.

On the way back to their school in the bus Stanley tried to engage Zachye in conversation. 'Do those boys have work?'

'Of course not. They're half-educated. They didn't get their school certificate. What work can they get in town?'

'But they're looking for work?'

'What for? There is no work.'

'But they try – surely?'

'What does it matter? They'll never own their own cars, or wear a black suit to pick up the girls from the banks and the offices.'

Zachye was looking away out of the window. Stanley thought of Felice: she was surely a top office girl. 'We'll both get our certificates,' he said, but his voice trailed off. Even he could not make himself believe it any more.

Zachye shoved him in the ribs with his elbow, but said in a forgiving tone, 'Little brother, you don't have to look after me. Did I not look after you at one time?'

'I remember,' Stanley said in a whisper.

Zachye closed his eyes as if to go to sleep, but Stanley watched the terraced fields rising away above the red earth of the roadside cuttings.

Then Zachye spoke suddenly, without opening his eyes. 'Felice! I'll tell you something. One day she'll be mine. You'll see.'

Stanley looked at Zachye, astonished. Then he remembered how, those years ago, Zachye had been right when he told him that he would find a way to persuade his father to send him to school. In non-academic ventures Zachye always found a way. But now Stanley baulked at the thought of Zachye winning Felice. The match could hardly be less likely. With a heavy heart he felt that his brother would not be good enough for her. There was something else as well: Felice was three years older, and he held little hope of finding her love himself, but it would be painful indeed to imagine her and Zachye becoming intimate instead.

The bus slowed to pass a dead cow on the side of the road, a casualty of a vehicle – perhaps the army truck.

Rusoro Town
1957

Sweet Hope, ethereal balm upon me shed,
And wave thy silver pinions o'er my head.
Keats, 'To Hope'

ONE

Michael, aged seven, knelt beside his bed in boarding school at lights out, on a prayer mat made by himself in handwork. His end of term report was to note that he was four foot two and three-eighths of an inch, and three stone nine at the start of term; and four foot two and three-quarters, and three stone nine and three ounces at the end. 'Apart from a head cold Michael has been well, although he developed a marked and frequent batting of his left eyelid in the last week of term. I suspect he was worrying about something.'

Face buried in the blanket, teddy-like in its comforting powers where it curved taut over the edge of the mattress, Michael said some things to God. He strained to hear God say something back. When he had become quiet and had stopped thinking about Rupert Bear and stilts he could feel God noticing him – just a little: a quick pat on his head and letting him know that mostly he was pleased with him. He told God that he was 'cumbered with a load of care' since Thursday so, as the song said he should, he was taking it 'to the Lord in prayer'. It was up to God now to do something.

Michael found it difficult to concentrate on his prayers because Lewis was whispering the Apostles Creed loudly from a little red book. He always missed out the 'catholic' in 'we believe in one holy, catholic and apostolic church'. 'That's because we're not Catholics,' he had told Michael when he asked.

Simon also knelt beside his bed, but he was reading *Tintin, Destination Moon*. Michael felt a little sad for Simon, that he had not let Jesus into his heart, but he also felt a little sad for himself that he was not reading Tintin. Simon did not have to pray because his parents had told the aunties not to make him. Michael thanked God that his parents were normal, and not funny-odd, like Simon's. He was pleased that Simon learnt memory verses like everyone else because Jesus might say something to him one day in a verse.

Prayers ended, Michael could see a small bump of boy in each bed. Lumpy shadows moved across the walls as Auntie Cynthia took the paraffin lamp out of the room. He lay on his back, pillow puffed around his ears, looking through a gap in the curtains at the night sky beyond the eaves. Bats momentarily extinguished a star here, and a star there, as they swooped out from their roosts in the roof. Michael had once listened so hard that he thought he heard one squeak, but Lewis said, 'My dad says that's impossible.' Lewis's father knew a lot. He flew a Douglas DC3 Dakota for East African Airways and had flown the Queen around when she came to visit Uganda.

Michael heard a whirring sound and wondered where the moths went when Auntie Cynthia took away the light. He heard Simon get out of bed and then there was a tinkle sound. That was the sound when they aimed straight: it made a plinking at the end. When Simon pushed the potty back under the bed there was a scraping noise on the concrete floor. Simon had once drank his potty for a dare; he drank it all up and put his potty on his head. He said he could easily do it again but he didn't. Michael didn't drink his because he knew Jesus wouldn't be pleased with him.

When he closed his eyes he saw himself running for the school lawns as he had that morning when they had swarmed out of Nature Study. Rainbows under the sprinklers on the spongy grass made hoops of colour to dive through before cartwheeling down and down towards the end of the lawn where the grass slipped under the purple, thin-as-crêpe-paper, surface of the lake. The volcano on the opposite shore rose up like a giant green papier mâché cone. Fishing canoes made sparkling paths of light as they crossed between the islands.

Auntie Cynthia, the matron, was on play duty. 'Children, look at the swallows!' Michael looked up and felt dizzy from their dipping and looping. 'To see how God in all his creatures works!'

Auntie Cynthia was always saying things like that, from a poet called

Wordsworth. Michael did not like Wordsworth – his name was stuffy and his poetry books had lots of tiny words all bunched up together. But on Sunday afternoons Auntie Cynthia made them sit on their grass mats under the branches of the giant pepper trees on the upper lawns, so she could read Wordsworth to them. She liked him, she said, because he loved God's creation: flowers, birds, clouds, every pretty thing. Michael liked the birds because they zoomed. That they were made by God and cared for by God was as obvious as his mother's love, and therefore just as embarrassing to talk about.

It must be fun to be a bird and zoom. His friend, Simon, had put his arms back and ran down the lawn weaving from side to side. They all followed like a flock startled from a tree, swooping down, swerving and twisting through each other. When Michael turned at the bottom of the lawn and looked back at Auntie Cynthia she was smiling at them, her arms folded beneath her bosom as if she was supporting two water balloons. Her cotton dress was floaty and colourful in the morning light.

In his bed Michael looked out at the stars again. Auntie Cynthia is too old to zoom, he thought, but she might float. He imagined her drifting over the pepper trees and then out over the lake. He closed his eyes and then opened them wide again. He was trying to think about funny things, because if he thought about what might happen tomorrow he would not be able to go to sleep. This must be the 'needless pain we bear' that they sang about in the chapel. He watched Auntie Cynthia float about as the swallows swerved around her. She was holding onto the string of a balloon now, like Winnie the Pooh. She was quite happy.

When Michael woke the house martins were shooting past the window. Auntie Cynthia said they came from England so as not to freeze in the winter. When they got cards from England at Christmas they gave them to the Africans as they especially liked cards showing snow. His parents said that he had been to England once, but he couldn't remember being there. In England they had stairs in their houses and one day he would like to try climbing them.

Michael heard the gong being struck and wondered why he had

woken before it had sounded. Out of the corner of his eye, through the window, he saw Auntie Cynthia fall to the ground – she didn't need to be floating up there any more. She just bounced once on her water balloons and then sat on a swing reading poetry. Then he remembered what today was and why he should worry. He sat up straight, scrunched his face up so hard that only the tip of his nose was uncreased, and prayed a memory verse: 'Behold, O Lord; for I am in distress: my bowels are troubled.' He was happy that there was a verse for everything.

On his way to breakfast Michael's worry started to make a lump in his stomach. He stopped outside the kitchen door and looked in. The cooks were folding the porridge with enormous wooden spoons held in their chocolatey hands. Some of the pots were popping and hissing, and he smelt simmering milk. It reminded him of home and he felt the back of his nose get ready to cry. When Freda, the most buxom cook, saw him she wagged a finger at him, playfully telling him off, her palms shockingly pink: she was always washing her hands with the long green bars of Sunlight soap that sat on the sunny window ledge. He was not allowed to disturb the cooks. There were rules and Auntie Cynthia said they were there for a reason, but he couldn't think of any important reason for this one and auntie rules were not as important as God rules. Luckily God rules were very easy to keep, like not murdering people and not coveting your neighbour's wife. He would have to ask his father what that meant, but he was sure he would never do it and never want to do it.

He lingered to catch Freda's attention. They chatted together by making faces, having decided that the rules were only for talking. She cocked her head to one side and he answered by chomping his mouth while he gazed longingly at the pots of porridge. She rolled her eyes around and around as if she was rubbing her stomach. He made a face as if he was going to cry. Freda looked terribly concerned and tilted her head again. He screwed up his face and strained. He could discuss anything with her. She nodded wisely, picked up a spoon and then tiptoed to a cupboard. The other cooks made laughing faces. She had to bend over to reach into the cupboard and her head and shoulders were gone a long time, although her bottom stayed patiently outside, wobbling a little. She shuffled back, turned around and then came towards him with two large prunes balanced on the spoon. She would do well in sports day. He opened his mouth and in popped the prunes. She tapped him lightly on the cheek, as if to say 'swallow those quickly and go'.

Michael was glad that he could tell Freda anything – it was like having a mother at school. The aunties were kind but they had to be strict: they had to be a teacher or a matron or a headmistress and were too busy to be a mother. He grinned at Freda and ran off down the corridor to skid on the polished floor, past the big picture of Jacob wrestling with an angel by a wild shadowy tree.

In the dining room Michael lined up for breakfast with the other children behind thin benches made for small people. Auntie Beryl, the headmistress, led in singing grace. They all sang together, so loud, so clear; a beak-stretching dawn chorus:

All good gifts around us are sent from heaven above.
Then thank the Lord,
Oh, thank the Lord,
For or-or-all his love

Before the 'v' of love the children surged forward, clearing the benches as quick as hurdlers. At least once a week Auntie Beryl clapped her hands and shouted, 'Don't rush.' But it was as useless as trying to hold back the swine from bolting into Galilee. Outside the morning sun melted the lake mists and warmed the red tin roof of the school; the pied crows cackled, the sunbirds splashed in the light and the mousebirds scurried busily up and down the limbs of the custard apple trees. Michael drowned his porridge with cream and spooned on the sugar. Lewis bent over his bowl and blew a deep dimple in the surface of the porridge. When his glasses steamed up he wiped each lens with the tip of his index fingers in a careful circular motion and then blew again, harder, lifting a quiff of ginger hair off his forehead. Simon gripped a fork in his fist, raised his dark peaky eyebrows under his fringe and stabbed down into the bowl. 'Ugh. You must kill the slimy worms first.'

As the last gloops of porridge were scoured off the plates Auntie Beryl clapped her hands. Behind her winged spectacles she waited for the high hubbub to settle down.

'As you all know,' she said, pausing to let the first wave of excitement pass, 'because it's the last Saturday of term we're all going to climb Crystal Mountain.' She paused again to wait for the second larger wave of excitement to end. 'We'll all meet at the front of the school at nine o'clock sharp. Everyone is to wear their plimsolls and everyone is to wear their hats.'

Only Michael's cheer was half-hearted.

As he left the dining room Michael looked through the windows at Crystal Mountain. Lewis said that it was just a hill, but if Michael squinted it looked a lot like a mountain; the white rocks on top were like patches of snow. He thought of Tim in the san: he was going to miss Crystal Mountain. He might have chickenpox but Michael was doubtful; Tim was always saying he was ill so that he could have a spoon of malt. Michael had to squeeze his lips really tight to get all the malt off the spoon because Nurse Janine didn't let them lick the spoon. He thought that was a bit selfish of her.

But now he felt his left eyelid start to twitch and he felt sick. He would also be kept in today; all because of Ticking. He made his way to the bogs, saying 'Behold, O Lord. Behold, O Lord.' God liked His People to say 'Behold'.

He was only just in time for Ticking. Auntie Beryl looked at him rather hard and rather long. He held back tears thinking how unfair it was: all term he had been dying to go up Crystal Mountain and all term he had been able to say yes at Ticking except for the last two days. If they said no for two mornings in a row they were told off but if they said no for three mornings in a row they were given medicine, which tasted revolting – like broccoli – but it was much worse than that: Lewis had said that anyone who needed medicine would be kept in and would miss Crystal Mountain.

He had already said no for the last two mornings.

He squeezed himself into the circle of children in the hall while Auntie Beryl read out their names from a brown book. She had a pencil to put a tick next to their names.

'Annette?'

'Yes.'

'Simon?'

'Yes, sir.'

Squeaky sniggers burst through pursed lips.

'Simon! Do you want to be kept in today?'

'I'm sorry. I'm very, very sorry. I'm really, really sorry.'

'Judith?'

'Yes.'

'Lewis?'

'Yes, big one.'

Even Auntie Beryl smiled, but not Michael. He was going to say yes even though he should say no. He could not miss Crystal Mountain, or he would blub for the rest of his life. It would be very annoying if he found himself in hell when he died because he had lied at Ticking but he would just have to throw himself on God's Mercy And Grace. He decided to ask his father if that would cover this sort of thing.

Something made Michael look at the painting of Jesus on the wall behind Auntie Beryl. Jesus was holding a lantern in a dark forest and was knocking on a wooden door covered in weeds. He was looking sad, straight at Michael. Michael could see that Jesus was thinking of turning his head and walking away into the forest, lonely and disappointed.

'Michael?'

Michael stared at Jesus. Jesus, still sad, looked back at Michael.

'Michael? *Michael?*'

Jesus started to turn his head.

'No!' Michael said, quickly.

'Oh dear, Michael, that's most unfortunate. It's Nurse Janine for you today. Rosalind?'

TWO

Almost the entire school of thirty-three children – in red floppy hats, plimsolls with flip-flopping laces, avocado-green shirts and blouses, cherry-red shorts and skirts – gathered on the gravel drive like a flock of excited parrots. While the aunties did what aunties have to do to get themselves ready to go, a group of jumping, jerking boys gathered around Simon.

'Most of the crystals on the mountain are not real diamonds,' he said. There was sighing and groaning even from those who had not known, until that moment, that the summit glinted with diamonds. Simon looked to see that no adult was near. The boys pushed closer.

'But some *are* real diamonds!' The boys went quiet. 'Once a boy found a huge diamond.'

'A boy from our school?' someone asked.

'Yes, a boy on an outing at the end of term,' Simon said patiently.

'What did he do with it?'

Simon checked again to ensure that the aunties were still busy striding in and out of doors getting ready. Everyone leant in towards him. 'He sold it to an Indian and then went on lots of jet planes all over the world.'

Lewis looked doubtful.

'With his big brother,' Simon added.

The boys started jumping again.

'We'll all have to dig hard,' warned Simon.

'We'll all dig and then share it when we find it,' a first year boy shouted.

Lewis said, 'I think it should be finders-keepers.'

'I'm going to share mine with Michael,' Simon said.

Michael stuck by Simon. He pulled his hat hard down on his head to contain his happiness. He was sorry now that he had thought Auntie Janine was a bit selfish. She had been very nice and said that she expected he would go for a number two tomorrow and, as an extra happiness, as he had not lied, he was not going to hell when he died. That was 'a blessing', as his mother would say. But even better, in the picture in the hall Jesus was no longer looking sad: he was looking at him in a kind sort of way. It was a shame about Tim, still in the san, but it showed that it was better not to tell fibs. And now he and Simon were going to find a diamond. He remembered a memory verse: 'In the house of the righteous is much treasure.' He yanked off his hat and held it high above his head.

Auntie Beryl led the way up Crystal Mountain, pointing out cowpats to avoid on the narrow path. Strong smells marked their ascent: the dank air of a banana grove, a baked-cereal aroma of drying millet on mats laid out in small terraced fields, warm wafts of something earthy but homely from nearby thatched huts, whiffs of wood smoke. Bugs buzzed. They briefly collected a sizeable tail of local children shouting '*Muzungu, Muzungu*' before they reached the clean grassy-knoll air around the rocky outcrops at the summit. The children spilled from the end of the path, curving out over the hilltop like balls from a bagatelle chute, scrabbling to find diamonds amongst the crystals.

The aunties, to make themselves comfortable, laid out a blanket on a grassy slope looking out over the lakeside town. Thirty years before there had been no buildings, just a swamp, but now the town boasted Indian-owned shops, a Caltex filling station, government offices, a craft shop selling woven baskets and place mats, a dusty stadium with a tall concrete perimeter wall, and a whitewashed cathedral. On the summit the noises of the town rarely intruded: the occasional revving of a lorry as it climbed the hill across the valley, a hammer blow against metal from Mr Khan's garage, a whistle from a cowherd further down the hill. The red roof of the school below lay partially hidden under the pepper trees. Canoes lay on the lake like leaf fall.

The girls, uninterested in digging, held hands and spun in circles of laughter. The diggers went quiet, scratching away at the earth with sticks and stones until a wail of disappointment went up. 'The ground's too hard.'

'Don't give up,' Simon insisted.

Lewis cleaned a single crystal with his neatly folded handkerchief and peered into its milky interior with a magnifying glass. Becoming bored with digging, a boy rolled down a bank hollering, 'Look at me,' prompting Auntie Beryl to shout, 'David, don't do that, you'll pick up ticks!'

Michael was especially pleased that he and Simon were going to share the diamonds because Simon would know how to find their aeroplane at the airport and would show him how to get a BOAC Junior Jet Club book; after about a year he would have the signature of every captain in the world. He dug harder.

A bobbing tin debbi appeared lower down the hill, balanced on the head of Godfrey, the general hand and emergency night-watchman. He carried sandwiches from the kitchen in a canvas bag and orange juice in the debbi. He looked tired.

Simon looked up and shouted, 'Hey boy, bring them over here.'

Godfrey ignored him but Michael saw Auntie Beryl standing up like a collapsed crane righting itself. She went rigid, and the wings on her glasses became even more pointy. 'Simon, come here!'

The boys stopped digging and the girls stopped turning because Auntie Beryl was breathing hard and going tomato red. She filled her chest to speak and Michael could see that a detention or, worse, a letter to his parents was coming down on Simon like a steam engine. Michael understood: Godfrey was old enough to be Simon's grandfather, and he had seen Godfrey's grandchildren bend their knees when he passed.

One of Simon's peaky eyebrows looked worried. 'Please, my dad always says boy.'

Auntie Beryl held the steamy air in her chest. No one moved.

After a long time (towards the end of which Michael thought that Auntie Beryl could win a breath-holding competition), her chest emptied suddenly in a short puff like a tyre with a blow-out. 'At school we're to talk to everyone politely.'

'How was I to know the rules are different at school?'

'You're too smart for your own good, young Simon. Go and say sorry to Godfrey.'

'Why do I have to when my dad ...' Simon's voice trailed off as rapidly as Auntie Beryl's chest filled up again.

Simon turned and walked with a stomping step over to Godfrey, who had been flapping his hands at Auntie Beryl while she spoke to Simon as if he did not want her to make a fuss.

All the children waited. Michael put a hand to his face so that he couldn't see – his best friend was the funniest friend he had but sometimes he was just too funny-rude. It was not Simon's fault. Lewis had said that Simon's father was a giant man with hair as black as a crow and red eyes like a dragon, and Michael was sure that he had never heard of the Kingdom of God – so he wouldn't have told Simon about it. The Kingdom of God was very polite.

Michael heard Simon mumble something. He looked though his fingers. Godfrey turned his hands out towards Simon. 'You are welcome, Simon,' he said.

A short squeal punctured the pressured air. 'A snake, a snake, there's a snake!' Rosalind was pointing to the base of a rock. The aunties turned their heads, brows suddenly creased and eyes anxious.

Lewis ran towards the rock shouting, 'Let me see. Don't scare it.'

Michael followed, a little wary. A flash in the grass, quick as sun on a steel blade, and then it was gone.

'Did you see it?' Rosalind screamed.

'Nah. Why did you shout? You scared it.' Lewis pummelled his fists on his head.

Auntie Beryl came over to the rock. Michael thought she must be coming to check that the snake didn't have an angry father hiding in a hole. 'It's all right, it's gone.'

'It's not all right, she scared it away. Why did she have to scream?' Lewis pushed his hands deep into his pockets and swung his foot against the rock so that he nearly overbalanced.

'If you got bitten you'd scream,' Rosalind said. 'Snakes can kill you. They're creepy.'

'Eve didn't scream when she saw the snake in the Garden of Eden,' Lewis answered quickly.

'The snake was just talking to her, that's why. I bet Adam screamed when God told him to get out of the garden.'

Michael said, 'It doesn't say in the Bible that he screamed.' He knew when people made mistakes about the Bible; he and Simon were the best in the school at memory verses, even though Simon didn't have to learn them.

'Well, it doesn't say he didn't. Anyway, he would have screamed if he hadn't been so thick.'

Auntie Beryl had been standing there listening. She said, 'The story's a powerful allegory.'

Auntie Beryl was very brainy and Michael found he could not always understand what she said. His mother said that Auntie Beryl had been teaching at the cleverest university in England and given it all up to come out to Africa to be In The Lord's Service.

Auntie Beryl had a faraway look, but then her eyes squinted at the children. 'It's a picture story to tell us something important. It tells us that we're different from the animals because we can choose whether to be bad or whether to be good. That for us there are such things as bad and good.'

'But everyone knows that, Auntie Beryl,' Michael said.

Michael did not hear her reply because he had remembered something: he had never seen a picture story showing Adam and Eve with all their clothes off, and he had checked in the books in his father's office. He didn't think his Bible picture stories were much good. They never showed him what he really wanted to see: the things his mother didn't want to talk about, like people drowning in the bubbly water around Noah's ark, or John the Baptist's head on the plate, or Abraham spilling his seed.

A cloud cast a shadow on the mountain and a cool stirring of air forewarned of rain. The lake shifted as if brushed by dark forces. All the canoes pointed to the town. The aunties gathered up their blankets, put the thermos and plastic mugs in the grass basket from the craft shop and told the children to get ready to leave.

'Oh no, not yet.' Michael hadn't found a single diamond, although Simon had been stuffing his pockets. He returned to the scratchings he had made, stuck his fingers into a clump of grass and yanked as hard as he could. He felt his face go red, as it had that morning trying to do the number two before Ticking. The grass came up with some earth. They weren't that big, the diamonds underneath, but there were three of them. He picked them out and pressed them into his palm. They were hard and had flat edges like the diamonds in his mother's ring. 'Yes!'

'Quick now, it's going to rain,' Auntie Beryl shouted.

The cloud purpled. A thick chill moved over the summit. The aunties hurried themselves up but the digging party stopped and stared. Diamonds were springing from the ground. 'Hail, it's hailing,' Lewis screamed. They all held out their hands to cup the little balls of dancing ice.

'You can eat them. It's manna from heaven,' Michael said.

'No, they're diamonds, we're rich,' Simon said.

They all became frantic collecting the hail, even the girls. Michael put some in his pocket with his crystals, and then he put his head back and opened his mouth wide to catch and swallow them.

Simon said, 'Don't swallow them or you'll have to look in your poo for the diamonds. Your wife won't want to wear the ring you give her 'cause of where the diamond's been.'

Michael snapped his mouth shut. Funny-rude, that was what Simon was – that was why he was his best friend.

'We're going now,' Auntie Beryl said, and set off down the hill, although the squall had passed as quickly as it came. Michael fell into line with the others. Auntie Cynthia was behind them. Michael heard her say, 'Oh, my knees! It's possible to pray too much.'

The sides of Michael's shorts were becoming wet. He said gloomily, 'Our treasure's melting.'

'Our treasure in heaven won't melt,' Auntie Cynthia said as she bounced down the path behind him.

Simon drew alongside him. 'These haven't melted.' He opened his hand to show a palm full of stones. Michael fingered the three small wet diamonds in his own pocket and gasped at Simon's collection. Some were probably just crystals but the two chunky ones were obviously diamonds.

'I found them all under a rock. Now we must go and see Mr Patel to see which ones are diamonds. Then he'll buy them and we'll be rich.'

Something made Michael unsure about seeing Mr Patel; he had been so close to making Jesus sad already that day. 'But we aren't allowed to go to Mr Patel on our own.'

'We *are* allowed, because we'll just be passing his shop after church tomorrow. We won't be going to buy anything on our own, we'll just be walking by and saying hello, just being friendly.'

Michael looked doubtful.

'If they're diamonds your dad can get a Zephyr 6.'

'Yes! Then he can go in the East African Safari.'

Because Michael's parents were missionaries and were not selling Kenwood Chefs to the Africans like Simon's father, they didn't have a Citroën DS or a Zephyr 6. They had an Anglia. Some very kind ladies in a place called Box Hill – which he would like to climb some day to look for the boxes – gave them the money for it. It would have been better if the ladies had given them just a little bit more so they could get a Zephyr 6. Anglias were slug-slow and would never beat a Zephyr 6 in the East African Safari. His father had laughed when Michael said that he should do the East African Safari, but Michael thought him a daring driver. If he had a Zephyr 6 he could win easily. If he won then the ladies up Box Hill would be extra pleased. He had been praying every night for a whole term for his father to get a Zephyr 6.

He said to Simon, 'Yes, I think we should definitely ask Mr Patel to tell us if they're diamonds.' And getting his father a car wasn't selfish like going around the world in a jet plane. It was a Kingdom of God thing to do; he was pleased that Simon had thought of it.

Michael thought of something else: God must have especially put the diamonds on Crystal Mountain when he made the world so that he and Simon would find them later. God had very carefully placed each tiny diamond on the summit with his huge fingers, pressing each one into the ground a little to make them not too easy to find. Then he had sat back and waited a long time for him and Simon to find them. Now God must be very pleased. He would be even more pleased when his dad won the Safari. Michael thought it super that he was a big part of God's plan for his father. Even Mr Patel was in the plan, although he probably didn't know it. He pictured his father standing on the winning podium, with his big Bible in his hand, preaching a sermon, while all the Africans crowded around cheering and crying and giving their hearts to Jesus right there where they stood.

He imagined Simon admiring his father's winning Zephyr: the mud-splattered windscreen, the thousands of insects stuck in the radiator grille, the bashed-up wheelarches. He could see Simon turning to him and saying, 'If this is what God can do, I think I'd better let Jesus into my heart.'

They were almost back at the school now. Michael could not hold his thoughts in any longer. He said to Simon, 'These are definitely diamonds because God wants my dad to win the East African Safari.'

Simon looked at his crystals again for a long time and then nodded, as if Michael must know.

At the school Nurse Janine examined them for ticks and scolded them for the grass burrs in their socks; then they sat on the lawns by the lake and had orange juice and sponge cake. Nurse Janine took some cake to Tim in the san.

'He can't be very ill if he's eating cake,' said Michael to Simon.

'Maybe he just wants to die 'cause he didn't go up Crystal Mountain, and Nurse Janine's just trying to make him want to stay alive,' Simon replied.

That evening the children lined up in their fluffy dressing gowns and slippers and padded after Auntie Priscilla into the cosy wood-panelled prayer room off the hall. They all sat in a circle on small wicker-seated chairs around a peacock-blue Persian rug. The shuttered windows had peep holes, although at night they were hidden behind weaver-bird-yellow curtains. A black Bakelite telephone sat on a lamp table in the corner with its wires cut off. The school was not yet on the telephone, the end of the line being some sixty miles away. The aunties used the telephone to explain about prayer. Simon told Michael that once he had got through to the devil and he had to say he had got the wrong number. Michael didn't think that was so funny. They also make-believed the telephone was a public phone box, so they could get the second star of the Wolf Cub Scout badge. An auntie stood behind the curtain and pretended to be a policeman at the other end of the line. They all laughed at the story of the little boy who had said, 'Hello, can you tell my mummy to come and take me home?' and then blubbed.

In the prayer room, in the Presence Of The Lord and in the presence of an auntie, Michael became unhappy again about going to see Mr Patel without permission. He needed to have a sign from God that Mr Patel was also in the plan. In the Bible Gideon had put out a fleece from a sheep when he had wanted a sign. It was the only thing with dew on it in the morning. That was how Gideon knew. There was a fleece rug in front of the telephone table. Michael looked at it for a long time, wondering if he could sneak into the room at night and drag the rug out onto the lawn. But it looked clean and white. What if a dog chewed it in the night or the night-watchmen sat on it? Auntie Beryl was very clever but he doubted that she would understand. God was not exactly making it easy. Sometimes it seemed that it was easier to ask God for forgiveness than ask for permission. He had to ask for another sign. It was not much to ask of God.

Now they were singing again.

Jesus bids us shine
With a pure, clear light,
Like a little candle
Burning in the night.

In this world of darkness
So let us shine,
You in your small corner,
And I in mine.

Michael liked that song. He liked to think that he was a little candle shining in the corner of a dark room, but what did it mean, 'this world of darkness?' All things were bright and beautiful and there were crowns for little children above the bright blue sky. They sang those songs every day. 'Little children, little children ... black and yellow, red and white, all are precious in his sight.' Everyone he knew had let Jesus into his heart, except Simon and some of the Africans, but Simon was soon going to – when they got the money for the Zephyr from the diamonds – and his father and mother were telling the Africans. It was only a matter of time before everyone had let Jesus in and then the whole world, not just home and school and Crystal Mountain and the lake, would be shining.

They sang another song:

He will gather, He will gather
The gems for His kingdom:
All the pure ones, all the bright ones,
His loved and His own.

Michael shot up his hand.

'Yes, Michael?' asked Auntie Priscilla. Normally Michael avoided noticing her much – she had a wide straight fringe of thick brown hair and a round face with chubby cheeks like a monk that Michael thought should belong to a boy, not a grown auntie, and when she prayed she rolled her eyes up so they became white – but now he had to speak to her straight away.

'Are diamonds like gems?'

'Yes, Michael, diamonds are a type of gem.'

It was amazing how quickly God had spoken. While Auntie Priscilla read from a small book called *Daily Light*, Michael was thinking about whether he would stand on the podium with his father when he won the Safari; and whether his father would thank him for his part in Bringing To Fruition God's Plan. And then he heard Auntie Priscilla reading about jewels. He definitely heard her say 'jewels'. God had spoken again in case he had not heard the first time. Sometimes God shouted at him.

Rosalind put up her hand. 'What does that mean – detestable idols?'

Auntie Priscilla read out the verse again.

'They were proud ...' she said 'proud' slowly as if she was teaching them pronunciation, 'of their beautiful jewellery and used it to make their detestable idols and vile images. Therefore I will turn these into an unclean thing for them.'

Michael started to pay attention again because Auntie Priscilla had straightened herself in her chair and was fidgeting as if she wanted to go to the toilet.

The End Times were never far from Priscilla's mind. She had an apocalyptic faith and supped hungrily on such passages. Abominations hovered near: she felt the hot breath of the four horses of the apocalypse on her neck, heard them snorting in her ear. She spent her evenings studying eschatology: the red horse, the pale horse, the four beasts from the sea, the six seals, the sky rolling up like a scroll, the full moon become blood, the shaft of the bottomless pit. She started revealing some of these visions to the children, pulling back the veil a little, telling them about the depraved statues of bloated cows, the graven images of shameless women, the foul masks worn by frenzied men. She spoke of a woman in purple on a scarlet beast, drunk with the blood of the saints. A warm flow moved down the centre of her torso, a delicious kneading. She found herself panting and noticed that Rosalind looked as if she was going to cry; so she turned her attention to lambs lying down with lions, angels in soft raiment wiping away children's tears, city walls of glassy jasper, foundations inlaid with amethyst and carnelian, gates fashioned from single pearls. With a quiet ecstatic moan she subsided into the chair again.

Michael was confused. The message from God was strong, but what was it? What did it mean? Were jewels good or bad? God was being difficult again.

It was time for the children to take it in turns to pray around the circle.

Angela prayed, 'Thank you for my rabbit, that we will never eat it.'

Rosalind prayed, 'Thank you for dying on the cross and help Lewis not to be so awkward.'

After Rosalind had prayed, Auntie Priscilla said, 'Michael, don't pick your nose.' Someone sniggered. Lewis had told Michael that if you picked your nose you would get a hole between the nostrils. After that he only picked his nose in secret, or when people were supposed to have their eyes closed. He scowled. Auntie Priscilla should have had her eyes closed properly during prayers. Perhaps she could see through the whites of her eyes.

It was Michael's turn to pray. He concentrated hard, screwing up his eyes tight. His last memory verse came to mind and he said loudly, 'Send forth your light and your truth. Let them guide me.'

Priscilla looked across at Michael, startled, as did all the children, suddenly wide eyed. No child had spoken with such authority and conviction before, and although Michael had spoken words that might have been uttered, in a ritual tone, by any Anglican vicar, the words were far too precocious to have come from a relative babe. As Priscilla stared a transfiguration occurred; the tension in Michael's upturned face melted away and it was as if a transcending inner peace had come upon him. A luminous presence attended him. Priscilla knew that she was witnessing an epiphany, an anointing. It was as if not the child had spoken but the Holy Spirit through him. Would the child grow in wisdom to become a prophet? Could such an ordinary child, who picked his nose, be a Latter-Day Saint? As the silence extended, Priscilla saw Michael open his eyes.

'What?' he said defensively. 'I didn't pick my nose again.'

Priscilla collected herself, but made a mental note to observe the child in case an angel was in their midst. Now she thought about it, she had seen glimpses of the celestial in Michael's face before. True, with his fair pudding-bowl hair and big trusting eyes he looked like a cherubic choirboy, but she sensed more: a spiritual aura perhaps, as if he had been touched by the divine.

She gave Michael a little smile and then said, 'David, you're next.'

But all other prayers around the circle were trifling after Michael's supplication. When they said the Grace together Priscilla noted that all the children spoke louder than normal, as if they were keen to show that they were just as fervent as Michael.

Lying in bed after prayers, Michael guessed that God would tell him what to do during the service in the cathedral in the morning. Now that Simon was expecting him to be right about the diamonds he was sure that God would not let him down. He just had to Wait On The Lord. Tomorrow he and Simon would come back from Mr Patel's with their pockets stuffed with money. He wondered if he should take a duffle bag.

The bats momentarily extinguished a star here, and a star there, but Michael did not notice as he was asleep.

THREE

The drums outside the cathedral started at 7.30am while the children were scoffing their porridge. The poundings burst through the windows of the school, stamped down the hill to shake the leaves of the eucalyptus trees in the town, made dancing water-spheres on the crest of the wavelets lapping the shore, ribbled over corrugated roofs, agitated the fields of maize beside wattle and daub huts, stepped up the hillside terraces planted with beans and sweet potatoes and turned the head of a goatherd on a humpback summit. Far below the goatherd, in front of the whitewashed cathedral, drummers struck the great cowhide drums. The drums were bound tightly to a stake lest the old legends be true and they break free and go looking for their wives and cattle, or were stolen – the owner of such drums might hold immense power. But these beliefs were sinking away: over the preceding half century a tide of Christian faith had swept inland from the sea. At its high tide mark, hundreds of miles from Africa's eastern shore, the cathedral lay like a bleached driftwood crate.

Michael and Simon sat on the cement floor of the cathedral, pressed in by soft flesh and marinated in the scents of another race. They had somehow become orphaned from the rest of the school who sat in a block a few rows behind. The bishop gave a command in a voice which was given weight and ecclesiastical authority by the acoustics of the high space of the building. They stood, all rising as one – it would have been difficult to resist, so tightly were they compressed together. The wooden chairs of the clergy at the front of the church scraped and screeched on the floor. Then, without instrumental introduction, a lone voice rose high and wavering and was taken up by the congregation: a plaintive cry drifting out and away into the hills, sliding into a melody that had been composed in Victorian Britain, translated by the worshippers into their own musical dialect: an indigenous inflection, a collective sighing, a melodic wailing. The voices slewed from note to note, bar to bar: strong male harmonies, high and anguished female parts. Singing of redemption through blood; the spilling of blood. The congregation knew about blood: chicken blood spurting from the severed neck, goat blood drying on the stones behind the cooking hut, caked blood on cow skins, blood from the gash of the panga, blood from childbirth. Blood was the strongest metaphor for life. They understood the blood of the Lamb, why it had to be shed. Sin was serious unto death. Only a life offering was sufficient atonement.

Through the tall windows Michael could see a hill. It looked like the Green Hill Far Away and the path running down its side was red. He saw then that the children in front were just like him, that all the people squashed in around him, whether mothers suckling their babies, porters with roughened hands, old women with milky sight, robed clergy, beaky aunties or soft-limbed cooks; they were all the same to God. He saw that everybody – black and yellow, red and white – had to be washed in the same blood.

Feeling rinsed of his sins, Michael sank down to the floor again with everyone else. The bishop climbed the pulpit, pulling himself up by the rail because he wore such heavy robes of scarlet and black. Another man, slim and straight like a skittle, glided to the foot of the pulpit. Michael thought he might be wearing roller-skates under his long white nightie. The bishop's booming words filled up the cathedral. When he paused the words drained away quickly out of the glassless windows. Then the roller-skate man spoke, saying in English what the bishop had said in Rukiga, but his little voice was like a narrow beam which only passed over Michael now and then.

Michael was distracted by the heads in front of him; he wondered whether his own head was as bumpy under his hair as the African children's. They had tiny wiry curls for hair which he wanted to touch.

Simon, cradling his crystals in his cupped hands, put his head close to Michael's and whispered, 'Stay at the back when we leave.'

The roller-skate man was saying, 'Once we were in bondage to the spirits. We gave them our allegiance. We did nothing without fear. In the morning when we woke, in the daytime when we ...' His voice disappeared.

Simon said, 'I've cleaned them.'

The bishop spoke again and the roller-skate man said, '... who can break the power of the spirits over us? Who ...'

Simon was fingering a crystal. 'I think this big one's a diamond.'

'... there is only One that can free us ...'

'How much money is a diamond?' Michael asked in the sudden quiet.

'... a Greek woman came to our Lord begging him to cast out the demon ...'

Simon said, 'I think we can buy two cars with two diamonds. Mr Patel will know.'

'... it is not right to take the bread for the children and throw it to the dogs ...'

Michael said, 'Do you swear you'll share the money?'

'... even the dogs under the table eat the children's crumbs ...'

'I swear on Cub's honour,' Simon said forcefully. The heads in front swivelled to look at him.

'... for such a reply, you may go; the demon has left ...'

'What's he saying about demons? My dad says there aren't any,' Simon said.

Michael looked knowingly at Simon. 'It's because he doesn't believe in the Bible. If he did, he would know there are demons.'

Simon said, 'I think my dad has a demon sometimes.'

Michael suddenly wanted to wet his pants. 'Does he really have a demon? Is that true?' he asked. He was going to stay at Simon's house in the holiday while his mother and father were away at a convention for two whole days. He didn't think his parents would let him stay at Simon's house if they knew his father had a demon, even if he only had it sometimes.

He didn't hear Simon's reply as they were lifted to their feet again at the command of the bishop. The bishop read a collect and prayers from the Book of Common Prayer; the congregation murmured its responses. Michael felt a rising panic as they dropped to the floor again, but not about demons. He had not been listening out for the sign that would tell him whether it was right to go to see Mr Patel without the aunties' permission. What if God had spoken already and he had missed it?

He tried to concentrate hard. A Bible reading followed. When it was translated Michael heard at last what he had been waiting for.

'He said to them, 'If any of you has a sheep and it falls into a pit on the Sabbath, will you not take hold of it and lift it out? How much more valuable is a man than a sheep! Therefore it is lawful to do good on the Sabbath.''

Michael sucked in his cheeks and bit them, thrilled. God could not have been clearer. It was lawful to do good on the Sabbath. He was going to be doing tremendous good for his father, but everyone else would be happy as well: the aunties; Freda and all the fat cooks; his home friend, Tomasi; their cross-eyed night-watchman, Kapere; and their fumbling gardener, Silas. Everyone he knew. And if they weren't as happy as they ought to be (he found that grown-ups, except Auntie Cynthia, sometimes forgot to be Joyful In The Lord), then Rachel, his little sister, was sure to get excited enough to jump up and down until she fell over. No one but Rachel ever got *that* excited about what he did; he must remember to tell her when she was older not to worship him because Worship The Lord Your God Only. It was definitely lawful to see Mr Patel on the Sabbath when he was doing so much good.

When the bishop dispensed the blessing, Michael whispered in Simon's ear, 'We must go to Mr Patel straight away.'

The Boys' Brigade struck up outside as the congregation poured out through the big arched doorway. The noise of the bugles, drums and tambourines hurt Michael's ears. Sunlight flashed off their instruments, hurting his eyes. The band marched up and down one side of the cathedral forecourt. Michael longed to try on one of their dark blue pillbox hats; they wore them cockily on the side of their heads.

Auntie Beryl was trying to gather her flock for the walk back to the school. Michael and Simon waited behind the crowd. Nurse Janine was looking for stragglers but then became distracted in talking to the American Crossroader man. The Crossroaders were rebuilding a small clinic on a hillside. The last clinic got washed away in a mudslide but this time they were digging deep foundations. Freda had told Michael that the Americans were 'very fine' and Michael could see what she meant. The British missionary men had twiggy arms sticking out of buttoned shirts but the American men had big muscles and worked stripped to the waist. Michael noticed that the Africans were most interested in the black Americans: children let their hoops fall, women stopped hoeing in fields, men put down their wheelbarrows; to see black people, like themselves but not like themselves: cowboy hats, wristwatches with huge dials, Levi 'pants' (that made Michael snigger), white gym shoes, lipstick, eyeshadow, sunglasses and lots of money. And the Americans didn't care what they did: one man had put his hands on Auntie Beryl's shoulders and said, 'Well, well, if it ain't the Queen of England herself.' The Crossroaders hugged each other all the time, and when they shook hands with Michael they practically pumped his arm off. The previous year they had all blubbed like babies when they left.

Michael could see the tall American putting on his hat again which meant Nurse Janine was leaving as well. He was the only Crossroader who came to the cathedral service – the rest went to the Baptist Gospel Hall in the town – and he always talked to Nurse Janine. He wore his hat to church, holding it to his stomach during the service and replacing it when he came outside, only to remove it again when he spoke to Nurse Janine.

'I bet she would let him lick the malt off her spoon,' Michael said.

'My dad licks sherbet off my mum's titties,' Simon said.

Michael made a gagging face. 'How do you know that?'

'Seen it. Through the keyhole. My mum was in agony.'

'Why didn't she just push him away?'

'My parents are disgusting.' Simon turned away with a shudder.

Michael could see it: Simon's hairy demon-father hunched over his mother, slobbering like a hyena with rabies, his paws on her shoulders, the fur on the back of his neck raised; but worse than that: his mother letting him eat her, wanting him to, as if she were one of those wild and revolting pagan women Auntie Priscilla had warned them about. His visit to Simon's house was going to be the hardest thing he had ever done. He hoped Simon's father didn't like to munch on small boys.

Now they put their hands in their pockets to look as if there was nothing wrong and tiptoed off the edge of the crowd, taking the path down the valley to the shops. Michael held his diamonds tightly in his pocket.

In front of the *dukas*, which lined both sides of the street, was a covered walkway with square pillars. It seemed very quiet to Michael – just two tailors working the treadles outside Mehta's Textiles – until he remembered that the shops were not allowed to open on Sundays. He expected Mr Patel was asleep, or counting his money, or whatever he did on a Sunday – he certainly wouldn't be at church. Feeling conspicuous he followed Simon up the three concrete steps onto the walkway. The tailors looked up as they passed. The tic-tic whirring of their treadles slowed. 'Naughty boys, naughty boys, mistress will catch you.'

They hurried on past Kapoor Stores, selling framed images of Hindu gods, past Gupta and Sons, Grocery and Foodstuffs, then Jaz Shoe Repairs (Certified), then Jethas Motor Parts (Imports). So many Indians, thought Michael. Auntie Beryl had told them that there were lots of different types. He had written them down in his exercise book (as he had different types of cars): Gujaratis, Goans, Parsees, Punjabis, Sindhis, Hindus, Catholics, Sikhs, Ismailis, Sunnis, Shias; and they all spoke different languages: Cutchi, Gujarati, Punjabi, Hindi, Urdu. He wondered what type of Indian Mr Patel was. He would ask him and put a tick mark next to that type: to show that he had spotted one.

When they reached Patel, Patel and Patel (All British Subjects) General Stores they found the door a quarter open. They peered into the dim interior to see if Mr Patel was at home. The shop smelt of polished metals and strong spices, making the boys hesitate in the doorway. Pots, paraffin lamps, handles for hoes and brooms, wire coils, matches, string, candles, maize oil, bags of sugar and flour filled the high shelves on the sidewalls. A ladder leant against the shelves. On the counter was a glass-fronted wooden cabinet and behind the glass were trays of powdered spices of flaming hues. Behind the counter, bottles of boiled sweets – mauve, crimson and glassy white – glistened in their glass jars.

For a moment Michael thought no one was in the shop, but then a boy about their age appeared around the end of the counter. They stared at each other, Michael unsure who should speak first. The boy's large black eyes gleamed back at Michael under eyebrows so neat and dark that they looked to have been drawn with a felt pen. Oil in his hair deepened its blackness.

Eventually the boy said, in carefully pronounced English, 'You want sweets?'

'We've not come to buy anything,' Michael said hastily. 'It's the Lord's Day and should be kept holy.'

Simon looked at him as if he was mad. 'What?'

'Umm, sorry. I don't think he knows that.'

The Indian boy started twisting his fingers together. 'You come to steal something?'

'We British don't steal,' Simon said abruptly.

There was another awkward silence in which Michael felt uncomfortable with what Simon had said. Things weren't going very well. The boy put his arm out and held the edge of the counter as if to stop them getting through to the sweets.

'We want to speak to Mr Patel,' Michael said, and then, anxious to be friendly, added, 'Please!'

'I find,' said the boy and turned to go, but then thought better of leaving them unattended in the shop.

'Papa,' he shouted.

A sack curtain hiding a door was pushed aside. Mr Patel wore a long shirt not tucked into his trousers (or were they pyjamas?), which Michael thought was very slovenly. He had not even shaved.

'You boys want sweets?' Mr Patel asked.

'We've come to ask you a question,' Simon replied.

'Very good, any question, I can answer.'

'It's about diamonds. Do you know what a diamond looks like?'

Mr Patel's face darkened. 'Bandhu, go and see your mother.'

Bandhu looked crossly at Michael and disappeared behind the curtain. Mr Patel closed the door to the street but did not turn on the light, so at first all Michael could see was a green glow from Mr Patel's luminescent watch.

'Why you ask me about diamonds? Who has sent such young boys to ask such silly questions? I'm an honest trader. Small talking that Patel has diamonds hidden in his house and the next thing Patel is found face in the swamp and his house is robbered.'

Michael felt hurt. 'We only want our dads to be able to win the East African Safari. And I think we should say that we don't want to spend the money on wonton living.'

'What is wonton living, my boy?'

'It's when you spend all your money and then have to live in a pigsty like the Prodigal Son,' Michael said.

'Pigsty, ha? Like Bandhu's room, heh, heh. But that is bad, it's best to be tidy.'

Simon said, 'We have some crystals and we want to know which ones are diamonds.' He dug his hand into his pocket and displayed them to Mr Patel. They looked like gravel chips in the dim light.

'I'm a trader of household goods. What do I know of diamonds?' Mr Patel said.

Michael looked dejectedly at Simon. Simon started to put the stones back in his pocket.

'But my cousin in Kampala; he has jewellery business. Maybe he has taught me a few little things. Come, come, we'll talk.' Mr Patel motioned them to follow him behind the curtain. Stepping through it he collided with Bandhu. 'Did I not tell you to go to your mother?' he shouted. Bandhu started to move back. 'No, no! Now you must go in the shop. I have business to do with these boys.' Bandhu scowled at Michael.

Simon stepped forward to follow Mr Patel, but Michael froze. It was one thing talking in the shop – that's where the Europeans and Indians talked to each other – quite another to go through the curtain. He imagined that beyond the curtain he would enter something like Aladdin's cave, except instead of treasure there would be glossy idols, showy statues, shiny images and hypnotising smells – like the Roman Catholic church that his parents had steered him away from when they had gone for a walk in Kampala.

'What is wrong? Are you frightened of an honest trader?' Mr Patel asked.

'I'm not allowed,' Michael said.

'Boy, do you want your father to win the motor safari?'

Michael followed Simon through the curtain and then through a door off a short corridor.

'Reshma, here are my young friends. They wish to do business.'

It was not immediately obvious to Michael whom Mr Patel was talking to, but a colourful shape in the corner – which he had mistaken for a roll of cloth – moved, and all of a sudden there was Mrs Patel smiling at them. Michael thought her very kind with her soft smile and her watery Bambi eyes. Her silky sari flowed lightly about her small body.

'You like chapattis? I make you some,' she said, tilting her head as if taking a position in an Indian dance.

'Oh, thank you. That's most kind,' Michael said. He had heard how to speak like that on the World Service of the BBC which his father tuned into every night, adjusting the dial as carefully as if he was listening for the click of a tumbler in a lock, finding words in a whole sky of whistles, static and hiss. In the Patels' room there was a radio playing Indian music. Michael found it mesmerising and strange. Other than that, their room was not very different from the living room at home. There were no creamy statues or spangled pictures.

Mrs Patel offered Simon a chapatti as well.

'No thanks,' Simon said firmly, and put his mouth to Michael's ear, whispering, 'They chew the chapattis in their mouths before they cook them.'

Michael looked with horror at Simon, but Mrs Patel had already slipped out to the kitchen, the trailing pallu of her sari only just keeping up with her. Mr Patel motioned the boys to sit down. Simon put his crystals on the table and Michael did the same to make an unequal pile.

'Where you get these?' Mr Patel asked.

'Up Crys ...' started Michael but Simon stopped him, saying, 'We can't tell you where our mine is.'

'You will make good businessman,' Mr Patel said.

Mr Patel picked the crystals up one by one, curling his lower lip further and further over his upper lip and frowning more and more as he studied each in turn. He got up and went over to a cupboard, moved a lot of objects noisily around, and came back with a small metal plate and a hammer. He placed one of the smallest crystals on the plate and tapped it firmly with the hammer. It crushed into small splinters.

'No good.'

He picked up another. Michael found himself suddenly fond of his crystals, diamonds or not, and pulled them back towards him, but Simon said, 'Let him find the diamonds. You said God had told you.'

One after another the crystals disintegrated under Mr Patel's hammer, each making a crunch noise like a plastic toy crushed under foot. God is testing me, like Abraham with his son, thought Michael, but he will find out that I'm very strong. It occurred to him to offer the last stone to Mr Patel straight away, the one God must have chosen to be the diamond, but he remembered: Do Not Test The Lord Your God.

Mr Patel finished dispatching Simon's crystals and, looking bored, gathered the last three, Michael's three, all together on the plate. Michael craned forward; this was the moment when God was going to show Simon what he could do. Mr Patel's hammer would bounce back off the hard diamond and hit him in the eye. Then he and Simon would jump up and shout with happiness – or perhaps he should stay calm to show Simon that he had never doubted what God had said. Mr Patel lifted his hammer high, took a long time to take aim, and then hit the crystals hard. The boys jumped at the sharp noise. Pieces of stone scattered widely. Mr Patel lifted his hammer slowly, his lower lip almost touching his nose. A miserable pile of powdered quartz remained on the metal.

'Very sorry, that is that,' Mr Patel said with finality.

Michael looked at the remains of his dreams: a shattered Zephyr 6. He couldn't bear to look at Simon; they wouldn't even be leaving with any quartz crystals. Simon was making a half-hearted attempt to find any pieces that might have flown away onto the floor.

Mrs Patel had come back in just as the hammer had fallen, and now she leant across the table to put a hot chapatti down in front of Michael. He was enveloped in sweet scents and feather-light touchings of her sari which somehow reminded him of his mother. The chewed chapatti lay steaming in front of him. Now he was pleased that God was going to have to watch him eat it. He would show God that he didn't care what he thought; he had tried to do good on the Sabbath but God had stopped him.

He chewed lightly, swallowing pieces whole, but then discovered he liked it – Mrs Patel's saliva was spicy. He decided that he would tell Simon that it was revolting: eating a chapatti was as brave as drinking a potty.

Mr Patel traced a pattern with his stubby brown finger in the rock dust and said, in a no nonsense way, 'Those are glass rocks, not diamonds.'

'We're sorry to have wasted your time, Mr Patel,' Simon said. He shot Michael an accusatory look.

'No, don't be sorry. Boys like you, you'll become rich one day. Maybe you'll have a big factory like Maneesh, my cousin. He has a sugar refinery. You like that? Sugar candy, jaggery, golden syrup, white granulated.'

He paused to smile widely at the boys. Michael was still eating his chapatti and making pretend disgusted faces at Simon to show him how much he was suffering.

'Manju, my brother, he has oil factories: castor oil, simsim oil, groundnut oil, cottonseed oil, vegetable ghee, oilcakes, sheanut butter, et cetera, et cetera.'

'You have forgotten Lalit,' Mrs Patel said.

'Ah, Lalit. Soda ash factory by the lake – for dye process, for glass, for soap. Also salt: cattle salt, coarse salt, crushed salt, crushed raw soda.'

'You have forgotten Mahesh,' Mrs Patel said.

Michael saw Mr Patel glance darkly at Mrs Patel. Mr Patel said, 'You're very nice boys but is not your school missing you?'

Simon looked at his watch – Michael had no watch although one was promised for his thirteenth birthday, an age away – and leapt up. They said a hasty thanks and bumped into the listening Bandhu as they went through the curtain. Not waiting to hear Mr Patel shout at Bandhu, they ran up the path towards the school.

'Oh, darn,' huffed Simon, but Michael did not hear – he was still furious at God, tears not far away.

Priscilla had seen the truants coming up the path, and her relief was turning to anger. She stood with her hands on her hips until Simon came to a halt in front of her. Michael came up behind, but he seemed not to have noticed her – she had to stop him running past her by putting out her hand.

The child said, breathlessly, 'We know that all things work together for good to those who love God.' She saw him take a deep breath. 'God is working his purpose out as year succeeds to year.'

A gentle light played on the boy's face. It diffused her anger. She glanced behind, expecting to see an angel casting its luminosity on Michael, but saw only the trunks of the eucalyptus trees, smooth and marbled, as if she was standing in the Courts of the Lord. Of course, she thought, we see through a glass darkly. I can't presume to see an angel's physical presence, but the child has surely spoken again.

Memory verses came to Michael at the height of his fury – they popped into his brain as if God had poked them in there with his finger. He clenched his fists in sudden recognition of what God was doing as he said the verses out loud. It was so obvious now. This was another test; a test that he only gave to Great Men Of Faith. Then he saw Auntie Priscilla. She was turning without a word to lead them back to school. That was worrying – it would be so much better if she had been angry straight away. She must be saving it up for a big punishment later on.

Auntie Priscilla took them straight to Auntie Beryl's office, and told them to wait outside in the corridor while she went in. After a while they heard Auntie Beryl raise her voice. She sounded fed up.

'Priscilla, that is highly speculative. We're Protestants, not Catholics – always seeing visions!'

When Auntie Priscilla came out she looked at Michael, and nodded her head ever so slightly in a knowing way.

Auntie Beryl called them in and told them to stand on the mat in front of her desk. She was busy writing something and did not look at them, as if she had better things to do. Her glasses were perched near the tip of her nose, so that she looked like a wise old owl. There were stacks of paper all over her desk. Some looked like end-of-term reports, giving Michael a sinking feeling. He tried to read the titles of the books in the glass-fronted cabinet behind her: *Strong's Exhaustive Concordance, Luther's Catechism, Selected Sermons of George Whitfield, Summa Theologica*. Auntie Beryl was very brainy.

Auntie Beryl was still writing but said, 'Whose idea was it to go to the shops?'

Michael hoped that Simon would own up, but then he remembered that Simon was not yet Saved, so he said, 'We were just doing some good on the Sabbath.'

'A disarming reply, Michael, but the Jewish Sabbath is Saturday, not Sunday.' She put some papers in a drawer and started looking through another stack.

Simon found his voice. 'No one told us that before. How were we to know?'

'Your aggrieved tone is hardly appropriate, Simon, and in any case breaking the rules is not allowed on any day.'

'Actually, Jesus did,' Michael said quickly. He was not going to let Auntie Beryl tell off a Great Man Of Faith like himself.

'You're not Jesus,' Auntie Beryl said and added, more to herself than to him, 'or some Latter-Day Saint.' She hunted in a wooden pencil box and took out a paperclip.

Michael pressed his point. 'I was Led By God to see Mr Patel.'

'And who led you, Simon?'

Michael looked down at the floor. That was the trouble with Auntie Beryl; she always had an answer, and she wasn't even concentrating.

Auntie Beryl folded her hands in front of her and looked up at them over her glasses. Her eyebrows were grey like rain clouds. 'You'll both have to stay on your beds for an extra hour this afternoon at rest time.'

She dismissed them.

Michael glared at her. Auntie Beryl was very clever but she would be sorry on Judgement Day when God showed her in the big book that she had punished them for doing God's work. He thought Auntie Priscilla understood, but she was a bit mad. God worked in mysterious ways.

'You said that God said they were diamonds,' Simon said as they made their way down the corridor. He sounded more disappointed than angry.

'I think I made a mistake.' He didn't think he could explain to Simon about Tests Of Faith.

'My dad says that God helps those who help themselves,' Simon said.

Michael thought about that. By the time he had reached the dining room he had had an idea on how to help himself so that God could help him; so that God could help him to help his father to get a Zephyr. He would do it as soon as he got home.

FOUR

S tella and Bernard, Michael's mother and father, woke at 5.45am for Quiet Time with God to a wind-up alarm clock inside a sock. The sock was Bernard's way of moderating its more shrilling tones. 'Brilliant academically, but so impractical he can't tie his own shoelaces,' was how Bernard had been described to Stella before they had met at missionary training college. Stella had been enthralled.

It was still dark in their bedroom so Stella blearily raised the glass of the paraffin lamp on her bedside table, removed the remains of a cremated moth, turned up a little more wick and lit it with a match. Out here in the hill country, twisting miles from any town, there was no electricity. Only the major towns were wired into a grid, although even there the electric light era was to be temporary, a false dawn, a short interlude between the long ages of fire-lit nights before colonisation and the long, snuffed-out nights of dictatorship to come.

Bernard, even at this sacred time of the day, set to work immediately, scribbling with a pencil in a hard-cover notebook, ragged along its binding from frequent use.

'Must you work during your Quiet Time? Can't you just listen to God?' Stella asked.

Bernard wrote on furiously.

'We have to talk about whether we're still going to let Michael go and stay with Simon. Miss Simpson took me aside when I picked him up. She said his friend Simon was not a good influence. Henry and Rhonda are very worldly. What do you think, Bernard?'

Bernard looked up from his notebook but Stella was not sure whether he had been listening. She found Bernard both frustratingly lacking in spontaneity and reassuringly considered in judgement.

'I'm listening most carefully to God. He places ideas into my mind and it's my duty to write them down before they slip my memory. I've just seen how I can better translate the concept of justification by faith.'

'OK, but what about Michael?'

'Michael?'

Stella repeated herself.

Bernard was silent for a full half minute and then said, 'He has to be exposed to the real world. We can't be the salt of the earth without being willing to be sprinkled out. What good are we in a glass salt cellar?'

'He just seems a bit young, darling. He's more sugar than salt. Not ready. Very impressionable.' She worried about Michael; he was so eager to please and so enthusiastic, but in that lay the danger: he looked on the Almighty as his personal and ever-ready assistant, recruiting him for all his schemes. She could see a fall coming.

Bernard said, 'There are two ways to learn to swim: thrown in at the deep end or paddling in from the shallow end. I agree that Henry and Rhonda represent the deep end, but I think we've equipped Michael with good water wings so he won't sink.'

On spiritual matters Bernard was the head of the household so Stella submitted. Had she profoundly disagreed she would have reclassified the issue as a practical matter, rather than a spiritual one, then made her own decision and not bothered Bernard with it. He had enough to cope with in his work.

Bernard always went straight to his study after breakfast although this was as reliably delayed by the ritual of looking for his black-rimmed glasses in any of many locations, in a track from bedroom to bathroom, to outside toilet, to dining room.

In his study, surrounded by heavily annotated books, Bernard was translating the Word of God from the original Hebrew and Greek into the vernacular. Each dialect required its own translation lest incorrect meanings became forever embedded in the consciousness of the recipients. For some dialects there was still no written grammar and no standardised spelling, so Bernard interrogated his native colleagues in the Theological College, testing every grammatical construction until he was sure that the meaning was pure. Stella would overhear Bernard verbalising his thoughts: 'The form of the simple imperative when preceded by an object prefix is the same as the subjunctive … that's a labial consonant, that's a palatal … that would explain the idiomatic use of the perfect stem …' She was used to Bernard periodically rushing out of his office and, unable to let emotion infect his speech, saying quietly, 'I've found a new tense,' or 'I've uncovered a declination rule. Most unique form.'

Word by word by word Bernard was disclosing the person of God to a people that had been in the dark since, well, since time began. Stella felt proud: her husband was revealing the very voice of God to the goatherd and the cattle owner, just as William Tyndale, four centuries before, had made known the same to the ploughman and the blacksmith.

After finding Bernard's glasses Stella took tea to her father, Arthur, who, long retired from his life's work as a doctor at a mission, lived in a small rondavel cottage in the garden. Stepping outside with a tray, she greeted Kapere, their night-watchman – afflicted with clouded corneas, and a squint that gave the impression that he was keeping half a watch for some danger from the heavens – performing his last task of the night (his only task, she thought): lighting the wood fire for the water boiler. Smoke gushed from the aperture in the blackened bricks and poured up over the top of the drum into the ocean of the lightening sky. Kapere wore a long fur-lined coat which had made its way to East Africa in a container full of winter wear from a Lutheran charity in Sweden. Stella was in charge of distributing the aid to the needy, although it was handed on again and again by barter or obligation. It was not uncommon even on the hottest days to pass a man or woman wearing a thick shearling or fox fur coat.

In the cottage Stella opened her father's curtains and went to see if he was still breathing. He increasingly occupied the land across the Jordan, deliberately uncurling his grip on this world and entwining himself in the arms of the Father. Every morning Stella braced herself to find that he had left his body lying in the bed and 'gone home', or even that the bed was empty; that he had vanished, taken by God like the patriarch Enoch. 'And Enoch walked with God: and he was not; for God took him.'

Her father had few visitors for his friends had all been 'promoted to glory' before him, although still some came from far for advice, for remembrance of lost times, for wisdom, for a blessing. Old men, barefoot and dusty, would come and stand patiently outside his cottage door. Stella would bring down sweet tea and sweet bananas and tell her father that he had a visitor. Later the visitor would leave as softly as he had come, walking down the road in the valley and then out onto the plain. When Stella asked him who these callers were he would say something like, 'That was Erasto Ndimbirwe. He also loves the Lord. I told him we must endure; that it wouldn't be long before we see Him face to face.'

On questioning her father further, he might add, 'He was the hospital driver in the late thirties. I first met him when he was brought into the hospital with a spearhead stuck in his leg. He had walked to see me then as well.'

When her mother had died suddenly a few years before, Stella had considered moving her father to the Pilgrim's Repose nursing home in Dorset, close to a church that had supported the mission. There would be many faithful visitors from the church, but it would be subjecting him to a cruel exile for he had lived half a century in Africa. He had inhaled its air for so long that to deny him now would be as heartless as withdrawing cigarettes from a forty-a-day smoker in his eighth decade. The England he had sailed from had, in any case, sailed with him – two wars and wave upon wave of social change had created another country from the one he had left; a country increasingly hostile to what he represented, thought Stella. Not that he would have complained, for the source of his contentment had long passed from the 'things of this world'.

Stella went to empty Arthur's commode. She carried it to the back of the house where the path led to a purple-garlanded bougainvillea bush within which was a small outhouse: the toilet. The latch was broken so she pushed the door open, but had to put the commode down to lift the seat. She held her breath as she bent but the sewer smell swamped its way into her nostrils. No one lingered in this room. Large bluebottles squatted on the flaky whitewashed walls. Little red smudges of swatted mosquitoes specked the walls. Strange how the blood did not darken with time. The flies, drunk with the odour, spun noisily around and around in crazed loops when disturbed. She emptied the potty down the 'long drop': a distant slop sound marked the arrival of its contents below. Leaving promptly she headed for the house, taking a heady breath of the relatively perfumed air outside. The path skirted a stubbly lawn that sloped away to a luscious banana grove; below the banana trees lay a valley, moist and sleepy, swathed in mist and light smoke from the still smouldering compound fires of the previous night. The other side of the valley rose steeply in terraced plots except for a small ravine cutting into the hillside, filled to its brim with trees, from which emanated a dawn chorus: tropical style with squawks, rasps and booms. The head of the valley opened out onto the plain, honeyed in early morning light, where the cattle herders roamed.

'Long drop and view,' she exclaimed to herself. Their lives in Africa: the filth and the beauty, the pain and the elation, the excitement and the terror, the daily dramas. And now the day would fill with myriad complexities and vexations. For a start the house girl was away at another funeral, or was it another wedding or another visit to a sick relative? How would they ever build a new nation with so many time-consuming social obligations?

Stella felt that her mother's generation of missionaries had had it easier, for they had kept their home a castle into which they retreated when tired. Behind the walls her mother would rest, sew, arrange flowers, read or write – undisturbed. The gap in the fiery-red hibiscus hedge surrounding the house was the gate through which her parents had, early in the day, travelled out and then, when the night reasserted itself, journeyed in. Out to cure the sick and feed the hungry, in to receive their own balms. Nowadays that smacked of snobbery for 'There is neither Jew nor Greek, slave nor free, male nor female, for you are all one in Christ Jesus.' She felt it right that the new generation of missionaries had rediscovered a Christian imperative for inclusiveness.

The African Christians were now 'partners in mission' and 'brothers and sisters in Christ'. They were all 'one at the foot of the cross'.

Eager to right previous wrongs, she and Bernard had metaphorically torn down the hedge and opened the door. So the English habit of restoring the self through withdrawal from the world came up against the African way of rejuvenation through sharing the self. Now they were suffering a fantastic invasion. She would find strangers ironing their clothes in her laundry, a pot of animal parts simmering on the hot plate, a mother in labour in her sitting room begging for a lift to the hospital many miles away, or a man with a bicycle on the porch hoping to sell her the bunch of chickens hanging by their legs from the handlebars. Each person had to be greeted, the well-being of the other (as well as near and far family and friends) fully established before the salutation process ended in a drawn out mutual liturgy of praise to God and his works, personal and general. The extrication was as protracted, but Stella constantly reminded herself that these interactions were where the soul of the Bakiga community resided – what was missing in her own culture – and to enter that community she must immerse herself in its interactions. Still, she sought out the occasional place to hide. Even if it had to be inside the bougainvillea bush.

Now she saw that trouble was coming to her early in the day. Silas, the gardener, was approaching with the grin of a man possessed and the stride of a man with a purpose; worrying, because normally Silas moved only when pushed, and then in random directions – a Brownian motion. He would have been sacked long ago by other expatriate employers, an Indian employer or even the Ministry of Works whose workers sat beside the potholed roads in their laterite-stained uniforms observing the slow passage of time, one of them occasionally chipping at a culvert with the only available spade. She consoled herself by reminding herself that her role as an employer was entirely charitable, so there was no risk to Silas.

'Madam, greetings this morning, and how did you spend the night?'
'I spent it well.'
'And how is your good husband?'
'He's well.'

'And how is the good doctor?'

'Fine, fine. Silas, is there a problem?'

'There's not a problem but there are no wheels on the car.'

Stella hurried with Silas to the drive. There were no wheels on the car. It sat on little brick towers under its axles. Very neat. Stella stood rigid, running through alternative explanations to the obvious: Bernard, absent-mindedly generous, had let someone borrow the wheels; Bernard had asked Mr Khan, the mechanic in town, to replace them in a two-stage process; the government had removed them for disinfection; it was a practical joke, and Silas was about to roll around laughing instead of standing around grinning.

Accepting the truth, Stella called for Kapere. At the urgency of her shout, Kapere came running around the side of the house holding his spear firmly in his right hand.

'I'm here quickly, madam.'

'Did you hear anything last night?' she asked. His eyes as they were, there was no point in asking if he had seen anything.

'No, madam.' He sounded a little unsure.

'I don't want you to say no if you did. Did you not hear anything at all last night?'

'Yes, madam.'

'I don't want you to say yes if you didn't. There's no need to say what you think pleases me. The truth has sufficient pleasures. Oh, never mind, I'll fetch Bernard.' She let out a little choked noise.

'I'm so sorry, madam,' Kapere and Silas said together, shaking their heads.

'It's OK; lots of people in Africa have cars without wheels. It's just … it's just going to be very inconvenient.'

Bernard took some time to surface from deep contemplation, but as soon as he had registered Stella's distress he leapt up and dashed for the door.

'No need to run,' she said. 'The robbers have left.'

They stood looking at the car as if studying a sculpture in an exhibition, occasionally moving to look at it from a different angle.

'It does appear from the scene of the crime that this was a well-planned heist,' Bernard said, bending down by an axle.

'We know that, darling. The question is not whether it was well executed but what we're going to do about it.'

Michael appeared with his shy friend Tomasi. 'Hey, who's taken the wheels off the car?'

Something in her son's voice sounded false. Almost as if the missing wheels were no surprise. 'We're just discussing that, dear. Your window is nearest, Michael. Did you hear anything last night?'

'Only Kapere snoring,' Michael replied.

Kapere looked sheepish. Stella made herself calm while Bernard stayed calm. To show anger in Bakiga culture was a sin worse than theft – or falling asleep whilst on night duty. A wrong could not be righted by the other wrong of anger.

'I think we'll talk about that another time,' she said to Michael.

She looked over to the flowerbed to see that Silas had decided he could not help with the car and was furiously weeding out the geraniums she had planted at the weekend – showing his sympathy by trebling his gardening efforts.

'How are you going to get to the convention?' Michael asked. He turned to Tomasi and said loudly and slowly, 'Now my dad's going to have to get a Zephyr 6.'

Stella looked at Bernard. Bernard was looking up the valley, clearly lost in thought, but she guessed that he was not solving the wheel problem but was likely cracking the particular translation dilemma that she had broken him away from. Bernard's physical site and circumstance rarely bore relationship to the location of his thoughts. Early in their marriage she hoped certain situations would bring Bernard's mind and body together, but even in these she was frequently frustrated – even when she tried to seduce him away from the missionary position. The conception of Michael had been a rare occurrence of internal fusion in Bernard, resulting in two more successful fusions; the first their bodily union and the second a fertilised ovum. The conception of little Rachel, still asleep in the house, was similarly wondrous.

A shrill bicycle bell announced the arrival of the Milk Man. More trouble. She would have to leave Bernard to sort things out in his own time. When he finally brought his supertanker brain around it could be unstoppably effective. She told Michael that Daddy would work something out, and to go and play.

'Hey, Dad! You'll have to get a new car, a Zephyr 6,' she heard Michael shout as she left.

A milk delivery could not be missed as it happened haphazardly and infrequently. The Milk Man, the Chicken Man, the Banana Man, the Pineapple Man, the Egg Man, all arrived on black bicycles with curvaceous chrome handlebars. Their wares dwarfed their cycles and did credit to the strength of the frames. When the Banana Man lost control, crashed and knocked himself unconscious in the village down the road, the stolen bananas, it was said, fed the entire village for a week.

Strapped to the back pannier with strips of inner bicycle tube was a large plastic milk container, which had once contained something combustible judging by the aftertaste left on the tongue. The Milk Man used a smaller container to ladle milk into Stella's saucepan. She would boil it before she put it in the larder. First she dropped in her densitometer to check that the milk had not been diluted. It disappeared under the surface.

'This milk has been watered down,' she said.

The Milk Man looked downcast for a moment, and then he looked accusingly at the milk. 'How can this have happened?'

'My husband and I have other more pressing investigations this morning so I'm not very interested in looking into that. I'm awfully sorry but I can't buy this milk.'

'Maybe you will pay half. Then you will not pay for any water.'

'A generous offer but no thank you.'

Stella often found herself converting anger into sarcasm. Delivered amiably it did not translate bitterly but it gave her a little satisfaction. Bernard did not approve, hinting that it was not a sign of a Renewed Mind. 'How do I know that the water is clean?' she added.

'Madam, the water is too clean.'

'I don't know why I'm asking if the water is clean. I don't care if the water is from an Elysian spring. I don't want diluted milk.'

'The water is from Bakoto spring,' the Milk Man said hopefully.

Stella felt her well of inner peace, filled at Quiet Time only an hour ago, draining away. 'My son is home for the holidays and I want to bake him a cake. When will you return with proper milk?'

'I'll be here tomorrow.'

'If you mean the day after tonight, then I'll be here if you come early. And I'll have my water finder again.'

The Milk Man rode away, ringing his bell and whistling. A few seconds later he was back, his bicycle wobbling under his excitement.

'Madam you have no wheels on your car.'

'Thank you for pointing that out. We were just thinking what to do about it when you came with the whitened water.'

'This morning, on my bicycle, I stopped to … to go to the bathroom … in some bushes, you understand me, and there I saw them. Now you will praise God that I brought you milk this morning.'

'I don't understand.'

'Your wheels, madam. They were hiding there. In the bathroom.'

Michael and Tomasi had returned and were hovering, listening. 'I don't expect they're our wheels,' Michael said, shaking his head dolefully.

Bernard walked the half mile with the Milk Man, Silas and a chastened looking Kapere to retrieve the wheels. When they returned, the Milk Man said to Stella, 'There are many bad people these days. But me, I'm an honest man. Perhaps you'll buy milk tomorrow, madam.'

She said she would happily do so. 'But I'll still have my water finder.'

Silas lifted the first wheel onto an axle.

'Those wheels must be fixed on in some way; screw devices I would say,' Bernard said, stroking his chin. He adjusted his glasses as if seeing more clearly would present a solution.

The Milk Man appeared pleased to have another opportunity to help. 'The robbers have thrown them away.'

Stella suggested that Michael and Tomasi help look for the screw things.

Michael seemed reluctant. 'I expect the robbers have taken them,' he said. 'It'll be better just to get a Zephyr 6.'

Stella gave Michael a hard look.

Kapere was standing nearby, shifting from foot to foot and twisting his face into all manner of contorted expressions. At first Stella had been pleased to see him squirm but now she took pity. 'Do go home, Kapere, we'll finish this off ourselves,' she said.

Kapere's eyes co-ordinated for an instant to look directly at her. 'Madam?'

She felt she had better say something. 'Well, Kapere, it is a disappointment. We don't ask much of you.'

'Maybe I was confused.'

Stella struggled to contain a rising irritation. 'I would say "confused" is not the correct word, although I suppose a deep sleep is a form of bewilderment.'

Kapere's face started to buck again. Then he reached inside a deep pocket in his coat and pulled something out.

'The little master told me you wanted me to do this, madam.' He opened his hand to display a heap of shiny wheelnuts. 'They are washed, madam.'

Stella saw it all. She turned to Michael. He was standing still, not jiggling as he normally did. He hung his head while he looked dejectedly up at her.

'I think I'd better have a word with you inside, Michael.'

Tomasi had been watching Stella with a wary expression. Now he turned suddenly and ran off as quick as a pursued rabbit, the pale soles of his bare feet flicking up and down like a scut. Stella watched him go, then turned back to face the others: there was Kapere, looking to the sky, still holding out the wheelnuts, a hopeful smile breaking out; the Milk Man leaning on his bike looking baffled, absentmindedly ringing his bell; Silas standing watching now, a fistful of magenta geraniums in his hand; Michael, big eyed and pensive; Bernard adjusting his glasses again to better look at Kapere. All trying to understand each other, all not quite succeeding. Stella started laughing.

FIVE

Until he had met Tomasi, Michael had been repeatedly frustrated when he tried to play with the local children – they either wanted to squat and stare, or laugh and jeer, or they took fright and ran away. All except Tomasi. He first met Tomasi when he was exploring a banana grove, looking for big leaves to make a house. He came across a boy widdling against a tree. The boy turned towards him unabashed so that Michael had to step back to avoid being splashed. They tried to outstare each other while the boy waited for his stream to finish. Then Michael said, 'Go away.' But the boy did not go away. He let his only clothing – a dirty white vest – fall to his knees, beckoned Michael to follow him and set off through the trees. Michael had seen a gleam in the boy's eyes and followed. They entered the thickest part of the banana grove where the ground was black from rotting leaves and the green-lit canopy was high above them, as if they were at the bottom of a lake. Michael heard the sound of water trickling down a rivulet. The boy squatted next to a small pool and pointed to a twisted copper pipe lying partially submerged in the water like a gold serpent. On the edge of the pool a pile of still-hot charcoal made an occasional clink sound as it cooled. A rich, fruity smell lingered over the surface of the water.

'*Waragi*,' said the boy as he lifted the pipe, being careful to keep it level. He lifted one end to his lips and tipped it gently. A few drops of clear liquid wet his extended tongue.

'It's good, drink it,' the boy said in Rukiga.

Michael reached for the pipe but the boy pulled it back and indicated that he should open his mouth. He saw that the boy was not to be dictated to and, just as interesting, knew secrets.

Michael tilted his head back and opened his mouth as the boy tipped up the other end of the pipe. He waited for – what he imagined from the sweet smell – would be bubble-gum-flavoured water. Nothing came from the pipe until the boy became impatient and tilted it to near vertical.

The *waragi* found its way around a bend in the copper and gushed from the end of the tube. Michael thought his mouth had been filled with ice; and then with fire. He spat it out; it ran like a hot blade down his chin; he scooped water from the pool, swilled out his mouth and splashed his chin and neck. When he looked up he expected to see that the boy had run off to tell the village about how he had tricked the *Muzungu*, but the boy was busy twisting the pipe above his own head, trying to coax out another shot of the *waragi*. Michael felt a rush of excitement. He ran his tongue around his cheeks; his mouth had cooled and he was left with a sickly, tangy taste – with a hint of rotten banana. He didn't like it. He preferred chapattis.

'It's the black man's Holy Spirit,' the boy said solemnly. 'That's what my uncle told me. He says it comes to the men like a fire on the head, like the spirits in the Bible.'

Michael felt he knew better but he was not going to give the boy a scripture lesson. He wanted to show him that he had secrets to match. They introduced themselves.

'Come with me,' he said, and Tomasi followed him home.

When Michael went through the front door, Tomasi stopped. When Michael insisted he come he followed warily, staring around him. Michael led him into his bedroom and took down the screw top jar from the shelf above his bed. His preserved appendix floated in formalin. It took him some time to gain Tomasi's attention for he was looking with astonishment around his room, poking the bed, peering intently at the picture on the cover of the *Boy Adventurer Annual*, and laughing out loud when he saw the Corgi miniature car on the windowsill.

Michael had difficulty explaining the thick, worm-like object in the bottle – his Rukiga failed on medical terms.

'Should I taste it?'

Michael shook his head, laughed, hitched up his shirt and displayed his scar. 'The worm came from here.'

Tomasi took a step back and looked respectfully at the worm as if he looked on a fearsome creature indeed to have made such a hole in Michael. Michael wondered if Tomasi thought he had single-handedly killed it.

And so Michael and Tomasi played together every holiday, initially trying to impress each other: Tomasi giving Michael fried flying ants to eat, Michael giving Tomasi a boiled sweet, Tomasi showing Michael how to climb the giant avocado trees, Michael showing Tomasi his Spirograph, Tomasi showing Michael a civet cat his brother had caught in a trap. This game continued until Michael showed Tomasi how to make a chameleon change colour; Tomasi recoiled with fear when Michael picked the chameleon off the bush.

'Are you afraid of chameleons?' Michael asked, pleased to have found he could out-impress Tomasi.

Tomasi shrank back, bravado flying away. 'They have evil spirits,' he said, and waved his hands frantically at Michael, pleading with him to put it back in the bush.

'Jesus is stronger than the evil spirits,' Michael said, and to prove that Jesus would let no harm come to Tomasi stretched out his hand to bring the chameleon near to Tomasi's face. Tomasi shrieked, then turned and ran home as if pursued by every spirit in the hills. It was three days before he returned to play.

After his mother had told him off about telling lies to Kapere and involving him in his scheme (she had been angrier about that than the bother they had all had fetching the wheels), Michael wanted to be with someone who wouldn't look at him with a worried frown (his mother), or as a little red man from the moon (Tomasi), or as an annoying buzzing bee (his father); someone who thought him clever and funny and brave. They had no dog, but he did have a sister.

Rachel was sitting cross-legged on the porch opposite Floppy, her teddy, who sat propped up against the wall, one ear furless – she sucked on Floppy's ear when she went to sleep. When she saw Michael she shuffled beside Floppy and said, 'Let's play schools. You be teacher.'

Rachel and Floppy were looking at him so eagerly that he put his arms behind his back like Auntie Beryl, walked up and down, turning quickly on his heels, and said, 'Today we're going to learn about diamonds.'

'Mummy's got diamonds.'

Michael looked over his imaginary glasses and said, 'You can only talk when I ask you a question.'

'Naughty Floppy! Wait for teacher.' She put Floppy's floppy arms across each other in his lap. Floppy slumped forward so that she had to sit him up again.

'You have to dig in the ground very deep to find a diamond and … ' He stopped.

Rachel nodded as if her head was on a spring. 'What other things?'

'Hey Rachel, this is a secret. Promise you won't tell Mum.'

'Floppy, don't tell Mummy.'

'I'm not teacher any more, Rachel. This is very serious; say, I swear on the Bible I won't tell Mum.'

'Floppy can't say that.'

'Doesn't matter. Listen, this is the secret: if we sell Mum's diamonds we could get Dad a Zephyr 6.'

Rachel leant down and put her ear to Floppy's face. Her hair was the same dark-bear colour as Floppy's. 'But Floppy says, then Mummy won't have a diamond.'

'Tell Floppy I could get her another one, easily.'

'Floppy says it's going to rain.'

Michael had also noticed a change in the air. He turned to look down the valley. The rain was coming like a battle: a wall of gun smoke and the cannon rumbling. Rachel picked up Floppy and held him hard to her chest so that the bear's arms and legs stuck out like a squashed creature. A single raindrop, as large as a bullet, hit the brick step of the porch with a sharp slap, hurting an ant which started going round in circles before it was washed off the step. There was a roaring from the roof like a furnace. On the road near the house Michael saw children running for cover; old women tried to protect themselves under goatskins, only to be splattered with the bursting of the rain on the hot ground, making their legs run red. Banana leaves pattered, sputtered and split. His mother's black-eyed susans were stripped of their petals.

Rachel screamed, 'I don't like it. I want to go in.'

When Michael opened the door he saw his mother. 'It's raining,' he shouted. Then he saw his mother's Bible class girls. 'It's raining,' he whispered.

The Bible class girls, from the boarding school down the road, sat on the worn sisal mat, smart in their white blouses and blue skirts. They were all gazing with happy faces at his mother. Rachel ran to sit on a girl's lap, then rocked back and forward with excitement. His mother was telling the story of Ruth, using her Flannelgraph kit. Michael had heard his mother and father discussing the class, and his mother saying firmly, 'I know I can get across the gospel with felt.' He decided to stay and listen until it stopped raining. His mother was sticking the soft figures of Naomi, Ruth and Boaz on the backcloth of blue sky and lush grass. The girls laughed when Boaz fell off just as Ruth lay down at his feet. His mother laughed with them and said that it showed what a fright Boaz got when he woke to find Ruth beside him. Michael found it difficult to understand everything: she spoke in Rukiga, which she had learnt when she was little at her father's hospital on the plains beyond the hills. Michael's father always said that she spoke like the cattle people. Listening by the door, Michael understood enough to know that she spoke of sheep and goats, of the wise and of the foolish, of immoral foreign tribes, of brides, of wedding feasts, of important ancestors and of the creator. The girls would understand all those things. And then she told them what the stories meant: of widewideastheocean, deepdeepasthedeepestsea love; telling of burdens rolledawayrolledawayrolledaway; of Peace That Endureth, Bright Hope For Tomorrow. The girls burst into a chorus about being washed whiter than the snow – the snow that they had never seen but was whiter than their blouses.

Michael looked at his mother and got a proud feeling that he was her son. On the outside she looked like anyone else's mother (except a little smaller and her eyes darker and her lips more smiley), but on the inside she was like all the best women in the Bible in one. She was especially good at explaining God's Kingdom – all anyone had to do was listen, and then they would understand and be happy. Outside, Michael saw that the rain had swept on and a rainbow marked the return of the sun, as if wrong things had been washed from the world.

When his mother said prayers with him that night, Michael wondered whether to tell her what Simon had said about his father having a demon but, although he had started having nightmares, he decided against it – he did not want to be prevented from going. Only one more day to wait. As his mother finished praying he took her hand and touched her ring. There were three diamonds in a row – he thought them small but they shone out bigger than their size.

'Can we sell just one diamond so Dad can get a Zephyr 6?'

'I don't think Dad would like us to do that.'

'He would, I know he would.'

'One day my ring may pass on to Rachel, so it would be a shame if it's missing a diamond.'

He dropped her hand in disgust. She ran her fingers across his hair and smiled.

He said grumpily, 'What will Rachel do with it?'

'She might keep it – to remind her of her mum – or she might want someone special to have it.'

'Someone special?'

'Yes. Maybe she'll have a daughter of her own one day and she'll give it to her.'

'If she doesn't, do you think she'll give it to me? I'm going to ask her.'

SIX

As Arthur, Michael's grandfather, remembered less of the events of the present, simple though they were, he found he could bring to mind more of the past. Sitting quiet in his cottage, he could return to a time when the giant landmass of Africa was still alone, following its own rhythms. A time when there were no highways into the interior and no wheeled transport. He saw again the tracks that crisscrossed the continent. Some were well worn by the Arab caravans that traded blue cloth and beads for ivory and slaves, but many were indistinct, dissipating in the grasses, smattered away by muddy rain, blown away as dust in violent stirrings of hot air, or broken up by animal tracks that had their own compelling destinations. The experienced traveller could distinguish animal track from human track for each had its own rhythm of line; its own cadence.

It struck Arthur that the routes into the interior were not visualised in the vertical view, from the cartographer's perspective, but by a journey re-enacted in the mind, a horizontal prospect: the scenes a traveller would see and remember as he walked the path.

When Arthur was small his father would tell him of the first men from Europe to find their way along those tracks. They ventured in from the sea, sometimes breaking away from the path to reach some rumoured lake or river, intimated by the wave of a tribesman's hand to the horizon. If there were many horizons to cross to reach this cryptic destination, the tribesman might repeat the gesture several times, clicking his fingers between each motion.

The explorers discovered peoples living by the power of their imaginations; living not by the written word, the book, but by their speaking and hearing, by the histories of their ancestors told to them by their fathers. So, like the tracks, there was no vertical view, no library view. The people could only be known by travelling beside them, understanding the cadence of their lives, hearing the stories they told. It was a ground-rooted outlook and was limited by a horizon; beyond this were those times past which had not been revealed by the older generation to the younger. Those times were unknowable, lost to memory.

Arthur's father had told how the explorers pushed further and further inland, searching like Jason for a Golden Fleece: the source of the Nile. They disappeared into the blank places on the maps, striking into the interior in blind hope, forewarned by the ancient Egyptians and Romans that the treacherous swamps and hostile tribes of the Sud would block their way if they attempted to follow the Nile upstream. Men like Burton, fluent in twenty-five languages, expert swordsman; Speke, fervent to be the one to 'settle the question of the Nile'; Livingstone, scourge of the slavers but having to depend on their assistance; Baker, finding a paradise to satisfy his lust for hunting; Rebmann, reporting snow on the equator to a disbelieving Europe. For months, sometimes years, Europe awaited news of their heroes. Until they reported back, wild beasts were drawn on the maps to fill the spaces: a vacancy at the heart of the globe waiting to be filled, the very blackness of the inhabitants nullifying them, thought Arthur, making them invisible – insignificant – to the European eye. The native population blended with the landscape too well; had not separated themselves from nature like the Europeans.

Arthur's father had spun out the stories he told of those men so that Arthur would wait anxiously for the next instalment (as fretfully as Europe had waited not many years before for news of their idols). Were they dead? And what was the manner of their death? A spear in the heart, blackwater fever, drowned in cataracts? And who would return triumphant? Would the source of the Nile be a trickling brook arising in pleasant upland meadows, or a mighty inland sea, or even the fountains of Am Kaam, King of Egypt, at the foot of the Lunae Montes?

And then his father, Mr Thomas Price, had left home himself to go exploring, following hard behind those first adventurers and looking for a different glory, hoping to be feted on a different shore; wanting to draw marks on the map of the hearts of men. Arthur believed that it was the Robert Moffats, the David Livingstones, men like his father – the men of faith – who were most loved by the native peoples. That was their reward, and his own.

Bending over his desk, Arthur looked through his old letters and diaries. In hands that shook he took papers to the light of the window, or the glow of the hurricane lamp, letting dates in diaries, jotted entries, or the text of letters open his memories. He had listed important dates on a sheet of paper at the front of a folder of papers.

'January 19, 1890 – the last surviving letter from my father before his death.' He recalled swinging his legs on the piano stool in the drawing room of the family home in Reigate in 1890. His sister sat beside him while his mother read the letter from their father.

Arthur picked up the letter and read it again.

My dear Ellen,

This letter brings the joyful news that the Rev. T. Johnson and I, after all these months, during which we have learnt patience and to wait on the Lord, will be leaving Zanzibar island on January 5th for Bagamoyo on the mainland. Last night Johnson and I stood on a rock at the far end of the beach outside the town and looked out across the dark waters towards the unlit shores of Africa. What a great harvest of souls awaits us there. What light the gospel of Christ will bring to the poor peoples of Africa whom for so long have lived in the fear of death. I wished you were standing beside me, but I remembered that you are faithful in prayer, and that brought you closer.

There was a stir last week when Mr Henry Stanley arrived in Zanzibar after travelling the entire width of the African continent from west to east. I did not speak to Mr Stanley myself but we had the good fortune to have an agreeable discourse with the reformed slave trader Juma bin Said, an occasional companion of that less than reformed slaver Tippu Tip. Juma bin Said has accompanied Mr Stanley on his expedition. What stories he has to tell of the distant lands so long unknown to civilisation. On the far side of the great lake they call the Victoria Nyanza, many weeks' march from the coast, Mr Stanley received hospitality from a proud race that can raise over two hundred thousand spears in defence of their kingdom. They believe that their ancestors were divine, had pale skin and came from the north, so when Mr Stanley and his party marched through their lands they honoured them as gods.

One of their princes was sent by their king to undertake a blood brotherhood ritual with Mr Stanley. Juma bin Said witnessed the ceremony in which Mr Stanley and the prince sat opposite each other on a fine rug clasping each other's left hand, while the master of the ceremony cut their forearms, mixed each man's blood with butter and rubbed the mixture into the forehead of the other. Stanley's men fired a rifle volley and then the Maxim gun, creating quite a spectacle of ejected earth and splintered rocks on the opposite hillside. The prince was exceedingly impressed.

By all accounts they are well disposed to the gospel and their kingdom is troubled little by the Arabs or other tribes. Their king sent greetings to Mr Stanley saying that no subject of Nkori would refuse him the right hand of fellowship.

But I fear that the ground Johnson and I are to tread is of a more stony nature. Perhaps God will one day grant us the privilege of venturing into that region beyond the great lake.

It is most likely that the next occasion I will have the opportunity to write to you will be on our arrival at the mission at Mwapa, three days' march from the coast. There we will join Mr and Mrs K. Barnes. I will then make haste to submit a report to Bishop Green concerning the financial requirements for the school and for accommodation at the mission for yourself and the children. The bishop has told me that the Barneses have recently returned to Mwapa from Bagamoyo, and they consider the climate at Mwapa far preferable to the hot and fever-infested coastal region.

My children are always in my thoughts. Arthur will find much to amuse him in these parts and Alice will find bountiful example of the delights of God's creation.

Arthur looked at the next entry in his chronology: 'January 26, 1890 – letter – now lost – from my father. His arrival on Africa's shore.' The letter had been misplaced, but not the image it evoked in Arthur – the strongest memory of his childhood even though he had been five thousand miles away. He saw his father wading ashore through warm surf onto virgin sand. Behind him the overladen dhow which had carried him from Zanzibar to Bagamoyo on the mainland was foundering in the blue water, the crew throwing off baggage to save their boat. Arthur's mother, his sister and he, had laughed at the description of the Rev. T. Johnson's attempts to retrieve a lost shoe.

Then came an entry that he had returned to again and again: 'May 24, 1980 – letter from the bishop concerning my father's death.' He did not keep this letter with his other papers: it lived in a pocket at the back of his Bible. He unfolded the heavily creased page; its black ink script was as clear as when first penned.

Dear Mrs Price,

It is my affecting duty but one which I pray will bring you godly pride and consolation, to give you a fuller account of your husband's death than you have already received from the mission committee.

The new mission at Mwapa presented a further threat to the slave traders and, wishing to prevent the mission taking root, the slavers stirred up the natives against the mission, making the most heinous threats. Your husband was sorely troubled by a recurring fever and I advised that the mission be abandoned until order and health could be restored. The Rev. T. Johnson and the Barneses arrived in Bagamoyo from Mwapa on February 8th, greatly disturbed, saying that Mr Price had declined to leave the mission. He had insisted on the others making haste to the coast but would not go with them, saying that he must not abandon the Lord's call, at any cost. It appeared at first that this steadfastness by your husband so inspired the natives that they desisted from their antagonism, but it was a little later that the African chief Manwa conveyed to me, by his own mouth, that action by your husband which turned the hearts of the people.

The chief's son was ill and near to death. His medicine men had predicted the child's demise and were powerless to ward off the powerful curse placed on him, so the chief brought his son to your husband to test the power of his God. When the chief returned with his men the next morning, prepared to pillage the mission and slaughter every soul if his son was dead, he found the child sitting up in bed, well and fully restored. Your husband was sitting beside the bed but, alas, had passed away by the fever. His hand still held the hand of the child. I think on the scene now, precious to me as I hope it will be to yourself, of your husband restrained from leaving Africa by the hand of a child.

Arthur recalled the day his mother had silently given him the letter to read. When he had finished reading he had vowed that when he grew up he would go and work amongst the tribe of two hundred thousand spears.

The night before Michael was to go to stay with Simon, his mother had told him he could have bedtime prayers with his grandfather. Michael paused in the half-open doorway. He wanted to go straight in but knew he had to ask first. Looking at his grandfather dozing in the chair, with his chin resting in the baggy knot of his tie, he felt sorry to have to wake him. He wondered if one day he also would have eyebrows like furry caterpillars that drooped down over crinkly eyelids. His grandfather's mouth was hidden by his bushy white moustache; one long hair was trembling as he breathed as if it was a butterfly's feeler. Michael couldn't imagine how his own skin might one day hang in loose folds from his cheeks. His grandfather's white shirt seemed too big for him as if his chest had sunk away. His large leather-bound Bible had slipped a little from his oversized hands. Michael thought he had hands like Jesus – so he could cure sick people.

'Granddad!' Michael said suddenly, in a loud whisper.

His grandfather first lifted his eyebrows and then opened his eyes. He stared blankly ahead for a moment as if he was wondering where he was, as if he was not sure whether he was still in the world. Then, seeing

Michael, he lifted his head. His moustache straightened and stretched as he smiled. His eyes welcomed Michael in.

Before prayers his grandfather sometimes read to him – books like *Montezuma's Daughter* or *Call of the Wild*. Sometimes Michael saw that he had his eyes closed behind his reading glasses as if he didn't need to look at the words to tell the stories.

That night he did not read, but talked of Africa. 'It's going now, Michael, that old Africa, but its echo will remain as a bittersweet legacy for tomorrow's Africa.'

'Oh,' Michael said, 'I see,' although he didn't.

He lay back across a chair, legs over the arm, and rested his eyes on the line of the hill across the valley, clear against the star-pricked sky. While his grandfather talked in deep and cracked tones of those far-gone days Michael saw shapes on the skyline. At first the shapes looked like bushes and trees but then, as his grandfather spoke, they changed into men, some in robes, some carrying curving elephant tusks, some leading other men with chains. He saw tribesmen with spears, cattle swinging their long horns, men sitting listening to stories, kings with high hats, wise men gathering to talk.

He pointed out a shooting star. 'Oh no, you didn't look quick enough. It's gone now.'

'Ah, tell me if you see another,' his grandfather said, and carried on speaking of the old days, his eyes closed.

On the skyline Michael saw thickset buffalos, creeping leopards, laughing hyenas. He saw queues of his grandfather's patients, crippled and bent at first and then straight and tall against the sky.

When his grandfather had finished talking, Michael sprung lightly from the chair and picked up a folded paper that had slipped out of his grandfather's Bible.

'You've dropped this, Granddad.' He gave it back to him.

'Ah, that. It's something I've kept since I was a boy about your age. I'll tell you about it another time.'

When Michael had gone, Arthur closed his eyes. He saw again his father wading onto Africa's shore at Bagamoyo. He wondered what shore his grandson would have to cross to find his path in the new world. He could not guess, and did not dwell on, for soon, very soon, he would meet his own father, Thomas, again; would tell him stories of the tribe of two hundred thousand spears that he never lived to see, but he, the son, worked among for forty years. Soon, very soon.

SEVEN

'Bloody hell!' shouted Simon's father. 'Where are my cigarettes? Who tidied them off the sideboard? Rhonda?'

'Shut up, Henry, the missionaries' kid has arrived. Try controlling yourself for just a minute.'

Simon's mother, Mrs Adams, stood in the doorway, half turned away from Michael as she yelled back at her husband. She seemed to Michael to be all twisting curves, from her hip-tight skirt, to the swell of her breasts under her silky blouse (he tried not to think about the sherbet), to her flicked-out blonde hair. She turned back to examine him. First he noticed her lips which were as red as coral, and then he couldn't not stare at her eyes: they were as pretty as a cat's – but also scary. She was looking at him as if he was a mouse that someone had dropped on the doorstep. She bent over him, gliding her polished fingernails down the front of her thighs. He was reminded of something he had heard somewhere: *nature, red in tooth and claw.* Some sort of perfumed vapour fell heavily onto his face. It would easily kill mosquitoes.

'Please forgive Simon's dad. He's a real devil sometimes,' she said with a purry voice. Her fingernails twitched.

Michael had not expected to have confirmation of Simon's warning so early in his visit. He was thankful that his father had told him, that morning, that he was an Ambassador For Christ and this would be his first posting. He had prayed the previous night for Jesus to help him fight The World, The Flesh And The Devil. Here was the Devil bit. He would be strong.

'You must be starving, poor waif. Boarding school is only one up from the workhouse. Come in and have some cake and ginger beer.'

This was awkward; she didn't know that missionaries didn't drink beer. This was the World bit.

While Michael wrestled with such closeness to sin, Simon pushed past his mother.

'Hello, Father.'

'Hello, boy. Have you seen my Players?'

Mrs Adams said, 'How can he possibly have seen your Players, Henry? He's only just arrived.'

'What? You've been away, son?'

Michael was not sure if Simon's father was joking.

'Just got back from Lewis's, Dad, and before that I was at school.'

'Teaching you to bat, are they? Got to learn to impress the girls, son.'

Simon had told Michael that his father used to look like a handsome airline pilot but then he had a terrible accident playing rugby which had smashed his face. 'To smithereens' was all Simon had said when Michael had asked exactly what had happened, leaving Michael imagining horrible facial deformities under the devil's horns and the hyena hair. Looking at Mr Adams now, Michael was a little disappointed for although his nose was a distance from the midline, the rest of his face was not caved in at all and his eyes, lips and ears were exactly where they should be; in fact Michael hoped he would look a bit like him when he grew up. He had a black pencil moustache which he kept running his finger along, and if he wasn't doing that he was stroking the tight ripples of his shiny, black, Brylcreemed hair. A manly chest was hinted at by the puff of hairs in the V of his unbuttoned safari shirt. Michael bet himself that he wore Aertex underpants.

'Aw, can we play with these?' Simon asked, picking up a heavy pair of binoculars from the sideboard.

'Don't get your grubby fingers on the glass,' Mr Adams replied.

Simon generously handed the binoculars to Michael who lifted them to his eyes. A milky disk bobbed about.

'You're looking at the ceiling,' Simon said.

Michael shifted his view and gasped. He was looking straight into Mr Adams's face. Mr Adams was looking straight back but Michael could see behind the handsome mask. His squoncky nose was missing but there were openings in the centre of his skull for breathing and his eye sockets were stretched sideways. Dark cracks had replaced the whites of his eyes. His lips made a rude hole. A devil unmasked.

Michael almost dropped the binoculars, his arms weak with shock. But Mr Adams was no longer in front of him. He had moved away and was looking under a cushion on the sofa, still searching for his cigarettes. Directly opposite Michael on the wall, a mask stared back. It was surrounded by other hollow-eyed masks, sticks stuck with feathers, and gourds hung with strips of leather and little bones. A wooden female figure squatted on the platform beneath the wall, her hands gripping her breasts which were shaped like ice-cream cones, except they were black. Michael had never felt scared of any of these things before – he had seen them in Tomasi's village – but now they seemed revolting; as if them being in Mr and Mrs Adams's house had made them so.

'My mum and dad collect that stuff,' Simon said. 'There's stuff to frighten away ghosts of ancestors, and there are things that witchdoctors use to find out whether someone's a murderer, and there are knives for throwing at people. I'm not allowed to play with them – it's crap stuff.'

'Language, son!' Mr Adams said. 'And be careful; one day something's going to crawl off the wall and get you. Ah, found the blighters.' He lit up immediately.

Mrs Adams was still arguing over payment with the driver who had collected Michael from his parents. It had been a forty mile journey and they had made a detour in town to collect Simon from Lewis's home. Simon had spent the first three days of the holiday with Lewis's family so that he could go with them to a game reserve. He had told Michael that his parents didn't mind at all if he was away as they went out a lot to clubs. His father went to the Great Lakes Golf Club and the Crested Crane Cricket Club, while his mother went to the Bateleur Bridge Club and the Hepburn Film Society.

The argument with the driver was becoming heated but Mr Adams had sunk into the sofa with his cigarette and had closed his eyes.

'Come and see my Meccano,' Simon said.

He opened his bedroom door. Michael's eyes widened; for a moment he wished he did not have poor missionary parents. On the polished-wood floor a large Meccano crane and two ships gleamed red, green and gold. When he stretched out on the floor to look closely he felt like the happy rich boy on the front of the Meccano box.

'Did you make these?' Michael asked.

'Not really. My dad did. He plays with my Meccano when I'm at school.'

'My dad doesn't have time to play,' said Michael ruefully.

'It's because my mum doesn't like him hanging around in the living room when he's at home. She shouts at him and he shouts back. Then she says something like "nothing for a month if you carry on", which I think means she won't let him have his cigarettes – and then he always shuts up.'

'I'm lucky – although there is no such thing as luck – because my mum loves my dad,' Michael said.

'What, they don't shout at each other?' Simon was amazed.

'No, never. They say good things about each other. They're like Christ and his Bride – I think.'

'That's sissy.'

'Why did they get married if they don't like each other?'

'I don't know. They met each other when she was a stewardess on a BOAC jetliner. My dad stroked her arm and she liked it, so they got married.'

Mrs Adams brought in the boys' drinks and a chocolate cake on a tray. Michael decided that it was better to drink the ginger beer than upset Mr and Mrs Adams. Later he was surprised how little the beer affected him: he didn't say or do anything silly afterwards at all.

While Michael wound pulleys and marvelled at real gears, Simon pulled his complete set of Tintin books and boys' annuals off the shelf onto his bed. He jumped on the bed and started bouncing, sending the books scattering. Leaping off, he pushed the crane over.

'What are you doing?' Michael asked, rolling out of the way.

'I'm bored. Let's do something else,' Simon moaned. He seemed to be getting poked – by Satan probably. Or maybe it was his ginger beer. He had ants in his pants. Michael thought Simon might be mad at his parents – he would be if he was Simon – and that it was making him want to break things. He felt sad for him. He wondered if his own parents could adopt Simon so that he could be happy. It might be the kindest thing.

Simon kicked his scattered books and said, 'Let's fly the water rocket. No, it's broken. Let's play with my dad's Bull Worker. I can't even pull it one little bit.' He made a bubble of spit between his lips. 'No, let's do an East African Safari.'

Dinky models lined the window ledge. They selected their cars, attached string, and marked out a route around the house. When Michael rounded the house onto the back lawn he saw that there was a girl in a crinkly blue swimsuit, lying face down on a bright-yellow towel on the grass, reading a magazine. She looked like a miniature Mrs Adams although her hair was turned under, rather than flicked out, and she had freckles so big that Naaman, the leper, could not have looked blotchier. The girl looked at him though her fierce, yellow, horn-rimmed sunglasses.

'What you looking at, you little bleeder?' she snarled.

This may be the Arrows Of The Evil One, thought Michael.

Simon said quickly. 'She's my sister. She was nice until last hols and then she changed. Her name is Angeline and we called her Ange, but now we have to call her Angie.'

'This is my friend, Michael,' Simon said to Angie in the kind sort of way that grown-ups did when they were talking to a sick little child. Michael smiled a worried smile at her.

'Welcome to the house of boredom,' Angie said, and let her head suddenly fall on the towel as if she had been whacked with a pole.

'She wants to leave home but she's only thirteen,' Simon said. 'She wants to go to London where she can get a boyfriend.'

'Shut up and go and play, Si.' She rolled onto her back and pulled her swimsuit down her chest so that the sun shone on the top part of her small white blubbery breasts. Michael felt a bit sick.

The cook sounded a gong for dinner. Michael sat with his back rigid and with his hands on his lap – an ambassador must be very polite – but Simon bent forward with his elbows on the table driving a fork around his plate. Mrs Adams rang a little brass bell. The cook, in white jacket and trousers, a red band around his waist and a red hat brought silver servers to the table, opened their serviettes and poured their drinks: Pepsi for Simon and Michael, beer for Simon's father, water for his mother and Angie.

Michael opened his mouth a little and sucked in the steam from his plate of steak, mash and squash. A curl of butter melted on the squash. His spit glands hurt with longing. Simon had told him that they never ate goat, and never would. This was just what he imagined the Banqueting House Of The Lord would be like.

'Do start, Michael,' Mrs Adams said. He saw her pull her lips into an encouraging smile.

'He's waiting for us to say grace,' Simon said.

'Oh, how quaint, er … Henry, can you say grace?' Mrs Adams asked.

'No, I bloody well can't. The hypocrisy would cause a lightning strike.'

Mrs Adams started to ask Michael to say it for them but Simon said excitedly, 'I'll say it.'

He put his hands together above his plate. 'God bless this bunch as they crunch their lunch.'

He laughed loudly. Michael also laughed, although afterwards he felt uncomfortable as he remembered that God Is Not Mocked.

'D'you think you could remember that grace, Henry? It's not in Latin, it's quite neutral and it won't perjure you,' Mrs Adams said.

'Will you stop sniping at me, Rhonda. We're unlikely to need it again.'

Michael kept his eyes on his plate.

'Aw, flip!' Angie said. 'This family stinks.'

'Angie! Please! We have a guest,' Mrs Adams said.

'I'm just telling the truth. I'm sure he can smell us whether I said it or not,' Angie said.

Mr Adams struck his plate with his knife, making Michael jump. 'Go to your room, young madam.'

Mrs Adams leant forward. 'No, don't, your father's overreacting. She's not five any more, Henry.'

'Michael's parents are kind to each other,' Simon said loudly.

'What people do to each other in their own homes is their own business. I'll not hold it against them,' Mr Adams said.

'They're like Christ and his Bride,' Simon said.

Michael saw Mr and Mrs Adams exchange glances. Angie said, 'Huh?'

'Christ and his what?' Mr Adams sneered. 'You've gone soft in the head, boy. Toughen up. If you're ever to get a woman like your mother you've got to be a man.' Mrs Adams looked across at Mr Adams, her eyebrows raised. 'Like she was when I first met her, of course.'

Mrs Adams rolled her eyes and said, 'The kid has a point.'

'Very well,' Mr Adams said, 'so what's the secret of your parents' marital bliss? And don't say it's religion because that's not going to help us.'

Michael found that everyone was looking at him. Simon had stopped his gravy-and-mash dam building. Angie was waiting for him with her upper lip twisted in a frozen sneer. Mr Adams was no longer chewing his steak with his muscley jaw. Mrs Adams had swivelled her neck and moved her face towards him. Michael feared that she might pounce if he squeaked. A fly stopped buzzing on the windowpane behind the Venetian blind. He puzzled over what Mr Adams had said about religion. Jesus was a friend, not a religion.

The fly started buzzing again as if it had got bored waiting.

'I don't know,' Michael said, and then, sensing that this fell well short of what everyone expected, added, 'That's what mothers and fathers are like.'

He saw Mrs Adams' smile slump; Mr Adams coughed.

'A very sweet sentiment,' Mrs Adams said eventually. She touched her lips lightly with her serviette and rang the bell for some more water.

'I got the specifications on the latest Kenwoods,' Mr Adams said. 'They've got extra power and extra blenders. But I'll have to find better distributors than the Mehtas. They sold only six Chefs last month and all of those to Europeans. It's the mass market we've got to get. Once the Afs catch on that they don't have to beat their millet in a pound all day or break their backs mixing their *matooke* with some goddamned pole, they're going to shift in their thousands. Imagine, a Chef in every hut!'

'So what happens when they have the big *ekiihuro* with thirty uncles, aunts, brothers, sisters and their *picininis* milling in as well, and the electric's down?' Mrs Adams asked.

'They're going to pressure the government to get their act together. Get things working. Once they're hooked in to modern appliances they're not going to accept the old pounding and grinding again.'

'Yeah, I can just see them marching in the streets 'cause their Chef won't work,' Angie said.

Mr Adams ignored her and poured more beer – slowly and with a smile on his face, as if he was sure he was right.

'Kid has a point, Henry,' Mrs Adams said.

'Kid has a point, huh? Well, I guess she does. Just got to be patient. It takes time to turn a primitive people into mass-market consumers. You've got to find the hook; then you've got 'em. You'll never find a civilisation that abandons a technological advance. Imagine – what about it, chaps? Let's not bother with pens any more; let's chisel marks on rocks. Let's not bother with umbrellas any more; let's go back to banana leaves. No, once the Afs have got their Chefs they'll never go back to big sticks, or whatever they use.' He snorted at the end of his speech, sounding to Michael like a buffalo, pleased it had trampled something down.

'Your mother got a Kenwood Chef yet?' asked Mr Adams to Michael.

Michael had hoped not to be asked any more questions but now everyone was looking at him again. He had his mouth full of juicy steak – he had been wondering if this was the Flesh he had been warned about, and that he would end up wanting more and more until he became a Glutton And A Sinner. He had not come across a single glob of gristle to retch on, unlike the goat meat they had as a treat at home. The Flesh was undoubtedly the most difficult and dangerous temptation yet.

He swallowed and said, 'I don't think so. I've never seen one in the kitchen.' There was an awkward silence. He sensed his family might have let everyone down. 'But it's a bit dark with smoke because our oven doesn't work properly.' Then he remembered something his mother had said which might be a better reason. 'My mum says she doesn't want to have too many things that the Africans haven't got.'

Mr Adams banged his beer down on the table. 'How wrong headed is that? How are they going to want appliances if we – we Europeans – don't show them.'

Michael pulled his shoulders in. He was worried that Mr Adams might hit him.

Mrs Adams said, 'Bernard and Stella are not "we", Henry. They've got different priorities. They don't see everyone as a potential consumer.'

'Sure – they see everyone as a potential convert. Bloody hypocrites.'

Michael had never heard anyone attack his parents before. He felt hurt, and then angry. All his mother and father wanted was for everyone to be happy by knowing Jesus. He imagined Mr Adams and his father having a fight. It was a bit worrying to think that his father might not win. He would have to use a Bull Worker first and then he could easily knock Mr Adams flat.

Mrs Adams said, 'Enough, Henry. It's not Michael's fault his parents are religious, and I don't think you know what a hypocrite is.'

But Mr Adams wasn't finished. 'What did that guy say? Religion's the opium of the people?' He cut his steak clean in two.

'Come on, Henry,' Mrs Adams said. 'You've just been going on about how you're going to get the Afs hooked on appliances. Your goods are just another opium. We've all got our opiums to anaesthetise us from what's coming. Maybe the missionaries have got a better opium.'

Angie groaned and slumped. 'Yeah, like I said, we stink, even though we've got Kenwoods and automatic washers.'

Mr Adams banged down his beer again but Mrs Adams looked fiercely at him. Simon said loudly, 'Wish we had smoke in our kitchen like Michael does.'

Mrs Adams rang the bell for dessert. The cook came through with a pavlova.

'Oh, well done, Isaac.'

'Yummy!' Simon said.

'None for me,' Angie said.

Mr Adams said, 'That's what your mother could do if she had a Kenwood, Michael. You tell her, huh?'

'Would you like some, Michael?' Mrs Adams asked, cutting the meringue.

He would, but he was close to tears and said nothing in case his voice came out quivery.

'Please don't worry about Simon's father,' Mrs Adams said, sending her husband another withering look.

Mr Adams leant across and ruffled Michael's hair. 'We're going to take you on a special outing after lunch.'

'I'm not coming,' Angie said.

'You're not invited,' Mr Adams replied.

Mrs Adams said, 'You boys can have some sherbet on the journey. Special treat.'

Michael and Simon exchanged looks.

The long Citroën DS, with its shark-like bonnet, sped out of the town, pedestrians and animals running before it like a bow wave, throwing themselves out and away at the last second. Mr and Mrs Adams sat in the front, not talking, while Michael and Simon sat in the back licking sherbet and grinning out of the windows. As if he were in a vicious presidential cavalcade, Mr Adams never slowed down. A woman screamed, 'We're saved!' as she pulled her young child from the vehicle's path.

Mr Adams chuckled and said, 'We're the cavalry, you're the infantry; we ride, you walk.' Then he added grimly, 'They'll learn.'

The scraggly outskirts of the town gave way to scabby land pocked by the makeshift dwellings and the scratched smallholdings of those attracted to the town but too poor to live in it; the beginnings of the shanties that would stow the cheap labour for the next century's cities. Soon they were away from the town, and the few small fields of millet and maize petered out as the land opened out into undulating grassland.

Michael felt cocooned from the outside world and spread his arms out on the seat, luxuriating in the space. His parents were always stopping to give people lifts and would continue to pick up anyone who waved a hopeful hand until no more bottoms could be wedged in.

Mr Adams said, 'This will make wonderful cattle ranching country but the government will have to clear out the nomads first. Can't have pest control without fences.'

'They've got by for thousands of years without fences, Henry.' Mrs Adams's voice sounded as if she'd got a stuffy nose.

'Yes, but they die off when their cattle are wiped out by rinderpest or drought.'

Simon exclaimed, 'Look, people camping!' He pointed to small, grass, tent-like structures on a hillside.

'Those are the nomads,' Mr Adams said. 'They don't bother with houses because they've got to move every few weeks.'

'Hmm. Wonder where they'll put their automatic washers,' Mrs Adams said.

Mr Adams changed gear. 'It's the march of history – you can't stop it.'

They caught up with a bus, crabbing its laden way, trailing a smelly cloud of exhaust and dust. Mr Adams shifted himself to see past. Michael became anxious, worried that they hadn't prayed for safety – his family never set off on a journey without asking for protection, and it was always given. As his father prayed he imagined God's hand holding their Anglia like a Dinky car and guiding it along the road. God could flick obstacles out of their way if necessary or slow them down at junctions if he saw a drunk coming the other way. He wondered what would happen if his father tried to throw off God's hand by out-accelerating him or taking an unexpected turn. But now he was in a car travelling at speed without any request for God's help.

'Can't we just drop back a bit? One can never be late for a picnic,'

Mrs Adams said, closing her window and placing a handkerchief over her nose and mouth. But Mr Adams was already accelerating out of the dust and the car was swooshing down the side of the bus. Michael could see three hens and a cockerel ahead on the side of the road. He was sure their little eyes widened in terror. They stretched out their necks and started out for the other side of the road. Then Michael saw the child. He looked a younger version of Tomasi and was running after the chickens – towards the road. Michael barely had time to think out the whole thought: the little boy's family has only got those four chickens and he wants to save them.

Mr Adams spat 'Damn it' as he swerved this way and that. Mrs Adams had covered her eyes with her handkerchief and sat rigid with her head bowed. There was a dull thud. Michael and Simon turned, open-mouthed, to look behind. Their own dust cloud billowed out, already hiding the bus and the road, but on its peripheries red, black and bronze feathers turned in the hot sun like the glowing ashes from a fire.

Mrs Adams screamed. 'Stop, Henry! You've hit the kid.'

'Nah, don't think so. Would have been a bigger bang. Got the chickens, though.'

He sounded casual but Michael saw him blow out through his lips.

'Good driving, Dad,' Simon said, then turned to Michael. 'That's how they drive in the East African Safari.'

Michael laughed with Simon. They had survived and missed the boy, without God keeping an eye on them. Simon's father had got them out of trouble all on his own by his own clever driving. Michael felt that he had joined in something daring and it had paid off. God was a good friend, yes, but it was exciting to get away for once; to go somewhere without him; to spread his wings on his own.

'Why did the chicken cross the road?' Mr Adams said. Even Mrs Adams joined in the chuckling.

As soon as Michael had laughed a disturbing image came into his mind from his Picture Bible. He saw the disciple, Peter, standing warming himself by a brazier at the first pink of dawn – red sky in the morning, shepherd's warning. Behind him a cockerel was crowing its head off. Peter had already disowned his best friend, Jesus. Michael remembered the cockerel on the side of the road, and how it had looked at him as if it knew.

They slowed slightly as the road narrowed and became corrugated. Michael and Simon held imaginary steering wheels and threw themselves from side to side, negotiating the course. Miles passed with no sign of permanent habitation. The land opened out into rolling arid pastureland.

'It's down here,' Mr Adams said, as he braked hard and turned off onto a boulder-strewn track.

Mrs Adams folded out the camp chairs under a thorn tree with a view. Mr Adams removed a large plastic coolbox from the boot of the car. Simon and Michael raced towards the pools of water amongst the rocks in a shallow cut in the land. They put their fingers in the water.

'Hey, Dad,' Simon shouted. 'It's hot!'

'That's why they call it Hot Springs.'

They took off their shoes and jumped on the rocks, but jumped back immediately because of the heat. The water slipped over a flat boulder at the edge of the water so they started to construct a causeway for their cars. When they looked up they found two young herd boys were looking at them from the slope above the pool. The older was big and strong but was hanging on his spear, which he gripped with both hands. The younger boy had light bones and was small, but stood straight as if ready to run.

'Ignore them,' Simon said.

'Why?' Michael asked. Everything was new and strange in Simon's family: he had to learn the new rules.

'For a start they'll want our cars and then they'll ask for money,' Simon replied.

'Tomasi doesn't ask for money.'

'Who's Tomasi?'

'Just a friend.'

'OK, you ask them to play and see what happens,' Simon said, 'but my mum and dad won't allow us. I think they're worried about disease.'

Michael shouted to the boys, but they just stood there gawping at him. He wanted to go up and ask them their secrets, the places where the snakes sunned themselves and the places where illegal distilleries were hidden, but the boys remained motionless, just staring – as if they were looking at Queen Elizabeth herself.

'There, see? They just stare; they don't even know it's rude to stare,' Simon said triumphantly.

'I think they haven't seen white people before,' Michael said.

They heard Mrs Adams call them to come and eat. She had positioned their camp chairs in the shade and placed their sandwiches and cake neatly on plates. They ate in silence, listening to the bubbling of the water, the lazy croaks of a toad and the pure clear calls of a bird.

'Do you think they're going to watch us eating? I understand now how a lion must feel when a tourist bus stops to gawp,' Mrs Adams said, looking at the herd boys.

'That reminds me, I'm going to take a picture,' Mr Adams said.

'Get one of the picininis to do it. Make them do something as payment for their front row seats.'

Mr Adams set up the camera on a tripod, pressed the shutter and hurried back to his camp chair. They looked into the lens and waited for the shutter to sound, putting their best face forward, except Simon who stuck out his tongue. 'That was silly,' said Mrs Adams. 'A waste of a picture.'

When Mr Adams sat down again he sighed and said, 'Us in Africa. We'll look back from our retirement home in Worthing and say, "those were the days".'

He ran his finger along his moustache. 'Yes, these really are the days. We're royalty for a short while longer, and then we abdicate and hope the natives don't chop off our heads.'

No one said anything. It was hot. Michael saw Mrs Adams lazily stretch her hand across towards Mr Adams and place it on the arm of his chair. Mr Adams didn't look at her, but he put his hand on hers and squeezed it gently. Mrs Adams smiled a little and looked happy. They're being kind to each now, Michael thought. There were lots of things he didn't understand.

While the boys picked the last crumbs off their plates Mr Adams became restless, got up and fetched his portable radio from the car.

Mrs Adams was napping, her eyes closed, but she jerked her head up as the radio came on. 'What the hell is that, Henry? Excruciating. Change it to something civilised.'

'I like it. It's got beat.'

'Change it, Henry. Don't spoil the picnic for Michael.'

Mr Adams looked at Michael but Michael did not look back; he didn't want to upset either of them. Mr Adams changed station.

'Those kids are coming closer. I really would like some privacy. They're giving me the willies. Tell them to scuttle off,' Mrs Adams said.

'Tell them yourself. They're not doing any harm,' Mr Adams said. 'Maybe I can interest them in a mixer.' He winked heavily at Michael.

'I've had enough. Go away! *Kwenda*!' Mrs Adams shouted.

The two herd boys fled.

That evening, after Mrs Adams had turned out the bedroom light and said a bedtime prayer – sleep tight, mind the gremlins don't bite – Michael got out of bed when Simon had gone to sleep and knelt down and prayed. He felt bad about feeling good when they had hit the chickens and so he asked God to forgive him. Then, as always, he knew God's kind pardon. He was glad God was a friend who knew him and not some sort of gruff judge. On balance Michael thought he had done well as God's ambassador, considering that it was his first full day on the job. He reminded God of that. What worried him was that he didn't know whether Simon's family had noticed; whether Mr Adams was saying to Mrs Adams in their living room as he poured himself a beer, 'Well I never thought I'd say it, Rhonda, but Michael's a great ambassador for Christ.' He doubted it. The chorus 'In this world of darkness ...' played itself in his head. Then he cried a little, as he had the first night he went to boarding school.

Kampala
1962

Cast from our course, we wander in the dark.
Virgil, The Aeneid

Michael, aged twelve, and his mother made their way out of the teeming ticket hall at the railway station in the capital. They left his father in the hall, pinned against a wall by Mr Adams, with his Bull Worker arms, who was suggesting that a man who truly loved his wife as Christ loved the church would buy her a stainless steel kitchen sink and built-in appliances. It was the Christian thing to do.

Michael tried to hurry his mother down the platform to find his carriage. It was the start of his second year at senior school in Kenya and he wanted to lay claim to the prized middle bunk in the compartment for the twenty-four hour journey. A middle bunk meant being able to lie awake and watch the shapes of the night slide by, see the great Beyer-Garrett steam engines being watered in the shunting yards and see proud station signs announcing their altitude: Tororo 3086 feet, through Eldoret, Sosian, and Kaptagat, right up to Timboroa at 9001 feet and then on to Equator and down to Nakuru. He liked to see the orange-illuminated bustle on the platforms – families catching the train in the middle of the night having made their way along unlit roads from far-flung farms and villages.

But making haste was as difficult as in a dream. Obstacles impeded every route: oversized suitcases, scuffed and bulging; spicy scented Indian women with insistent voices, flesh hanging in rolls from their midriffs, their gold-trimmed bright-red saris contrasting shockingly with the dull-grey platform; mail-lumpy sacks on squealing trolleys dwarfing the sweating porters leaning heavily into their loads; small boys in khaki-brown shorts and stained hand-me-down shirts getting in everyone's way, pleading a few coins for peanuts in small newspaper cones.

When he pulled ahead of his mother a little he found himself wanting to hang back again as if, although he desperately wanted the bunk, he was not yet ready to leave her. Not yet ready to make the transition from the snug care of his parents to the equally dependable but aloof care of the school; from being at the hub of a family, to being one of a crowd; from days where he need think of nothing but projects and games, to months where the first priority was to keep alert to avoid being last in every queue. Another nine months away from home. His parents could only afford to bring him back once a year. The Lord's work required sacrifices. In the holidays away he stayed, like a wartime evacuee, with a dreamy and bookish friend whose parents owned a coffee farm, kicking around, missing Tomasi, missing Rachel and his parents, missing home.

He saw Simon and his mother ahead. Simon was going to get to the middle bunk first.

'There's Simon. Why didn't you want to invite him to stay with us this holiday?' his mother said.

Michael's sockless feet felt gummy, confined in his shoes again, the straps too tight, the concrete platform hard and hostile.

'I think he hates me,' he said weakly.

His mother frowned at him. 'I'm sure that's not true.'

'Oh yes it is.' He held back hot tears and felt his eyelid start to tic.

'What happened?' she asked, putting a hand around his shoulder. He shrugged her hand away.

'I sort of ratted on him at school. He was nearly expelled. He got detentions and I wouldn't be surprised if his father beat him when he got home.' He hadn't meant to get Simon into trouble; it had all got out of control when he had refused to give Simon an alibi.

'Perhaps telling on him wasn't such a good idea?'

'I didn't, but what am I supposed to do? I should have fibbed.'

Ahead, Simon and Mrs Adams had stopped while Mrs Adams looked for something in Simon's kitbag. She seemed agitated; Michael could see her lips moving colourfully. She pulled out a packet of cigarettes. His mother raised her eyebrows in a question to him. He nodded.

'If he smokes that's his business. It's something for his parents – not you,' she said.

'I know that!' he hissed fiercely, suddenly angry. He tried so hard but God never helped. It was God that confused him (although he now felt his early attempts at second-guessing God – the quest for a Zephyr, for example – were babyish). But mostly he was angry at himself – for not knowing what to do; for looking like a goody-goody.

Mrs Adams straightened up, pulled a cigarette from the packet and a white lighter from her white handbag. She drew heavily and put the packet back in Simon's kitbag. She saw Michael and his mother.

'God! Such a strain all this. Kid tells me he's got to hide the bloody cigarettes behind his locker. But next year he'll be safely in Bedales where boys can be boys – and with girls. So good for children to be free to find their own way, don't you think? Not to have to be devious.'

Michael's mother puckered her lips a little. Mrs Adams noticed and blinked her heavily mascaraed lashes as if making a conscious decision to reformulate the world from another angle.

'Of course there have to be limits: murder and … er … adultery and … such things. The Ten Commandments …' she trailed off.

'Oh, I don't think they really matter,' his mother said.

'What, not murder?' Mrs Adams's eyes flashed cerulean.

'Rules and laws are very … Old Testament,' his mother said, casting her hand to the side as if chucking something away.

'How extraordinary! My dear Stella, we should get together. I didn't know you were such a rebel. I wasn't expecting such radical views from a missionary. You must be corrupting the Afs terribly.' Mrs Adams flicked the cheekily angled cigarette she held in the fingers of her lolling arm. The smoke entwined itself around her hips.

Michael's mother smiled and said lightly, as if she was just reminding Mrs Adams of something everyone knew, 'We're not under law, but under grace – Romans six.'

'Say! You've lost me. I just read *Vogue* – when I can get it.'

'It's about *love*, Mother,' Simon said, glaring with malice at Michael. He looked more and more like his father now, his crow-black hair rippling backwards; except his nose was more like his mother's: small and delicate – not squoncky. A boy at school had started to call him Sniffy – until Simon punched him in the face.

Michael saw Mrs Adams look at her son as if she were flummoxed, as if wondering what impracticalities Simon's religious schooling had taught him. It was not the first time he had heard Simon use his reluctantly received spiritual knowledge to shoot barbed comments at his parents.

'Well, I'm sure I've misunderstood something. But we mustn't linger. Simon seems very anxious to get to his carriage. It's divine – literally! – to see you, Stella.'

She swept them with a smile and swung on down the platform. Simon hurried ahead of her. Michael thought of running to overtake them but it was already too late, and his mother was leaning close to say something.

'I hate being stereotyped,' she said, with a hardness in her eye that Michael rarely saw. 'You must think this, disapprove of that, you're two dimensional, can't think for yourself, need a crutch to lean on.'

He gave his mother a quick smile – her battling spirit restoring him a little. She returned his smile and he thought he would make an effort to remember it if things got tough in the year ahead. He took some strength from their fellowship against the hostile secular world. Since leaving junior school and starting at senior school it had become plain to him that being a child of missionaries, and having religious belief, was considered distinctly odd – at best a quaint leftover from the traditions of the past, at worst a pitiful eccentricity. Nothing fitted together as it used to. He felt caught between loyalty to his family – their dogged faith, the circle of their love, a sure God-given framework for living – and the world of his school friends.

As they reached the carriage his mother said, 'I'll be praying that you and Simon make it up.'

That was all he needed to hear because God listened to his mother's prayers more than anyone else he knew. He realised now that he wanted Simon's friendship as much as God's.

The steps up into the carriage were steep and he struggled with his kitbag. His father had somehow escaped Mr Adams – with what Michael hoped was an unexpected upper cut – and had caught up with them, carrying Michael's suitcase, his mind on some translation riddle. Michael shuffled down the hot corridor towards compartment F while his father lifted the suitcase into the luggage racks at the end of the carriage.

Simon was waiting in the doorway of the compartment. 'I've bagged this middle bunk and I've bagged the other one for Lewis.' He sounded triumphant.

Michael said nothing, dumped his kitbag on the floor and went to the window in the corridor. Lewis was shambling towards him with a dreamy expression, picking at a wart on his thumb; Michael didn't think that Lewis cared which bunk he had. He raised one hand a little in a quick and off-hand gesture, and Lewis raised his eyebrows in a brief acknowledgement. Michael prided himself on being just as good as his friends at keeping an even face whatever the circumstances – he felt it a mark of having left childishness behind.

His parents were on the platform by the window saying obvious things like, 'Don't forget to put your tuck straight in your locker when you get to school,' and questions which he could not possibly know the answer to, like 'Will Ma Crickenhowe still be your dorm matron?' or – his father – 'Er, Michael, let's limber up on your Latin. What's "The queen killed the slave with the spear"?'

Michael kept glancing up the train; waiting for something to happen. He hoped his mother wouldn't blub, otherwise he might blub as well. Lewis was leaning out of the next window looking sombre, but he would never blub. It was annoying that his parents had left Rachel at a friend's house nearby – he would have been brave for his sister. She played with him and Tomasi all holidays now: they dissected dead birds, swung on the rope over the river, hunted for *waragi* distilleries in the banana groves. It was as if he was going to sea, or to war, the way she asked him so many questions before he left for school; her eyes became huge, like fried eggs, when he told her all the most scandalous and funny stories from senior school. It was OK to fib a bit to little kids.

Now he could hear the engine snorting and hissing at the far end of the platform; a brooding, heavy presence. He imagined it as the head of a monster, the leathery-brown carriages its body sprawling out behind.

What was happening to them was big and it needed something equally big to do it. When the monster started to pant it was ready to go, and no one could stop it.

A shrieking whistle sounded. The crowd panicked, shouting and running about, dragging their overweight suitcases, throwing bags and small children through the windows. The porters, upper lips wet with sweat, heaved the last sacks into the guard's van. The peanut boys pleaded for one last sale even as they were pushed aside. Relatives inside the train fought to get off as the stragglers fought to get on. Coins and peanuts scattered.

Soon the suitcases were gone and there was a slamming of heavy doors. For one brief moment all movement on the platform ceased. A hush descended on the crowd and even the distant noise of the engine was stilled, as if it were drawing breath. In that moment Michael saw that everything was fixed and that everyone was resigned to what was going to happen next. He saw that some things will happen whatever you hope for and it's no good blubbing, as it won't make a difference.

The engine started panting and stirred. His carriage gave a lurch. It was a small movement but Michael felt it in his stomach. Even the people on the platform sensed it: they started frantically waving and shouting again. He took a quick look at his parents. They were trying to smile and his mother was saying something about letters. The harsh breaths of the engine sounded like some gigantic saw – severing him from home. As the whole carriage started to rumble he could hear the wheels rolling; metal against metal. The steely growls of the train grew louder and louder until he could no longer hear his mother or the shouting on the platform. An irresistible force was pulling him away. Everyone on the platform became smaller. Then they turned a corner, and his mother and father were gone. He always remembered how small they looked. It was the last time he saw them.

They clanked past marshalling yards grubby with coal, broken pipes, rusty coils of wire and oily sleepers – scattered like the burnt dead on a battlefield. He choked on a tarry gas that hit the back of his throat. He went and sat in the compartment. The seat plastic was coldly smooth against his bare thighs below his shorts, like snake skin. Simon was eating a corned beef sandwich, stinking the air. Michael felt an immense and aching solitude.

'You know,' Lewis said, 'if they stopped all the trains from here to the coast and then you put your ear to the track and someone hit the track in Mombasa with a hammer, you'd hear it one hour later.'

Michael put on a half-interested expression but he wasn't ready to talk. To take his mind off leaving home he thought instead about what his grandfather had told him of the building of the railway; how hundreds of workers had come from India to lay down iron bars – seven hundred miles of them – from the steamy coast right up to Kampala. He tried to remember more: it had been two years since his grandfather had died. It was easier to remember if he imagined himself sitting in his grandfather's cottage again, looking at the line of the hill against the night sky. His grandfather told him that the land was a place of hard rock, escarpments and ravines. Those Indians had to hack, slash, dynamite and grade a straight way across the terrain because the carriages couldn't go around sharp corners. Then there were the man-eating lions that roamed in the shadow-black nights. Nights that fell as 'quick as doom', his grandfather said. The man-eaters took the coolies in their hundreds; dragging them from the light of their fires, yanking them from the grasp of rescuers, snatching them out of their tents and even stalking down the corridors of the railway carriages to pull them off their bunks, still clutching their sheets. Their sheets were all that were found, ripped and bloody.

Michael felt better, thinking at least he was not a coolie. He wondered why he had not been born a coolie and why he had been born a missionary's child instead. His father had said that God had a plan for everyone, whatever they were born as, and if they asked God he would show them what it was. Michael decided that if he had been born a coolie, he would have asked God for a plan that didn't involve building a railway.

Simon took a Fanta from his kitbag. Michael had watery orange juice. His mother had said that although they couldn't have Fanta or

Pepsi they had other things – like knowing Jesus. Michael once shared a Fanta with his sister when they stopped for petrol on a long car journey. It was the best thing of the holiday, that Fanta: so fizzy, so sweet, so impossibly orangey. When he was grown up, if he got rich, he decided he would buy hundreds of crates of Fanta and keep them for himself and Tomasi in a secret place in the banana grove, but give the rest of the money away to people like Freda and Godfrey.

'Hey, we saw *Lawrence of Arabia* last night,' Lewis said.

'Yeah, saw that and *Dr No*,' Simon said.

The only time Michael saw films was at school at the end of term. Oh, the excitement as the day neared, but the nagging worry that he might fall ill and be confined to the san. When the day arrived the blackouts were pulled down in the hall and they sat cross-legged on the wooden floor with bare knees touching bare knees. At the back of the hall Pa Boyce mounted the huge reel on the projector, and the screen would light up and be spattered with black dots and numbers before the orchestra blared out, a little flat. A lion appeared on the screen, looked beyond them regally and roared a slightly wavering roar. It was a fitting expression of the fragile thrill of the occasion. When the reel needed changing they had an interval and drank hot chocolate from gigantic urns brought into the hall from the kitchens.

In the train compartment Simon and Lewis whooped over the exploits of Lawrence, but Michael got up and leant out of the window. The train voyaged on, marking distance from home with the regular clack, clack of the wheels on the tracks. The night had started to close in. He heard the cry of an animal somewhere out in the darkening bush. It sounded lonely.

Simon had not spoken to him again. His anger must be deep and well nursed, thought Michael, but he could see that it was not just his own refusal to collude with Simon that had broken their friendship. Simon was becoming hard edged; his behaviour embarrassing to Michael, his settler-boy friends rude and bullying. He had started making remarks about God Squads and Bible Bashers. At junior school he and Simon had competed for gold stars in memory verse recital. Once they had recited a whole Bible chapter by heart; they had never needed to look at the hymn book when they sang in the cathedral. But now Simon sang crude songs to hymn tunes to tease him.

Michael thought, with some pleasure, that he could get Simon expelled if he wanted. Simon's night-time excursions to meet Veronica in the cricket pavilion had not yet come to the attention of the teachers. He allowed himself to imagine being thanked by the headmaster in his study as Simon was picked up by his father to get his just punishment. He got a satisfied feeling, as if he had scratched an itch.

Then a Still Small Voice spoke to him and said that he should forgive Simon because God had forgiven him for other things, like being too goody-goody and for laughing at Tomasi for still being terrified of chameleons. He blinked away a piece of soot from the smoke of the engine and wondered whether the soot was like a mote. Maybe I've got a plank in my eye and Simon has a mote in his, he thought. But what exactly was a mote?

He rubbed his eye and asked God for pardon. He prayed that Simon would forgive him as well. Feeling better, he pulled his exercise book out of his kitbag. The cover was blue, fading to grey around the edge. While the silhouette of the boy and girl holding hands and walking towards a mountain on the cover was sissy, it was the only book he had to write in. He chose a clean page and wrote in pencil, frequently crossing out words or full lines, but a poem emerged that he was proud of. He would show it to his father in the holidays and ask if he would translate it into Rukiga.

East African mail train, warm tropics night;
Bulk of the engine, red flickering light.
Smoke pushing upwards, black velvet sky;
Huts and bushes, train clatters by.

When he finished the Still Small Voice said something else – something gulpingly hard. It said quite clearly that he should apologise to Simon to his face. He balked at that. Simon was likely to see it as pathetic cringing. But the Still Small Voice said that Simon's reaction was irrelevant. Michael steeled himself to obey. All that remained was the timing of his repentance. Then everything would be all right; if not with Simon, at least between himself and God. He decided to wait until he got to school: there would be some gratification in letting Simon carry on scowling at him for the time being. He would bear it in the knowledge that Simon would feel more inclined to accept his apology if Simon felt that he had already meted out enough punishment.

A gong rang out along the corridor, announcing that their dinner was ready. In the dining car Michael found that the weight of leaving home started to lift. The waiters, haughty in their white jackets and black trousers, checked them in two by two. Michael gasped at the starchy finery. If heaviness meant quality, then the dining car's interior was first class: chunky silverware, robust linen on the tables, substantial white china plates with satisfyingly stout white cups and saucers, rigid napkins. Teak-framed, black and white photos of the largest and tallest of big game hung between the windows. The pea soup was viscous enough for the chunks of white bread to lie proud on the surface, like swimmers in the Dead Sea. Hunks of beef followed, smothered in black gravy that battled for supremacy against a white sauce that flowed like a warmed-up glacier, slowly but inexorably, down a mountain of cauliflower.

They ate in silence until it became clear that the food was more than a match for their appetites. Michael was about to tell the others about a deadlier design for arrows when Simon said, to no one in particular, 'Ah, Veronica! She's so bloody beautiful.'

He burped and lolled back in his chair.

Michael tried to think of something funny to say, but then decided against it: Simon might not think it so hilarious. Lewis and David said nothing, Lewis suddenly finding his fork interesting. Michael knew that men and women came together when they got married but that was a long way off. Pa Peacock had talked to them one evening about husbands and wives and how a baby should be planned and some confusing stuff about how the baby was made. He had told them something surprising:

that it was enjoyable, the making bit. Michael had puzzled over that, as he could not imagine how it could possibly be enjoyable snuggling up close to Ma Peacock. She was practically spherical and her hair was going grey.

David suddenly said that his crystal set could pick up Soviet radio and they could listen when they got to school. Lewis said he had CCCP stamps showing rockets. Simon pushed himself back in his chair, put his hands in his pockets and yawned.

Back in the compartment they lay satisfied on their bunks, digesting their meal. At 10pm the parent guardian looked in to ensure that their lights were out. They waited a little and then Simon turned on the lights again.

'Are you going to tell on us, Michael?' Simon asked.

'No, of course I won't,' Michael said, making himself sound cheerful.

They had a pillow fight, Michael being careful to let Simon land a few, until the parent guardian knocked loudly on the door and said that they 'had better stop larking about'.

They waited patiently for a minute and then, leaving the window open to make it harder to hear each other's movements, they pulled down the flimsy blind to black out the compartment and turned out the light. They played 'blindy', one of them being the 'It' who had to find and name the others, climbing stealthily from bunk to bunk in total darkness, senses straining for signs of movement. Michael curled himself up tightly in the corner of the middle bunk by the window. He avoided being tagged for several minutes. A hand brushed his arm and then returned, feeling for his face. He buried his face in his knees. The 'It' was Simon, and Michael was sure Simon knew whom he had found; hadn't they lifted each other up trees, squeezed into hiding places together and arm-wrestled each other? Simon's hand went away. He's going to ignore me, thought Michael.

He started to uncoil himself in the silence in readiness to dive across to the other middle bunk before Simon changed his mind. Then Simon's hands were back, but this time a sharp fist pushing hard into Michael's shoulder, his knuckles digging in. Michael remembered, 'Unto him that

163

smiteth thee on the one cheek offer also the other.' Simon's fist slipped, or was driven, off Michael's shoulder and into his windpipe. Michael gasped; a clamp obstructed his breathing, a hard knob of pain grew in his throat. Simon moved away again but Michael reached out, a volcano of fury welling, pent-up emotion forcing itself past the compression in his throat. Simon's slights against him now seemed monstrous.

'I'm not a weakling, you know,' he shouted.

Michael found the neck of Simon's pyjamas and pulled. Simon overbalanced, swivelling and falling away towards the window. A grey wash of light showed Simon's form as the plastic blind gave way against his back. A rush of sooty night air forced itself into the carriage. The blind snagged precariously on the frame. Simon cried out. His hands reached for Michael. For a moment Michael did not help, wanting Simon to feel scared, wanting him dead, never wanting to see him again. With a quiet snick sound the plastic broke free and then exploded outwards. Simon fell away, his hands scrabbling at Michael's sleeve. Michael lunged at him in sudden terror, trying to take hold of him. His fingers hooked on Simon's clawed hand. He was wrenched through the window.

The train crossed a network of points, making a sound like the hooves of the horses of the apocalypse.

Kampala
1983

Behold, I take away from thee the desire of thine eyes with a stroke: yet neither shalt thou mourn nor weep ...
The Book of Ezekiel, Chapter 24

ONE

In the British Airways jet Michael reconciled himself to having to sit beside a corpse for the remainder of the flight. The stewardess had gone to notify the captain and her colleagues of the sudden death. She returned, breathless. 'You're right. The captain says we should leave him just as he is until we've landed. I should've known that. It's in our training, but when it actually happens …'

She met Michael's eyes, and he could see she was looking for acknowledgement of her distress – but his claustrophobia was pressing in hard again so he just nodded once, and handed her his tomato-stained glass. She took it, stared again at the dead man and then, her face turning as pale as the overhead locker, sat down heavily on the bulkhead seat opposite.

Michael resumed his window-gazing, trying not to be oppressed by the dead man beside him, trying not to think about the constricting cylinder of the aircraft. The man's death was certainly spooky, but there would be a natural explanation. Maybe a belief could set off a patho-physiological cascade that could kill. Perhaps he should have engaged him in conversation, allayed his subconscious fears. But he had had his own pressing preoccupations and he was a surgeon, not a psychiatrist. Superstition was likely to win over rationality in any case. People were wired up for that.

The aircraft banked steeply and slowed, crossing a corner of Lake Victoria. Lake Victoria – Michael considered the name too English; a name to tame and familiarise an alien place, to domesticate it and bring it within the national domain, like a Windermere. But the lake he saw stretched beyond the curve of the earth and violent pewter-grey waterspouts united with the sky where stormy showers fell. Soon the perspective changed rapidly. He was no longer the God-like observer of a place apart but a participant. He saw a canoe on the lake. The dark forms of the oarsmen turned to watch the aircraft. Images followed in quick succession, like a slide show from his childhood: the thin shore bordered by reeds, tin roofs bright as sun on flints, banana groves, smoke from a village compound, the shell of a car in a ditch, a cyclist on a black bicycle, the tar of the runway; and then came the jolt of the landing and the roar of the reversed thrust.

As the other passengers disembarked, unaware of the corpse in first class, Michael covered his dead companion with his blanket. He was satisfied that he had left him trim and tidy. After tightening his shoelaces – a secure surgical knot before throwing the bow – he stepped around the body in as dignified a manner as possible. Slipping on his light tan sports jacket (a recent purchase), he gave its hem a tug to smooth its lines. He turned his Royal College of Surgeons cufflinks so that their rectangles were lined up parallel with his arm, and collected his calfskin briefcase from the overhead locker. He felt lean and ready. Naomi had told him that he should have been a naval officer, 'perhaps a submarine commander' she had said as she mock-saluted him. Michael had no strong objection: he accepted that his bearing and manner came across as military at times, and his compact build would have suited a submariner. He had never told her about his claustrophobia.

The open door beckoned, but there was to be no quick exit: he had a tedious hour in the cabin repeating the undramatic story of his seatmate's death to a string of officials of increasing seniority. He didn't bother them with the curse angle, out of common sense.

At the foot of the aircraft steps, out in the open again under an ample sky, the day infused with light and warmth, he suppressed an unruly impulse to step out jauntily onto the tarmac, but he kept a measured gait as he walked towards passport control. Now, at last, he could enjoy his visit.

'Welcome to my country, my friend. May I see your passport? Have you visited before?'

'A long time ago.'

'You are very welcome again. You're here for business or pleasure?'

'For a conference.'

'Everyone is welcome. Have a good trip.'

The passport officer swung his stamp hard down onto the virgin page. The sharp noise ricocheted off the bare walls and concrete floor, triggering a visual overtone, a long ago memory: an unwelcome image of himself standing with his parents in the hall of a railway station in this same country, collecting a ticket for a journey to school. For a moment he stood looking at his passport, held out to him.

He came to as the official lost patience and thrust his passport at him, waving forward the next person in the queue. As he left the room, Michael heard other stampings of passports and papers, and found it pleasing that the terror the country had just emerged from had left some things unchanged – some order remained. In fact, he considered it instructive: it stiffened his resolve. He would hold his remembrances in check whatever the provocation; three days was not long.

Outside the terminal he stood looking for transport. He had declined the offer of a car from his hosts; a small act of philanthropy on his part to save them the trouble and expense.

'Taxi, sah?'

The beaming driver squatted down and encircled Michael's padded suitcase with both arms in a reverential manner, as if lifting it by the handle was insulting to such a precious object. They passed a blue Zephyr 6, the car of his childhood dreams. He noticed, with a frisson of excitement, the dead insects in the radiator grille – a colourful massacre – although it looked as if they had deliberately committed suicide: the vehicle could not have sped anywhere in a long time. The sign across the top of the cracked windscreen read like a desperate plea: 'Jesus Saves'. There was a substantial rope wrapped around the front of the car, holding down the bonnet, and along its doors was scoured evidence of more than one scrape. Rivet holes marked the original run of the chrome side-stripes. It leant back on its rear springs like an exhausted dog. Michael almost collided with the taxi driver as he suddenly stopped at the rear end of the Zephyr, put the suitcase down and went to open the boot.

'Er, no, I'll …'

It was too late, the taxi driver laid Michael's suitcase gently in the dusty boot, closed the boot lid on the second attempt by slamming it down with considerable force, and then opened the rear door with opposite, but no less vigorous, exertion.

'Make yourself comfortable, sah.'

Michael sat on the springy seat, positioned his briefcase flat on his lap and turned to give the taxi driver instructions, but he found the driver had turned his attention to the airport lobby again.

'Taxi, madam?'

He tried to get out, to tell the driver he had thought the car was a private taxi rather than a bus, but reached in vain for the door handle; it had broken off. Michael sensed an encirclement of his chest again – a gentle squeeze for now, but hinting at a latent strength of hideous proportions.

Ten minutes later the taxi was full. Next to the driver (who was still grinning as if they were about to have the best fun imaginable) sat a Ugandan man in a black suit, Daz-white shirt and sheeny blue tie, making Michael feel that he had noteworthy competition in the tailoring department. A large nun sat next to Michael, and beyond her ballast-like mass a fortuitously thin Indian couple struggled to make themselves thinner still. The seat lost its bounce.

Their driver's optimism was catching, for the passengers, except Michael, nodded affably at each other. Michael, still wondering if he could get out, swore to himself at the minor loss of control and the forced bonhomie of the cab.

'Now we'll go,' the driver said as his head disappeared under the steering wheel. He fiddled with some wires and the starter motor cranked once, a metallic cough, followed by an ominous silence. He tried four times. 'Ah, sorry, we'll have to push.'

'This is bloody ridiculous,' Michael said loudly. 'Is there no other way of getting into town?'

The driver and passengers all pivoted to look at him. The nun clasped a hand to her bosom, while the well-dressed man in the front seat looked hurt and said, 'I'm so sorry, good sir,' as if willing to take responsibility for the decrepitude of the car.

The driver said, 'Sah, we will go soon. You'll be happy again.'

The nun smiled soothingly at him. Michael saw that he, the visiting white man, had become the problem, not the car. He felt like a child with a temper tantrum.

Sinking back, he muttered with poor grace, 'I'm all right. Just tired.'

'Ah, OK,' the driver said, and then shouted out of the window to a group of men – who were slapping hands in fond greetings – to come and help.

Michael told himself off. Why had he let his feelings explode like that? Everyone else around him was almost deliriously cheerful and he had let a small adventure unnerve him. He put it down to sitting with a corpse on the plane, and the dissociation, effected over many tension-filled hours, between his reliable and regulated London environment and this chaotic attempt to leave the airport. He had wanted his return to Africa to be on his own terms, under his own command. Go in, do the job, get out.

The men pushed with considerable gusto and soon the taxi was being propelled forward at a tidy rate. Just as Michael began to think they were to be pushed all the way to town the driver released the clutch, and the engine engaged with a jerk that threw them all forward. The motor fired and they were vectored against the back of their seats again. Michael turned to see the pushers, choking but happy, in a thick pall of exhaust fumes.

The clouds had cleared and the sun scorched his neck. Several turns of the window winder almost fully lowered the glass before it jammed. He leant out until his face caught the slipstream. He had come back to Africa but now Africa came back to him with an overpowering physicality: the heated air; the little black flying insects stinging his cheek in tiny impacts; the prismatic flashes of colour, poinsettia as red as wounds, purple-bracted bougainvillea, silky-white frangipani; the heat-shimmered sounds, the loose rattle of a worn, poorly tuned engine, the sticky sound of rubber on hot tar. Fragrances swished past, dearly familiar, like old friends met again: honeysuckle, giant granadilla, wild calabash. Starting to feel more at ease, Michael took a deep breath and, somewhere in his chest, the tropical-house air of warm foliage perspiring in the sun charmed away the last lingering of sour London vapours.

The road tunnelled through a forest towards the capital. Michael could not determine where the city began, for such was the feverish power of nature in this fecund belly of the earth (as far from each frozen pole in distance and condition as it is possible to be) that it seemed humanity was unable to fuse the city into a cohesive uniformity of solid slab and structure. Bushes and trees had thrust themselves between the buildings, overhung the roads and seeded themselves in every crack. They passed a run-down suburb of wide bungalows, vestiges of the colonial era, now crushed under heavy weights of creeper and climber, their lawns volcanoed by termite mounds. He saw Marabou storks, urban vultures, in the few open spaces; ugly scavengers finding their niche in the messy tracts of the city.

In a shanty district the car slowed. People were waving them down. What now? More passengers to load? His left leg was numb under the weight of Catholicism beside him. As they came to a halt he saw, in the crowd, two men supporting a young woman. She held her leg in flexion, a bloodied tourniquet made out of someone's white shirt around her thigh. The car was quickly surrounded by people banging on the metal. It felt threatening and confusing: should he get out and offer to help, or was this some sort of hold-up? Faces filled the window, pressing inwards. He became acutely aware of a closing in of space and tried to wind up the window. The handle came off in his hand.

He turned to the nun. 'What is it?'

'Oh! Holy Mother! A lady's been shot.'

'Shot? Who by?'

'By a soldier.'

'Why?'

The nun looked at him pityingly. 'They can shoot.'

'But why?'

'They're saying he was drunk. God have mercy.' The nun gripped the seat in front and pulled herself forward. She shouted at the driver and then panted at Michael, 'I'll get out. I'll find a lift later.'

She rolled further onto him. He put his hand out of the window and released the handle. Their combined pressure opened the door, and he was swept outwards like a fish at the crest of a burst dam.

The injured woman's rescuers placed her on the back seat, amidst fierce discussion and shouted instructions from the onlookers. She grimaced, but did not cry out. Several hands shoved Michael back in next to her and then the car was away, the passengers rolling sickeningly from side to side as the driver negotiated the potholed road at a velocity reminiscent, thought Michael, of the glory days of the East African Safari Rally.

He found himself making a rapid assessment. He was alarmed by the amount of blood loss. The tourniquet was soaked.

'It's her femoral artery,' he said (pointlessly, he immediately realised) to the Indian couple, who sat frozen, mouths in a pouting expression of fixed surprise. 'I need to apply more pressure.'

Michael pulled a silk handkerchief from his jacket pocket, folded it into a pad and pressed it hard against the top of the tourniquet where the femoral artery would be finding its way down and around her inner thigh. He touched the top of her foot with the fingers of his other hand, feeling for the dorsalis pedis pulse. It was absent. Her foot was cool. Either the artery had been shot to bits or he had succeeded in occluding it.

Michael looked at the woman. 'I'm sorry. My pressing may be hurting you.'

Her head was back. She breathed through her mouth (a soft panting), her lips were retracted, revealing pale gums, and her eyes were wide open staring at the roof as if in a trance.

'This is the second time today my medical skills have been called upon,' he said in a reassuring tone, 'although the first time ...' he added, under his breath. No one asked him to continue.

The car sped through the streets, its old suspension clonking and its bearings shrieking, its driver making liberal use of the horn – the only part of the vehicle in fine health. Michael kept his grip on the woman's leg, hoping they would not crash. At least he was working again, he told himself grimly. He would make sure that the woman survived. His grip tightened further as he imagined it was Naomi bleeding to death beside him. He felt now how desperate he would be to save her, but his unexpectedly intense feeling could do nothing to change their unsatisfactory parting. It came to him that she would always perceive something about him as inscrutable; it would inevitably abort their relationship, if it had not done so already, and there was nothing he could do about it.

At the hospital the driver ran in and came out almost immediately with two orderlies and a trolley. Michael released his hand long enough to scoop the injured woman onto the trolley.

'Damn, it's still coming!' he exclaimed, as a fresh rivulet of blood found its way out of the top of the blood-soaked wrapping. 'You must press here; exactly here,' he instructed.

The orderly tried to take over but the woman twisted her head forcibly away from him and pushed against his hands. The orderly shouted at her. She closed her eyes and released his hands but spoke in a rush of emotion, tears welling.

'What's she saying?' Michael asked.

'She says she's already died. She knows her leg is finished.'

'Maybe – but her life is saved. Tell her she's lucky. Not many people would have known precisely where to press to stop the bleeding.'

The woman spoke again in short, weak gasps.

'She says her life is gone,' the orderly said, as Michael took the man's hand and moved it an inch higher up her leg.

As the orderlies tried to move the trolley the woman took hold of the hem of Michael's jacket, and looked at him for the first time. Her voice came in high-pitched rapid bursts. The orderly translated as he tried to prise open the woman's grip.

'She thanks you anyway. Her life is gone because without her leg she'll not be given in marriage, so she'll never have children. She'll be barren.'

The woman released Michael, collapsing into a flaccid state. The trolley party disappeared through the hospital doors, and was left holding his bloody handkerchief. He let it fall to the ground, dropped back into his seat in the taxi and stared at the crescents of dried blood under his fingernails; he noticed his fingers were trembling.

'Welcome to my country,' he muttered.

The Indian woman turned to him and made a silent offering, with both hands, of a British Airways face wipe. She nodded at him when he thanked her, looking relieved to be of some help and then said, 'I don't know why we've come back. We were expelled in 1972. My husband wants to see what has become of his shop. Big mistake, I told him, big mistake.' She dabbed at the inner side of her eye with her finger. Her husband sat stone-faced.

They drove on, into the unknown, the driver and his front seat passenger taking it in turns to shake their heads, and competing with other to make the loudest tsch-tsch sounds.

When they reached the heart of the city Michael saw that its citizens colluded with the ways of nature, swarming about like ants so that he feared the taxi would be engulfed. The driver stopped to let his other passengers out. Michael stayed in the vehicle and the driver leant on his horn, revved the engine and set off at a pace, even though the road teemed with pedestrians. The crowd gave way as if it were a shoal of fish aware of a predator passing through its midst, re-forming as soon as they had passed.

They climbed a hill, failing to avoid the erosion gullies in the *murram* road. Michael bounced on the now-restored convexity of the seat. When they had climbed enough to rise above the mêlée of the city the road levelled off, and a thin coating of tar smoothed their way past white walls, manicured hedges of pink hibiscus and cropped grass verges. Here at last was a place with references to a predictable, more familiar world.

Michael was left, exhausted – more than that, he told himself: battered – at the high wrought-iron gates of a large bungalow, which nestled under a green roof with deep eaves. Birds flew in and out of a sprinkler on the lawn, its soft hiss welcoming and benign, its chill refreshing the air. He could see a wicker chair with thick cushions on the shaded veranda, a book resting on an arm. Thwarted by the padlocks on the gate he stood waiting, both hands gripping the fretwork, unsure whether to shout for attention. Two Alsatian dogs lay on the grass. One picked itself up in a half-hearted fashion, barked once – more through duty than conviction – then flopped down again and stretched itself out with a wide toothy yawn, tongue lolling. Michael was envious. Passing the time he checked his pockets to ensure that his passport and wallet were still there, and found himself holding the feather he had picked off the dead businessman's lap. He released it but then gripped it again, pulled it out and inspected it. The barbs had broken. He twizzled it in his fingers. A strong urge came over him to arrow it into the hedge but, setting his jaw, he stuffed it back into his pocket.

A man in a green overall appeared from along the side of the house.

'Good afternoon, bwana. I'm Winston.'

His winning smile did not fade as he opened the gates and took Michael's suitcase. When he set out for the house Michael hesitated, tempted to make sure that the padlocks were fully clicked home.

Before they reached the front door it flew open, and a wiry man burst out.

'My dear fellow! Dr Lacey, I presume! Welcome. I'm James McCree. Glad you've got here safely.'

His sleeves were rolled halfway up his forearms and his handshake was so energetic that Michael braced his shoulder to protect it from dislocation. McCree had a narrow face which swept back from a sharp nose. His skin appeared seared, as if he had spent years in a merciless desert wind; the deep lines that radiated back from his eyes could have buried grains of sand. Michael wondered what travels and postings had scoured such marks.

'None the worse for wear, I hope?'

With weary effort Michael fought a desire to sink to his knees, but said, 'One or two incidents, but I'm here.' He rallied himself. 'It's most kind of you to have me to stay. I dare say you've been terribly overworked with the organisation of an affair like this – in a place like this.'

James was signalling to Winston to leave Michael's suitcase on the veranda, and then moved to pick it up. He seemed the kind of man who was never still, although perpetually and purposively active rather than fidgety. 'Och, we wouldn't live here if we wanted the quiet life. It's a grand opera in Africa and anyone can be big on our stage – although,' his tone darkened, 'we have to accept that, as in opera, high drama is the norm.'

'I've had a little drama already,' Michael said.

He turned out his wrists to show the blood on the sleeves of his shirt. One of his cufflinks was stained.

James froze for just long enough to take that in. 'My dear fellow, come straight in. What happened? On second thoughts, have a clean up before I debrief you.'

He led Michael across a tastefully furnished hallway: a Persian rug on the teak floor, a rosewood sideboard, a shower of pink flowers in a blue porcelain vase, silver photo frames with Celtic-patterned edgings, a dark oil of some plethoric tartaned landowner-ancestor, and a mounted deer head of a curious bonsai dimension to fit the modest size of the room. It was a hallway that a retired well-to-do couple – Edinburgh solicitors, say – might aspire to in their Highland cottage. There were no African curios. The only reminder of location was the window to the side: heavy burglar bars were welded into its metal frame.

James took him through to his room. 'You're not hurt, are you?'

Michael wanted to spill his story straight away, and told James about the death on the aircraft. James returned his smile when he heard how the man believed himself to be cursed, but then said, 'What nonsense, but don't tell Audrey, my wife. She finds all that very credible.'

Michael told James about the injured woman. When he described her ingratitude James nodded and said, 'It's true – about her marriage prospects, and if she's poor it'll be disastrous for her economic prospects.'

After a change of shirt Michael found his way to the lounge, expecting to meet James's superstitious wife, but although James was there, energetically digging out bottles of spirits and crystal glasses from a walnut cabinet, Audrey was absent. Michael's eye was drawn to the enormous gold-framed portrait of the young Queen Elizabeth II that dominated the room.

James noticed his interest. 'Haven't lived in Britain for nearly twenty years – that's why I'm so loyal.' He warmed to his theme. 'Frustrating for us Scots that she's so often referred to by our African friends as the Queen of England. Same for Queen Victoria: her most devoted followers were the Scottish diaspora. Have a look in my bookshelves while you're here. Ah, meet my wife.'

A petite woman with large sad eyes had come quietly into the room. Her dark hair was drawn back into a tight bun, exposing greying strands over her temples – although Michael guessed her to be a little under forty. Movement seemed an effort to her, as if she were wading through a glutinous swamp.

'Audrey, there you are. This is Michael Lacey – somewhat bloodied by an incident on the way here.'

Audrey's eyes started to flick about; she picked at the nail of her left index finger. Her chest rose and fell rapidly like a frightened bird. Michael thought she might turn and drag herself back out.

'Audrey, dear, there's no need to fret. He's here – nothing fatal.' He turned to Michael. 'No good beating about the bush, as we say in Africa.' He paused to laugh, and then as quickly became sombre. 'Doctor to doctor, my wife is suffering from … a melancholia. We've lived through hard times – it does have its effects. But you've been better recently, haven't you, my dear?'

Audrey seemed to steel herself against some inner difficulty, settled her gaze on Michael, and said softly, 'It's so nice to have visitors from Britain. We've been dreadfully isolated the last few years. Oh, and congratulations on your appointment. You must feel very secure. This is what we miss: security. Well, James doesn't, but I crave it. But perhaps it's my condition. Are you married?'

'No, I'm not,' Michael said. He recalled, with a renewed sense of foreboding, his parting with Naomi: her stiff lips. Then, because Audrey appeared to be waiting for him to say more, he added, 'Too many hours in theatre to meet anyone, and all the women in theatre are masked. That does make getting to know each other difficult.'

James laughed. Audrey did not. She had not taken her solemn eyes off him.

'I don't believe that. A successful man like you, in your mid-thirties I imagine, on the threshold of riches and adulation – you should have found a wife by now.'

She seemed to have no need to blink.

'We're not living in a Jane Austen novel,' Michael said, trying to sound amused.

'Are you attracted to the opposite sex?' she asked.

Michael saw James give a look of desperation at his wife.

'I adore them,' he replied.

James laughed again. 'Hear, hear, well said.'

Michael was bringing himself to mention Naomi, but Audrey said, 'You're looking for something in a woman that you haven't found so far. Maybe something your mother has.'

Michael started to phrase a non-committal response, but when he looked at Audrey he was taken aback: although her body still trembled as if it was only a few quivers away from disintegration, her eyes remained focused on him but not at his face, at some distance through him, looking not behind him but into his past. He found himself saying, 'Not likely. My mother's dead.'

Audrey nodded gently. 'She died when you were a child.'

He felt compelled to dip his head slightly to affirm her knowledge. Now she readjusted her gaze, and he thought that she gave him a momentary expression of approval – as if he had passed a test. He had not tried to lie to her.

James rescued him. 'We really ought to get to know our guest better before embarrassing him. Anyway, as I was saying, we Scots are heavily represented in the hall of famous Africa pioneers.'

He pointed to a set of framed prints hanging on the opposite wall. 'There they are – all extremes of human endeavour. Take Mungo Park: the quest for knowledge; Karamoja Bell: the life of adventure; or Kirk over there: practical action against the slave trade.'

James drew breath to continue with his Who's Who of pioneering Scots, but Michael stopped him.

'Karamoja Bell? Must have been larger than life with a name like that.'

With a slight curl on her lip, the motions of a wry smile attempted with effort, Audrey interjected, 'Do you want to be embarrassed or would you prefer to be bored to death? It's the choice you have in this house.'

'Ah yes, Karamoja Bell,' went on James, 'he chose the outdoor and the outlaw life. Did his hunting where some of my patients come from: far north, far west. Said he looked for a country where a man could still slit a throat or grab a native girl without being badgered by the law.'

Michael saw Audrey leave as silently as she had come, her long cotton dress, more fifties than eighties, hanging limp off her shoulders as if soaked in her melancholy.

A shadow crossed James's face but he said, 'Used to live up in Karamoja myself before I met Audrey. Not much has changed up there. Isn't that right, Blessed?'

The McCrees' maid had appeared in the doorway to the kitchen. She paused there, eyes averted, hands clasped in front of her, waiting for James to finish.

'Blessed, this is Mr Lacey, a VIP all the way from London. Bring some tea, my lady.'

Whether it was the unaccustomed heat, the strange encounter with Audrey or a delayed reaction to the traumas of his journey, Michael suddenly felt faint.

'Do you mind if I take a bath first? I feel a little shaky.'

James looked at him sharply. 'So sorry, old chap, how unthinking of me. You do look a touch pale.'

He escorted Michael back to the bedroom but when they entered the room, and Michael had reassured him that he was going to be fine, James suddenly said, 'Terrible thing, depression. Please don't be offended.'

Michael searched for the right blend of emollient and facilitating sentiment. Not easy: his forte was cutting his way out of difficulty. 'Not at all. No doubt been tough for you both.'

James walked over to the window and said, 'Let me take a page out of Audrey's book and be forthright. It's what I admired – still admire – in her.' He paused, looked out and gripped the burglar bars like a man trapped. 'I married the wrong woman. Or I should say she married the wrong man, because I love her dearly, but she always wanted a safer life; a garden to tend that isn't completely eaten every few days, close family down a shaded lane and a circle of friends who can meet to talk about their children, rather than a fragmented laager of heat-shocked women whispering about the latest armed robbery.'

Michael would have furrowed his brow if he had been given to facial expression. Outdoors it was dangerous, indoors it was a psychological minefield; and it was not yet nightfall. 'You've not considered leaving?'

'We should go back but I can't. I came out here on a British Council-sponsored contract for a year. That was in sixty-six. I became addicted. Going home is like stepping into a shallow grave. Tried it a few years ago.'

James continued to stare out of the window. Michael saw him shudder, and wondered if some men might go and stand beside him, putting a hand on his shoulder in masculine alliance. But straight away he knew that he had heard enough, had already been party to more than he wanted to know. He should have stayed in a hotel. He lifted his suitcase onto the bed.

'My dear fellow,' James said, releasing his hold on the bars and swinging around. 'I'm out of order with all this. You've caught us at a difficult time but I'm delighted you're here. From now on we'll concentrate on the success of the conference.'

Michael nodded emphatically. 'It's what I've come for.'

James straightened himself. 'Of course. Quite right.'

Michael asked what he should do with his laundry.

'Och, put it in the basket. Winston will wash it, and then iron it with the coal iron. Makes it too smooth for the bugs to get a foothold.'

He laughed and gripped Michael's upper arm amiably, crushing a nerve.

Michael turned on the cold tap of the bath to swill a battalion of insects with extraordinarily long antennae down the plughole, but their limp filaments formed a dense mesh over the drain, refusing to rinse away. After a moment's hesitation, wondering whether he should scoop out the sodden and faintly twitching mass of unlucky life and drop it out of the window, he pressed the plug home with resolute force; an action that gave him the small pleasure of reasserting some control over his environment. When he turned on the hot tap, scalding water – stained brown from the wood-fired boiler – sputtered out.

He lay back in the bath, stretching out, the tinted water lapping his body. He closed his eyes: it felt like an act of containment. Then, remembering his promise to himself to keep his three days in Uganda free of introspection, or pointless reminiscence, he rehearsed his forthcoming lecture to the twelfth conference of the Lake Regions Surgical Association; rattled it out fast in a low murmur. Soon finished, he started on a passage from 'Hiawatha'. The rhyme of the verses was soothing. Michael's talent for memorising text came in handy when he had to attend a party – a trick to compensate for his lack of small talk. He could recite long passages from 'The Rime of the Ancient Mariner', *Gray's Anatomy*, even the three chapters of the prophet Habakkuk or some other obscure part of the Bible. He wondered whether his gift was innate, or whether – a dark thought rising again – it was acquired through having to learn memory verses at his religious school.

The stains of his travels soaked away, Michael cast his eye along James's books while buckling his belt. Tiredness blunted his will to decipher faded titles, or pick out anything heavy or tightly packed, but at the end of a shelf a book entitled *In Search of Paradise* lay on its side. He stared with a cynical eye at the blue and yellow watercolour on the cover: a man in a straw boater, reading in a deckchair under a palm tree, a full-breasted mermaid with shell necklace resting on a rock by the water. Someone's idea of paradise. There were others: the oasis garden of the Mohammedans, the nirvana of infinite light of the East, the bejewelled city of the Christians. He preferred more concrete aspirations, less intangible; like the mitigation of disease. It gave him satisfaction that his work gloved in with that modest creed, although he would welcome a little less shapeless unease. So far his return to Uganda had been disquieting (the unexpected, the violent and the McCrees – there was something of the soothsayer about Audrey), but it was a sense of proximity to malign ghosts that he found most disturbing. He struggled to grasp at what seemed a valuable insight but it flew away before it became substantive: that peace of mind might not depend on freedom from the memories of the past but on ... what was it, freedom from guilt? A guilt that to a contemporary man, wedded to reason like himself, seemed a relic of a past age of foolishness.

He snatched up *In Search of Paradise* and opened it at random. It appeared to be a travelogue. Some place in Uganda was mentioned: in the Rift Valley to the west – the far west, Karamoja Bell's hunting grounds. Where a man could freely slit a throat and pick up a native girl. He flicked through the pages, but found he was too tired to concentrate.

T W O

'Surgery is grievous bodily harm,' Michael said.

The surgical trainees sat taut at their desks, scribbling his words down in frantic haste, lest they miss that essential tip. James McCree had told Michael that he, the visiting maestro, would be addressing the elite survivors of a hard and long journey: from their mothers' perilous giving of birth, through an infancy where one in five died, via exposure to a myriad body-invading creatures, biting reptiles, arachnids and arthropods, via miles and miles on bare feet to school, via the eye of the needle to get into medical school, via the volumes of books imbibed in dimly lit nights, via scarce patronage and tenacious grit to get onto the surgical training programme.

Michael had woken that morning at the McCrees' house to see the first rays of the sun lancing through a chink in the curtains. Above his bed, on the wall, the light cast a bright feather-like shape. He recalled the previous day's troublesome events, but now, looking at the light playing a little as if filtered by leaves, he felt that he had slept away an oppression. Any notion of having been jinxed had vanished. He lifted his hand to the sunbeam and sensed its warmth, noticing the pattern change to a crescent moon on his palm. How the mind's eye hunted for meaning, and how the heart also, seeking significance and implication, making associations that were as ephemeral and futile as the conjuring of his eye on the pattern of light. Thinking back, he saw now that he had let a few incidents (regrettable as they were) and Audrey McCree's intrusive questioning disturb his equanimity. It was time to get a grip.

By the time he entered the classroom of surgical trainees he was in particularly good spirits and relished the chance to teach and to inspire. The conference had started at last, he would be giving it his all, and then in a couple of days he would be on his way back to work.

'We surgeons cut, saw, burn, bruise; we wound; we traumatise; we violate. We split the skin, breaching the body's primary protection against a hostile environment. Then we spill its blood, dehydrate its tissues and dissipate its hard-won heat.' The students' pens slashed across their notebooks. 'My job today is to teach you how to repair the damage you've done on your way in, as you come out.'

A refrigerated pig's trotter, pale as exsanguination, lay on a wooden platter on each student's desk. A surgical blade, needle holder, scissors and forceps were arranged around each trotter like a dinner setting.

'Never forget that to make our craft possible we rely entirely on the body's remarkable restorative powers. Very rarely, an unlucky person is born with a profound defect in the mechanism of healing. The smallest injury fails to knit; no amount of suturing, by the most expert of surgeons, can fuse the tissues together. Death comes in childhood. Our sutures and clips only approximate what we've rent apart; the healing is nature's work. We surgeons must have humility.'

He paused, waiting for the ripple of amusement that would have run through a British audience, but there was no cynicism in the room that day. Michael thrilled, sensing his listeners were captivated. Here was a thirsty audience, eager for his help; so much more emotionally engaged than the students back home.

'Our job is to make the body's work easier. Our skill is to create the right environment for healing. How do we do that?'

Pens poised while he came around the front of his table. Every head was down, waiting.

'We do it by art.'

The students looked up, scribbling still suspended, panic welling in their eyes. A hand shot up. 'Excuse me, sir. You said, "by heart"?'

The class laughed, but Michael saw that they did not laugh at the student who had spoken, but at their own humble, collective by kinship, misunderstanding.

Michael smiled. 'With your heart, of course, but most importantly by art. Great art. We make art with our hands. We practise until we can effortlessly create a four-dimensional work. Three dimensions of space and the other of time; the movements of our fingers through time.' He was surprising himself with his flowery address, but his audience had given him a sense of release. They were approving of zeal; he could express his passion without embarrassment. 'We choreograph a flowing opus; an aspiring to perfection of motion, like ballet. You will know from your own culture that the best practitioners make great art of their dance.'

A deep murmur of appreciative agreement swept the room. The harmonious sound, almost songlike, reminded him of a sighing singing in a whitewashed cathedral long ago, but he pressed on.

'The wounds you make must be repaired as if you've violated Mother Nature's handiwork and don't want her to know. Hold the tissues with feather-like gentleness so that when the patient wakes the nerves don't jangle with a thousand coarse pluckings. Each penetration of the suture must be accurately spaced. Only stab once: don't make rehearsal stabs. Apply enough tension to your knots, but not too much. You mustn't inhibit the blood supply, so make the wound edges kiss lightly; don't make them snog hard.'

He saw the scribbler who had raised his arm before start to lift his hand again but just as quickly put it down, whispering 'snoggard, snoggard, snoggard', and with a puzzled look underlining what he had written.

'There must be no wasted hand movements. Can you think of a good dancer who lets his hand wander; whose every action is not purposeful and graceful?'

He returned behind the table to where his own trotter stood proud on its hoof, in contrast to the students' trotters which had been placed on their sides. 'Before you is the stage on which your fingers will perform.'

The students looked awed as they inspected their own platters.

Michael picked up the blade, feeling its delicate weight, and then, with a deft movement, cut a deep wound in the skin of his pig. Taking the needle holder, he positioned a needle between its thin jaws a third of the way along the needle's svelte, curving length. The silent class heard the click of the securing ratchet. Taking a fine pair of forceps in his fingers, Michael closed the wound, both hands moving nimbly in a smooth, interlocking rhythm. It felt good to be working with his hands again, to be in control. This was his craft. He did not need to boast; his art proclaimed itself. There were surgeons who had climbed the career ladder through publishing research but were all fingers and thumbs in the operating room. He had published profusely as well, but he was pleased to be a surgeon's surgeon. His colleagues sought him out if their wives or daughters needed the knife. He was a cabinetmaker, not a joiner.

The class cut and stitched until the pigs' feet bristled with sutures, like five-day stubble. Michael moved from desk to desk.

'Take equal bites of tissue.'

'Smooth hand movements.'

'That's a granny knot. Undo it, and make a reef knot with a double throw on the first tie, and bed that first throw down.'

'Take your second bite closer to the skin edge. Nine cells out is enough.'

At the back of the room, windows opened onto a dusty lawn. A gardener was roping a bed of canna lilies on the far side with water from a hose, the stream slapping the broad leaves. Flying insects drifted in and out of the windows, taking a keener interest as the pig feet warmed up. One made straight for Michael as if on assignment.

'Sir! There's a hornet on your collar. Don't move, sir.'

It made no difference. A sharp stab made his neck muscles twitch but he held himself composed and did not wince. He flicked the hornet off with his hand. The scorching afterburn made his eyes water. 'It's stung me!'

'Ah – we're so sorry,' the class groaned, and Michael saw their pain. He had travelled to their country, at his own expense, was their honoured guest, and had been mugged in front of them – and they had been helpless to prevent it.

One student, face contorted with rage, got up and chased the hornet, waving his surgical blade. It disappeared out of the window and for a moment it seemed that the student was going to jump out after it, but instead he shouted something at the gardener. It sounded to Michael like an accusation.

He lifted his hands to calm the atmosphere. A searing pain travelled down to his fingertips. 'Please – it's nothing. We must carry on. We're engaged in a most important pursuit which requires our total and undivided concentration. When you're operating nothing must get in the way of your work or take up your thoughts – only how to perform better than the last time.'

The students quietened, looking at him as if overwhelmed anew at the privilege of studying at his feet. He felt ennobled and humbled, although he wondered how much worse the pain could become.

Back in his room at the McCrees' house, Michael took paracetamol and recited memory verses to himself – a distraction technique. The more obscure, the better. 'And they returned, and came to Enmishpat, which is Kadesh, and smote all the country of the Amalekites, and also the Amorites, that dwelt in Hazezontamar.' It was not much help. The hornet had punctured his equanimity with its sting. The pain had reached a peak and he had a tightness in his throat, but he was more disturbed by the hornet's abnormal behaviour than the pain. Pain was just physiological, attenuated or damped by the psychological – he could understand that – but the hornet's actions seemed deliberate. It was as if the insect had exhibited human sentience, as if it had been going about its business, seen him through the window and thought, 'Great bats! There's a white man with a pink neck. I hate them and I have a sack full of venom to unload. What am I hovering about for?'

He smiled grimly to himself at his anthropomorphising. If this was what the human mind could ascribe to a winged insect, no wonder it readily ascribed sinister intent, with the slimmest of pretext, to peoples of a foreign culture. Wars started that way.

At least he had reacted in a controlled manner. Reaction to an emotion was so destructive, and set off further events – perhaps the gardener would go home and beat his wife out of frustration at being unjustly accused by the irate student. Michael's own past proved that it was quite possible to generate ill consequences. Far better to apply logic, analyse, make rational decisions and then act to turn the event to benefit – after all, when attending crash victims in casualty, or stemming the blood loss from a ruptured abdominal aorta in theatre, his coolness under pressure had saved lives.

He could see himself coming to the conclusion that it was not only controlling behaviour that was possible, but that emotion itself was voluntary. It might be possible to turn it off. He wasn't alone: he had read about a father of a young girl killed in an accident who chose not to feel grief. Her father was extremely sorry she was gone and would have given his life for her; but now she was dead what was the point of torturing himself with grief? Want was another powerful emotion, but the Holy Men of the East attained a state of not feeling want at all. They achieved a peace of mind that culminated in something they equated to paradise.

James knocked at the door and came in with a sock filled with ice. 'The sock's clean,' he said.

Michael turned his head stiffly and attempted a lopsided smile. 'Thank you. I'm sure it'll settle soon.' The woollen sock felt cold and wet on his shoulder, like a bedraggled guinea pig.

James said, 'Would you like to go down to the lake for a walk this afternoon? It's a pretty sight. I'm tied up in a conference committee meeting myself and supervising preparations for this evening but my driver will take you. He has an errand to run for me that way.'

Yesterday's shooting incident came to mind. Michael hesitated; he had promised himself not to take any pointless risks.

'Alternatively you could have a cup of coffee with Audrey on the veranda. She loves having visitors – perks her up no end.' James's loud and enthusiastic voice was giving Michael earache. James leant towards him. 'Be careful, though – she's a fine one for finding out every wee secret.'

'If Audrey doesn't mind I'll stretch my legs by the lake.'

Michael walked along a dirt track that afforded irregular views of the lake between thick reed beds, stands of broken bulrushes and scraps of forest. James had told him that Lake Victoria was the size of Scotland. Looking out at its limpid expanse under a heavy haze of sky, he thought it little wonder that when the explorer, Speke, had seen it, he reported that he had found the source of the Nile. Such a vast inland sea had to be the giant mother-reservoir for the river that gave birth to Egypt.

Small waves slapped the shore but, further out, curiously isolated patches of choppy water formed shadowy agitations. A long way out a solitary canoe with a single oarsman made its lonely way across the water. Michael was surprised to see a cloud of black smoke hanging over the surface half a mile out until he realised he was looking at a dense swarm of flies. He did not find the lake as beautiful as he had hoped and put this down to altered perceptions induced by the hornet sting: his senses had become abnormally raw and nettlesome; every few steps he found himself ready to retch or shiver at some rank fish stench or fetid miasma coming off the lake that he could taste as much as smell. He felt mosquitoes landing on the hypersensitive skin of his face. Near the water's edge a crow with untidy feathers plucked the eye out of a rotting fish. Startled at his approach, it scrabbled into the air with a deafening smacking of its wings.

For reasons he seemed unwilling to discuss, the driver had insisted he go another way, but he had not gone far along the driver's suggested route when he saw that the track came to a dead end by the lake. He turned back and took the forbidden route, desperate to get a little exercise and walk off the pain.

Michael strode on, skirting the lake but sometimes losing sight of it in thicker vegetation until the track became indistinct. Needing to relieve himself, he took a small side path into the trees. He was midstream when the buzzing of flies made him turn his head. By the ashes of a small fire near his feet he saw a dead cockerel with its belly slit open. Hello, he thought, someone was having a barbecue here. Then he saw the rodent nailed to the tree whose roots he was soaking. The desiccated creature was stretched thin and wrapped in leather strapping, which held in place a straggly covering of feathers – black feathers with a suggestion of a bronze sheen. A pricking sensation travelled up his back. He said to himself forcibly, 'It's only a fetish.'

And then he noticed the flies had gone. The grove had become eerily still. His urinary stream sounded torrential in the silence. Michael redirected his stream into the ashes to try to quieten it but that only amplified the sound. It occurred to him that there was sure to be some taboo against desecrating a spiritual site – particularly in this way. Then he noticed the entrails strung out on a flat stone at the edge of the clearing. There was a movement in the long grass nearby. He splashed his shoes.

All was still again.

'Hello! Is anyone there?' he said loudly, and added, 'I'm British,' as explanation for his blundering. His privates were still exposed and he shut the stream off without completely emptying, hastily zipping his flies.

'Damn it!' he exclaimed, and unzipped again to free the nipped skin.

The grasses shifted once more, an ominously wilful movement towards him. His heart thumped, his hands came up. He took a step back to use the tree as a shield. As he did so, he heard the sound of beating wings. Some large bird lost itself in the reeds by the water. Michael exhaled, relieved at first and then annoyed that he had started to panic. He turned to go and then turned around again to face the small clearing, backing away, watching for anything unusual until he got back to the main path.

He hurried along telling himself that there was no need for fear, but disturbed at the way a little hocus-pocus had taken power over him – its grip on his emotions. He wondered if humanity could ever break free from superstition and if so, how humanity would change. It must have some evolutionary explanation, but he could not imagine there would be much to lose.

He glanced at his watch. It was getting on. The driver would be wondering where he had got to, and he had to be back in time to give his lecture. When the path gave him a view of the lake again Michael was surprised to see that the canoe had disappeared. That was strange: it had not been ten minutes since he had last seen it making imperceptible progress across the vast expanse of water. Perhaps the oarsman had fired up an outboard motor. He looked again. Something dark lay in the agitated water. It bobbed in and out of view. Was that an arm raised, or the head and neck of a cormorant? Perhaps he was imagining things – his over-sensitive state playing tricks with his eyes. Scanning the lake again, he saw nothing. If the oarsman was in the water he was miles out. There would be next to no chance of rescue. He had read somewhere that few Africans, even lake dwellers, could swim. Time was passing; he had done enough rescuing in the last twenty-four hours, and it had not been appreciated. Worse, he had broken his vow to avoid putting himself in potentially unpredictable situations by taking off on his own down a forbidden track. James had reminded him of the operatic dimensions of life here. He must not get caught up in it. The dense grasses and thick groves pressed in behind him. He convinced himself he had seen a cormorant and walked on.

Putting a hand in his pocket to find a handkerchief to wipe his brow, Michael felt the feather he had picked off the dead man's leg in the aeroplane. An intense irritation welled, turning to anger. His action in keeping the feather, far from being a snub to superstition, had given credence to it – as if he acknowledged its power and was fighting it. The sane action would have been to ignore the thing. He scooped it out of his pocket and let it drop, but then had to flick it off his trouser leg when it attached itself as it fell, as if by static.

When he got back to the road the driver was waiting, pacing a small distance to and from the car, as if tethered.

'That is a bad place, down there,' the driver said.

'I didn't find it so. It was … anthropologically interesting,' Michael said.

'There's some water in the bottle. Have a drink, Dr Lacey. You'll feel better. Remember that Jesus is stronger.'

He was thankful of the water, as he felt sweaty, but who wouldn't with the heat and the sting.

'I don't believe in any of that.'

'That is a shame, sir. You'll die sad.'

'Why's that? Superstition causes fear.'

The driver looked at him as if he felt for him. 'Sir, there are good spirits and bad spirits. If we make peace with the good spirits we can die happy. If we bow to the bad spirits we die fearful. If we don't know any spirits we die sad.'

'Why do we die sad?' Michael asked.

The driver took his empty water bottle and put it on the back seat. 'Maybe, sir, it's because we're lonely.'

'Well, I hope I've found a good companion – a flesh and blood one – by then.'

It seemed a long way back to the McCrees' house, and he was racked by uncertainty concerning the oarsman: whether he should have raised the alarm. Logic dictated not, emotion pleaded otherwise. He supposed his decision was in keeping with the naval submarine commander that Naomi saw in him.

Later, when he was being driven to the university for his lecture, Michael thought he could still smell the lake on his hands: fish guts and rotting weeds. It was only when he took the lectern and saw the crowded audience that he put the memory of the lake behind him. To illustrate his lecture – Latest Innovations in Bowel Anastomosis, Illustrated with Slides – he had brought from London an example of the latest staple gun for joining the colon. No more tedious double-layer stitching in the deep and miry pit of the pelvis. The staple gun was passed around the audience, its smooth white plastic form stroked by most and its trigger squeezed by all.

'When you fire a gun you don't pull the trigger weakly, in two minds, hoping you will only half kill your attacker. So it is with the staple gun. Pull the trigger firmly and completely, otherwise you will repeat the error of my registrar who spent an hour removing three dozen half-closed staples from the wall of the sigmoid colon last month.'

The Minister of Health, himself a doctor and clearly pleased to encourage links with the outside world after years of isolation in the terror, led the audience in a standing ovation for the informative and captivating lecture. Michael looked out and recognised many of the students from the morning's workshop. Afterwards a good proportion of his audience stayed to ask questions. He started to relax again. His neck felt better and he was touched by the warmth of the students; he wanted to do something for them that would extend beyond these three days. Perhaps he would set up a trust fund to offer scholarships to James's most gifted students, so they could come over for extra training in London. He made a mental note to speak to James about it later. He hoped that his motive was not merely an attempt to convince himself that he was not a callous man – someone who might have left an oarsman drowning without raising the alarm.

THREE

The conference dinner that evening was held at the McCrees' home. Guests spilled off the wide veranda at the back of the house onto the candle-ringed lawn. Audrey McCree had emerged coiffured (her hair out of its bun and flowing in a lustrous black tide down her back) and perfumed. She wore a pepper-red gypsy blouse and a loose green skirt with a frilly hem. Michael had to look twice to confirm that it was her. The sodden languor of yesterday had vanished and another Audrey had burst forth: voluptuous, glossy, in bloom. Michael noticed how her eyes sparkled, although when she glanced across at him he found their dusky shine a touch wild for his taste. In a previous age he could imagine her being denounced as a witch. She busied herself around the tables arranging napkins and instructing the cooks. It was probable that an event like this had not occurred since before the years of terror. Maybe things were going to improve for the McCrees now that they were able to receive visitors again: life might become a little more predictable, and ordinary.

James took Michael by the arm, his sandy complexion flushed from rushing about, and guided him through the reception room towards the garden doors. He leant towards him and said, 'Between you and me, my dear fellow, we have a zoo of eccentrics with us this evening. Everyone here, to a man, would be considered oddball in a stable institution. But here they're institutions in themselves.'

They stopped on the veranda where a faint smell of grass cuttings, wood-smoke and gum from bleeding branches told of a day of frantic preparation in the garden beyond. James discreetly pointed out the guests. 'That's John Grey. He goes around the country weighing human excrement. Ask him why yourself, although I can tell you that heavy is good. He says our western stools are too light – not enough roughage in our diets. Wouldn't need any bowel surgeons if we took his advice. Talking to him is Peter Simms – bush doctor from Tanzania. Done thousands of operations using fishing line as a suture, and doubtless his teeth as scissors, to save money. I exaggerate only a little.'

James indicated a mountain of a man parked on the lawn, whose hand almost completely enveloped a bottle of beer. 'That's Leo Karwemera – specialises in the delicate repair of vesico-vaginal fistulas. It's a terrible problem in some districts because of late presentation of obstructed childbirth. Does more repairs in a week than all the surgeons in Europe do in five years. By the door over there is Crawford Clarke – flown in from Kenya – treats the president. That makes him Surgeon for Life. Gupta, by the drinks, chatting up my wife, is an orthopaedic surgeon – gets polio victims walking again with clever tendon transfers. Next to him is Stanley Katura. With the thick glasses. He's a mission doctor out near the Rwenzori Mountains – the legendary Mountains of the Moon in the Albertine Rift Valley. Serious chap. Frighteningly dedicated.'

The lights on the veranda faltered and then steadied again.

'Excuse me a moment. I'm going to check we've enough fuel in the generator. There's a power cut tonight. Frequent occurrence.'

Michael walked out onto the lawn, away from the house, past the citronella-scented candle flares to where darkness lapped the edge of the grass. He listened to the raspings, clicks and susurrus rustlings of the African night and sensed furtive movements, momentary flarings of strong winged insects, sudden and unexpected small deaths of small creatures in the darkness beyond. He looked down into the valley. Apart from the orange glare of a few fires there were no clues to the city's existence in the power cut. He thought he heard a gunshot. 'Popcorn' they called it. No wonder the guests had needed a police escort from their hotels.

He turned back into the lawn, the arena of a safer place, and wandered towards a tree in the centre of the lawn where a woman stood on her own. The tree glowed softly from lights strung in its thick foliage, like luminescent fruit. As he approached, the woman turned her head and looked straight at him. If allure is the beauty that arouses hope and desire then Michael saw in an instant that he had stumbled on the allure – he struggled to think of a fitting expression – given by God to Eve herself. If the woman that he approached had held out a fruit, plucked with her lissom arm from the boughs of the tree, and invited him to eat, he would have willingly accepted – just to please her. She wore a halterneck gown, a deep fuchsia colour, made of something silky (charmeuse, chiffon, something like that). Her eyes had the seductive lines of a Pharaohonic princess; her lips were full, kissable. Her face was exquisitely set off by her earrings: a pendant of three small pearly-white cowry shells.

Beautiful, yes, but there was more. She held his captive stare with such a deep-welled self-assurance that Michael, himself used to projecting confidence, felt his gaze faltering and had to stop himself lowering his eyes in deference to a purer, uncontrived composure.

'Good evening. I'm Michael Lacey.'

The woman did not proffer her hand, but she smiled, still holding him with her eyes, and said, 'I am Felice.'

'I'm … charmed. Call me Michael.'

Felice dipped her head slightly but said nothing, although Michael, with a clinician's attuned eye, thought he detected a transitory dilation of her pupils. They stood facing each other, Michael all of a sudden feeling wonderfully relaxed, free, with no imperative to make forced conversation. A curious but comforting feeling grew in him: that he and Felice shared something in their past. Something about her was familiar – more than that: was dear – but he could not think of any occasion when he might have met her before. It came as a relief that his sudden bedazzlement had more complex roots than simply a Pavlovian response to her physical appeal. She smiled at him again. He asked if she would like her drink filling up; he noticed that she wore no rings.

'That's kind, but I'm OK. Just enjoying this lovely place.' She spoke softly but with a clear, clipped accent, as if she had had an expensive English education.

He found himself saying, 'Yes, it's, well … I thought … oh, damn it, I'll say it: you make it lovelier still … you really do.' Propriety caught up with him: 'I mean … under the tree here …' He stopped. Or anywhere, he thought.

Now she looked down for a moment, but recovered quickly enough, looking up at him again with what he felt was a quizzical eye. He couldn't quite believe that he had spoken like that, and was about to apologise for embarrassing her when she smiled at him. He found himself trapped again in her gaze.

He searched for something safe to say. 'Do you live in Kampala?'

'Thank you. You don't know how nice it was to hear someone say that,' she said, and then when he opened his mouth to ask the question again, she said, 'I used to, but not now.' She suddenly became animated and came a little closer. 'See if you can guess where I live, if I give you some clues.'

He would go along with anything. 'Let me try.'

'OK, listen carefully. Your first clue is … I'm often bathed by the Cloud King.'

She seemed eager to hear his reply, but not in the fawning way of someone intimidated by him, but as if she wished to intrigue him; to entertain him, and to be entertained.

'Hmm – could be near a waterfall.'

She laughed. 'Good try. Your second clue is … my place is hidden from the eyes of Europeans.'

Her gaiety was infectious; intoxicating. Michael screwed up his eyes and said, 'Very mysterious – take me there.'

They laughed together. He was surprised not to feel foolish at his playful conduct. They stood in their own small and private pool of candy-coloured light, the rest of the party having slipped away into the darkness.

'My third clue? Let's see … in the moonlight there are white fields in the sky.'

'Oh, gosh! It's impossibly romantic.' At any other time in his life, an utterance like that would have been tongue-in-cheek, bordering on sarcastic, but not tonight.

Now she came closer still. If you touch me, I shall melt, he thought. My final clue …' He saw her notice something over his shoulder. She pulled back. 'Ah, our game's over. Here's my husband.'

'Your husband?'

Making mental adjustments, Michael wrenched his attention away from Felice. The small thin man with the thick glasses that James had pointed out – he reminded Michael of a rather intense laboratory officer at his hospital – had joined them, and was holding out his hand.

'Stanley Katura. I enjoyed your lecture.' He held Michael's hand in a steady grip.

Michael, still settling from the sensations of a moment ago, said absentmindedly, 'Good. Was it useful?'

'In the city, yes, but I work in the bush and we don't have the technical facilities. That's a way of saying we don't have the money.'

Michael loosened his handshake, but Stanley failed to do the same and relaxed his arm as if he was going to hold Michael's hand all evening.

'I'm sorry,' Michael said. 'You must be looking forward to moving to somewhere that does have the money – the amenities.'

Stanley glanced at Felice but Michael saw that she did not reciprocate. Still Stanley held his hand. He said, 'We've already moved to where we want to be. We're very happy there, thank you.'

Michael relaxed his hand further. 'Forgive me,' Stanley said as he released him. 'You're new here so you won't know that we Ugandans like to come close when we greet, to hold each other and take our time over the introduction.'

Felice said, 'I think it's our way of seeing into the soul.' She tilted her head as if she was particularly interested in his reply – willing him to reveal himself.

'We Europeans don't have a soul nowadays. It's unscientific.' He liked to counter irrational sentiments, even if it meant being pedantic, although he immediately regretted sounding so cold.

'Oh, how dull,' Felice said lightly. 'My friends all have souls. Isn't there an old Middle Eastern proverb: man cannot live by bread alone?'

Michael was pleased she could counter him; here was someone sharp enough to parry with. 'We have a mind, of course.' And sometimes a wonderful body as well, he thought.

She shrugged. 'So does an elephant.'

'Indeed – but ours is more complex. It gives us that subjective phenomenon some call the soul, but it's all generated by that physical entity we call the brain. Science will find an explanation for any sense of soul some day.' He felt he had sounded pompous, and added, with a jovial tone, 'Everything else is mumbo-jumbo.'

She said, evenly, 'Are you sure you meant to bring our Mumbo-Jumbo into this?' She turned to Stanley, and with a shocked air said, 'I'm sure he didn't mean to be blasphemous. But perhaps we ought to advise him to sacrifice a white goat; we don't want any bad juju coming his way.'

Stanley squinted at her, as if he had not understood.

Michael started to apologise (perhaps Felice and Stanley venerated Mumbo-Jumbo) but Felice's serious expression melted and she laughed, a delightful belly giggle, and said, 'Don't worry, Mr Lacey – Michael – I'm teasing you. And anyway, I don't think you're without a soul. Other people's perception of us is more accurate than our own.'

She smiled at him again and then glanced at Stanley, but he was looking away as if his mind was on other matters. Michael saw a tightening in the corner of Felice's eyes – betraying a disappointment perhaps. An overwhelming need came over him for Felice to believe that he had whatever she considered to be most admirable in another person. A soul, for example. Whatever that meant to her.

He said, 'I'll bow to your astute judgement on my soul.'

Felice sipped her drink, looking satisfied with his response.

Stanley intruded again. 'How long are you here for?'

'I have leave, but I'm booked to return to the UK on Monday, and then I may join some friends skiing in France.'

Felice spoke excitedly to Stanley, 'Shall we invite him to see what Europeans call the real Africa?'

She turned back to Michael without waiting for Stanley's reply and said, with what he make-believed was a smoulderingly seductive invitation, 'Why don't you come and stay in our home? We'll take you to the Queen Elizabeth National Park in the Rift Valley. It's not far from us. I'm sure you can change your plans.'

Even as Michael found himself saying, 'That's most kind. Are you sure?' he thought of the disturbing events of the last two days and the need to cancel the skiing holiday. He was astonished at his unhinged acceptance of the invitation – as if Stanley was not there; as if Felice was going to lead him to that place he had seen mentioned in the book that he had picked up in his bedroom at the McCrees: *In Search of Paradise*. With a jolt of guilt he thought of Naomi; but then he remembered her parting kiss: her tense lips more a peck than a kiss. As he recalled it now it seemed like a dismissal. A danger presented itself, although he immediately discounted it: he would be many miles away from his childhood home. They had lived in the south; this was the west, the far west. There was little risk of meeting anyone he knew from those days.

Stanley was looking at Felice, his eyes small, bead-like, behind his myopia-correcting lenses. 'But – our work. The patients,' he said, frowning.

Michael immediately regretted his haste. He tried to give Stanley a way out. 'Perhaps I'd better not; it's too short notice.'

But Felice had puckered her cheeks and was staring out Stanley.

'It's too much trouble – I'll be getting in the way,' Michael added.

'Ah! There could be trouble,' Stanley said, and then exhaled sharply. Michael was not sure whether he had laughed.

Stanley left the words hanging until Felice said, 'Stanley?'

A hint of a smile pulled at Stanley's cheek. 'The trouble will not come from us.' He stopped again.

He's hard work, Michael thought, and to fill the silence said, 'Travel here seems a little hazardous. Is it safe to come with you?' He tried to sound nonchalant.

Stanley took off his glasses, studied them, put them back on and then turned to face Michael squarely as if he had come to a decision. 'Safe most of the time. And if you come with us it'll be safer for me and Felice at the roadblocks on the way home. There's something of a taboo against harming a white man. For a start, your government makes a tremendous fuss about it.'

'I'll be pleased to be the token taboo.'

Stanley didn't smile, but said with polite formality, 'It'll be a pleasure to give you hospitality. Forgive my hesitation – I seem to have my mind on my work too much.'

Michael thought that Felice relaxed.

The McCrees joined them.

Audrey said brightly, 'I hope you're enjoying getting to know each other.'

Michael was struck again by her transformation from the frightened woman he had first met the day before. Even her movements had become liberated.

'Michael's coming to visit us,' Felice said, sounding triumphant.

'My dear fellow, I thought you were returning to the UK,' James said.

'So did I, but I've been persuaded otherwise. An invitation that I can't refuse.'

Michael looked at Stanley as he spoke, rather than Felice. He feared his rapid intoxication might be showing like a flashing red light on his head. He wondered if Stanley was used to every man falling for his wife, got a closet pleasure from it, knowing that it was he (the antithesis of a charismatic, well-physiqued man) who had been the one to marry her.

Felice said to Audrey and James, 'We're going to show Michael the real Africa. He'll not regret it.'

Audrey said, 'Beware, Michael. Africa's a siren to white men. They end up shipwrecked on its ancient spirit-filled rocks.'

'That's a bit melodramatic, Audrey. Look at me,' James said.

'Exactly.'

James threw back his head and laughed loudly.

Audrey said to Felice, 'I do like your dress.'

Felice mouthed, 'Borrowed.'

'Wonderful fit. And your earrings, lovely too.'

'Oh, thanks, it's a family tradition – my mother and grandmother always wore shells.'

'Symbol of fertility,' James said.

Audrey coughed and said, 'Such a beautiful evening – not too hot.'

James stuttered, 'And ... er ... were used as currency until the beginning of this century. Inflation caught up with them; in the end it required seven men to carry the value of five pounds. When the shells were banned they were incinerated in their millions. The first District Commissioner's house in Kampala was called the Shell House because of all the lime from the burnt shells used in its construction.'

'Sort of boring thing James knows,' Audrey said, her tone giving away a hint of pride.

James was getting into his stride. 'I heard of a boy from the interior in those days who accompanied his master to the sea. It was his first time at the coast. When he saw the beach he fell on the shells, crying "Money, money, money!"'

All the guests gathered around as James entertained them with stories from his archives. All except Stanley. When Michael looked away from the group he saw him wandering, restless, around the lawn. Michael glanced at Felice. She caught his eye and smiled at him again. Out of the corner of his eye he thought he saw Audrey watching him.

As the guests dispersed, Michael helped clear up, and found Audrey stacking plates alone in the kitchen. She spoke as he put a tray of glasses on the sideboard. 'Michael, I know it's none of my business – but I don't think you should go to Lwesala with Stanley and Felice.'

He turned to look at her, but she was facing away from him. 'Really? What makes you say that? Is there something I should know about them?'

'It's not them. It's ...' She seemed unable to go on.

'Too dangerous?' he prompted.

Audrey was running the tap, still busy. He felt irritated: she was behaving as if she could see into his life and knew what was best for him, delivering hints obliquely, like a fortune teller.

'Is it ... me?'

He was thinking about asking her if she had read the tea leaves at the bottom of his cup, but James came in whistling the Skye Boat Song.

He clapped his hand hard down on Michael's shoulder, causing him to catch his elbow on the edge of the sideboard and setting off his funny bone.

'Fff …' He stifled it.

James was oblivious. 'Thanks for your help, old chap.' He swung round towards Audrey and placed his hand on her waist. He was less clumsy with her. 'Audrey, my dear, do go to bed; we'll finish off. You made this evening a spectacular success.'

She flicked the water off her hands in a satisfied way, and dried them on a towel. 'I think I will. So much excitement all of a sudden.'

That night Michael dreamt of a place in the Rift Valley where the moon cast a silvery light. White fields hung in the sky, like some imagined country. At the entrance to a house made of sheaths of grass cut from those fields stood a woman adorned with white shells, hair plaited with red beads, a smile of perfect teeth and white shoes on her feet. But when she turned to lead him to her bed of downy pillows, a child appeared in the doorway and blocked their way. The woman picked up the child and swung him around playfully. The child laughed and was happy. Michael woke restless and unhappy. In the calm of the night he reflected on his agreeing to go with Felice and Stanley: a foolish crush on the black woman; a married woman, even if he was right in detecting that she was a frustrated one. Then there was Audrey's warning. It was too late now; he had committed himself in a moment of foolishness. In the heat of an emotion.

FOUR

To their relief, Stanley, Felice and Michael reached the Rift Valley before nightfall. Travelling by day had its dangers but these were multiplied at night. Stanley had earnestly recounted tragic misadventures on the roads: variations on a theme of drunken soldiers, potholes, trucks with no lights, or all three combined.

They dropped down a forested escarpment of ironwood, thick with leaf and vine and moving with feathered and furred creatures, into a geological playground. Blue-watered explosion craters, rimmed with red aloes, punctured the wide valley floor; deep-silted plains spread far south and north glassed with the lakes and rivers that feed the Nile. Michael would not have been surprised to see an Arab caravan or a Victorian explorer's train of porters tramping their shores. Ahead, the sun had been swallowed whole by the clouds of the Rwenzori massif. Vapours advanced like pale-gloved fingers down the thick-forested buttresses as if the hand of God was gathering in the mountain's secrets.

Nearing the foothills of the mountains they took a twisting track through dense banana groves, compact fields of dark-leafed coffee, heavily fruited mango trees and bloated gourds; the soil as black as congealed blood. Hushed by a land fit for the gods, they had been silent for a long time, when Stanley said suddenly, 'It's fertile country; they say that even a toothpick will root. Be careful not to fall into the toothpick bushes.'

Michael saw Felice shoot Stanley a startled look. He had found Stanley polite but, until then, lacking in humour. Perhaps his tribe were the Prussians of Africa. In contrast, Felice had been voluble and sparkled with wit.

As they got near to Lwesala they slowed frequently to return the greetings of brightly clad women returning from market. It was obvious that everyone knew the Katuras. When they arrived at the hospital, nurses hurried towards them as they parked at the edge the compound. The women formed a crescent in front of the Land Rover and danced to the accompaniment of an impromptu song. Michael heard a drum start up, like a church bell heralding a cause for rejoicing.

'This is a very kind reception,' he said.

As soon as he said it he remembered that it was unlikely anyone at Lwesala could have known about his arrival. He felt foolish and self-important. The welcome could only have been for the returning Stanley and Felice. No one here knew him from Adam. Stanley and Felice must think him conceited.

Stanley got out and stood by the vehicle door as the staff continued their song of welcome.

Felice said cheerily, 'They're just pleased we've arrived safely,' and then soberly, 'When Stanley's away some patients die, so now he's back some will be saved.'

'Is that so?' Michael said. 'He's that critical here?'

'Of course. There's no other doctor.'

'How can he ever go away then?'

It seemed the weight of all humanity's ills came to Felice as she shook her head slowly and said, 'It worries us a lot.' Then she shook the burden off as if it was an impediment to doing something about it and opened her door. 'But everyone knows he can't be here all the time. They accept it. For a year there was no doctor here at all but we've good assistants and nurses. They do the best they can.'

Michael was about to commiserate when they were interrupted. A nurse was approaching, at speed, from the hospital. She stood to attention in front of Stanley.

'Doctor, there's a female patient who's in obstructed labour. The baby is dead and the mother is sick.'

Stanley made off down the path to the hospital with the nurse trying to keep up.

'I see what you mean,' Michael said.

Felice sighed. 'He may be gone some time or he might come back straight away. Sometimes when it's reported that the patient's sick, he finds that they've already passed away.'

Felice made her own greetings to the welcoming party. They each genuflected to her in turn. Michael saw love in their eyes. At least he thought it was love: it might be subservience or jealousy. Reading the shifting nuances of muscular tension around the eyes and the mouth in a far-removed culture was an inexact science. Felice introduced him, in the local language, and they shook his hand formally, looking down in respect to the stranger.

'Come! I'll show you where you're sleeping,' Felice said.

He followed her along a path that plunged into a banana grove and then emerged in front of a small square bungalow with roughly pointed brick walls and a rusting corrugated-iron roof. There was no veranda but the earth outside was hard-packed and swept clean. The front door led straight into a sparsely furnished room: three square-framed wooden chairs, a small bench and a four-legged table; they might have been cast-offs from a school. A beaded blue and white bowl, brimming with miniature bright-yellow bananas, had been placed in the centre of a white cotton tablecloth. Above the grass mat on the concrete floor a wire hook for a paraffin lamp hung from a roof truss. All was spotlessly clean. Through the door at the back of the room Michael could see a wood stove in a tiny kitchen. Felice opened the door to the left and led him into another simply furnished room: a bed with a turned down sheet over a plain brown blanket; an upturned packing case for a bedside table with a hand-embroidered cloth draped over it; a soot-free paraffin lamp on a wooden stool in the corner; a neatly tied mosquito net hanging ready for use over the bed.

'This is your room. It's always ready for visitors,' Felice said. She ran her hand over the blanket to smooth a small crease.

'It's a cosy guest house,' he said, and was about to ask how far it was to the main house when Felice giggled and said, 'Guest house? This is our home.'

Its simplicity reminded him of his childhood home, and afterwards he realised it was that unwelcome intrusion of remembrance that made him say, 'You live in this tiny house? Have they not built you something bigger?'

'Bigger?' she asked, with a look of puzzlement.

He had said the wrong thing, but found himself trying to extract himself by flattery. 'Yes, of course, educated and important people like you and Stanley: the medical superintendent of a hospital. You deserve some proper comforts and ... er ... some visible sign of status ... in case ...' He stopped before he made a further fool of himself.

Felice took a snatched breath, dropped her smile and looked momentarily confused. Then he saw a fire in her eyes as she said sharply, 'Who are the *they* that you refer to? Everything is done by our own effort: this house, the hospital. We can't build what the community can't afford. But in any case we only build what we need. Our friendships and community are our wealth – they're our big house.' She faced him square as she talked, chin projecting, arms akimbo. 'We have strong ambition, Mr Lacey, but the size of our house is not linked to that ambition.'

He was taken aback. Stung by her reaction, he tried to justify his comment to himself: he wanted his hosts to have success. Here were Stanley and Felice, stuck in a dank banana grove in a house hardly bigger than a garden shed, in the deepest backwater of a third world country with a major law and order problem. Intelligent people should maximise their opportunity for advancement. And Stanley should be providing better for Felice. If she had been his own wife he would have lived to give her his best. Why, even in her anger she was achingly lovely.

But he had upset her. He was no longer Michael, but Mr Lacey, the unappreciative and patronising guest.

'I apologise. I'm not used to the sort of life you have here.' That wasn't strictly true, he remembered: only true for his adult self. 'I was just concerned for you – and Stanley. Also, all the dangers here. But you're right; I'm sorry.'

Felice relaxed, although she glanced around the room as if seeing for the first time its spartan and cramped nature. 'Your concern's appreciated,' she said, without sarcasm, 'and your apology's accepted, but maybe you're looking at me as if I'm a coconut.'

'A coconut?'

'Brown on the outside, white on the inside – European inside.' Michael thought a coconut, with its coarse, hairy shell, an inappropriate association with Felice, whose skin was lustrous and smooth. 'I'm sorry: I've put my foot in it again.'

A hint of a smile tightened the corners of her eyes. 'You're out of your element. That's all.'

'That's it.'

She gave him a forgiving look and said, 'You're just a bit lost in Africa, Mr Lacey.' She turned to lead him back to the living room.

'Please call me Michael, or I shall start calling you Madam Katura.'

She turned back to him, her spirited disposition restored. 'I think we shall be good friends, Michael.' Their eyes met for a moment and he was transported back to the tree in the garden at the McCrees, he thought she had flown there with him too, the last few minutes of gaucherie excused as merely an awkward but necessary prelude to ... what? She was a married woman, a pillar of the mission, and he, although he had spent two decades trying to bury it, was a missionary's child. Thou Shalt Not Covet Thy Neighbour's Wife.

They went on into the kitchen, heading for the back door. 'Let me show you our bathroom facilities. They would be en suite if you were sleeping in the banana grove. Perhaps I should make you do that.' She was laughing again. He followed her out, across another swept-earth yard, and she waited for him to catch up. When he drew alongside she said in a low voice, as if confiding a secret, 'Stanley's very dedicated.'

He was not sure how to respond – it seemed that she expressed a regret – but he had little time to think, for she was pointing out the two outhouses.

'This is the shower and that's the long-drop. You don't have to flush – that's high technology, don't you think? Stanley will show you how to work the shower. The water's heated twice a day from the wood boiler.'

The day was closing rapidly. A maid had appeared and was lighting the hurricane lamps in the kitchen, pumping them vigorously, an urgency against the fading light. Soon the gauze element brightened, making the door frame glow welcomingly.

'Sorry there's no electricity – the hospital generator's faulty again,' Felice said as they returned to the kitchen.

She introduced the maid, who bowed theatrically, and then left him to unpack.

Michael heard Stanley's footfalls on the path well before he arrived at the house. No doubt the earth was well compacted from his going to and fro at all hours of the day and night.

When Stanley came in, he nodded at Michael, and sat down wearily at the table. 'Contrary to the first report the mother has passed away but the baby survived. If we'd arrived earlier I might have saved the mother.'

Felice handed Stanley a mug of tea, putting in four or five spoonfuls of sugar as if it would make a cup of kindness that would salve his troubles, and said, 'There are always many what-ifs. You shouldn't blame yourself – think of those you've saved.'

Stanley said, 'If only there were enough doctors. If only the patients were able to reach the hospital earlier.'

'I've been showing Michael our facilities,' Felice said. 'Could you show him how the shower works?'

Stanley didn't seem to hear. He took off his glasses and sipped his tea.

'If there's anything I can do to help while I'm here, I'm more than willing,' Michael said.

Stanley took some time to answer. 'Thank you, but we'll not make you work on your holiday. Tomorrow I'll work and then we'll go to see the animals. Tonight we'll be eating at our friends' house.'

'Do you go out a lot?' asked Michael, uncertainly; wary of saying something that could be misinterpreted by the sensitive Felice.

Felice answered, 'We're as we've been since Ham: no television, no cinema, not enough light to read.'

'So our evening entertainment is each other – eating,' Stanley said, looking revived.

Felice burst into laughter. 'Don't give the *Muzungu* an opportunity to reinforce his darkest fears about us.'

Michael smiled at Felice.

'Why's that?' Stanley asked.

Felice said flatly, 'What you've just said. He'll think we eat each other.'

'Ah, yes. That's funny,' Stanley said soberly.

Michael felt a prick of anger towards Stanley – that he did not appreciate Felice's vivacity. She'd laughed more with him than with Stanley over the last two days. Stanley had the demeanour of someone who carried a heavy burden – his medical responsibilities too onerous, perhaps. But it seemed to Michael that there was more: he had the melancholy air of a man pre-occupied with some persistent sorrow. He wondered if it related to his marriage, although there was no compelling evidence of a serious ruction.

They had walked in the deep night for twenty minutes, Michael following closely behind Stanley who held a dim-beamed torch. Felice followed behind Michael; her presence like a sylph. He was drawn by the magnet of her attraction, but what destruction would ensue if he did not resist that pull, if he nurtured the scenarios and situations where he would feel her breath on his cheek?

Stanley spoke suddenly, breaking the silence. 'There are snakes but I'll let you know.'

'Thanks, please do,' Michael replied. He wondered how they would get back if the torch gave out.

They walked on in silence. He peered to his left and to his right to see what sort of countryside they were walking through. Ambiguous forms metamorphosed in his mind's eye into luxuriant vegetation hung with succulent fruits sleeping plumply until dawn.

A well-lit building came into view and a generator droned.

'The house of the district chief,' Stanley said.

On the edge of the compound, light spilling from the windows traced the form, in chrome trim, of a Mercedes. White-painted stones marked the edge of the driveway.

'Mr Magara likes his comforts,' Felice said.

A large man wearing a black jacket over a loud yellow and green, swirly-patterned shirt came to the door. His eyes were lost in the slits of his puffy face, his nostrils as widely spaced as a buffalo's. He expressed his pleasure at seeing Stanley and Felice and then pressed Michael's hand. Michael was introduced to Mrs Magara who sumptuously filled the billows of her floral, cotton dress. She clasped Michael's hand softly in both of hers and curtsied graciously.

'You're from London. That is fine, fine,' Mr Magara boomed. 'Do you know John Kabera? He's a famous doctor in Harley Street. Do you practise in Harley Street?'

'Not yet,' Michael said, but Mr Magara had turned to his wife and was signalling instructions. She disappeared into the back of the house.

'Good, very good,' Mr Magara said. 'The best doctors are there. Our Dr Katura here would make a superior Harley Street doctor but he has dedicated his life to us poor people here and has sacrificed a fine career.'

'We don't see it like that,' Stanley said. 'It's a privilege …'

Mr Magara cut in, looking at Michael again, 'Perhaps you could arrange for Dr Katura to work at your Harley Street clinic, Dr Lacey. I can assist with paperwork this end: character reference, letter of commendation, proof of competencies, reportings of patients cured, testimonials. My secretariat will make the arrangements.'

'I'll bear that in mind,' Michael said, and saw Felice grin.

'Fine, very fine. Now, Dr Katura, come in and let me give you news of our community while you've been away.'

The sofas in the Magaras' sitting room were draped with colourful knitted throws. Fading, out of date calendars lined the walls: Transafrica Trucking, 1979; Mufugu Beef Products, 1974; East African Breweries, 1980; and, ribbed and curled but catching Michael's eye, Agents for Kenwood – Electrical East Africa Ltd, Takes the hard work out of housework!, from 1963. Michael wondered how many kitchen appliances the Magaras owned; whether Mr Adams had ever won his battle against sticks for pounding, against great wooden spoons.

Mrs Magara came in with a tray of Cokes, Fantas and Schweppes. Mr Magara talked on while Mrs Magara put a straw, with delicate precision, into each bottle and offered them around. There were problems as always, said Mr Magara, over the border in Zaire; fuel was short again; he was pushing the government to restore the electricity lines but certain other districts were getting priority; a bus had wedged itself across the road in the valley; bandits had held up a lorry and robbed it of beer.

A maid brought the food through in three large steel pans and a smaller woven grass basket. Plates followed but no knives and forks. The maid placed a blanket on the floor. Michael followed the others in washing his hands in a pink plastic bowl, the maid offering her arm as a makeshift towel rail. Mr Magara waved Michael expansively to the table.

Stanley said to Michael, 'Mr and Mrs Magara are generous with food. This is mutton stew, this is *matooke* – steamed plantains, this is groundnut stew, and in the basket is millet. You take a scoop of millet or *matooke* with your hand and dip it in the stews.'

Michael made way for Felice and Mrs Magara.

Mr Magara said, 'No, no, Dr Lacey. It's the custom for the men to take first.'

Michael did as he was told and then hovered, unsure where to sit; there were only three chairs at the table.

'Please sit down, Dr Lacey,' Mr Magara said.

Michael sat down and Stanley and Mr Magara joined him. Felice and Mrs Magara sat on the blanket on the floor, Mrs Magara lowering herself with all four limbs while Felice slipped down gracefully, tucking her legs to the side. The women talked happily to each other, ignoring the men.

The hole in Michael's stomach felt large enough for the meal ahead, and he took to the earthy juiciness of the stews and contrasting textures of the smooth *matooke* and gritty millet. It reminded him of eating with Tomasi in the dim interior of his family's hut. He finished his plateful to the evident delight of Mr Magara.

'You like my food?'

'Yes, it's very satisfying, thank you.'

'I find it so. My wife and I are hoping that we can feed up Felice to make her beautiful. She would be the second most beautiful woman in Uganda if she would gain fullness. Fullness is pleasing in a woman. Do you not think so?'

'What is it in a man?' Mrs Magara asked from the floor, and then covered her mouth as if shocked at her own audacity.

'In a man it shows success. The problem for Felice is that Stanley is not earning enough to feed her. That's the problem.'

Felice protested mildly.

'It's the fashion,' Stanley said, rather quickly.

'European fashion! European fashion!' Mr Magara wailed. 'What's the good of following European fashion here? Here, where we have pygmy people in our mountains that have never seen an advertisement for Coca-Cola. Think of that, Dr Lacey.'

He scooped more mutton stew onto Michael's plate, including body parts that Michael had seen in the operating theatre but had never seen served up.

'I've had enough, thank you,' he said, too late.

Stanley gave a rare smirk. 'If you're full you should leave some food on your plate. If you clean your plate then it's assumed you've not had enough. That's another custom.'

Mr Magara piled on more food. 'No, no, he needs to put on weight. You'll gain respect from your Harley Street patients, Dr Lacey, if you go back a big man.' He stood up and belched, paused to recover his digestive system's equilibrium and went to the sideboard to turn on the radio. 'Let's have music. This is the shortwave from Zaire.' After some white noise and octave-tracing whistling, the tuner picked up an optimistic jangle.

'How do you like our Western Rift Valley, Dr Lacey? It's not the Happy Valley of Kenya, I think. There are no white settlers here, you see. Personally I would welcome them but I fear we don't have the creature comforts.' By now Michael had understood that conversation would be one way, so he didn't reply. Sure enough, Mr Magara was off again. 'A man came looking for you, Dr Katura, when you were away.'

'I see.'

'He gave his name as Zachye.'

Stanley's hand stopped on its way to his mouth. Felice looked up abruptly from the floor.

'Zachye?'

'Correct, very correct,' Mr Magara said, tearing a sinew off a bone with his teeth.

Stanley and Felice were looking intently at Mr Magara.

'Did he leave a message?' Stanley asked.

'No.' He paused to suck on the cartilage at the end of the bone. 'He just came to the door and asked where you were – but he called you Stanley, as if he knew you well.'

He waved the bone about. 'When I said you were in the capital he said nothing. He just walked away.'

'Walked away?'

'I shouted after him, "Mr Zachye, what do you want?" But he was gone. Do you know him?'

'My brother – it might be my brother. It must be my brother.' Michael thought that Stanley struggled to keep his voice from fracturing. 'I've not seen him for many years.'

'He was taller than you, although not as wide as me,' Mr Magara said, slapping his flanks and looking round for appreciation. None came.

'My brother was – is – taller than me. If it's my brother then it'll be an answer to our prayers. He's estranged. He was missing. I believed he could be dead. Did he look well?'

'He looked fit, but he was not well dressed. His clothes were shabby, very shabby. A man doesn't come to speak to the District Administrator in those clothes unless he has no others.'

'We must find him. Maybe he needs help. He just left?' Stanley sounded incredulous.

Mr Magara replied, 'I'll instruct my secretariat to ask if anyone has seen him but no one has reported him to me.'

Michael saw Felice and Stanley acknowledging their hopes and fears with a glance.

'He was a prodigal son, then?' Mr Magara asked, tackling the next bone.

'The prodigal son came back,' Stanley said, 'Zachye never did. My father would have killed any number of fatted calves in celebration if Zachye had returned.'

The conversation never recovered after that, Mr Magara at last too satiated to speak and Stanley and Felice stunned by his news. Mrs Magara busied herself serving sweet tea. Michael had a pleasant discomfort from his stretched stomach. He tried to fill the silence by telling Mr Magara about the proposed excursion to the national park.

Mr Magara guffawed. 'Why pay to see animals? Pay to eat them, of course. But just to look? The world has become strange. Would you pay to look over your hedges in your country to see your Jersey cows and your Aberdeen bulls? Would you go on safari to your Lake District in a bus painted black and white to see your sheep dogs?'

Stanley said, 'We'd better go. Do you have any spare batteries? Our torch is nearly dead.'

'I'll walk you to your vehicle, have no fear,' Mr Magara said, lifting himself with difficulty from his chair.

'We came on foot – the hospital fuel's running low.'

Mr Magara tutted loudly. 'I'd drive you back myself if my driver wasn't drunk and asleep in his bed.'

He found a powerful torch. As they left he came to the edge of the compound with them and said in a whisper, 'Be very careful, there are bandits.'

They walked back in silence, the torch providing what Michael knew was false comfort. Stanley swung it away from the path once to look for the source of some noise he had heard. As he swung it back Michael saw a black cockerel hanging from a branch.

'Did you see that?' Michael asked, a crawling sensation spreading across his shoulders.

'Did you see something?' Stanley asked.

'I thought I saw a chicken.'

Felice found this funny. 'You're going to get very excited in the game park.'

'There are many chickens in Africa,' Stanley said.

'I assume they don't roost by hanging upside down from a tree,' Michael replied.

Stanley scanned the bushes. 'Where did you see it?' He handed the torch to Michael.

Searching with the beam, Michael saw nothing but an illuminated lattice of branches and their shadows behind: a ghostly tracery of dark matter.

'It's easy to mistake shapes for anything,' Stanley said.

'Must have been my imagination. I'm completely out of my element.'

But he was convinced he had seen another fetish, and its disappearance when he tried to find it again was, quite frankly, disturbing. He remembered the incident on the aircraft, the grove in the forest by the lake, the vanishing oarsman. He speculated about a link between the cursed man with the feather and two identical feathered fetishes hundreds of miles apart. Then he got a grip. He firmly discounted the paranormal; the only linking factor was his irrational fear. Nevertheless, he was disturbed to be glad that it was Felice and Stanley with him as he walked on into the night. Ironic, really: his rational and scientific self feeling protected by the mission couple with their naïve religious faith; they who believed in a force bigger than whatever was out there in the night, and therefore that they were shielded in some way, or at least part of some greater purpose, whatever happened. Jesus is stronger, the driver by the lake had said. He remembered the child again. The torchlight created a tight tunnel of light along the path. He fought against a constriction around his chest – a black serpent of the night.

When they arrived back he went straight to bed. He could hear Felice and Stanley talking in the living room. Stanley said, 'Zachye could come back any time.'

The door muffled Felice's words but not their soothing tone. He imagined her putting her arm around Stanley, her skin warm on his.

FIVE

On glass slides in the hospital laboratory smeared blood teemed with parasites, mycobacteria clogged slices of lung, cysts pocked sections of liver, faecal blobs moved – alive with worms. But the air was sharp and clean, sanitised with methylated spirits. At the other end of the microscope the eye of the lab officer flicked about: a hunter, out early, looking for microscopic raiders. Outside the lab a concrete path (protected from the mountain's anabatic downpours by a roof of iron sheeting) ran between the single-storey brick wards that stepped in an orderly line down the hillside. Smaller buildings edged the compound: blackened kitchens, smoking from every vent, where relatives prepared food for the patients; a washhouse behind lines of tired white linen, spewing rivulets of soapy-grey water into a soak-away drain; and, at the far end of the hospital, the latrines, where the cyclical life of enteropathic parasites finally came to an end in the deep pits beneath.

A woman sat on the grassy slopes below the path, cradling her sickly child in the puffs of her gaudy wrappings, while an elderly man leant on his stick, still as an old stork watching fish. The valley mists lay unwarmed but already mothers queued beside the outpatient and dispensary block to have their babies weighed in a sling suspended from a scale under the eaves. Nursing staff, in purple dresses and white aprons, crossed the compound hurrying to their duties, having received a short inspirational message from Stanley at morning prayers.

In the cottage in the banana grove a short walk from the hospital a black cockerel crowed in Michael's dreams. It continued crowing as he startled awake – fearful of its bronzed plumage. He heard hens clucking contentedly outside his window. A fresh light percolated through the mosquito netting, the suffusion bringing with it the dusty taste of the net and a faint aroma of baking bread. He stretched himself out from an embryonic position and let himself float on the soft mattress, coddled and relieved, the net like a veil over a cradle. The prospect of seeing Felice again delighted him. He made a half-hearted effort to suppress impinging thoughts of adultery. Then he surfaced to full wakefulness and curbed his fantasising, reminding himself that he was at risk of breaking trust with his hosts.

When he passed through the house on his way out to the shower he saw that his breakfast was on the table. He lifted the fly-net to find a boiled egg (brown as a cappuccino), fresh bread, a rich yellow cube of butter and a sliced pawpaw, its jellied black seeds slipping down its juicy surfaces. Stanley and Felice had already gone to work. The maid was in the sunny kitchen, singing to herself while she wiped the draining board of ants with the side of her hand.

Michael found a note from Stanley on the table to say that if he was interested in seeing the hospital he was welcome to join him on a ward round at 8.30am. Felice would be spending the morning in the dispensary but would be returning home at midday. If he preferred to go for a walk, then the hill behind the hospital afforded spectacular views of the Rwenzori Mountains – on the rare occasions that they revealed themselves.

Michael saw Stanley striding towards the topmost ward and caught up with him.

'Ah, good. You've come to see the bush hospital.'

Stanley looked like a man with a purpose, showing none of the anxiety of the previous evening. He wore a spotlessly white medical jacket with a pen and a mini-torch in the top pocket and a thick-piped black stethoscope in the side pocket.

They entered the ward. Michael took some time to adapt from the glare outside, seeing first the whites of the patients' eyes as they looked towards him. The beds resolved themselves next, packed tightly down each side of the ward, all occupied. Then he saw the patients on the floor lying on thin mattresses between the beds.

'The very sick ones are on the beds. The rest sleep on the floor but spend most of the day outside,' Stanley said as he flicked through the treatment charts on a table by the door. 'We don't turn anyone away.'

Stanley made his way down the ward with Michael close beside him. Michael noticed that a deep reverential hush had fallen, as if Stanley was the chief's medicine man and the patients waited for his augury. Michael remembered seeing a diviner at work when he was a child. He could picture Stanley in the full regalia: a tall leather hat, a long robe, bead anklets. Even in his white jacket, Stanley might be considered as inscrutable as any diviner of old: hearkening for malignant air in the lungs with his ear pipes, pulpating for lumpen infestations in the abdomen, sniffing for mephitic fetors, spying the mouth for violaceous eruptions, prying the genitalia for pestilent discharges. Michael wondered if he, the white man, added a priestly authentication to Stanley's rituals. He and Stanley discussed the cases in a deeply sacerdotal language: trypanosomiasis, Wasserman reaction, transvesical prostatectomy, schistosomal, seroconversion, necrotizing gingivitis.

'Maybe you can help me with this young man,' Stanley said, stopping at the foot of a bed at the end of the ward where a gaunt patient, eyes large in their fleshless sockets, gave Michael a grimace for a smile, wincing at the movement – perhaps hurting his dry lips.

'He's wasting away, as you can see, and has chronic diarrhoea. Whatever I do he gets worse. We call it Slim.' Stanley turned away from the patient. 'These patients with Slim all die. I saw my first case two years ago but now we have many.'

'Are other parts of the country affected?' Michael asked.

'Oh yes. In Rakai district near the border with Tanzania they're burying many young people – male and female.'

'An infective agent?'

'I think it's sexually transmitted but some theorise it has a mosquito vector. Many people here believe it's the curse of witches – that's why the hospital treatment can't cure it.'

'Well, I hope it doesn't become a full blown epidemic.'

'I fear it's already become that,' Stanley said. He described the investigations, the futile treatments, 'and we've prayed'.

Michael said, 'I'm damned if I know what to suggest – unless he has something I can cut out. What are you going to do next?'

They stood studying the patient for a moment and then Stanley said, 'I'll give him leave to take his last journey. His relatives will take him away on the bus this week. They wish to bury him at home. It's cheaper for the relatives to transport him as a passenger than as a corpse.'

The man lay there expectant, his large eyes adding poignancy to his plight. Michael felt unusually impotent: in his surgical practice he was able to pass on the hopeless cases to the radiotherapist or oncologist. He wanted to look away; to move on quickly; to give attention to the curable. He was a lemon in these situations; he had nothing to offer. Stanley stood quiet. He must be praying or something, thought Michael. Still Stanley stood there. The patient turned his gaze on Michael. Perhaps the white man had access to special technologies.

'His name is Tomasi,' Stanley said, quietly.

Michael's heart thumped. Tomasi? Surely not. But no, he was younger than Tomasi would be now. If he was still alive. Perhaps he was dead with the rest. A sucking emptiness opened up inside him; a void. He found himself blurting out, 'But you're a mission hospital. Don't you try to convert him before he leaves? Save his soul, even though you can't save his body?' He was surprised at his outburst, and tried to wink at the nurse to show he was only teasing them, but she was not looking at him.

Stanley turned slowly towards him with a puzzled look, as if having difficulty understanding the question. Eventually he said, 'This man knows why we've tried to help him. Ruhanga will do the rest.'

Michael looked on stiffly as Stanley sat down on the man's bed and spoke to him in his language, quietly and without haste, all the while looking into the patient's hungry eyes. The man lay still as he listened to Stanley, but Michael saw in his face the moment of shock, the recoil of fear, the collapse into resignation and then, as Stanley stood up, the giving out of something else; it could have been gratitude.

'This is the men's tuberculosis ward,' Stanley said as they stepped into the next building, Michael having to move fast to keep up with

Stanley's brisk pace. 'In this ward you've stepped back into your country in your grandfather's generation. These men have to rest here for six months so we can make sure they take their medication each day and complete the course of treatment. Many live over a day's walk away and we don't have the field workers to visit their homes. The nurses watch each man swallow his tablets: in the markets tablets are sold individually.'

'It's magical stuff then,' Michael said.

'Yes, but if a man under our care dies then the traditional healers say it's proof that the medicine doesn't work or that it's not enough on its own.'

'It must work the other way around – when the traditional healer is unable to save a life,' Michael said.

Stanley shook his head emphatically. 'No. The medicine man is only a medium. He'll not claim he can cure; he claims only to uncover the offended ghost and tell what might appease it. He doesn't say he's more powerful than the ghost.'

Stanley ran his hand down the tubes of the stethoscope that hung from his neck, thinking, and then said, 'But Western medicine – scientific medicine – we claim its power over the unseen. When it fails the people conclude that a divination is needed as well. They like to get help from both worlds. My mother used to say, "We're a shrewd people." A small smile broke through. 'I think you also have alternative medicines.'

Michael smiled back. He was warming to Stanley.

'Have you ever sought a divination?' he asked, and then wondered if Stanley would welcome such a question in front of his nurse.

Stanley seemed unabashed. 'When I was young ... it was sought for me.' He pulled a shiny, green and yellow capsule out of his pocket and held it out in the palm of his hand. 'When I first saw modern medicines I was fascinated. They looked like exotic beads from a far away place; like the beads that my ancestors bought from the Arab traders. The traditional healer's medicines were ordinary in comparison: just familiar herbs wrapped in skin and bark – everyday objects. But these new medicines in their silver foils and glass bottles with strange colours were a wonder – irresistible to me because I'd lived only with nature until then. I understand that it's the opposite in your country: people seek the natural.' Stanley pointed to an X-ray on the nurses' desk. 'That's another wonder: to see with such a penetrating eye.'

'I didn't expect you to have an X-ray machine,' Michael said.

'It's very old. I try to avoid using it because I fear it shoots radiation in all directions. I've made a long lead so that I can fire it from outside the building.'

Michael smiled, imagining Stanley with a cable stretching to the other side of the mountains to avoid the radiation flash.

A man coughed down the ward. Stanley jolted as if suddenly aware that he'd been wasting time, and moved quickly to the first bed. He greeted each man briefly, passed a few words, checked the charts, asked questions of the nurse, listened to the men's chests and wrote on the treatment cards.

Michael found himself introduced to many medical antiquities as they passed on through the wards: a tetanus victim restrained by tight blankets, the crater-like ulcers of yaws, a case of rabies behind screens, a bubo of syphilis.

'In Africa man has lived for the greatest number of generations, so the microbes have had plenty of time to learn how best to exploit us,' Stanley said. 'They've been successful: when my father was a child only fifty per cent of children reached five years.'

When they stepped out of the lowermost ward into the sunshine, Michael saw that a multitude had surrounded the outpatient building and were hustling for a position by the door. A male dresser was trying to bring order, shouting out names, pushing back some while he pulled forward others. Babies cried. On the periphery of the crowd men lay patiently on bamboo and grass-mat stretchers, their bearers resting after long treks. The crowd saw Stanley and stopped jostling in order to follow his progress as he made his way to the door at the back of the clinic.

'There must be three hundred people here,' Michael said. 'You're not going to see them all, are you?'

Stanley did not answer straight away. Michael saw that he had lost his purposeful expression and was looking about him, as if looking for someone. He collected himself soon enough. 'I have assistants but end up seeing about half. Come in and observe if you wish.'

They had almost reached the door when a woman rushed towards them and knelt down in front of Stanley, holding out her baby, begging him to reach out and touch it. Stanley sidestepped around her to reach the door.

'They venerate you,' Michael said.

Stanley grunted. 'It's an embarrassment to me.'

Inside the clinic Stanley went to wash his hands in an annexe. As Michael hovered behind him Stanley suddenly turned and said, 'I think it would be polite to warn you, if Zachye comes back I may not be able to go to the National Park – but you could go with Felice.'

'Just with Felice?' A sweat broke out. Lead Us Not Into Temptation.

'Perhaps we could persuade the Magaras,' Stanley said, and Michael thought that he almost smiled again.

Michael said, 'I do understand the situation – about Zachye.'

It must have sounded as if he did not understand, because Stanley said, 'You see, I don't know Zachye's state of mind.'

'His state of mind?'

Stanley appeared to struggle with how much more to say. 'By that I mean that Zachye is unpredictable.'

'In what sort of way?' Michael found himself intrigued by Stanley's errant brother.

Stanley took off his glasses and studied them. His wet hands dripped onto the frames. Now that his eyes were not warped and diminished behind thick lenses, Michael thought that he looked warm and personable, although weary.

'When I married Felice, Zachye wanted me dead.' Stanley turned away quickly as if the remembrance alarmed him, and went to dry his hands.

Michael re-examined what he had thought about the prodigal Zachye. After listening to the conversation at the Magaras he had assumed Stanley and Felice were anxious to bring Zachye back into the family circle; that Zachye needed to eat humble pie (although he doubted that this was exactly how the Katuras would have put it). It had not occurred to him that Zachye might represent a threat, that Stanley's brother might be criminally insane. The statistic about most murders occurring within the family came to mind. He said, 'Do you think you're in danger?'

'I don't worry for myself,' Stanley said. He looked towards the full waiting room. 'From what I've said you may believe that Zachye's not a good man, but when he was young he looked after me, protected me. He's my brother.' He put his hand to the stethoscope that hung from his neck and squeezed the tubing. 'Michael, please forget this, it's just a … difficulty for me, to think that I might see him again – of course, I want to, I need to, but … how he will react … his intentions.' He replaced his glasses and looked like a brainy scientist again. 'Enough. Let's see a few patients.'

Michael stood in the corner of the clinic as a nurse brought each patient in turn to Stanley – speaking in English to present the complaint to Stanley, who then questioned each patient in their native tongue. This man cannot see well … this woman has head pains … this baby has diarrhoea … this man has a cough … this boy has a swelling. The common language of symptoms gave little away, for when Stanley exposed the offending parts Michael was reminded of the grosser pictures in old medical textbooks – ulcers the size of side plates, swellings to fill a bowl, spleens like a rising moon, elephantine growths on the limbs.

Stanley doggedly worked through, writing prescriptions for the dispensary, instructing some patients to be taken to a ward, sending others to the health education nurse. At midday he insisted Michael go and get lunch. He would be finished in outpatients at two and then had a tooth to pull, an abscess to drain and a fracture to set, but he refused Michael's offer of help, saying Michael must have his holiday.

When Michael returned to the house he found to his delight that Felice was alone. She welcomed him with a courteous inclination of her head and informed him that there was a bowl of water in his room to wash his hands.

She would be pleased if he would join her for lunch. She had an air of formality about her: a correctness of speech and deportment, a playing of the genteel host to an honoured guest, as if the bonhomie of the previous day – the easy laughter, the light teasing – had been unseemly; as if yesterday she had forgotten herself, or had got a bit drunk, and now she wanted to show that to be an aberration. Perhaps Stanley had admonished her and told her not to be so familiar. She was quiet as she folded a linen napkin, placed it with care next to his plate, and then stepped back through the door to the kitchen, the smooth curve of her calf catching his eye.

Michael took his seat, and said, 'Your husband's devoted to his work. He's got a huge workload.'

She replied from the kitchen. 'It's always been his ambition to do as he does now, although he might have become a diviner if he'd been born in a previous generation. When we visit his home village we go and pay respect to the old diviner. Stanley gives him some financial support: return of a favour given to him as a child.'

She brought through a pan of sweet-smelling chicken stew and placed it on a grass tablemat. Hot droplets of oil bubbled up, coalescing on the surface. Michael's salivary glands contracted painfully.

'Africa's a better place because of people like my husband. But there are few like him; most of his colleagues from medical school are working in Britain or America, or have a private practice in the capital.'

'I shouldn't be too harsh on his colleagues. You have to be extraordinary to do what Stanley does,' Michael said, raising his voice to reach Felice as she returned to the kitchen.

She came back with warm bread from the oven on a wooden board.

'We all go where our heart leads,' she said, and then added, with what he thought was not a question directed at him, but the voicing of a riddle that had puzzled her for a long time, 'but what determines our heart?' She sat down but then got up again immediately saying, 'Oh, how forgetful of me! I've not brought cutlery.'

'You were going to eat African style?' he asked.

'Yes, but when the Romans come to the peasant village it's the peasants that must adapt,' she said.

'Please, that makes me sound like a colonial governor. Relax with me, Felice. Let's do as you normally do; after all, my hospital canteen doesn't get out chopsticks if we've a visit by Far Eastern medics. I want to fit in with what you do.'

He reached up to guide her back onto her chair. Felice smiled back, sat down less stiffly than before and exhaled a soft sigh of release. She gave him a wily look and said, 'If you wish to fit in, then you must know that in my house we pray before we eat.'

'Be yourself. Do whatever you normally do. I insist.'

Felice bowed her head. Michael waited, but as the silence extended he glanced at her. Her eyes were closed, her face serene, completely unselfconscious. She spoke at last, 'My Father, thank you for this food, for your gifts and for my guest, Michael. Amen.'

Brief and simple, but in the short silence that followed he felt that something disagreeable had happened. Felice had not prayed as if observing a ritual, but as if God himself was there at the table, an unseen guest whom she could turn to at any time and address intimately. He had heard it all before. It disturbed him, the intelligent Felice believing it. He remembered the goddamned child, the trusting child, but then saw an image in silhouette of his mother, head bowed like Felice, the same turning to something beyond the troubles of the day, receiving sustenance beyond the physical. It was either ludicrous or the most necessary and profound achievement of the human heart. A choking feeling welled. But Felice was inviting him to eat. Her voice made him put aside his objection and his disquieting vision: it bubbled with happiness to the point of childlike excitement. It came to him that her spirituality, naïve as it might be, was a vital ingredient of her charm – made her independent of, not beholden to, whims of want and need.

She took the fly-net off the water jug and filled his cup. 'Water from the Fountains of the Nile.'

'Gosh,' he said, swilling the water as if tasting wine.

'Yes – from the melting snows of the mountain.'

Felice broke the bread and gave him half. They dipped pieces in the stew, Michael enjoying the sensuousness of eating with his fingers from the same bowl as Felice. Their arms crossed back and forth. Only a week before he had been in the clattering canteen of his big-city hospital, and now he was here in a fairy tale: a tiny house in a banana grove, beneath the Mountains of the Moon, in the Lands of Zinj, drinking the crystal-clear water of legendary fountains, sitting opposite a princess. He smiled to himself as he remembered his companion of the previous week: an ill-humoured, hirsute registrar who wanted to be an orthopaedic surgeon but was having to learn haemorrhoidectomies and other unclean bowel operations in order to pass his Surgical Fellowship exams.

'The food is good?' she asked, stopping her hand in mid-motion and smiling eagerly.

'Excellent, and such delightful company as well.'

She laughed. 'You're very polite.'

He looked at her. 'You don't know me well, Felice. I'm not given to false sentiment.'

She raised her eyes to him and, with a shy smile he had not seen before, whispered, 'Thank you. It's really nice to be appreciated.'

Her eyes drew him in; he felt a little flustered. He said, 'Well, I'm sure Stanley appreciates you.'

She looked away. 'Stanley? Oh, yes, I'm sure he does.' She took a sip of water. 'But he has to work so hard. I don't think I help him as much as I should.'

'Well, you've got your own work to do in the dispensary.'

She did not seem to hear him, saying, 'He hopes to serve here for the rest of his life. It's his calling.'

'And what about you?'

She swallowed and took some bread. 'Have some more, Michael.'

'Er, thanks.'

'I can't complain,' she said, with what Michael thought a brave smile. 'Please don't think I'm ungrateful; we have a good community here.'

'It is a bit isolated.'

She nodded slowly. 'OK, I'll admit it; it's not what I expected. You see, there are not that many people who I can really relax with here: there's Beatrice – she works in the dispensary with me – that's about it.

And Stanley's always working. I love having lots of friends, going out, maybe even the opportunity to see a bit of the world. What's Britain like? Is everyone happy there?'

Michael chuckled. 'Delirious!' Then, more seriously, 'No … if anything, I suppose people carry their own happiness with them.'

She stiffened her back a little and spoke with finality. 'It's not to be. I made my decision when I married Stanley.'

Michael felt uncomfortable. 'Any news of Stanley's brother?'

'Oh, I asked everyone I saw in the dispensary this morning if they'd seen a man looking for Dr Katura.'

'Any luck?'

She shrugged. 'They wondered why I asked: everyone's always looking for Dr Katura.'

'This Zachye, he and Stanley were close?'

'Once, yes, very.' She said no more.

'I'm sorry – if you'd rather not discuss him.'

She pursed her lips for a moment. 'Maybe it's OK. Stanley doesn't like to talk about him, but he's not here, so I don't think he'll mind.'

'It sounds like the two brothers could hardly be more different.'

Felice laughed, a little caustically. 'I'm not so sure. They're both headstrong. Both ambitious – it's just Zachye wasn't academic, so with the good jobs going to those with the certificates he joined the army.'

'Uh-huh.'

'And then Idi Amin came to power. Zachye stayed in the army.' She cast him a look, as if he would know what that meant.

'He's had no contact with the family all these years?'

She shook her head. 'After Amin was overthrown some soldiers deserted and resorted to banditry. Maybe Zachye also. There wasn't much else for them. Stanley says that a herder saw him about five years ago watching the cattle from a long way off. That's as close as he ever came back.'

She wiggled her fingers in the washing bowl, dried them with a napkin and touched the side of her glass with the tips of her fingers. Michael found himself feeling their light stroke.

'I really can't understand him. Family is everything to us, Michael. Everything. To have cut himself off like this, cut himself off from his family, from the roots of his life.'

Her words jolted him. 'Cut himself off?'

She looked at him.

He said quickly, 'Very tragic.'

Felice lifted her glass and sipped, and then dabbed her lips with her napkin. He put aside the previous disturbing moment – the cutting off comment. She leant back in her chair and took a deep breath. He wished she wouldn't make movements that drew his attention to her figure.

She said, 'It's so hard for Stanley, because he loved him – his older brother. I think Stanley would forgive him anything. He's always hoped to meet him again; to bring him back to us.' She bent forward again and slipped her fingers down her glass.

The door opened a little and a young woman peeped through the crack. 'Praise be! You're in.'

'Come in,' Felice said, springing up. 'How's it going?'

The women embraced. 'Too well – I'm having my afternoon off. Ha, you've company.'

'Sit down. Eat with us,' Felice said, 'Michael, this is Beatrice.'

Beatrice looked delighted to meet him, and said, 'The famous surgeon from England! Nothing as big as this has happened to us since a certain explorer, Henry Morton Stanley, came around the corner of the mountain about a hundred years ago.' She had a direct, sunny face and wore a well-cut bright-yellow blouse. Michael could see why Felice got on well with her.

A few seconds later another figure appeared in the doorway. Mrs Magara came through with a folding chair in her hand.

'Good! I'm in time for some food,' she said, 'I've brought a camp chair and my own cushion with me. These are the necessities until Stanley moves into Harley Street. Fine, very fine.'

They all laughed.

The women tried to include Michael in their conversation, Felice in particular, but he soon felt as he had on previous occasions when he had been the only man in a female group: an impediment to the desired directions of the conversation; a stone in their shoes. He excused himself, saying he would take a walk up the hill, and collected his binoculars and bird book. Felice sent him on his way with a couple of bananas as a snack. He felt a little mothered.

He climbed a well-trodden path through banana groves to a small ridge above the hospital. A group of children watched him pass.

'*Muzungu*!' they called, giggling, hiding behind each other.

He smelt drying millet and woodsmoke, and raised the lid on his memories a crack: a grassy knoll, diamond seeking, Mr Patel's *duka*. He smiled at his guileless hopes. Nights in the dorm, voices of children, voices of the aunties, songs sung with the gusto of angels, the smell of approaching rain, the taste of fire-roasted maize cobs. Happy days before ejection from an Eden; before being condemned, like all men, to want to go back but finding the way barred by the terrible truth: its impossibility, its absurdity, in the face of hard facts. He saw a tree on the ridge ahead and it struck him forcefully that if only circumstances were different, if he and Felice were together, he would be in his own Eden. Another impossibility.

When he got to the tree he inspected its trunk for ants (some instincts from his childhood days remained), and then leant against it, scanning the view with his binoculars. Perhaps I should try and locate Stanley's lost brother, he thought, smiling to himself. He's out there somewhere. A rogue, hiding in paradise. A description would have been useful although he imagined that Zachye looked like an army oaf. He picked out figures walking on a road: bright-red skirts and headscarves against the dark-green vegetation, straight necked against the loads they carried on their heads. Tracking over the iron roofs of the hospital he thought of Stanley toiling away. Raising the lenses he followed the forest canopy – shadowy, deep – up the slopes of the foothills until it vanished in the cloud wrapping the mountains. He had yet to see the snow-capped peaks. Stanley had said that Rwenzori meant Cloud King. It was little wonder that the first European explorers passed close by and failed to find them, or their coy fountains.

He let his binoculars down and gazed at the great bulk of cloud; the land rising into that silence – blotted out. Lwesala felt like a place on an edge. He had experienced the same sensation in otherwise prosaic seaside towns in Britain: an abyssal wilderness just a short walk away, a pervading sense of the close presence of something untamed – a frontier. He felt a little vertiginous, as if he was in danger of being spirited across.

Back at the house Mrs Magara and Beatrice were gone but Felice was saying goodbye to a family with several small children. He waited as she kissed the children. For a moment she reminded him of his mother seeing off the girls from her Sunday school class. It brought a sudden sense of intense longing. When the children had left he expressed his surprise at all the visitors.

'Oh, but this is our life,' she said, 'we like to be together. The more we are the happier we are. But is it true that in Britain you must have an invitation before coming to a meal – that a time is specified?'

'Well, yes, I think it would be.'

Felice looked astonished. 'To us that would be impolite; as if the guests were unwelcome at other times.'

He shrugged. 'We have schedules; the price we pay for an industrialised society. The price we pay to have shiny goods, electric lights, food mixers.'

She considered what he had said. 'I think I would like to have both. Perhaps it's not possible.'

One of the children ran back and gave Felice a newly laid egg she had found near the path. Felice thanked her, waved her goodbye and then started clearing the table.

'You must be looking forward to having your own children,' Michael said, crossing to his room to put away his binoculars.

He heard her say quietly, 'We cannot.'

He stopped in the doorway – mortified. He remembered the injured woman on the road from the airport; this was a society where childbearing defined being a woman. What had Felice said about the importance she attached to family? He turned towards her. She had stopped clearing the table and stood with her back to him, her head bowed.

'I'm sorry. A very intrusive question. I should've realised.'

She took a deep breath. 'It's OK.' She took another deep breath. 'Sorry … seeing the children … and then your words. Stanley had mumps … we had tests … it's unlikely. Maybe with treatment; but it's expensive. I don't know.'

He fiddled with the focus ring on his binoculars, unable to think of any comforting comment. Felice started tidying up again – with vigour. She marched into the kitchen with her load and said, 'It's not so bad. We share children in our community. That's ample comfort.'

Michael was still standing, feeling stupid, in his bedroom doorway as she came back and gathered the glasses.

'Mrs Magara thinks it's because I'm too thin. She says there's nothing to feed a growing baby.' She cast him a forced smile and then turned away. 'Stanley's accepted it, so that's good.' Her voice cracked on the last word.

She left the glasses on the table, hurried into the kitchen and stayed there.

SIX

About an hour out from the hospital, on a stretch of road bordered by tall grasses, a wooden boom blocked their way. They stopped and Stanley turned off the engine.

'What's this?' Michael asked.

'It's the entrance to the National Park,' Stanley said.

They waited; Stanley and Felice seemed content to sit until something happened. Stanley looked worn out: after getting up in the night to attend a patient, he had been at the hospital until late morning. Michael moved forward in his seat to ventilate his back from the heat. Still Stanley and Felice remained silent and stilled. To Michael they appeared to have settled into a state of suspension; entered it together; he felt their unity. Lonely, he could wait no more and said with a jocular air, 'Is the barrier automatic?'

'Maybe we've not been heard,' Stanley said, starting at Michael's voice. He blipped the horn. The grasses to the right parted and an elderly man in a tatty, khaki uniform and floppy hat came out.

Long greetings ensued, followed by a chat in the local language which looked likely to go on for hours. Michael heard his name and the warden said, 'Ah,' and nodded his head towards Michael. Michael noticed that the top of the man's hat was missing; just a frayed rim where the top had been fixed in long bygone years.

Losing the gist of the conversation, Michael asked Felice, 'What's he saying?'

'He says that you're the first tourist to pass his gate in one year. He says that we've made him very happy by coming to the park. He's hoping that many tourists will follow. He remembers Queen Elizabeth when she visited Uganda in 1954. He hopes that one day she'll return so that he can open the barrier for her.' Felice suppressed a smile before she translated again. 'He'd like a job as a keeper of the entrance boom to Windsor Safari Park.'

Stanley seemed to reassure the warden of Michael's endeavours on the latter point and then launched into a pressing enquiry. The warden frowned – Michael thought he conveyed uncertainty in his reply.

'Stanley has asked about poachers and bandits but it's all right; the warden says they've had no serious incidents in a long time.'

'But?' Michael asked.

Felice's attention had been drawn to the warden. He had became animated again and pointed towards some location over and beyond the grasses ahead and started snorting, then danced around in a circle, holding both hands up in front of his face. When Michael leant forward, grinning at the warden's antics, the warden minced into the grasses and came out in a crouch, at speed.

Stanley intervened, thanking him, but the warden was not to be interrupted and pawed the ground with his right leg whilst making hissing sounds. Flailing arms followed, indicating some sort of pandemonium. The warden then snapped back his head and rolled his eyes.

Felice translated again, barely containing her amusement. 'Stanley asked where we can find lions. The warden says there was a kill yesterday, quite nearby, and he's given you a demonstration of how it happened.'

Stanley thanked the warden again and the man relaxed, exhausted from his exertions. He beamed at Michael, who clapped his hands a couple of times to show his appreciation. The warden disappeared into the high grass again. Michael expected him to reappear in an encore, perhaps from another angle and on all fours, but he came back shortly in a formal mood, with an enormous cashbook.

The warden passed the book through to Michael, opening it as he did so. A large, pressed spider fell onto Michael's lap. 'Ah, a fossilised spider from the Miocene epoch. It must be more than a year since anyone filled this in,' he said, gingerly lifting the spider by a leg but losing it on the floor when the limb broke. At the top of the page 'Year of 1983' had been written in faint charcoal and the columns renamed: 'date', 'vehicle registration', 'name', 'nationality' and 'passport number'.

The warden examined Michael's entry carefully and was satisfied. He spoke to Stanley again.

'He would be happy if you could give him a pen or a pencil,' Stanley said.

Michael felt in his camera bag and passed a ballpoint to the warden.

'He says he's now ready for all the tourists,' Stanley said.

As they drove away, to a salute from the warden standing to attention by the lifted boom, Michael remarked, 'He was jolly!'

Stanley signalled his agreement with a tightening of his cheek muscles, but Felice said, 'He's a faithful man; a good man. He didn't leave his post through all the years of terror. Many good people didn't leave their posts at that time. They ...' She stopped and swallowed. Michael waited for her to collect herself. 'Sometimes he hid in the grasses while the soldiers came through with their machine guns to kill the elephants. In an African country, when soldiers start shooting the elephants you know it's time to hide.'

'Are there any elephants left?' Michael asked.

'A few. Some hid in the forests, but they're still afraid.'

'Did you have to flee as well?'

'We stayed low and prayed. We were spared. God took some others; others we knew well,' she said, speaking louder, as if to prevent emotion cracking her voice.

'You mean the soldiers killed them. You can't bring God in,' Michael said, and then wished he hadn't. Why couldn't he resist scoring points on anything religious?

She paused and then replied, 'What I said is what it means for us. Don't shoot hope, Michael. It will backfire on you one day. No one can live without hope.'

Michael wasn't sure about that. He felt that once upon a time he had relied rather too much on hope.

Stanley said something to Felice in their language. He seemed cross. Felice answered succinctly in what sounded like an acceptance of whatever he had said.

Then Stanley stopped the vehicle to let a dung beetle struggle across the road rolling its oversized load. 'One of my teachers was shot dead during those years,' he said. 'It's always the elephants and the teachers.'

As the high grasses thinned out a wide vista opened up: a gently undulating plain of richly hued savannah, dotted with the delicate forms of acacias looking like ballet dancers in pirouette. The sky above had altered, as if they had burst through into a vast, glassy dome; entered a bubble from a primordial past. A sliver of brightness, miles away, marked the location of a lake. Behind the thin gleam were the suggested forms of hills and mountains. Michael considered it a uniquely African landscape and it made him want to take wing and soar; to gaze and gaze, knowing that he would never be satiated. He thought the sight might represent an archetype of landscape perfection, lighting up some long-dormant neural network in the visual cortex; a plexus laid down many millennia ago when humanity was young and looked out for the first time with a nascent appreciation of beauty, and considered this landscape sublime.

But his guidebook said that there was a 'sting in this vale of paradise'. The human population had long been 'forced out by the tsetse, a fly that carries trypanosoma brucei'. A parasite with the power of hypnosis, thought Michael, the power to cause men to succumb to the fatal slumber of sleeping sickness. A Gaian guardian against humanity.

They drew up beside an intensely green pool sunk in the plain. Stanley said, quite animatedly, 'Let's walk on the stepping stones to the other side.' He paused. 'But look again – the stepping stones are hippos!'

A hippo raised itself with a sucking sound, extracting itself from the jelly-like pond. It yawned, jaws infinitely expansive, displaying the cavern of its peach-coloured mouth before sinking back again with a contented grunt. Birds stepped precisely amongst the water hyacinths around the edge of the pool: egrets, white as lilac; shimmering ibises; jet black crakes; jacanas (handsome in their tightly fitting chestnut waistcoats). A small flock of powder-blue cordon bleus flitted on the bank, dipping their rose-thorn-like beaks into the water. In a stand of bulrushes canary-yellow weaverbirds threaded their nests with grass braid.

'It's nature exuberant, unbound,' Michael breathed.

'There you are – we've brought you to the *real* Africa,' Felice said. 'Not that we Africans get to see much of it ourselves. You have to have spare cash to come here.'

Nearby they found the site of the lion kill that the warden had enacted, but the remains had been left to squabbling vultures and a hopeful jackal.

'That's a jackal, Stanley; not a hyena,' Felice said. Michael saw Stanley glance at Felice with a half smile. Some private joke.

Large trees marked the location of the rest camp: six thatched rondavels, two grass shower enclosures, a lone flagstaff with no halyard, a simple outdoor barbecue grill made of stone. They parked by a sign which read 'All visitors must report here. By order', their tyres pressing crisp lines in the pristine dust.

A young man in a warden's outfit, well ironed – particularly along the crease of his shorts, the epaulets at his shoulders and the flaps of his shirt pockets – stood gawping at them in the doorway of the camp office. He appeared frozen to the spot. Stanley got out to greet him. The slam of the vehicle door closing activated the warden as if it had provided proof that he was not seeing an apparition. He ran forward with arms outstretched to embrace Stanley, but then gripped Stanley's proffered arm, bending at his waist as if giving supplication to a long-awaited rescuer.

'Thank the Almighty God, I'm saved!' the warden cried.

Michael looked around a little nervously for whatever they were saving the warden from.

'What's happened?' Stanley asked.

'That's the problem. Nothing's happened. I wish for happenings. Every day I get up, wash in the shower, iron my uniform, put on my uniform, make sure no animal or insect has entered the guest cottages and then – nothing. I sit in my uniform. I walk up and down a little in my uniform. No one comes. The animals graze. The insects buzz. The sun gets hot. The same; every day.'

Michael felt some sympathy. 'You're as isolated as a man in a lighthouse out here.'

The warden turned to Michael, transferring his hold onto him. 'Ah, I've seen pictures of lighthouses! I'm the lighthouse keeper. This empty place,' he swung his arm out to encompass the wavy plain, 'is the sea.'

'Have you no transport?' Stanley asked.

'I have that – over there.' The warden pointed with his chin at a dilapidated Land Rover with its bonnet in a thorn bush. 'There's not enough fuel, but even if I had enough I cannot leave, in case a tourist arrives when I'm gone. Then I would lose my job.' He frowned, contemplating his dilemma. 'I'm ready to lose my job but the tourist may die. Right here.' He bared his teeth at Michael to indicate the type of death a tourist might suffer. 'I was due to be relieved in February but my relief never came. Have you books? Don't leave without giving me books. I'm an educated man.'

They were interrupted by a piercing scream. Felice had been inspecting a cottage and now came hurrying towards them. 'Ooah, there's a snake! There's a long big snake!'

She went to Stanley as if seeking comfort, but he had turned to the warden who was saying, 'Ha, there are many snakes – this is a national park for snakes! Let me identify it. Just give me your description. I came top of the class for identification. The most dangerous is Dendroaspis jamesoni kaimosae, the black mamba. You'll need twelve ampoules of anti-venom for that one, but we've only two ampoules in the first aid.' He turned to Michael. 'It's disgraceful, sir. I've written this in my reports.'

Felice still looked shaken. Michael wanted to go and put an arm around her but Stanley was looking impatiently at the warden. 'Spare us your nature lesson. You've not been checking the cottages often enough. Your boredom has made you lazy. My wife is frightened.'

The warden looked mortified. 'Please, let me receive your forgiveness.'

Michael understood: it was not the African way to display wrath. Stanley must have been especially provoked.

'Come, please,' the warden said. 'We'll go to another cottage and see if it's free of snakes.' He indicated the rondavel next to his office.

'No, that's the best cottage,' Felice said, composed again, pointing back to the cottage she had run from. 'It has a good view for our guest. If you chase the snake away then we can go there.'

The warden's eyes widened. He held his hands together as if in prayer. 'The cottage over here is more suitable,' he pleaded.

'We'll stay where my wife prefers,' Stanley said, and started striding towards the cottage.

The warden hurried after him. 'Sir! It's dangerous.'

'Get a stick,' Stanley said.

The warden ran to his office and came back clasping a long barrelled gun with a cracked wooden butt. 'It has no bullets but the snake will be frightened.'

'Get a stick!'

The warden returned again with a wood pole, which Stanley seized. While Stanley strode forward the warden followed closely behind, making pleading expressions to Felice to stop her irritable husband. They arrived in time to see the snake gliding away, taking on an angular form as it slid down the steps of the cottage, its skin like a sequined cloak of tiny, dark, lacquered stones. Michael was stunned at its length: its head had long disappeared around the side of the cottage before the tail snatched off the porch.

'Now you're safe,' said the warden, his voice squeaky with relief.

'You will check the rooms before we go in,' Stanley ordered.

'There'll be nothing alive in there, sir, if the snake has been living there. You're safe to enter, please.'

Stanley turned on the warden again but Felice put her hand out towards the man. 'I think you're afraid. It's OK. What's caused you to lose your courage?'

'Madam, you've identified the problem! I'm fearful of the animals.'

Michael found himself chortling. 'A game warden who's terrified of animals? I'm going to dine out on this for years.'

They all turned to him as he shook with laughter. Felice giggled, and then they were all away, the warden baying like a rutting zebra, and

Stanley acknowledging such absurdity by nodding his head.

The warden lit fires for washing and cooking, and attended to them keenly, making amends for his previous failings. Night fell fast, and they sat around a fire under a glittering sky, roasting chicken and sweet potatoes. Stanley was quiet, looking out into the darkness. Michael guessed that he was wondering where his brother was now: out there somewhere. Cut off.

Felice was melancholy until they had eaten, but then said, with what came across as forced cheeriness, 'This reminds me of those days when our elders told stories around the fires in the kraal.' She looked up. 'What story do you want, Michael? I can tell you of beasts that swallowed whole villages, or of men who fell into the lands of the dead through holes in the ground, or of the girl who wanted the new white teeth. You choose.'

Michael looked at the girl with the wide white smile. 'The girl who wanted the new white teeth.'

She looked into the fire and recited her story. 'In the time of our ancestors, the young girls of a village made a journey together to ask our God, Ruhanga, for white teeth. But there was a girl of the village whose stepmother was cruel and kept her hard at work, never gave her enough to eat and dressed her in old tattered skins. She worked her so hard she could not go with her friends. But one night the girl slipped away on her own. She walked all night, and as the dawn was breaking she met Ruhanga himself, looking like a kind old chief.

'Ruhanga said to her, "Little maid, where are you going?"

'She answered, "I have been living with my stepmother and she wouldn't let me come with the other girls to ask you for new teeth, and so I have come myself."

'Ruhanga took pity on her and gave her not only new white teeth but the smoothest skin, oiled and scented, and clothed her with new clothes, brass armlets and anklets, and adorned her with beaded ornaments.

'Then, like a good father, Ruhanga saw her safely back to her village, but as he left he said, "Little maid, I command you to never smile or laugh again." This he said to test her obedience to him.

'Her stepmother accused her of stealing, or of selling the family cattle, in order to afford such finery, but the other villagers were impressed and soon a man of good standing wed her. But the girl never smiled or laughed.'

Stanley was no longer looking out into the dark but was listening to his wife. Michael thought he looked on her with pride; and so he should: his wife who forgave his stolid solemnity, his wife who forgave his infertility, his wife who was loyal and faithful.

'Soon a child was born and grew to be happy, although her mother never smiled. The stepmother now plotted to make her stepdaughter smile and made the child plead with her mother to smile at her. But she wouldn't smile, so the child grew sick with sorrow and died. The same thing happened with the second child. When the third child was born the woman went to the graves of her two older children in anguish, and cried out to Ruhanga, "I have never once disobeyed you; will you not save this little one?"

'Then Ruhanga appeared and said he had heard her cry. Because she had obeyed him, even to the death of her children, he called her dead children back from the grave. After their joyful reunion Ruhanga touched the woman and she was transformed into the beautiful woman she had been before her grief. He even gave her new white teeth again, and to her husband he gave many cattle. Ruhanga released her from her vow so that for ever more she smiled at her husband and her children; but now she was also filled with a very deep joy, which only those who had obeyed Ruhanga could know.'

Felice pushed a stick a little further into the fire. The cicadas played on a sustained note, while every now and then some beast or night-bird bleated or called.

'That's the story of the girl who wanted new white teeth.'

'Curious,' Michael said, 'it has elements of the stories of both Cinderella and Abraham. There must be universal fables.' A stick in the fire flared. 'But it's a very moral tale: blind obedience and you'll be blessed.'

Felice said quietly, 'Obedience is not always blind.'

He glanced at her but she was staring into the fire, her eyes shining in the firelight; wistful. Stanley had closed his eyes.

She said, 'What about you, Michael? What stories did you hear when you were a child?'

He moved himself back from the fire a little – it had become too hot. A log hissed violently, steaming superheated sap. 'Mainly fairy tales.'

'OK, tell me,' she said.

'I don't remember much. Religious ones.' He dismissed them with a wave of his hand.

'Surely they had meanings?'

'I can recite poems.'

'But didn't those stories mean anything to you?'

'What sort of meaning were you thinking of?'

She bent, picked up a stick and turned it in the flames. 'Oh, things like … that the sacrifices we make are …' Her voice faded.

'I can recite poems.'

'Poems?' She looked surprised and then intrigued. 'Oh, yes, I'd love that,' she said, and turned to Stanley, but he had dropped asleep, his chin on his chest, the firelight liquid in the rims of his glasses. She leant towards Michael and said in a whisper, as if they were plotting together, 'Carry on.'

It took Michael a few seconds to choose a poem, acutely aware that Felice was not some half-drunk party guest, eager to be astounded at his recall faculty, but that she would be listening for the words; would want to be moved. He was struck by the realisation that he had always avoided reflecting on what he recited, and wondered why. Perhaps it was because taking words too seriously had got him into trouble as a child.

He chose Keats.

'My heart aches, and a drowsy numbness pains
My sense, as though of hemlock I had drunk …'

Through eight verses he made no errors, his voice even and unaffected, and finished with,

'Was it a vision, or a waking dream?

Fled is that music – do I wake or sleep?'

The fire glowed contentedly.

'That's beautiful,' Felice said. 'Really beautiful.'

She let the stick she had been revolving catch light and said, 'You've brought back some memories. Zachye was as talented as you at reciting. He could remember all the Bahima songs. I once saw tears in his eyes when he recited a verse about a drought that starved the cattle. But I imagine he would despise those old ballads now.'

She glanced at Stanley but he was still fast asleep. 'I'd love to hear another poem.'

'Well, I don't know that many,' he lied. 'But I can tell you some medical jokes.'

'Oh, OK! That would be fun.'

He picked his best medical jokes – he could recall jokes as easily as poems – telling them with a dry inflection, rarely having to interpret for her. She laughed freely and leant towards him as they talked on. He saw the fire's last flames cast new wraiths of beauty about her face. He could not gaze at her long, lest he find himself reaching out to touch her. That night he found it easier than he had ever known to chat about little things.

'Michael, it's probably a silly question,' she said dreamily as the firelight ebbed, 'but you've not been to Uganda before, have you?'

'Why do you ask?'

'Oh, it's nothing … never mind.'

He couldn't think why Felice would know him from childhood. He felt an urge to tell her about it. It came to him that she was the right person; the only person likely to comprehend; that it would somehow reconnect him to something necessary to break the difficulty he had with his relationships, so that those he had wanted to love, like Naomi, would feel they could understand him; might stay with him. The moment passed.

Stanley slept on.

SEVEN

Michael slipped out of the cottage early the next morning with his binoculars and guidebook, being careful not to wake Stanley and Felice. He walked past the white ashes of the previous night's fire and found a broken termite mound, which he used as a vantage point. The sun had not yet risen above the horizon. In the short transition between night and day the scene was as peaceful as an English country park touched by a light morning mist. Nearby two female gazelles grazed, unaware of his presence, their tawny skin velvety over their delicate forms, their lips nuzzling the milky grasses. He imagined stroking them, running his fingers from their firm snouts back over their yielding flanks. A Bible verse came back to him from his junior school days when the class had to learn one verse a week and occasionally, as a treat, could each choose their own. When he had recited his chosen verse to his scripture teacher she had gone crimson and sent him away to learn another; but it was that first verse that had stayed with him: 'Your two breasts are like two fawns, like twin fawns of a gazelle that browse among the lilies.'

He saw the quivering of the gazelles' highly tuned muscles when the sun, a molten brilliance even at this early hour, burnt through the mist and lit the taut curves of their haunches. His guidebook said, 'If pursued by a predator for over two minutes the gazelle may fall dead, the vessels feeding its heart muscle rupturing, pressured beyond tolerance and broken down by a toxic build up of lactic acid. Fortunately for gazelles, a predator has usually given up well within this time frame.'

When he closed the book the gazelles startled and bounded effortlessly away. He sat down and enjoyed the quiet, feeling near to contentment. He allowed himself the remembrance of holidays as a child when he had visited similar places. It pleased him that he could now recall aspects of his childhood without it triggering pain.

He walked back to the cottage, hungry for breakfast having watched so many animals eating. The shower was running in the grass enclosure. Passing the open entrance he saw Felice, naked, beaded with water as if dewed by the dawn. She was reaching across to retrieve her towel from the small bench outside. He could not look away. She saw him as she straightened, the softness of her flexed form firming. When he met her eyes she lowered hers but made no attempt to hide her nakedness. He had the notion that she looked down not for shame, but accepting his gaze, relaxed and receiving – inviting his admiration. Or was it nonchalant disregard? An instant later he had walked on out of view. His step faltered. He wanted to turn back, but he heard a whistling and saw the game warden ahead of him preparing the fire.

Stanley was in fine form at breakfast, no longer tense and tired. 'We've given our problems to God in prayer,' he said. 'He'll worry about Zachye and we'll appreciate his creativity here in this wilderness. You see, Michael, God has his plans and we must rest in those.'

Michael ignored the sermon. Felice seemed distracted with other thoughts. He feared she was avoiding talking to him.

The warden had exceeded his job description again, insisting on cooking their maize meal porridge himself. 'Today I'll show you what I know. I'll take you to see the animals,' he said as he spooned out the runny porridge with a twirling motion, creating a sludgy spiral in their bowls. Michael smelt alcohol on his breath.

'Are you not going to be afraid?' Michael asked.

'In your vehicle, with such brave men, I'll not be afraid. And I'll bring my gun.'

'But you have no ammunition,' Michael said.

'We don't have to shoot to show them who's boss.'

'I don't think we should take a gun,' Felice said, frowning.

'Madam, it is regulations. It's UP56.7 1981. This superseded

UP56.6 1972 which itself was modified in 1974. UP stroke Master Appendix 5b is the …'

'That's all right,' interrupted Stanley. 'We understand you must follow the rule book.'

The game warden's class work made him an effective guide. From the safety of the vehicle there was no creature he could not name in English and Latin. He described their length of gestation, survival chances to their first birthday, their social behaviour and their mating habits – in unnecessary detail. He even ventured out of the vehicle onto the road to study some tracks, which he declared as belonging to a leopard, before returning rapidly to his seat and closing the door firmly.

'Why don't you take pictures?' asked Stanley to Michael, as they watched a fine male waterbuck.

'I haven't got anyone back home who's going to be interested in looking at them.' Naomi might have, he thought, with a pang of regret, but he would not have wanted the inevitable questioning from her that would have required him to mention Felice. Naomi had shown herself to be sensitive to any hint in his voice of admiration for other women, however innocent the aside.

Stanley said, 'I'm sorry to hear that. You must be too busy with your work. But I thought all Europeans took pictures to remind themselves of their experiences.'

'I've a good memory – for most things. The things I want to remember.' He had an urge to confide that which he had tried to forget, but this was not the time, and Felice was pointing excitedly to an ostrich walking along like an enormous Donald Duck in a frilly, oversized, black tutu.

'Michael, look! There's a large chicken. Be afraid!'

They were returning to the camp when Stanley said, 'There's smoke over there.'

The game warden leant forward and looked ahead, intently, as if identifying another animal, but said in a high pitched voice, the voice they had heard yesterday when Felice had disturbed the snake, 'It's a bush fire. It may have been started by poachers – or bandits.'

He fingered the barrel of his rifle.

'They're driving out the animals so they can shoot them. Go fast to the camp. They'll not come there.'

As they neared the top of a small rise in the road Michael could see ahead a shimmering heat haze in which ashen ghosts of grass and twig tumbled and twisted in the agonised air. The fire came into view: less a line of flames, more a zone of flarings of brilliant, amber light. Amber for danger. Dark-silhouetted against the burning, a group of ragged men walked unfalteringly down the road towards the vehicle. Their baseball cap peaks jutted out aggressively; their rifles gripped purposefully.

'No, no, bad, bad! Bandits!' the game warden said, in a strained whisper.

Stanley braked to a stop. Felice, sitting beside him, put a hand to her mouth. Michael moved instantly into that clear-headed decision-making state that he knew so well, although this time he was acutely aware that it was his own life that was at stake, not a patient's. Even as Stanley was slowing the vehicle Michael had seen that diplomacy was now the only strategy. He felt a movement against his leg and noticed that the game warden was no longer sitting next to him but had slipped into the footwell and huddled face down, legs folded tightly underneath him. What does he think he's doing? He's bound to be seen, thought Michael, his heart kicking at the implications of this display of cringing terror.

The bandits swung their rifles up as they approached. Three of them stopped a few metres in front of the vehicle, lining up like a firing squad. The fourth came round to Stanley's side. His movements were slow and careful. He said nothing, just inspected them, moving his barrel from person to person. Michael had the chilling sensation that they were being sized up by something insentient: an unblinking reptile with a snake-cold stare. Something without a soul.

Stanley said, 'Is there anything you want?'

The man scanned the vehicle again. He looked hard at Michael but then rested his eyes on Felice.

He spoke slowly and deliberately, 'I want that woman. Tell her to get out.'

'You'll have to kill me first,' Stanley said. 'But remember that God will judge you.'

The man turned his gun towards Stanley. Michael found himself unable to take his eyes off the hole at the end of the barrel; as if he could warn Stanley when the bullet appeared. Then he remembered Stanley's comment about the white man giving them some protection. He would play whatever card was available. He said urgently, 'Excuse me, mister. Do you know who I am? Before you harm us, you should know.'

The man turned the gun slowly towards Michael. 'Who?' he said, conveying contempt in one word. He had still not blinked.

'I'm Her Majesty's ambassador. These friends are taking me on a game drive. If you do us harm my government will not rest until you're found and brought to justice. But if you let us pass on our way you'll be safe.' The bandit blinked. 'I'll also give you money. Dollars and sterling.'

Michael stared unwaveringly at the man, trying to project himself as the embodied presence of a world power.

'Where's your escort, Mr Ambassador?' the man asked, with the beginning of a sneer.

'They're near, we were expected back before now, so soon they'll come looking for us. Take my money now before they arrive.'

Michael leant sideways and reached into his pocket for his wallet, trying to appear like a man who has acquiesced with reasonable grace to a less than perfect deal. His mouth dried as he realised its contents would confirm him as someone other than the ambassador. He hoped that the bandit would just take the wad of notes he was extracting.

The bandit kept his gun on Michael but turned to Stanley. 'Is he the British Ambassador?'

Stanley did not answer.

The bandit bared his teeth and turned the gun to poke the barrel into Stanley's shoulder. 'Is he the British Ambassador?'

Lie, Stanley, for pity's sake, lie, thought Michael. You can ask for forgiveness afterwards.

'No, he's not the British Ambassador, but he's a good man. He's trying to protect us.'

'Ha!' the bandit said in derision, and then Michael saw his face harden, his eyes narrowing as if a scaly slit was shuttering down. He was going to do what he was going to do.

Felice cried out, but she was not looking at the bandit; she was looking ahead at the men in the road.

'Zachye! There's Zachye!'

One of the three men had lowered his rifle and was staring back at Felice.

The bandit looked back at his companion, and then at Felice.

'You know him?'

'Yes, he's … our brother.'

The bandit shouted at Zachye.

Zachye nodded, still staring.

The fire had worked its way down the side of the road, jumping from bush to bush, the smouldering grass creating a dense smoke, the front of which now wisped around the men.

'He's my brother!' Stanley said excitedly. 'Let me speak to him.'

The bandit strode back to Zachye and shouted in his face. Zachye answered without expression, his eyes still on Felice. The leader hesitated for a moment, then spun around towards the vehicle and waved his arm to motion them forward.

'Go!' he shouted.

They drove forward as the bandits parted to let them pass, their rifles now held at ease. Stanley slowed when he got level with Zachye, leaning out to speak to him, but the bandit leader screamed again, 'Go!'

They picked up speed towards the smoke across the road. Another five seconds and they would be hidden from the bandits' view.

The game warden lifted himself from the foot well. 'We're saved,' he cried, hoisting and shaking his rifle in triumph.

The panicked shouts from behind made Michael turn. All the men were taking aim. He did not hear the shot above the noise of the revving engine, but heard two sounds from within the vehicle, both quiet, like a light tap on metal. A shard of metal fell hot against Michael's leg creating a tiny smouldering hole in his trousers. The smoke of the bushfire enveloped the vehicle but Stanley kept going. Michael looked behind again. The game warden was pointing to a hole in the rear door of the Land Rover. In his other hand he still held his rifle to the roof as if it was a spear.

Michael asked, 'Is everyone all right?'

'I'm hurt,' Stanley gasped.

He was bent forward, supporting himself against the steering wheel. Michael saw that the bandits were hidden by the smoke and said, 'Stop the vehicle. I'll take over.'

Stanley braked, groaning with the effort. Michael jumped out and opened Stanley's door. A fan of blood was spreading on the side of Stanley's shirt. Michael yanked it up and saw a small entry wound in the right side of his abdomen. Pressure would be pointless on that. He looked for an exit wound but there was none. Michael shouted to the game warden to get off the floor again and help him lie Stanley down on the rear seat.

'Felice, sit in the back with him.'

The smoke choked Michael as he took the driver's seat. He smacked the gearstick into first and accelerated away through a kettle-black landscape dotted with stark skeletal remains of bush and sapling.

In the mirror he could see Felice kneeling beside Stanley, holding his hand, her face close to his, saying in a fearful voice, 'It's OK, you'll be OK.'

Michael headed for the park entrance, concentrating on keeping to the middle of the narrow track, fists tight on the wheel. A warthog scampered across the road, legs a blur under its stout body, upright tail rigid with fright; a panicked flock of francolins launched themselves away over the grasses, wings beating noisily, shrill calls like a chorus of expletives. Half a mile from the gate Michael sounded the horn to summon the warden gatekeeper. He turned on full-beam lights. They approached the boom at speed.

'You must sign out,' said the game warden, agitated. 'Regulation UP75.6.'

'Regulation ML1 takes precedence,' spat Michael.

The gatekeeper appeared, took one look at the approaching vehicle and leant heavily on the end of the boom to open it.

Good man: a sixth sense that protocol must be ignored in this instance, or perhaps he was sensibly preserving the boom; after all, there were no exit fees to collect.

'Where's the nearest hospital with a trauma surgeon?' Michael shouted.

He heard Stanley respond weakly, 'It's too far, Michael, take me to Lwesala. You must do the surgery. We have instruments.'

'What's his pulse, Felice?'

'It's fast. It's not strong.' He could hear the suppressed panic in her voice.

'Do you have blood at Lwesala?'

'We've no blood bank. We crossmatch the relatives before surgery and bleed them if we need blood,' Felice said.

The game warden said, 'I have nausea.' He took out a well-ironed handkerchief and placed it to his mouth.

Michael ignored him. The only relative of Stanley's nearby was Zachye. He might as well be at the other end of the earth.

Felice said, 'Sister Dorakasi's the same blood group as Stanley. She'll donate.'

Stanley was speaking again to Felice. She lifted her head and said, 'Stanley asks that we don't tell the police that Zachye was with the bandits.'

'I must report this Zachye in my report,' the game warden said, his voice muffled by the handkerchief.

Felice touched Michael on the shoulder and said, 'Please!'

Michael glanced around. She was looking at him as if only he could deliver what was likely to be Stanley's last wish.

He looked sharply across at the game warden and said menacingly, 'If you ever speak Zachye's name, I'll ensure that your role in provoking the shooting is made known to the police.'

'Me?' the game warden said.

'Think about it,' Michael said.

The warden thought about it. He lowered his gun to the floor. 'But that Zachye,' he pleaded, 'he shot at us.'

'We don't know which of them shot at us. Let me make myself clear. If you mention Zachye to anyone I'll take you back to the park and kick you out, at night, on the plain. Do you understand?'

The game warden dropped his handkerchief and fingered the barrel of his rifle again. 'You can rely on me, sir.'

They stopped directly outside the small theatre building at the hospital. Michael leant on the horn. Staff came running from every direction.

'Stanley's shot. I need to operate straight away.'

While many hands, desperate to help, carried Stanley to the operating table, news spread as if winged, into the district. Their doctor had been shot. A silent crowd gathered in no time outside the theatre. The hospital chaplain arrived to lead supplication. Inside, Michael barked orders: 'I need a Venflon, I need a giving set, sterilise the instruments, someone take this blood for crossmatch. Are you Sister Dorakasi? We need your blood. I need gauze packs.'

Michael found that his hands were steady, moving with unhurried but efficient purpose. Idiot man had broken; rational man would repair. The thought came that this was why he had come out to Africa again: to save Stanley. Fate (impassive, blind, but wise enough to have generated every living thing on the planet) had ordained it. He picked up the knife and ran through possibilities, through technical scenarios, as he cut down through the layers, varying the pressure on the knife, weighting each cut to the texture, density and thickness of the tissue. There had been no exit wound. With a high velocity rifle round that could only mean that the full energy of the bullet had been attenuated dramatically before entering the body. At a kilometre per second the energy transfer to a body that stopped the bullet dead would liquefy its innards; the shock wave bursting blood vessels far from the bullet's resting place. Not survivable. Maybe he would find a shrapnel shard. What if a liver resection was necessary? He might need gallons of blood. Sister Dorakasi could only be asked to give two pints although he guessed she would be willing to be completely exsanguinated for Stanley's sake.

The last layer, the peritoneum, he tented up with forceps and then held the knife, poised, ready to enter the abdominal cavity.

'I'll need suction.'

He nicked the peritoneum with the blade to make a small hole and then slid a pair of scissors up and down, protecting the bowel under the lower blade with his fingers. When he let the abdominal wall fall back, blood and thin bowel juices spilled out of the wound.

'The intestine's perforated.'

But first he had to identify the source of the bleeding.

'Pass me the sucker.'

'It's broken, sir,' a nurse said, 'but I'll make it work.' She pulled the vent tube out of the top of the sucker bottle and sucked, soon filling the glass jar with murky, brown liquid.

She's got guts, Michael thought. I might get a smile out of Stanley with that one – if he pulls through.

'I need packs.'

'We've no sterilised packs at the present time.'

'Damn it.'

He pressed the bowel away with his hands, placing the sucker nozzle in the deep recesses of the abdominal cavity looking for fresh bleeding. Loops of bowel slid around his fingers, obstructing his view.

'Damn it!'

He worked his way methodically down a checklist. Spleen OK, liver OK, mesentery OK. No obvious source for the bleeding. He lifted the large bowel onto his patient's chest and explored the recesses where the first part of the intestine, the duodenum, formed a loop as it left the stomach, enclosing the head of the pancreas and critical vessels carrying bile, pancreatic juices and blood to the intestine. Blood washed around the complex anatomy: paraduodenal fossa, inferior duodenal fold, mesentericoparietal recess. He struggled to prevent the twenty feet of small intestine from worming its way into his field of vision. He asked the nurse to suck again and, with the tip of the nozzle, touched the bloody pools at the base of the intestine, draining them from their surface to avoid disturbing any fragile plugs of clot beneath. A purple swelling, a haematoma, precariously contained by the semi-translucent peritoneum, emerged at the root of the intestine like jellied pond life. Through a laceration at its apex seeped a small, but confluent, stream of fresh blood.

Choices: gentle packing of the area in the hope of sealing the bleeder by inducing a stable clot – but there were dangers in shifting the underlying structures; or dissect down to find the vessel to repair it, risking making the bleeding worse by disturbing the clot already formed.

Complicating factor: a bullet, or shrapnel, might be sitting in the blood clot and if not removed might cause overwhelming infection. The abdominal cavity was already awash with bacteria from the perforated bowel.

Decision: he would pack the area, get the patient haemodynamically stable with the blood transfusion, and would then weigh the risks further. He wished he had an X-ray. The hospital radiation-spreader was not transportable.

Someone had found a sterile pack on the obstetric ward and he pressed it, with the gentleness of a hand of blessing, onto the haematoma.

As Sister Dorakasi gave up two pints of blood in the corner of the theatre – the whites of her eyes turning as pure as egg white – a compelling but guilt-inducing thought slipped as smooth as liver into his head. If his patient were to die, despite his heroic efforts of course, Felice would be alone. He swallowed awkwardly as if struggling with an unchewable piece of Mr Magara's stew. What sort of man had he become to play with such thoughts? Karamoja Bell? Slitting a throat, grabbing a native girl. Damn it! He could offer her a different life; probably with children; certainly with money. She could indulge herself at last, adorn herself from Oxford Street – it was plain that she loved to dress well, making the most of what must be a limited wardrobe. He could save her. He saw her naked in the shower. He saw her accepting look. He remembered her easy laughter and their repartee. He felt his solitude. Damn it!

EIGHT

It was gone midnight on the second night after the operation when Michael saw the mountains. He had returned wearily from the hospital to the cottage but, being unable to sleep, he dipped into a book he had borrowed from James about the explorer Henry Morton Stanley. He read how on the morning of 9 May 1889 Stanley and his caravan of Egyptians, Sudanese, Zanzibaris and plateau natives had snaked their way around the south-western flanks of the Rwenzori Mountains. Stanley lay back in his hide hammock – held in suspension by two of his porters – marvelling at the luxuriant cultivations of plantains, sweet potatoes, yams, colocassia, beans and sugar cane. Looking up, the explorer saw, for the first time, the mountains emerge from their 'mantle of clouds and vapours ... resplendent with shining white snow; the blue beyond was as that of ocean – a purified and spotless translucence'. Strangling his excitement with Victorian self-discipline, Stanley took measurements and drew sketches. Now, at last, the world at the far end of the Nile would believe what the ancients had told: that the great river's fountains sprung from a mountain range whose brightness matched that of the moon.

Still unable to sleep, and remembering that the moon was up, Michael put down the book, left the cottage and followed the path a short distance to see if the mountains were still covered in cloud. High in the sky he saw an unearthly whiteness, like a shroud over a celestial body – or like fields of white in an imagined country. The peaks had revealed themselves.

He stood transfixed, but jumped when a voice hissed at him from the banana grove, 'Mr Ambassador, stand still!' He froze. 'Mr Ambassador, do not move!'

He had no intention of moving. He looked straight ahead and turned out his hands to give the bandit no excuse for hasty action. He remembered the sneer on the bandit's face. Yet again he was at the mercy of the unpredictable. For a few seconds there was not a sound. Was he taking aim?

'Where's Dr Katura?' the bandit asked coldly.

Options for reply, each with their repercussions, presented themselves like a flicked-through card index: in the mortuary, gone to his home village, been flown to London. Or the truth. Would that put Stanley in danger? Was the bandit going to eliminate witnesses? Stanley was in a critical enough state as it was. Thank God that Felice was in the hospital, and not alone in the house.

'I can tell you, but may I ask who you are?' Michael said, offering co-operation while trying to build a rapport.

The silence stretched out, every second pregnant with menace. Then the bandit said with a snigger, 'If you're the ambassador, then I'm Idi Amin Dada.'

Michael dared to play along. 'I ask the ex-president for permission to go about my duties.'

'First I command you to tell me of Dr Katura's whereabouts.' The bandit had abandoned any effort to keep his voice down.

'I'd like to comply, but he's a friend of mine so … I wouldn't want him to come to any harm.'

'I wish to speak to him.'

Michael risked not replying.

After a long pause the bandit said without emotion, 'I'm Dr Katura's brother.'

Michael caught his breath, then said slowly, 'Your brother wishes to speak to you as well, but he's very ill.'

'What illness?'

'He was shot.'

'Shot! Cho! Who shot him?'

Michael suppressed a sarcastic response.

There was a long silence. Michael saw again the fields of white in the sky – some other country; of the imagination only.

When Zachye spoke again, his voice was slow and deliberate. 'And Mrs Katura?'

'She's not injured. But she's very distressed.'

Zachye was quiet. Michael kept still.

'Where's my brother? I'll not harm him.'

For a moment Michael felt that Zachye spoke honestly, that he was not in the habit of doing anything other than what he promised; then he remembered he was speaking to an outlaw who prowled around at night, who consorted with violent men, who had likely been involved in all manner of atrocities. However, it seemed news to Zachye that Stanley had been hit in the shooting. Or was he in denial that he could have shot his own brother?

'Come with me to where I'm staying,' Michael said evenly, 'and then I'll go and ask Mrs Katura whether she's happy for you to see him.'

There was no reply. Michael waited, remaining perfectly still, looking up at the mountains. The snows faded from view as he watched. He felt the night empty of a presence. Michael said, as calmly and as clearly as he could, 'I'm going to walk on now to my bed.'

He waited a little longer and then, thinking better of returning to the house, turned and hurried back to the hospital in case Zachye was on his way there. He strode down the ward to the side room where Stanley lay, but all was quiet, the patients sleeping. Felice was coming out of the room.

'You're back already. I'd like to thank you,' she whispered. 'I'm told by Sister Dorakasi that without your expertise Stanley would not have survived.'

Michael took a deep slow breath, determined to act in a measured manner. 'He was lucky as well,' he said quietly. 'If the metal splinter had ended up a few millimetres in any other direction ...'

They stood close together by the door to the room. 'Felice, he's not safe yet; he's still critically ill.' He did not want her under the impression that Stanley was out of danger. 'I'd like him moved to somewhere with better monitoring facilities, but I think he's still too ill to travel.'

'He's in God's hands,' she said.

He let it pass. What sort of man takes away another's basis for hope?

Felice was saying, 'His mother will be coming to see him. I've sent a message. I hope she arrives soon.'

She made to walk up the ward but Michael put out his hand to stay her. 'Something else has happened.' He told her about his meeting with Zachye. She looked up the lamp-lit ward, absorbing the news, but said nothing. 'I think you'd better come back to the house and sleep,' he said. 'You're exhausted – you've been awake for more than thirty-six hours.' He looked at her weary form in the lamplight and wanted to wrap his arms around her.

She slipped back into Stanley's room but came out again after a minute and nodded at Michael.

As they walked back along the moon-traced path she said, 'Stanley's at peace.'

'Good. He needs all the sleep he can get,' Michael said, with half a mind on whether Zachye might spring out on them.

'No, I don't mean restful. I mean he fears nothing.'

'Uh-huh … I see.'

When they arrived back at the house they found the maid had left the stove well stoked and a lamp burning on the table. Felice turned up the wick, stood watching it for a few seconds and then reached over to turn on the radio. The song reminded Michael of an occasion long ago when he played with his school-friend Simon by a hot spring in the pasturelands of the Bahima, and saw two herd boys on the slope above the spring listening to Mr Adams's radio. Felice went to the kitchen and put water on the stove.

'Stanley told me that Zachye loved this song. It's Franco – a Congolese singer. Zachye loved music. Stanley says that if Zachye had joined a band of musicians instead of a band of brigands things would've been different.'

'What's the song?'

'He's singing in Lingala but we all know the words. It tells how love makes us suffer. It's called "Infidelite Mado".'

'Do you like it?'

'Yes, it's our own voices, our own rhythms.' She started swaying slowly, sadly, to the music. She caught herself almost immediately and looked across at him with a smile that died as swiftly as it came. 'So you see – it moves me.'

Felice fetched a saucepan of pre-boiled milk from the cupboard, but when she transferred the pan to the sideboard Michael saw her body wilt as if this last task had drained her of any remnants of energy.

'Can I help?' he asked.

She shook her head and made a click noise with her tongue. 'I'm just so sorry your holiday has not turned out well. Zachye!' She spoke his name heavily, weighted with years of exasperation, years of hurt. Michael saw it now: Zachye, the ulcer that gnawed at her husband, never left him, and distracted him … from her.

He said, 'Do you think Zachye will come back again?' Felice tensed, but he went on. 'Perhaps what's happened is bringing him to his senses.'

Felice picked up a long metal spoon, dipped it in the milk and started stirring slowly. 'Stanley will hope so. For myself – I don't know. Stanley is lying in pain on account of Zachye. Zachye's caused much suffering. His mother grieves for him. His father died sorrowful.' Michael said nothing while she finished making the tea, her movements languid, spent. Now she stared down at the tin cups. 'Stanley's wrong to protect Zachye from the consequences of his actions.' Her voice caught. She took a deep breath, and impulsively took the grey dishcloth hanging over the taps and wiped down the draining board, although it did not need it. 'I'm going to report him to the police.' Her voice wavered.

'But … Stanley asked …' Michael said, disconcerted.

She left the drinks and crossed quickly to her bedroom, saying, 'Your tea's there. Please excuse me, I'm very tired.'

He glanced at her and saw wetness in the angle of her eyes. She closed her bedroom door hard behind her. He found himself standing outside the door and was going to call her name. But then what? What could he say that would help? Any oil he tried to pour on the choppy water of her emotions might ignite in his face. He returned to the radio; he did not have to understand the words to hear that the songs were about heart-stopping infatuation. He felt his own infatuation with Felice; nothing good could come of it. He tried to analyse it dispassionately: it had driven him to fantasise about the death of Stanley; imagining Felice saved from a life of privation. Damn it! Whose satisfaction was he after? Guilt slashed at him. He took in a calming breath and made an effort to get a grip: the picture of himself that had emerged was an exaggeration; after all, he had stepped back from his dangerous thoughts in the operating theatre, had hardly forced himself on her and, surely he had not been mistaken, there had been moments when Felice seemed to crave his attention – had given him mixed signals. Adultery had been in the imagination only and, he reassured himself, the private life was harmless as long as the public life was seen to be proper. Everyone nowadays agreed with that.

Michael had a restless night. He kept waking, thinking he heard movement outside the window. He heard Felice get up at least once and go through to the kitchen. At six he was woken again by a loud knocking. After a brief struggle to pull the mosquito netting out from under the mattress he went to the door, turned the large key and peered anxiously at the nurse outside, suddenly aware that he was naked apart from lightweight pyjama shorts.

'Dr Lacey, come quickly! Dr Katura is not so well.'

He dressed with the haste of a house officer answering a crash bleep, pulling his trousers over his pyjamas. He left his cufflinks on the bedside table, forewent his socks and threw his laces with a surgical knot. Felice's door was open – she must have gone down to the hospital again in the night. The nurse was moving off as fast as she could without running. Michael buttoned his shirt as he followed her, feeling a chill in the air on the skin around his waist.

'What's happened?'

'His breath is leaving him. Maybe he's already passed away.'

'Is Mrs Katura with him?'

'She came not long ago. To bring him milk.'

'Milk? What the …? He's nil by mouth.'

'It's a custom … the Bahima … the wife brings milk to her husband.'

'A custom?'

'She wished to bring him a gift. To honour him.'

He tried to run through a checklist of possibilities, but his clarity of decision-making had splintered. He felt something akin to panic; as if his mental faculties had abandoned him. Please God, I'm terrified she's about to be hurt. As he hurried down the dim ward he was aware that all the patients were sitting upright in their beds and those on the floor were supporting themselves on their arms, all looking at the door at the far end of the ward. In the room Felice sat holding Stanley's hand. Stanley lay as still as the air.

Michael took Stanley's other wrist, felt for his carotid pulse, then listened with the stethoscope handed to him by the nurse. He stayed listening for a long time – much longer than he needed to. He could not bring himself to straighten up and meet Felice's eye. How would he break the news? What exactly would he say? He wanted to remain bent over Stanley and wait until something else came along – some other situation. This was an in-between moment: when the world did not know, but he knew. Before long he would have to say it, and all the consequences would roll.

Then he heard Felice's voice. 'Michael, I know.'

He could not look at her. He glanced at the central venous pressure line that he had inserted to help monitor Stanley's fluid balance. A trickle of blood and saline spilled from its end. 'The line – it's been disconnected,' he said, more loudly than he had intended.

The nurse stepped forward as if ordered by a drill sergeant. 'I fear it fell out in the night, sir,' she said, a tremble in her voice.

'Was no one checking it?'

She did not answer.

'How?' he asked.

He heard Felice again. 'Please, Michael. It's of no importance now.' She was gripping Stanley's hand tighter, as if she could change things by just holding onto him a little harder.

Michael lifted the end of the line. A disconnected line could give rise to an air embolus: the air finding its way to the heart, to then be forced in a fatal froth up into the arteries of the brain, starving it of oxygen. I'm sure I connected it securely, he thought, remembering the difficulty he'd had finding compatible connectors for the tubes. Then he saw the open window. 'Was this window open all night?'

In his mind's eye he could see Zachye climbing through, pulling apart the tubing and then blowing into it. But would Zachye have known its fatal effects? Would a stupid bandit know that?

Felice had started to sob. She looked up at him and said, 'Please, Michael!'

The nurse was moaning, leaning against the wall. Another nurse was at the door muttering something agonised, over and over again. Michael saw that the consequences had started to roll but that he was an obstacle in its path, preventing it gaining proper momentum. He had to get out of the way.

As he left the room and retraced his steps up the ward – aware of his hair dishevelled, his shirt half-buttoned, his sleeves flapping: he felt every eye on him. Leaving the compound, he saw something that he had somehow missed on his dash to the ward: a crowd huddled, wrapped by a cold mist, on the slopes of the hospital grounds in the dismal light of the early dawn. It was like a Galilean, Sermon-on-the-Mount scene from his old Picture Bible. Eerie waves of wailing rippled out. Staff passed him, running to the ward, not seeing him. Their beloved physician, Dr Katura, was dead. Michael saw that he, himself, was a nobody: an expendable technician, replaceable immediately with an eager senior registrar if he should drop dead. Stanley was a one off; a Messiah to his people. Michael found himself speared by remorse, blaming himself for Stanley's death. If he had not yielded, like a teenager with a crush, to Felice's allure, the Katuras would never have found themselves in the game reserve; perhaps he had misjudged the tension on one of his sutures and it had given way, causing sudden massive internal bleeding; perhaps he should have got Stanley moved to the capital to be properly monitored in an intensive care unit – whatever the risks of the journey. It struck him with horror that this would be the second time he would be going back to the UK following a death in which he was implicated. How ironic to come out to Africa, determined to put behind him what had happened, and to return having as good as killed again.

He passed the road running to the hospital before taking the path to the house. A bus had drawn up. Tired people stepped down including an old woman in long white robes, thin and bent. A broad-shouldered man, not unlike Zachye in build, supported her. Michael knew at once that he was looking at Stanley's mother and some other relation. He hurried on. The maid nearly collided with him as he neared the house. She looked at him, fear in her eyes.

'It was too late,' Michael said.

She cried out and ran on.

Michael quickened his pace, his footfalls reverberating on the path as he passed the spot where Zachye had spoken to him. Bloody Zachye. Felice was right. The psychopath should be locked up. Even if he'd not murdered Stanley in the night then his was the hand that pulled, or as good as pulled, the trigger. He looked forward to giving his statement to the police.

NINE

When he got to his room Michael changed into his pressed trousers and a fresh white shirt, slipped on his well-cut jacket, shaved his face ultra-smooth, wet his comb to slick his hair, vigorously polished his shoes and clipped in his cufflinks, lining them up symmetrically. He was keen to recreate Mr Michael Lacey, Consultant Surgeon; to return to order in his dress, his bearing and his thoughts. He felt thirsty and strode to the kitchen. The stove was cold but Felice had left milk in a pan. He poured himself a glass and gulped it down, remembering on the last swallow that he was drinking the dregs of some sort of sacred offering that Felice had taken to Stanley. It's just milk, he told himself.

When the maid returned, moving on automatic, she said that Stanley's mother and cousin had arrived and it would be appreciated if he would move out to make way for them. A room would be given him in Mr Magara's house. Michael asked if there was transport back to Kampala and she replied that there was the bus. It would leave mid-afternoon and arrive in Kampala in the evening after dark – she did not recommend it. She also had to tell him that the police had arrived and wished to question him about the shooting.

He returned to the hospital. From the crush around the chapel it was clear that Stanley's body had been moved from the side room. The Ugandan flag over the chapel was at half-mast. A steady stream of people entered the hospital compound – a mass migration from the surrounding hills. He imagined Felice with her mother-in-law and her late husband's relative in the chapel, pressed in by mourners. She would not feel alone – a grief shared with a multitude. Surely that would make the heartbreak less keen? But grief was infinite – he knew that. It could not be reduced by division.

He saw the crowd part to make way for Felice. She was coming through with Stanley's relative. Michael could see the police waiting by the administrative office, but Stanley's relative raised his arm to signal that they wanted to speak to him. They stopped on the path away from the crowds.

'I'm so sorry,' Michael said.

Felice was far away, not registering his presence. Now that she was out of public gaze she leant heavily on her helper's proffered arm.

'Words are not enough, of course,' he said. She looked towards him but he could see that she had not yet seen him. 'I wish I could have done more.'

Stanley's relative spoke. 'I'm Kabutiiti. A distant cousin of Stanley. We're all grateful for your efforts. Felice will give her thanks at a less difficult time.'

'None are due,' Michael said, and sized up Kabutiiti. The man was calm and strong. He could see that Kabutiiti would carry Felice through.

Relieved to be able to excuse himself, he said to Kabutiiti, 'The police want to see me now. They'll want to question me about the shooting. I shall give them a full account.'

Felice gasped as if a bucket of cold water had been thrown in her face. She said in a rush, 'Michael, I'll be respecting Stanley's wish. I ask you to do the same.'

Now she was looking into his eyes. Michael took his time to reply, thinking through the implications for his statement to the police, and then said, as gently as he could and hoping to sound as he felt: a friend giving kind council, 'I don't think that's wise. You were right last night.'

Felice recoiled, and said, 'Michael, please respect my request. For my late husband's sake.'

She had let go of Kabutiiti's arm and had clasped her hands tightly in front of her, twisting her palms against each other.

Late husband; how the dead so quickly vanish into the past. 'I understand, but he'll not know. He's ... not here.'

'He's not dead,' she said immediately.

Michael did not reply but nodded sympathetically: the recently bereaved have their defences. Did she mean that she thought Stanley had become an ancestral ghost or was this her Christian belief in the resurrection of the dead? It occurred to him that she might hold a fusion of both traditions.

Felice turned herself away from Michael towards Kabutiiti and said to him, as if he at least would comprehend, 'What we believe is not destroyed by Stanley's death. My pledge to him honours that.'

Kabutiiti put his hand gently on her forearm and said, 'You're right.'

She turned back to Michael and took a step towards him. 'For my sake, Michael. Michael?'

She spoke his name tenderly, almost intimately. It came to him that she was appealing to his feelings for her. That she knew their intensity. An incongruous regret came over him: that she could not appeal to his citizenship of a shared kingdom of belief. At this moment, he almost wished she could.

He met her eyes. 'I'll do as you ask.'

She grasped Kabutiiti's arm again and they walked on. Michael returned to his appointment with the police. Beatrice and the maid came hurrying past him, weeping.

Michael's meeting with the police was long and tedious. He had given witness statements before, as a casualty officer in London after he had attended stabbing victims, and now he discovered that their ponderous methodology was universal: one of the two officers, his stomach stretching his black jersey, wrote out Michael's witness statement himself, in capital letters, with a pen that required several strokes to leave a mark, and with cold turns of phrase: 'I OBSERVED FOUR MEN ... THE VEHICLE WAS BROUGHT TO A HALT ... WE MOVED OFF AGAIN ... WE PROCEEDED TO THE PARK ENTRANCE ...'

He told the bare minimum to avoid saying anything that might conflict with the other witnesses. It was harder than he imagined. With a frisson of worry it occurred to him that the police might have already interviewed the game warden, who might have spilled the beans on Zachye. So he emphasised how fast everything had happened and how difficult it was to remember the exact sequence of events. He said he was sure they would understand. They asked whether he had witnessed the quick actions of the game warden. He sensed a trap, but when he looked non-committal the police officer was eager to fill him in: the game warden had certainly saved their lives by his quick thinking in firing back out of the window, so scattering the bandits.

By the time the last word had been scratched into the paper he was happy to sign anything: further tinkering was too wearisome to contemplate. He asked a few questions of his own which the police were pleased to answer, as if anxious to show that they were well advanced in the murder investigation: Did they have any idea who these bandits were? Ex-soldiers probably. Would they be able to catch them? If the bandits stayed together the police would find them, but if they split up and left the district it would be difficult. How many bullets were fired into the vehicle? Just one. Yes, that was strange. Perhaps they only had one bullet remaining, suggested the junior officer. The senior officer looked doubtful.

The police thanked Michael for his help and apologised for the 'unfortunate incident', asking if he could mention their diligence to any officials he might meet in the capital: out here they got passed over for promotion. The junior officer started asking Michael if he would write a letter in support of his son to do a veterinary course in Great Britain, but Michael excused himself firmly and left.

He took the afternoon bus back to Kampala, despite the protestations of Kabutiiti and Beatrice. They told him it was the slow bus, it was uncomfortable, it might arrive late and he might have difficulty finding a taxi at the other end. But Michael was resolute, saying that he did not wish to burden them further. He left Felice a note, saying he would write when he got back to the UK. He put two hundred US dollars in the folded paper: 'A small gift as a token of my wish to help you in any way I can'.

Kabutiiti insisted on carrying his suitcase to the bus. They said little to each other. Kabutiiti looked distracted as he shook Michael's hand, and said, 'All the best for the future.' It sounded as if he assumed he would never see him again.

TEN

M ichael squeezed his briefcase into the small space under his feet. His suitcase was on the roof of the bus, conspicuous amongst the sacks, crates and sticks of bananas. He had to rest his left foot on his briefcase, his hip and knee uncomfortably flexed. Despite his discomfort he had a sense of relief that he was on his way, tempered a little by the fear that his troubles were not yet over.

To take his mind off the gloom he allowed himself a mental indulgence: once back in the white rooms of his town house in Ealing, he would devise a strategy to woo Felice; to bring her to him. He would take her to the best venues in London: shows, clubs (he would become much more sociable) and restaurants (she would never have to sit on the floor again). She was a jewel that he had stumbled upon in the forest, a diamond he had come across on a mountain, and he longed to display her. She would want for nothing.

It did not take long for his rosy daydream to be muddied by the appearance of Naomi, not because he thought she would be waiting for him (he was sure that he had failed to live up to her expectations; convinced now that the airport goodbye had been a farewell), but because he couldn't see why Felice, in the end, should see anything more in him than Naomi had, or Annie or Jo for that matter? Enjoying each others' company was one thing, but he seemed to be drawn to women who wanted more than good repartee, good sex, or goods and chattels. What was it? Honesty? Openness? One thing was sure: if his relationship with Felice grew, she would demand whatever was missing. But if he revealed to her his childhood secret – that he had killed his friend; had been granted a moment's wish – how could he expect her to accept him? If he could not forgive himself he saw no reason why anyone else should.

There was also what happened afterwards – after Simon's death – which he refused to think about.

Next to him sat a diminutive old man, hair like a thin frost, who clasped the head of a cane with his shrunken, breakable hand. The old man looked out through whitened corneas but held his head up with a private dignity. When Michael manoeuvred his right shoe to the floor beside his briefcase he noticed that the side of the old man's bare foot had rubbed away the dust on the shoe leather, to reveal the polished lustre that had been buried yet again by Africa's dust. He looked forward to getting to the end of a day untarnished.

The aisle filled with standing passengers carrying wicker baskets and cloth bundles. Chickens clucked in alarm somewhere up ahead. A baby, strapped to the back of a woman in the aisle, pressed against his shoulder when its mother turned. He tried to get up to offer her a seat but he was too wedged in. The air was thick with the organic odours of peasant people. He feared he would start to feel panicky, but for now the coiled serpent of his claustrophobia lay dormant.

The bus stopped every few miles; passengers shuffled in and out. Michael dozed, opening his eyes from time to time to see small birds on the telephone wires, bunched in tight groups like beads on an abacus. He tried to count them, to take his mind off the operation; thinking about where he might have gone wrong. Analysing adverse events was a habitual and dispassionate part of his surgical practice, but on this occasion it made his stomach tighten. Stanley had died suddenly, having been haemodynamically stable for several hours after the operation. It was quite possible that he had had a secondary haemorrhage that might have been prevented by different decisions, but there was the disconnected venous pressure line. Had he failed to secure it properly? Could Zachye have done it? The telephone wires rose and fell, rose and fell. Michael saw a large eagle perched on a pole, silhouetted against the reddening sky, and was thankful it was not a bronze-feathered cockerel.

The next time he opened his eyes it was dark. The bus had stopped and the old man next to him was trying to get past. Michael pulled his knees up further and to the side to let him out, and found himself covered with a blanket. It reeked of stale milk, and his thumb was poking through one of a number of holes. For a moment he could not think how he had come to be covered but then he remembered the bundle in the old man's lap. He gathered the blanket up, lifting it gingerly between thumb and index finger and, thanking him, gave it back to the man, who took it with a brief nod of his head before making his way slowly off the bus, the other passengers taking trouble to make way for him – his age revered. Michael moved to the vacated window seat and noticed a sign on the road junction that pointed to a town near his childhood home. The old man was walking down the road towards the town, soon disappearing into the night. Michael regretted that he had not attempted to speak to him – to ask what ghosts in his past gave him such dignity and kindness. There was something of his grandfather about him; he wondered if he might have known him.

An hour later the bus stopped again. This time the driver killed the engine, and with it its sleep-inducing monotony.

'Half an hour,' he shouted, and repeated it in Swahili.

Michael could see lights outside and heard excited voices and radios vying for attention. They had joined a major route. *Matatus*, the ubiquitous minibus taxis of Africa, trucks and buses were parked untidily along the verge. A group of young men leant against the wall of the Dance Bazaar, their heads bobbing to the sound of a Congolese beat. One of them saw Michael and began a dance, crouching down and gyrating his hips whilst he held his bottles of beer high above his head. Michael gave a thumbs up sign – he meant it ironically – and then hoped that the gesture was not a crudity in the native culture. The man bent his knees even more and gyrated violently, pumping his arms back and forward.

In the ill-lit doorway of a small building set back from the road a woman leant against the frame, motionless, ignoring the men. She was looking at Michael. When he met her eye she smiled pleasingly, sliding down the frame a little with a slight dropping of her hip. She reminded him of Felice – at least in figure. A man in a hooded tracksuit top, whom Michael thought had got on the bus at an earlier stop, came up to her and tried to engage her in conversation, but still she watched Michael. An overwhelming desire to be comforted gripped him. He had not been able to take Felice in his arms, to console her, but whilst he longed for that he also ached to be held himself – and not only on account of recent events. He regretted seeing the signpost to his childhood home at the road junction at the previous stop. He regretted the old man's kindness. He regretted his own rigid heart; but he could not think of any key to unlock it.

Michael got off the bus, now almost empty, and found himself lingering near the woman. He half-hoped she would come and talk to him, to pass the time, but when their eyes met she invited him to follow with a discreet movement of her hand, and melted into the room. It was simple to follow her in, telling himself that perhaps she just wanted to talk inside, away from the road. The room was dark, although there was enough light to show sacks of millet stacked against a corner, a heap of flattened cardboard boxes against a wall, a pile of stripped maize cobs on the floor. The room appeared to be used for whatever purpose would generate a little cash. For a moment he could not see where she had gone, and then he saw her in the entrance to another room at the back. She smiled at him with an understanding tenderness, as if she knew his troubles and wanted to help. The noise of the street deadened as the door behind him swung silently closed.

The woman came unhurriedly towards him and leant gently against him, melting into him, her arms lightly embracing him, her breasts warm and soft as down on his chest through her thin cotton dress. It was all so easy. So comforting. So dreamlike. She put her head on his chest and raised her hand to unbutton her dress. The wallet in his jacket pocket pushed against his ribs. Poking him. He pulled back, jolted out of his trance. Condemning words came to him: two hundred dollars down payment for Felice; how much for the prostitute?

The woman noticed his retreat. She reached out to take his hand but he pulled it back. 'Do you wish a protective?'

Michael recoiled again. He remembered the man in the ward, dying of Slim. How could he have forgotten? 'Sorry, this is a mistake,' he said, and made for the door.

272

'No mistake! I have protectives,' he heard the woman say plaintively as he fled to the street.

Walking briskly away, he wondered why he felt shame and self-loathing instead of mere annoyance at an error of judgement. For years he had regarded such emotions as vestiges of a primitive nature that had rightly been eradicated by modern thought. It was since his arrival in Africa, but particularly since meeting Felice, that these feelings had been induced. Consenting liaisons (with protectives of course), with whom he pleased, should not be of any concern. Felice was not his wife.

He needed something to drink. The acrid but fruity smell of *waragi* enveloped him as he hurried down the road away from the brothel. He shook his head at the vendors who thrust packets of charcoal-roasted meats, peanuts and other less identifiable foods at him. As he passed a bar a girl shouted, 'Hey mister, buy me a drink.' He ignored her. Lorry drivers leant against their vehicles, smoking and yawning, their trucks laden with goods from as far as Mombasa, seven hundred miles away on the Kenyan coast, bound for Rwanda and Burundi, another three hundred miles beyond. Cheap hotels, small bars and kiosks were strung out in a strip along the road to service the international trade; including trade in whatever caused Slim, he thought.

An adolescent boy tagged on to him, holding out the haunch of some small animal. 'Bush meat, sir. Very good. Make you strong. Make you good with women.'

Michael waved him away and bought a Coke from a stall. He decided to drink it in the bus, along with the bread that the maid had put into his hand as he had left Lwesala.

As he approached the bus he saw the hooded man come out of the brothel. Their eyes engaged for a moment, and then reengaged in surprise. At first he thought, with disbelief, that it was Kabutiiti but, although his face was similarly shaped, the man wore a tension in his expression absent from Kabutiiti's. His eyes had been hunting about furtively, lips puckered as if about to blow a whistle, or perhaps breathless and sucking in the lively air. Michael had no wish to meet Zachye; it would be another situation replete with risk. He headed straight for the steps of the bus, but Zachye caught up with him and, putting a firm hand on his shoulder, said, 'Ambassador!'

Michael turned, irritated and a little frightened. Zachye stank of *waragi*.

'Yes? What is it?'

'It's your friend, Zachye.'

'Take your hand off me.'

Zachye pulled him closer. 'I'm Dr Katura's brother. God is bringing us together.'

Michael shifted his shoulder, attempting to pull himself away.

'I need help.'

'Not from me,' Michael said.

'I've killed my brother,' Zachye said, spitting the words into Michael's face.

'It's none of my business. Let go.'

'The police will find me.'

'You should turn yourself in.'

'They will hang me.'

'You deserve it.'

Zachye's arm fell off Michael like a dead weight. He dropped his pleading look. His expression became neutral, verging on cold; as if he had changed to a new strategy on the failure of the first. 'I'll tell you something. We're alike, you and me.'

So preposterous was Zachye's statement that Michael sneered back, 'What the hell do you mean?'

'We're both trying to get things that we cannot have.' Michael stared blankly at Zachye. 'Yes, I watched you and Felice; through the window of the house; talking together. She's a fine woman. But proud – and she is self righteous.'

'You're completely wrong. You've a chip on your shoulder; a bloody great plank in your eye.'

'Do you want her, Doctor? You think you have a chance now?'

'What do you want?'

'Let me tell you, Doctor, I loved her before you did.'

'What do you want?'

'Money. That's what I need.'

'Just be thankful you're still free – go and hide somewhere.'

'You're to give me money,' Zachye said, maintaining an even tone. Michael turned to go but Zachye held onto his jacket and said in his ear, 'I'm suggesting that a man like you, who has a respectable position, who also wishes to impress a moral woman, wouldn't want anyone to know that he has gone with a prostitute.'

'I did not go with a prostitute.'

'There are plenty of witnesses. A white man is like a glow worm; his path is clear for everyone to see. The woman said that you were good, and paid well – green dollars.'

'You're mistaken.' But Michael's throat tightened. A dispassionate receiver of such a rumour might have some suspicions. It was better to shut Zachye up. 'You represent everything that's wrong with this country.' He reached inside his jacket. 'You can have what's in my wallet. Just leave me enough money for my taxi when I get off the bus.'

'No, Doctor! You misunderstand me. I want you to send me money. Four hundred pounds sterling each year. I'm being merciful to you – I could ask more.'

Michael grasped Zachye's arm, trying to tear it away, and said, 'If you don't let go I'll shout that I'm being assaulted. You wouldn't want me to draw attention to you, would you?'

Zachye said calmly, 'Do you not know that Felice will marry Kabutiiti?' Michael's grip on Zachye's arm gave way involuntarily. He met Zachye's eyes to hunt out the truth. 'Kabutiiti is a widower – his wife died of malaria two years ago. He has children who need a mother.' Michael felt the wind knocked out of him. Zachye leant into him so that their faces were inches apart. 'Unless Kabutiiti meets an accident.'

'What?'

'Then you could have your way with her.' Zachye made a crude gesture with his tongue.

Michael turned his head away, disgusted, but stood rooted to the spot. He saw the open window in Stanley's room again. 'You mean, like

Stanley met an accident? Did you come back and kill him? Failed to get a good shot the first time?'

Now it was Zachye who pulled back. His jaw muscles trembled, the set of his expression wavered. 'No, no! I did not.' Michael said nothing. Zachye looked down. 'I was not always like this, Dr Lacey ... when I was a boy ... my brother ...' He raised his voice, a hint of desperation in it. 'I cannot grieve...' He trailed off and looked through Michael as if focusing on some other world. Michael felt a brief and strange sympathy. They stood there for a few seconds, Michael fighting his own remembrances.

'Let's make a deal,' Zachye said, face impassive again, releasing Michael and holding out his hand. 'We're brothers now.'

Michael thought of Felice in Kabutiiti's arms. Gone forever. Life would be intolerably bleak. To have found, by the lottery of life, someone like Felice (to feel she could somehow redeem him; but much more than that, to know that he would hide nothing from her, that she would be the first to understand him), and then to have it all snatched away. But Zachye's suggested solution was grotesque, unspeakable. He was on the point of making a break for the bus when it struck him that Zachye might hold a key. Just might. Perhaps some knowledge of their traditions that would help him to woo Felice.

He declined Zachye's hand but said, 'We need to talk; how we can help each other.' He had kept his voice even and icy, but a flicker of satisfaction crossed Zachye's face. Michael instantly regretted what he had said – love was making him blind – and was about to make a retraction, but Zachye was looking over his shoulder, suddenly alarmed. Then Zachye turned and darted between a parked bus and a lorry. Michael looked around and saw two policemen strolling in his direction. They passed by. He bolted for the bus.

ELEVEN

At the McCrees', Michael found that the news of Stanley's death had gone ahead of him. Audrey had withdrawn to her room and had not come out to welcome him when he arrived, late evening. He suspected that she blamed him for what had happened.

'Bit of a state, poor thing. She doesn't want to know the details,' James said, pouring a whisky for Michael and himself.

Michael recounted the events of the last two days, omitting any reference to Zachye. In the home of a fellow Briton (drinking from cut glass, one hand on the back of a high-back, green-leather chair, a violin concerto playing softly in the background), his meeting with Zachye now seemed absurdly theatrical, and Stanley's death an event he had read about, rather than experienced first hand. Nevertheless, he was not fooled: each passing hour presented new opportunities for the malign. He would not risk giving the curse that clung to him in Africa like a static-charged feather the opportunity to cause himself, or others, further grief. He could not stay for the funeral; he would have to hope Felice understood.

'I'd like to get the earliest flight out. I'll ring the airline first thing in the morning if you don't mind.'

'Why don't you rest here a couple of days?'

'That's kind, but I need to get back to my routine as soon as possible.'

'Quite understand, dear fellow. It'll be therapeutic.'

They talked quietly, so as not to disturb Audrey. As Michael went over the medical details of Stanley's treatment James reassured him that he could not have done more.

Michael made a casual enquiry. 'I saw Stanley's cousin, Kabutiiti, accompanying Stanley's mother to visit him in hospital. Do you know him?'

'I've met him. He came back from exile a couple of years ago. His father was outspoken against the Amin regime and was a good friend of Archbishop Luwum; Luwum was Uganda's Desmond Tutu. Amin had him murdered.' Asking more about Kabutiiti now seemed inappropriate, but James continued, 'I think he has a post in government – not sure what. I understand his father has a publishing business. They've got money, I believe – plenty: could buy Edinburgh Castle.' James offered Michael another drink, which he accepted. 'Kabutiiti needs to be careful if he's following a political career. But he'll not be naïve. He fled in the mid-seventies after he was forced to watch two of his friends being executed in Rusoro stadium. I'm told they made him applaud.'

Audrey did not appear until the following day, when she came out of her room to see Michael off. Her hair was contained in a tight bun again; she wore a dress of muted colours; her dark eyes were grave and moist.

'It wasn't your fault, Michael,' she said, as she reached towards him to brush a beetle off his sleeve.

'That's kind, but how do you know?' he asked. 'I haven't told you about it.'

'It would've been the ancestral ghosts,' Audrey said firmly. 'They cause more than we know.'

'Yes, well …'

'Could have been theirs – or yours.'

'Mine?'

The taxi was waiting. Michael shook James's hand, but Audrey still had one more thing to say. 'Don't think you can come back for Felice, will you?'

James said, 'Please, Audrey, the man's got his own life.'

Michael smiled, pretending Audrey was just trying to be amusing. She kissed him lightly on the cheek as he said goodbye.

He wrote to Felice as soon as he got home; or rather, he posted his letter when he got home, for he had written it on the aeroplane. Its careful composition had kept his claustrophobia in check and he wanted to reach out to her immediately, to build their relationship before Kabutiiti got any ideas. He expressed his heartfelt condolences and praised Stanley and his work: 'a unique person ... a true saint ... my admiration'. As he wrote, it seemed that his previous assessment of Stanley as a dour husband holding back a vivacious woman was grossly simplistic. This was a man for whom flags fell to half-mast and for whom a whole region mourned. Michael had no allusions; he could not compare himself to Stanley. He hoped that Felice would eventually see that his love for her was different; it was total. He would love her above all else: his work, his responsibilities, his ambitions. Stanley had divided his loyalties, at best. And yet, he concluded, Felice had certainly loved him.

The days would drag before he heard anything back from her, so he determined to keep busy. He was not expected back in the hospital for another week (because of the cancelled skiing holiday) but as soon as he arrived home he rang his secretary to say he would be back in two days, tidied his post, almost entirely medical journals, slept a dream-free night – as if his double-glazed, brick-walled Ealing home was impervious to ghosts – and then drove to Leicester to attend a conference of the Society of Gastroenterological Surgeons.

Sitting in the audience, with the lights dimmed, Michael found it impossible to concentrate, his mind wandering to Felice; but every time he saw her he also saw Kabutiiti standing beside her: strong, supportive and rich. With children for her to love. He had heard the presentation on colostomy-sparing pouch operations before so he left the lecture theatre and made his way out to stretch his legs. Walking through the city centre, mildly irritated at having to dodge the shoppers with their little chores, he soon found himself in a road lined with Asian shops. It was a drizzly winter evening but the street had a silvery patina and the shop windows burst with colour and dazzle: Zarah's Sarees, Asiatic Jewellers, Zanzibar Curry House, Bombay Fashions. He had passed Cash and Carry Mart and Bank of India when he came across Juicy Jalabis. A mouth-watering display of sweets caught his attention and, as it had started to rain again, he entered the shop.

'You want sweets?'

He looked up at the man behind the counter, startled; reminded of his quest with the crystals in Mr Patel's shop when he was a boy, although this *duka* was bright, modern and odourless, unlike the spicy, dark interior he remembered from his childhood.

'I might. I enjoyed having jalabis when I was a child in Uganda.'

'Uganda! You're from Uganda? We're from Uganda!'

The man was about his own age and had strongly drawn features: a triangular face with neatly trimmed hair, tidy eyebrows, glassy-black eyes and a sharp chin. A grown up pixie.

'Was your family expelled in seventy-two?'

'Oh yes, but bygones are bygones. We've made good business here.'

'I imagine you came with nothing?'

The man chuckled. 'Some of my compatriots had only the clothing they wore, but my family were able to cross the border with some possessions, some money. My father bribed the customs official with a diamond. Such a funny story.'

An elderly man came through to the shop. 'Bandhu! Are you serving this gentleman or are you talking?'

Well, I'm damned, Michael thought. 'You didn't have a *duka* in Rusoro, did you?' he asked.

'Yes, a very fine store,' Bandhu said.

'Patel, Patel and Patel?'

'Indeed! You know it?' The old man was examining Michael intently through his round, metal-rimmed, National Health Service glasses. The skin around his eyes had the dark, almost purple, pigmentation of older Asian men, giving him the appearance of having had a particularly bad night.

'I brought crystals to your shop with my friend,' Michael said.

'Wah! This is most fortunate. Reshma!' he shouted, 'it's one of the small diamond boys! He's come back to us.'

An elderly woman with a kind face emerged from the back. She took one look at Michael and cried, 'My, my! One of our little diamond boys. Your diamond saved us.'

'My diamond?'

'The one that flew off into my wife's sari,' Mr Patel said.

Michael remembered that final blow of Mr Patel's hammer. 'How extraordinary.'

They stood beaming at each other, the Patels no doubt marvelling at the bestowals of Sukra – planet goddess of diamonds – at the meanings of circles that intersect, at the multiple-armed powers of the gods; and Michael at the coincidence of this meeting. Mrs Patel, who had become even more of a light spirit inside her sari, was grinning up at him with all her gold teeth. The family appeared to be unabashed at having kept the diamond.

It was churlish to tarnish the occasion but he broached the subject anyway, 'Did you not want to return the diamond to us? I'm delighted, of course, that it was of use.'

Mr Patel laughed, and so did Bandhu and Mrs Patel. 'That was no diamond – but the customs wallah didn't know that. He was excited; so, so excited.' The three Patels laughed again at the memory. 'He let us go without searching us. That little stone was a diamond to us. It got us out with all that cash – in Reshma's brassière and Bandhu's panties.' The Patels broke into laughter again, except Bandhu.

Mr Patel insisted Michael come through for Masala tea, 'or perhaps you prefer lassi? With flavour. We have mango, papaya, guava, lemon, strawberry, coconut, savoury, or,' he paused to smile, a twinkle in his eye, 'you like bhang lassi? Make you very happy.'

Michael looked at his watch.

'You're a man now. You'll not be in trouble if you're late,' Mr Patel said.

Michael followed Mr and Mrs Patel through to their living room.

'No, Bandhu, you mind the shop,' Mr Patel said, as Bandhu turned to come with them.

It was when he was opening the door to his house again that Michael was struck by the thought that talking to the Patels was the first time he had reminisced to others about his childhood since the incidents he wished to forget. The Patels had no connection to the baggage of his home background and had opened a window to a world that had run in parallel to his own but cared nothing for its preoccupations. Thankfully they had not asked him what had become of the other boy with him in the *duka* that day. Or about his parents – his mother had probably bought provisions from the Patels when she came into town.

The phone rang when he was hardly through the door. He strode quickly to pick it up on the outside chance that it was Felice, although she was probably miles from a phone.

'Hello, darling. You OK?' It was Naomi.

He gripped the receiver tightly in surprise. 'Ah!' he blurted.

She said, 'I've been trying to get you.' He detected an anxiety in her voice and could imagine her twisting the telephone cable with her long white fingers; her lips thinning out as she stretched them across her teeth, the way she did whenever she became pensive. The crease on her forehead would be visible. 'Michael?'

'Yes, sorry, I've been a little shaken up. The vehicle I was travelling in got shot at.'

'Jeepers! You all right? You should've rung me as soon as you got back.'

'Yes, I'm fine, but ... the driver ... got killed. Unfortunately.'

'No! You don't say. I'll come around straight away.'

Killed! Stanley, why Stanley? Why not the game warden ... or himself. Why did the good people always die?

'Michael?'

'Yes.'

'You OK?'

'I shouldn't have gone back.'

'Gone back? What happened, Michael?'

'If I hadn't been there, it wouldn't have happened.'

'Why? What did you do? Where did it happen?'

An intense wish to be in the hospital came over him: in theatre past the 'No entry to unauthorised persons' sign, masked, sewing loose ends of gut together in the hush.

'What happened, Michael? Did you go to a dangerous area or something?'

He straightened himself. 'Sorry, Naomi, it's OK, just unexpected. The conference itself went like clockwork, just as you said it would. The students there are so keen I'd like to get some of them over here for more training.'

'You're not going to talk to me about it, are you?'

He squeezed the telephone cord between his fingers. 'It's complicated, Naomi, really complicated.'

'For God's sake, Michael, I'm a lawyer, complicated doesn't bother me. And it's normal to talk about these things.' He could imagine her yanking the telephone cord tight, and that vein filling on the right side of her lean neck as she vented her frustration. 'It's not going to work, is it?'

He had arrived there again: hurting those he loved. He said, with resignation, 'I just don't know.' He almost felt her releasing the cord. 'Look, you're smart, pretty, and deserve better.'

She sighed. 'That's some sort of compliment, I suppose.' He waited. 'There's a lot you won't talk about, Michael. Funny thing is there's a lot I don't tell you as well. Perhaps that's why we hit it off, up to a point.' He stayed silent. 'We'll meet up some other time then.'

He blurted, 'Shall I give you a call … next week?'

She took a few seconds to answer. 'I think you need to get yourself sorted first, Michael.'

She hung up. He stood for a long time, still holding the phone to his ear. Then he smacked it down. 'Damn you, Felice, this is all your fault.'

He went straight to his desk and started another letter to her. The first of a weekly routine. His letters contained no overt declaration of his love, but he beseeched fate that their regularity and frequency would establish a growing bond. He wrote of the details of his life: his teaching commitments which he relished, a scientific paper he was working on, the tedious committees, which of his junior staff had potential, his expanding private practice – 'Mr Magara will be impressed!', the antics of Doug – his Australian anaesthetist friend, a practical joker who sent his new juniors to the theatre stores for an anaesthetic device called a 'long weight'. Stores duly obliged. He imagined her smiling through her tears; he hoped he might be lightening her grief a little.

When he received no reply to his sixth letter it occurred to him that he was feeding her nothing but gossip about his work. It looked an unrounded life, one that she might feel would exclude her. So he wrote about plans for rearranging a skiing holiday with his acquaintances: 'such wonderful friends to have fun with – only missing a companion for me'! That was as close as he came to hinting at what he hoped for the future. He asked if anyone had ever attempted to ski in the Rwenzori Mountains: 'I can't see Mr and Mrs Magara on skis.'

Still there was no reply. He rifled expectantly through his mail every evening, looking for a gaudy stamp that would tell him he had a letter from Uganda. Once, on the ward, he saw a black nurse facing away from him at the nursing desk. She held herself like Felice and it stopped him in his tracks. The nurse turned and saw him looking at her. Her skin darkened as she flushed. She turned quickly back to her charts.

As time passed Michael concluded that Felice must still be in a state of shock; in secluded mourning. Perhaps she had not even opened her post. He borrowed a book on bereavement from the psychology section of the medical school library (an aisle he had never entered before), to better understand the emotions Felice would be experiencing; to find the right words to comfort her.

First denial, then anger, then bargaining, then depression – then acceptance.

What stage would she be at now? Maybe she was in a prolonged stage of anger. Possibly furious with God or, God forbid, resenting him, whose visit had been the trigger for Stanley's death. Perhaps she was questioning his surgical skills. Perhaps Kabutiiti had already taken her to his home. He wondered if it were possible to aid her rapid passage through the stages of grief. Shortcut the tedious process. Give her some advice that would propel her straight through to 'acceptance'. He wrote down some homilies, practising several turns of phrase on a scrap of paper.

'… it's not that you get over a loss like yours, but that the naked awfulness eventually moves out of the living room, into a cupboard …'

'… Stanley would have wanted you to find happiness again …'

But the sentiments did not read as coming from himself; it was if he had lifted someone else's words and copied them down, which was close to the truth. He made a ball of the paper and threw it, in one, into the bin on the other side of the room. He wished his ability to give counsel was as good as his co-ordination. For the first time in years he regretted his estrangement from his sister, Rachel. At a time like this a man needed family confidants, preferably female.

He restarted his letter and wrote:

I wonder if a break away from your own environment, with its reminders of what has happened, would be helpful. It would be a chance to relax. I know a charming hotel for you in Holland Park and would be very pleased to arrange everything – and some spending money for shopping in Knightsbridge nearby! I could take you to some London shows – show you the 'real' London, just as you wanted to show me the 'real' Africa – it might help a bit to laugh again. Of course, if you would prefer to be left completely on your own while you're here that would be fine as well – whatever you want.

When he took the letter to post, late that night, he held it dangling in the mouth of the post-box, suddenly unsure whether his offer was propitious; perhaps he should have offered to pay for Beatrice to come as well, as a companion. He was beginning to worry that Felice saw him as highly intrusive, an embarrassing problem for her to cope with, in addition to her bereavement. But he concluded that he needed to act, and sprung his fingers open to release the letter. He could not afford to be timid; time was not on his side.

Still the weeks passed with no answer. He became irritable at work: he snapped at a perfectly sweet theatre nurse for not being quick enough to pass the instruments as he operated, told his house officer that she had it easy compared to his day, and left his registrar to see the post-operative cases so that he could get home early to check his post. After six months his petulance changed to despair. He convinced himself that Felice had forgotten him. Recklessness took over. He found himself flirting with his secretary, who appeared pleased: she started coming in with a denser shade of red lipstick. He rang up Naomi but a man answered the phone, so he excused himself as ringing a wrong number. He drove to the south coast on a free weekend and sailed a yacht with a colleague. He went to the boat show at Earls Court and bought yachting magazines, attempting to generate a lust for something sleek and expensive. It was all pointless but he had to occupy every waking minute.

When Felice's air letter arrived – on a morning in April when the buds on the trees in his street were splitting their scales – he slit the letter open the wrong way in his haste, completely detaching its lower third, which fluttered to the floor. He retrieved it impatiently and read the letter, pacing up and down in the hallway. As he finished reading he shouted out, 'For Pete's sake!'

She was polite: thanking him for his correspondence, apologising for taking so long to reply, thanking him for doing all he could to save Stanley's life and for his financial generosity. He was a 'true friend'. She was unable to take up his kind offer of coming to London: 'I need to be with my family and friends.' The funeral had been 'difficult but, nevertheless, a joyful occasion'. Over a thousand people had attended to give thanks for Stanley's life. The archbishop had talked of 'a vision brought to completion', and said that Stanley had lived his life as if he knew it would not last long, that he had to achieve all he could in a short time. Then, at the end of the letter, 'Please keep writing, Michael. Your letters have been welcome.' She signed herself, 'Affectionately, Felice'.

When he re-read it he wondered why his initial reaction had been negative – as if he had assumed she would be straining to get on the next plane out of Uganda. The letter was warm; as warm as could be expected of a recently bereaved woman. It was encouraging that she had not mentioned Kabutiiti.

A few days later he received another letter from Uganda. The address was written in a precise masculine hand. For a moment he feared it was from Kabutiiti, politely telling him of their engagement, but the address on the back was the McCrees'. James apologised for taking so very long to send his appreciation of Michael's contribution to the conference, which all agreed was a success and had put Uganda back on the academic medical map after the destruction of the Amin years.

It went on:

I need to tell you that the accountant you met in Lwesala, Adoko Ojera, visited me in my office yesterday to ask me to pass on the bank account details (see below) of the charity you talked of setting up. You are certainly a man of action! Ojera seems a charming and reliable man – just the sort to administer the financial side of the charity. I note that you have changed the charity's remit from what I recall of our original conversation, but I was impressed with your idea of getting in early with helping the families of victims of Slim. I can tell you that the numbers of new cases are multiplying dramatically and the international media are now swarming all over us for the big story. Difficult for us expatriates as we have to be careful what we say. There are political implications and cultural sensitivities to this disease. You might be interested to read the emerging literature, particularly from the US, on the new disease dubbed AIDS. There are strong similarities to Slim – I suspect that they are one and the same.

Mr Ojera says he will implement everything you had discussed, as soon as the first payment is made into the account. I hope you will accept my making the first donation.

Michael found himself cursing aloud. A jinx had followed him; he looked up, expecting to see a black cockerel feather on the window ledge. He pulled out his diary and found the McCrees' phone number. As he waited, tapping his finger on the telephone table in impatience, he imagined Zachye at that very moment hunting Kabutiiti down. What if he had killed him already? But his heart jerked in a conflicting current of emotion. He moved the phone a little away from his ear – on the cusp of putting it down. Had anyone seen him and Zachye together that night at the transport stop? What to do? Still the phone rang. He was about to conclude that the McCrees were out when Audrey answered the phone.

'Yes?' he heard her say flatly.

'This is Michael here – Michael Lacey.'

'Oh, Michael, how nice to hear you.' She brightened. 'We were thinking of you today: we met Stanley's cousin Kabutiiti at the Uganda Bookshop having a coffee.'

'You did? Thank God!

'Sorry?'

'Er – how was he?'

'He looked well – he had a lady with him.'

'His fiancée?' His heart leapt.

'He didn't introduce her as his fiancée – just a friend. He's going to New York tomorrow for a year. Some post at the UN. Seems pleased with himself.'

Michael released his breath. He had an urge to open a bottle of champagne and invite Doug round to share it. The villain had been neutralised without the maniac, Zachye, lifting a finger. A close call.

'Did you ring for any particular reason?' asked Audrey, sounding remote.

'Did James mention a man who claimed to be operating an account for a charity? The charity I'm hoping to set up for the surgical training?'

'No, but then we're not talking much at present. I'm hard going again.'

'Unfortunately the man was an impostor. James was going to make a gift into the account and I wanted to warn him off.'

'That's typical of James. He's generous, but gullible. I'll let him know.'

'Thank you.'

'Were you ringing for any other reason? You sounded a bit anxious earlier.'

'No – just that.'

'You've put Felice out of your mind I hope?'

'Well, I would like to know whether she's all right.'

'Kabutiiti said she's coping well.'

'Good. Umm …'

'Did you say something?' Audrey asked.

'I do think about her.'

'I thought you might. Forget about her, Michael. Find someone from your own culture. So much less complicated. It's not just your different backgrounds, you know. Felice is steeped in her spiritual world – most Africans are – you can't begin to understand her unless you recognise that. You'll never be soul mates; you're oil and water, Michael, and I'm not making a judgement on you at all.'

Despite Audrey's reassurance, Michael felt a little stung. He said, 'I had exposure to the religious views that Felice holds when I was a child. I do understand it.' It was the first time that he had admitted that aspect of his childhood to anyone. He wondered if Audrey knew anyway through her – what was it? – clairvoyant powers or, more likely, her sharp intuition.

'No, I don't think you do. She doesn't have views, as you call them. That implies the holding of an opinion: looking out through a shade of glass that one holds up oneself. What Felice has is far deeper: it's something projected out; she emanates it, radiates it.

He thanked her for her advice and sent his regards to James. When he put down the phone he considered Audrey's words carefully. If he deeply loved Felice, should he not learn to swim in the same sea? The sea of faith. For her sake. Others had done more: some slain dragons, embarked on impossible quests, the biblical Jacob had worked as a slave for fourteen years to win Rachel. He sighed; faith seemed to be something given rather than self-generated, and he could not make himself believe, could not conjure up visions, feel religious. For the first time he feared that he was not the right man for Felice. That he might taint her in saving himself. Even destroy her.

TWELVE

Dear Michael,

I wished to write again to say how kind you were in writing to me so often in the early months of my loss. It was a help to me. I have been less than courteous in only writing back once, but grief did strange things to time. The weeks and their happenings fell haphazardly – in no particular order, or sometimes all at once. Now my orientation is restored and I have started to look to the future again.

I hope your work is going well, you sound as busy as Stanley always was. Find time to relax.

As for myself, I have had to make many decisions as to what to do next. There is no doctor yet to replace Stanley at Lwesala although the Central African Fellowship may send a retired general practitioner from the UK to help as a stopgap. Regrettably I am not qualified to take Stanley's place.

Michael looked up from the page. Would he go and work at Lwesala if that was what it would take to win Felice? Could love exist divorced from the world in which it found itself?

'My big news is … ',

He turned the page to read on, his heart missing a beat,

'… that I am to study for a Masters in Pharmacology in Nairobi – thanks to the generosity of Kabutiiti, although I have not seen him for a long time. He is in New York as a VIP! I start in six weeks.'

Michael bounded upstairs to his office and searched along his neatly indexed files. He pulled out the Proceedings of the Twelfth Conference of the Lake Regions Surgical Association. There it was: 'Minutes of the Committee'. Second last item in the minutes. 'The next annual conference will be held in Nairobi from the ...'

'Four months' time!'

She finished her letter warmly, hoping that they would be able to meet again.

Michael placed the letter on the shelf above the desk, sniffing it before he folded it in case a trace of her perfume had lingered, trapped in the creases. He touched the stamp – she would have licked it. I've gone crazy, he thought: emotions out of control; dangerous. But I don't care.

He wrote back immediately to say that, by happy coincidence, he was attending the surgeons' conference again, that it happened to be in Nairobi, and would she like to meet?

Until she replied the objective of his days was to reach the moment when he got home to look through his post. He woke one night in a sweat, seeing Zachye – about thirty feet tall and a bush fire behind him – on his way to find Felice. To whisper a lie. To destroy his future. He tried to run after him but Zachye's long legs made his own efforts hopeless. At the brothel he got on the bus to get to Felice more quickly but Zachye leant down, removed the keys and threw them over the Rwenzori Mountains. Zachye bent down again before he disappeared towards Lwesala and whispered in Michael's ear, 'I loved her before you did.'

He could not get back to sleep. By dawn he had decided that he must take a necessary precaution: to start a small monthly deposit into Zachye's 'charity' account to ensure that Zachye kept his mouth shut. These were critical times. It was a fraction of what Zachye had demanded – just enough, he hoped, to prevent him spreading rumours, and if it ever came to light he felt some justification in claiming that he feared Zachye would threaten Felice, or the other witness, unless he paid up. He could not go to the police because of Stanley's last wish, which he felt honour-bound to keep. A practical and logical case – and it would, ultimately, be for Felice's sake.

He did not have to wait long for Felice's reply to his request to see her in Nairobi. She would be delighted. After that Felice wrote regularly – an increasingly relaxed correspondence that replicated, as far as it was possible by the written word, the bonhomie that they had established face to face before Stanley's death. Her letters were long and detailed: her friends, her family, everyday events, small happenings. She picked up on the scraps of news in his own letters and asked for more: 'Hope your secretary, June, is better soon ... Did you enjoy your conference in Turin? I would like to see Italy one day ... How was your registrar's wedding? ... You must be pleased with your new car.'

Starting one of Felice's letters, Michael's eye was drawn down the page to Zachye's name. She had written:

I did not mention before now that Zachye failed to attend Stanley's funeral. That will hardly surprise you until I tell you that our traditional beliefs compel us to attend the funeral of friend and enemy alike, or forever suffer the wicked attentions of the ghost of the deceased. So Zachye will be fearful, although I believe Stanley, even in death, would wish Zachye no harm. I pray I will one day be given the grace to feel the same about Zachye ...

I was thinking today about your invitation to me to come over to the UK. Is it too late to take up your offer? It would have to wait until I've finished my masters. Perhaps we can discuss it when I see you. I'm looking forward to that, Michael – very excited to think that I'll see you again and laugh with you and have some fun. It seems as if it's been a long time since I could really relax. I think back to when we talked by the fire in the Queen Elizabeth National Park. Please don't forget your poems. I'd love to hear them again.

In theatre one morning, while scrubbing up, Michael started humming 'The Lion Sleeps Tonight'. His house officer, Jenny, glanced at him along the line of taps.

'You're happy this morning, Mr Lacey.'

'I'm in love,' he said, shocking himself with his unabashed reply.

He saw Jenny cast an eye at the nurse behind him unwrapping the sterile gowns, and could imagine her mouth falling open in silent return of his house officer's astonishment.

'That's nice. What's she like?' she dared to ask.

'Beautiful of course – and bloody hard to catch.'

'When's the wedding then?' the nurse said boldly.

Michael re-established order. 'What did you say earlier about the X-rays? They've not arrived in theatre yet?'

The operation – a gastrectomy for stomach cancer – was technically challenging but his hands worked easily amongst the metal retractors, swabs, clips, suckers and the lines of thread which came up from the wound like the ordered cables of a suspension bridge.

Doug, the Australian anaesthetist, was leaning over the towels at the head of the patient, watching him operate.

'Haven't you got anything to do up there, Doug?' Michael asked.

'I'm bored,' Doug said, holding his half-tied mask (colourful with Disney characters) to his round face. 'Nothing screws up in your theatre. I won't mention your colleague, Mr Barnabas Smithy Smythe, by name, but with him I'm fighting to keep the patient alive while he carries out all sorts of bloody atrocities in the abdomen.'

Michael heard the sniggering of the nurses. He would normally have stopped the banter at that point by his silence but he had released a tension and it felt cathartic. 'It works both ways. With your fellow antipodean gasman, I have to hold down the patient with one hand while I operate single-handed with the other.'

'No shit!'

'Language please, Doctor,' the theatre sister said. Michael thought that she looked like an eagle owl with her fiercely angled eyes and fixing stare. She reminded him of Auntie Beryl at his junior school.

'The patient's unconscious, no worries,' boomed Doug, rotating his mask up so that the lower half now covered his eyes, prompting open laughter from the nurses but a disdainful snort from the theatre sister.

The theatre became hushed once more. Felice came to Michael's mind again. She was never far from him now, like an entwining silk: lightly running, an erotic charging, sometimes a cool teasing, always a tugging.

He said, 'Did you know that John Hunter, the seventeenth-century surgeon, said that Eve was indisputably black?'

'What? Aboriginal?' Doug asked.

'Sure, African aboriginal.'

'Well, I'm whomped! My nana would never believe that.'

Jenny chipped in, 'They're going to find the Eve ancestor one day, if they keep digging for bones in Tanzania.'

Michael pushed a little on the retractor that she pulled on, to remind her to concentrate on giving him full access to his field of operation, then said, 'I've found my own black Eve already.'

'Your Sheila's aboriginal?' Doug pulled his mask under his chin.

'Yes.'

'Fuck me! Good on you, mate.'

Michael smiled under his mask. Everything was going to turn out well.

He felt nervous when he rang Felice's number as soon he had dumped his suitcase on his bed in the New Stanley Hotel in Nairobi. The irony of its name was not lost on him – his private joke. Felice had told him that she was staying with family friends in the suburbs. There seemed to be too few digits in the number for a capital city. He feared that she had inadvertently given him an incorrect number.

'Hello.'

'Ah, hello.'

'Hello?'

'Yes, hello. Could I speak to Felice Katura?'

'Hello?'

'Hello. Could I speak to Felice Katura?'

'Whom do you wish to speak to?'

'Mrs Katura. Felice Katura.'

'Hello?'

He assumed that the recipient of his call could either not hear him or could not understand him and so he reverted to a trick he had used on European holidays: to use any native word he happened to know to demonstrate just how futile it was for the recipient to attempt to communicate in anything but English.

'*Asante sana*, Felice,' he shouted down the mouthpiece.

'She's not in.'

'When will she be in?'

'Hello?'

'Please, is there anyone else I can talk to?'

'Felice is not in.'

'Yes, I know.'

'So why do you ring?'

'Look! When will Felice be in?'

'Maybe an hour.'

'OK, thank you. Tell her Michael Lacey rang. I'll phone back in an hour.'

He unpacked, set his alarm, had a shower, lay on the bed pretending to read and then rang back five minutes before the alarm was due. His heart pounded as he waited; he wondered if Felice would be able to feel the throbbing down the line.

The same voice answered. 'Hello.' He assumed she was the maid.

'Yes, it's me again. Mr Lacey. Is Mrs Katura back?'

'She came back.'

At last. 'Can I speak to her?'

'It's not possible.'

'Sorry?'

'She's gone away.'

'What?'

The maid repeated herself.

'Did you tell her I rang and was going to ring back?'

'I informed her.'

'Well? What did she say?'

'She said nothing. She went away.'

'You told her that Mr Lacey rang?'

'I informed her.'

'Did she not ask me to ring back?'

'She did not.'

He lay that night, alone, knowing Felice was still far away, still on another continent.

The university refectory was packed with students, and noise. He scanned the tables, working systematically from near to far. She was sitting with three other girls by a far window (the blinds half pulled down against the tropical sun), hardly distinguishable from the other students in her jeans and white blouse. As always, she wore her cowry shell earrings. He walked boldly to the table, catching the attention of a few students who followed his progress. He suspected they believed he was some tourist with a crush on a black girl he had met in a bar; or a foreign lecturer unaware that this was the students' domain.

She saw him coming, exclaiming, 'Oh!' so that her companions followed her gaze.

'Felice, I'm sorry to surprise you.' She had her hand across her heart. 'Is there anywhere quiet we can talk?' He waved a hand at the bright lawn outside with its honeysuckle hedge and low-boughed trees.

She looked away from him at a point in the middle of the table. 'I have a lecture in … ten minutes.'

'Yes, she has a lecture now,' said the girl sitting next to her, fast on the uptake.

Michael looked steadily at Felice. She glanced up at him, her face set. He found he had stopped breathing, was perfectly still.

She looked at the table again but he could see that she was wavering. Turning to her companions, she said, 'Will you leave us alone for a few minutes?'

The girls got up, scowled at Michael and leant against a wall nearby – watching.

'Thank you,' Michael said. He sat himself down opposite her. 'You have young friends.'

'Yes, I feel old.'

'So do I,' he replied.

There was a silence. He waited for her to explain her sudden change of sentiment. It occurred to him that there were parallels in what was happening with those occasions when Naomi had wanted to understand him – but now the tables were turned: it was he who wanted to make sense of the woman.

'Can I pour you some water?' he asked.

She nodded. The silence continued until he said quietly, 'Felice, I've come a long way. Why do you not want to see me?' He tried to look into her eyes but she was still looking down. Her long eyelashes curved seductively. 'I love you.'

He had not meant to say it. Not now.

She bent forward a little, an involuntary spasm, as if she had been punched in the solar plexus.

'Have I totally surprised you?'

'Michael, I cannot.' Still she would not look at him.

He blurted, 'What do you need from me, Felice?' What did she want most? He hesitated, and then said with as much tenderness as he could muster, 'I'd like children too, you know.'

She dropped her head, and he saw that she was fighting back tears. He wanted to reach out to her, but stayed cemented to his chair.

'What's wrong? Is it skin colour?'

She made a small shake of her head.

'Is it culture? My background is closer to yours than you think.'

She sat herself up straight. 'No – something has happened.'

'I can see that.' He leant towards her and opened out his hand. 'So let's not hide anything. Don't they say love conquers all?'

'Some love, yes.'

He sensed her regaining her self-assurance; he feared what might be coming. He almost hoped that their conversation would end in an inconclusive state and leave room for hope: the very act of asking Felice to explain might confirm her in whatever contrary state she had fallen into. On the other hand surgical incisiveness demanded action: expose it, fix it.

'Surely romantic love can do it? If that's not strong enough what the hell is?' He could not hide his welling exasperation. 'Felice, do you have no feelings for me?' He immediately regretted his outburst, and said gently, 'Is there another man?'

She seemed unable, or unwilling, to answer. Her jaw had hardened and she had fastened her gaze on the middle of the table again. He saw her friends start to move themselves off the wall.

She looked up and fixed him with steely eyes. 'Was it just flattery?'

Now Michael felt he'd been punched. Anger and confusion rose together. A ten thousand mile round trip for this.

'I have to go,' she said. She picked up her handbag and took out a small mirror, but then put it back without using it.

He became aware of the cross girlfriend squeezing past him to get to Felice. A kraal of feminine alliance was about to take her in.

He leant forward and said urgently, 'I'll wait for you. The rest of my life, if necessary.'

'Don't,' she said, her voice calm, resolved.

Felice's friend had put her arm around her shoulders, fixing an accusatory stare at Michael. The students at the next table were watching. He got up and left, side-stepping his way around students carrying their trays to the tables. A male student jostled him. 'Get your prick out of Kenya, *Muzungu*.'

He got out of Kenya that evening. He left a message for James McCree, who had come down to the conference from Uganda, to apologise and say that an urgent problem had called him back to the UK.

Suffocation accompanied him in the aeroplane. One word pressed in on him: flattery. He forced himself to face it: she thought his sentiments towards her were cheap, calculating and manipulative. She had precipitately reassessed him. But he was surprised that, as overwhelming as his feelings of loss were, he felt little indignation. She might be right – perhaps his infatuation had been nothing more than self-serving.

At home Michael washed and changed, and went straight to work. Keeping sane was his priority, and he decided that hard work was the only prophylaxis. If he stopped to think he feared he would howl like a demented animal.

He took the stairs up the nine floors to the surgical office, rather than jump into a cubicle of the paternoster that travelled in a continuous loop up one side of the lift shaft and down the other.

June, his secretary, jumped as he burst through the door. 'Oh, I've got you down as back on Thursday.'

'Sorry, June, change of plan. What's in my in-tray?'

'I've not sorted it yet – you've surprised me. Anyway, here it is.'

She handed him a wire basket full of letters to sign, memos from the administration, referrals from general practitioners and a few unopened envelopes marked confidential.

'You've got a letter from Uganda.'

He looked at the address. The hand was large, almost childlike, with some words in capitals and some in lower case:

Dr LACY
DOCTOR
SAINT Tomas HOSPITAL
London
GREAT Britain

'I'm surprised it got here,' June said.

Michael dismissed it. 'Probably someone asking for money.' As soon as he had said it, he froze. Fate grant it was not Zachye requesting more cash. 'I'll take the lot through to my office.'

His office overlooked the River Thames. When the wind was right he could hear the tour boats. 'To our right is St Thomas's Hospital, founded in 1275, but on its present site since 1871 … To our left are the Houses of Parliament …'

He closed the door, picked up the letter knife from his desk, took the envelope over to the window and turned it over. There was no return address but three strips of brown box-tape covered the flap as if the sender was determined that it should not reveal its contents accidentally. The envelope ripped as he peeled back the tape. He pulled out a piece of paper torn from a lined exercise book. The writing was uneven, like the address.

Dear Doctor

I hope you are well and romance is progressing to your satisfaction. K went away and so I could not fulfil my side of the matter hastily. Fortunately he came back this week for a holiday. You will understand me.

Michael looked through the razor-edged Venetian blinds at the slug of grey water beneath him. Understand? Oh God! He grabbed the blind with one hand but it collapsed under his palm. His eyelid started to twitch. He read the rest of the letter.

You are a honourable man so I am asking you to fulfil your obligations to me. The money you have been sending has been welcome but is not enough according to our agreement. Now I have complied most fully I am looking for your early convenience on the matter.

With felicitations and sincere greetings,

A Ojera (you will understand me)

He stuffed the letter and envelope into his trouser pocket and stared down through the slits of the blind into the river below. A barge was vomiting black smoke from its chimney. They might have been black feathers. He pressed his fingers against his eyes until they hurt. When he took his hands away the Houses of Parliament on the opposite bank of the river broke free of the earth like a giant airship, before crashing down again. Vertigo made him stagger back.

He made for the door and almost collided with June in the corridor. He heard himself say, 'June – apologies – not feeling well – picked up something tropical. Going home.'

'You shouldn't rush about so much, Mr Lacey. Knowing you, I'm sure you'll be back tomorrow.'

He nodded at her mechanically, made his way to the stairwell and threw himself into the paternoster. As he passed each floor he wondered if he could stick his head out at the right moment and decapitate himself. They said it was impossible, but he might succeed if he was determined. Somehow he missed the ground floor and went around the bottom of the loop through a grimy basement groaning with the meshing of teeth and the strain of belts and pulleys.

When he found himself at home again he immediately made a fire in the grate and burnt the letter and envelope. That's what a murderer does, he told himself.

'Human misery would be intolerable if it was not diluted in time,' he had read somewhere, but now time had stopped.

Sitting in a chair, rocking, he watched the letter and envelope burn; the tape on the envelope contorted and smoked heavily before melting. The shape of a feather emerged from the blackening letter. An ashy fetish had found its way in; had breached the walls of his white, ice-hard house. He carried on rocking for two days, only getting up to pee and to quench his thirst from the tap. On the second day he heard the phone ring several times. He saw visions of fire, of guns, of shapes in the night. He saw Felice trying to offer milk to her husband, but he found himself snatching the milk away from her before she could put it to Stanley's lips. *Nil by mouth, nil by mouth*, he heard himself scold. *Keep to the rules. Scientific rules. They're there for a reason.*

On the third day he drank the contents of his drinks cabinet.

They came for him – he didn't know when.

At first they told him that his precipitate psychosis arose from an encephalitic inflammation of the brain (not countenancing what Audrey told him in a dream – her black hair flew wild, her lips and fingernails a gipsy red – that it might be a combustion of the mind: the buried embers of grief, smouldering for two decades, blown on anew), but when his tapped spinal fluid had been spun of its secrets in the laboratory centrifuges and no pathology found he was transferred to the psychiatry department of his own hospital.

THIRTEEN

Michael felt himself emerging from a thick smog; dust, smoke, feathers clogged his nose and mouth, so that he had to blow and spit. He flapped his arms about to clear the air.

'Whoa, Mr Lacey, it's OK. You're OK.'

Two bulky male nurses were escorting him to a side room.

'Here we are, Mr Lacey.'

'And who are you?' he asked.

'We're here to help you.'

'You've got your own room.'

'I've never met you before,' Michael said. 'What the hell do you think you're doing? Take my money but leave me enough for the taxi. Lay off! Where's security? Look, you're making me late for outpatients.'

'Everything's OK, Mr Lacey, sit down here.' They had their hands on his upper arms and started to manoeuvre him around.

'Lay off!' he shouted. 'You're trying to stop me saving lives.' He shoved one of his assailants and lunged for the door. It was locked. 'Security!' he shouted. He felt their heavy hands on his shoulders and turned to face them. 'I'm not a weakling, you know.' He let fly with his fists.

They floored him and crushed him, big knees in the small of his back, his right arm stapled to the floor. They hauled down his trousers. 'You're perverted!' he screamed. He felt a hornet shoot its poison into his buttock.

He was a patient of a venerable professor who had taught him as a student; elevated enough for Michael, when calmer, to let him interview him. The professor's department held that, as the brain is jellied chemistry, all talking therapies are just holding devices until medical science advances enough to discover which colouring to add to the jelly to change its complexion. Michael was clearly lacking in molecules with hydroxyl and amine side arms. Agitated depression was its mental manifestation, the depletion triggered by some environmental event or genetic switch. But so what? Boost the chemical and the trigger was irrelevant.

In moments of relative lucidity, when the fire temporarily flared out, this professorial analysis made sense to Michael; it explained what had happened in logical terms that he could understand, although it troubled him that chemicals could not neutralise the past and what he had done, and could not alter Felice's opinion of him. He had already tried ethanol on the third day of his insanity.

A woman, whom he thought might have been his mother, appeared to him one night, a long way off, but she could not be reached.

An indeterminate time later the medication had dampened the flames enough for him to be allowed home under supervision. He was surprised, and found tears of gratitude threatening, when Naomi visited after she had finished work one day. She looked elegant and tall in her dark trouser suit, blonde hair cut short and neat, quite the lawyer. He was quiet and apprehensive but she came in cheerily, kissing him strongly on the cheek.

'Jeepers, Michael, you've given me a fright. I didn't realise when we last spoke that you were getting ill.'

She insisted he sat down (although he preferred to pace) while she made him a drink. He perched on the edge of a chair in the dining room next to the kitchen, trying to remember when his illness had started. Perhaps he had been ill for years.

'It's kind of you to visit. I don't deserve it.'

She was making such a noise with the cupboards, cutlery and cups that it sounded as if she was eagerly demolishing his kitchen.

'Oh Michael, you're not all bad, you know! Remind me where you keep your tea bags.'

'I might need a lawyer, Naomi. Will you represent me?'

'Found them.' There was the sound of pottery cracking. 'Oops.'

'Of course, if you'd rather recommend someone else ...'

'Don't worry, I'll replace your pot. Now you see why I always eat out.'

He heard the tap being turned on too far and splashing out of the sink.

'Aw, shucks.'

'Naomi, I'm going to need legal help.'

More slamming and banging. Eventually she said, 'They were just trying to help, you know. Just trying to make you better.'

'I'm serious, Naomi, you don't know the half of it.'

She came through with one mug of super-strong tea and placed it in front of him as if it was a medicinal gruel. She sat herself down opposite him, straight backed.

He said, 'Aren't you having ... ?'

She interrupted, 'I ought to say, Michael, I've got a new boyfriend.'

Michael stared into his mug. He thought she was going to lay a hand on his arm, but if she was she changed her mind, and flattened her thin fingers on the table. At last he said, 'I'm pleased for you. I'm sorry I wasn't able to be what you wanted.'

She looked as if she was about to contradict him, but he said, 'No secrets between you, I expect. That was our problem, but you know that, don't you? My inability to open up.'

'Oh Michael, I don't blame you at all. We all know it's hard to talk about ... mental illness.'

He glanced up at her. There was concern. She pitied him. There was no point in disabusing her.

She left soon after that and wouldn't let him walk her to her car. 'Best for you to stay in and rest, I think.'

He was sure he would never see her again.

Whether it was part of his madness, or a rational search for pardon, he set out as an explorer of London's churches. Most were empty but sometimes he found an island of faith. He sat at the back, ignoring any attempts by any worshipper to engage with him. He found African diasporas, come via the West Indies to the West End, singing of being washed in the blood of the Lamb. He fled when the minister yelled, 'there is someone here tonight who has been possessed by a devil. Yes, Looord, someone who has been to Africa, invited a spirit to enter. I see a fetish – a black fowl. The Looord is calling you to come forward to receive the laying on of hands.'

He found tiny Anglican congregations populated by people so old that they seemed to have grey socks pulled over the faces. He was startled by triumphant middle class evangelicals. He tried to make himself comfortable on the pews of small Baptist chapels where humble men sat next to gentle women, faces peaceful, bathed in the scriptures. He listened to alien chants in a Greek Orthodox church, although he retained a distaste for 'bells and smells' from his Protestant schooling. He read Chesterton, Weil, Kierkegaard, Barth. He dismissed the East as too far from the African soul. He shopped for New Age beliefs, closely studied horoscopes, read the writing on the walls of public toilets – until he was admitted back onto the ward.

He heard mention of ECT but the professor insisted that other medication be tried first. 'I don't want to risk electrocuting whatever makes his hands do their fine work,' the professor said to his senior registrar outside his room. Michael lifted his hands in front of him as he lay in his bed and saw them tremble. He doubted he would ever operate again.

For three weeks he lay there, or sat slumped, inert, in a chair, taking the pills. Sometimes faint voices came to him: people who loved him when he was a child, although he could not make out their faces or what they whispered. That made him anxious.

And then one morning he woke to find himself in a new calm – although detached – state. It felt, at last, as if the correct receptors had been stimulated. A switch had been tripped.

He dressed himself. When the professor dropped in on his daily round, Michael was standing by the window wondering who had been doing his work while he had been away, and feeling embarrassed at what had happened to him. How could he ever show his face again? The sooner he put on a mask and got back into the operating theatre, the better.

'Ah, good morning, Michael. Are you going somewhere?'

Michael's overnight bag was beside his bed, ready packed. He had paced up and down beside his bed for an hour, thinking that on his own ward rounds he would have seen all his patients by now; wondering where the professor had got to.

'John, I'm completely cured. Time for me to get back to work.'

'Well … good … but I think we'll need to take that slowly.'

'On the contrary, the sooner I return the less chance there is of a relapse. I'll ring June and find out if there's a list this afternoon.'

'I wasn't thinking of … quite that soon,' the professor said.

Typical psychiatrist: unable to make snap decisions, Michael thought, and said, 'Come on, John. Now I'm better you can't expect me to occupy some half-existence. It'll set me back.'

'Unfortunately, there are regulatory committees to convince.'

'And who chairs those committees, professor?'

'Point taken, but …'

He was interrupted by a bang on the door, and in came Doug. He was in his theatre greens and wore pink clogs and his Disney cap.

'Sorry – am I interrupting? Had a few moments before Smithy Smythe's list and thought I'd drop in to taunt the madman.'

'Thank God you've come,' Michael said. 'I'm trying to convince the professor here that I'm saner now than I ever was. I'm … well … purged, and – what do they say? – a rounded human being again. I want to start back at work today, but the professor's telling me that I can't even start tomorrow.'

'Prof, I'm whomped,' Doug said, 'The guy's a bloody genius. I'd let him operate on my nana, right now. Let him do a list with me first if you like.'

Michael and Doug were bigger than the professor, and it was two professional opinions against one. He looked intimidated. 'Well, perhaps we'd better sit down and talk things through.'

The professor had greater powers than Michael had anticipated: it was six weeks before he was allowed to operate again. At first he worked with intense concentration, and silently, a hush falling on those who worked with him. Even Doug pretended to be busy at the top end. Later, finding his hands dependable and their reuse restorative, he regained a work rhythm. The professor commented: 'Good. You've dug a rut; now stay in it.'

Months later, and with no relapse, he found that he had developed a spark of motivation to take up the McCrees' offer, in their Christmas card, to stay in their croft near Arisaig in the western highlands of Scotland. The croft overlooked the islands of Rhum, Eigg and Muck. The absurdity of the names drew him.

He stayed a night with James and Audrey in Glasgow on his way up to their croft. They were back for good now. Audrey had insisted on returning to look after her father who had suffered a stroke. She kissed Michael warmly and James greeted him like a lost soulmate. James could not stop reminiscing about Uganda but Audrey was more interested in showing off her garden. She had plumped out a little and was relaxed, comfortable in a knitted Fair Isle cardigan and a tweed skirt of old-fashioned earthy colours.

At dinner James said he was sorry to hear that Michael had been 'off-colour'. Michael made little of his illness, but Audrey was too perceptive.

'We've all been there, Michael.'

James told him he just needed a break. Audrey seemed to have guessed that his depression had been hooked into his feelings for Felice and avoided mentioning her, but James said, 'Felice got her masters, I gather. Bright girl.'

Michael nodded once.

'Before I forget,' James said, 'You remember that man who tried to con us into putting money into his account?'

'I do.'

'I saw his face in the newspaper before we left – arrested for armed robbery. That was curious enough to see, but when I read on I discovered that he'd been caught in Kabutiiti's residence. Mind you, crime's so rampant that very few escape being a victim. Still – I'd met the man myself.'

'What happens to those convicted of murder in Uganda?' Michael asked.

'It wasn't murder – armed robbery. Although I suppose it might have been murder if the night-watchman hadn't pinned him to the wall with his panga.

'So Kabutiiti was unharmed?'

'I believe so.'

Audrey said, 'Are you all right, Michael? You've gone pale.'

'Och!' James said, laying on the accent, 'he just needs some fresh Highlands and Islands air.'

Michael said, 'Excuse me, I need the bathroom.'

He bent over the basin waiting for the nausea to pass. Zachye had lied – must have sent his letter before he set off to kill Kabutiiti … in his eagerness for more money. For over a year he had believed himself to be an accomplice to murder. Believed that he should hang. Now he was reprieved; the victim had been resurrected. But he felt no elation. He had lost Felice anyway. She had probably married Kabutiiti by now. But why had Felice rejected him so precipitously? Maybe Zachye had confessed to the attempted murder and implicated him. He doubted it; the sentence for armed robbery would be long enough without volunteering for more. Something else must have happened. Of course it had – how could he have thought otherwise? Felice would hardly have been in Nairobi, going to lectures, if she had just heard that her benefactor had been murdered. How could he have been so blind? If he had known that it was not the murder of Kabutiiti that had driven a stake through his hope, he would have persisted with her: gone back, written, pleaded, until he could absolve himself or explain. The nausea welled again. He tried to remember the last time that he had been able to control his emotions.

The McCrees' cottage lay in billows of heather on a small bay overlooking startlingly white sands. When the sun appeared between the clouds (islands above islands), the sea swam with streams of blue, turquoise and green. Seabirds rode the fizzing water beyond the headland. Michael walked the lonely paths along the coast. When he came in from his walks he sat on a chair on a platform near the front window that allowed a view of the bay, and stared out to sea.

He had brought books to read, although he found that the shelves were full of discarded novels from previous guests. A stack of board games lay in a corner: none for single players. He picked up a Nevil Shute, *A Town Like Alice*. He had enjoyed reading it many years before, but put it down again when he remembered that the couple in the book got together in the end and, presumably, lived happily ever after.

Preferring the view to books, he looked out with his binoculars, following the passage of yachts between the islands, spotting seals, shearwaters and divers. Letting the binoculars down into his lap he recalled that dewy morning in the National Park with Felice. He remembered the evening before that dawn when they had talked long into the night while Stanley slept beside the fire. How relaxed she had been with him then; how happy. Then her eager correspondence, before whatever had caused her to reject him in Nairobi. There was a desk on the other side of the room. He searched it and found writing paper. Lowering himself slowly onto the stool in front of the desk he centred the pad on the desktop, took a pen from his shirt pocket and started to write.

Dear Felice,

You may be surprised to hear from me after so long and I ask for your forgiveness if this letter is unwelcome. I am sending it to Lwesala in the hope that it will be forwarded. I can't imagine where you are now, or what you are doing, although I heard from James and Audrey McCree that you have gained a masters. My congratulations.

You can picture me, if you wish, sitting in the McCrees' cottage in Scotland, overlooking the sea, and listening to the wind and the seagulls. This is a convalescence – I have not worked for many months, which is quite uncharacteristic – but I'm recovering now.

It may be that you have found happiness with someone new, but if that is not so, then I would like you to know that I have been faithful. I do not know what happened, so suddenly, to make you so appalled at having to meet me in Nairobi, but whatever the reason it would bring me some peace of mind to know it. Maybe I can receive your absolution. I need it. I have the same address in London.

Faithfully yours,
Michael

He left the letter on the desk and went to look at the sea again, its ever-changing surface hiding the mysterious stillness of the deep. Thinking of Felice, and seeing the water, brought the sea of faith to mind: troubled, choppy on the surface, treacherous currents; but beneath, in the depths, something quiet and still, something sustaining and powering. Perhaps just a primitive instinct – but an instinct for hope, for humility, for selfless love (far beyond a socially protective decency, he thought), for searching for transcendence. Something important to his lost family, and important to Felice. He had found a definition of faith that he could lean towards whilst reading the philosopher-theologian Simone Weil: the longing for an absolute good, directing attention and love towards that good. Yearning for Eden. Vague as it was, he wondered whether Felice might think this proof enough of a spiritual awakening – if that was what was important to her. If he met her again, he would tell her that he was sympathetic; he understood the human need; was much less cynical; had seen where his cynicism could lead – its logical consequences. Man cannot live by bread alone.

He returned to the desk and folded the letter. He could not deny that humans had an electrified jelly-mind, but neither could he deny that living as if that was the only truth was self-defeating. A paradox of the human condition. A curse, he felt.

'Is this yours, Mr Lacey?'

Mrs Craddock – hunchbacked, knobble fingered, sallow skinned, but eyes as sharp as a sparrowhawk's – was waiting for him, on the first morning of his return from Scotland, by the low wall that separated their properties. She held a small branch in an outstretched pincer grip, her face turned away as if she had picked up a used condom. In her other hand she held, as always, a hand fork; she spent hours stabbing at her garden. A tight black headscarf gave her a piratical appearance.

Today Michael had neglected, before going out, to look through his front door spy hole to see whether she was lurking. He believed himself to be a low-profile neighbour: polite, quiet, helpful when possible (he had taken out Mrs Craddock's dustbin since her husband died), but she clearly thought otherwise, and was threatening to live on for ever, powered by malice. He was not sure whether a psychotic dementia was creeping up on her, or whether she was innately wicked.

'Sorry, I'm not with you …'

'Are you blind? It's a branch. From your cherry tree. Keep your litter to yourself, young man.'

Her front garden rose behind her, dense as the heart of Borneo: stinging nettles, cow parsley, straggly dogwood, a thick stand of bamboos. Sharply bristling acanthus leant over the wall like a phalanx of spears. The neighbours called it Ealing Forest.

'Must have blown across.' He stretched over and took the stick. 'I'll get rid of it.'

'Another thing, you've got thistles in your back yard.' She never referred to his neat-as-a-crew-cut lawn as a garden.

'Have I?'

'Cut 'em down, Mr Lacey, or they'll seed in my garden.'

'Well, thanks, I'll do it as soon as I can.' He started to move off, nodding as if he much appreciated her advice.

'Another thing, a woman came looking for you.'

'Yes?'

'Yes, Mr Lacey, a *woman*. Yesterday, it was. She hung about your door, ringing your bell. Brazen, she was.'

'Tall with fair hair?' He couldn't tell if Naomi might take it on herself to reappear.

'No, not tall. Dark. Very dark.' She cracked out the 'dark'.

'Dark? Sorry, she was dark skinned or her hair was dark?'

'Not a *darky*, Mr Lacey. Not this one. I said she was dark haired. Are you deaf? Dressed respectable, she was, but it doesn't fool me.'

'Did she say what she wanted?'

'No, and I wouldn't like to think what she *wanted*, Mr Lacey. She asked when you'd be back. How would I know? I said.'

'I think I told you that when I left, but anyway, did she leave a message?'

'Wouldn't have taken a message, would I, Mr Lacey? That would be interfering. You keep your *business* to yourself.' She raised her nose and fought with her lips as if chewing a lemon.

'Did she leave her name?'

'Asked for it, I did, and that's when she took herself off. Ashamed of herself, I should think. Girls like that wouldn't leave a name, would they?'

'Well, got to go now.'

'Another thing.'

He backed down the path, his briefcase in one hand, the errant branch in the other.

'There was a little boy in the car.'

He reached the gate, nodded back, forced a smile and unlatched the gate to go through.

Mrs Craddock raised her voice, making a passing mother and her school-age children turn their heads. 'Looked a bit like you, Mr Lacey, that little boy. Yes, I could quite see the resemblance, I could.'

He closed the gate and strode to his car, a smile on his face; he was confident that he'd never fathered a child. A woman with dark hair? He placed his briefcase in the foot well of the passenger seat, contemplated dropping the cherry branch in the gutter but, fearful of being shouted at by Mrs Craddock, threw it in after the briefcase. Could have been Jo, but he'd not seen her for years. Perhaps it was a patient: someone with a bitter complaint about an operative complication, who had found out his home address. He got behind the wheel smartly – Mrs Craddock had shuffled to her front wall, shaking her head – and slotted the key in the ignition, but sat there for a few seconds arrested by another possibility. Rachel? His sister. She'd be dark haired – chestnut. He toyed with the idea of getting out again to ask Mrs Craddock if the woman had a scar in her left eyebrow – Rachel's face had been lacerated on that fateful, unthinkable day – but she would only assume that in addition to leaving his loose liaisons pregnant he assaulted them. He turned on the ignition. Rachel could well have a child – children – by now. If so, the little boy in the car would be … his nephew. A nephew; his own. A peculiar feeling of regret threatened. He threw the wheel and drew out fast, leaving rubber on the road.

When he arrived home he found a small white padded package face down on the mat. He picked it up and took it through to the kitchen, switching on the kettle before turning the package over. It had been hand delivered, no stamp, just 'Michael' written on the front. He opened it while he waited for the kettle to boil, although his mind was still on his work: he thought he'd return to the hospital later that evening, as there was a patient with abdominal pain whom he wanted to reassess. Since his illness he had become obsessively protective towards his own patients; after all, they were all he had left. When he passed his colleagues in the corridor or sat with them in audit meetings and committees he sensed a veil of embarrassment. But his relationship with his patients was uncomplicated: they needed him, and he needed them.

There was a miniature blue envelope in the package. He shook it out onto the sideboard and was about to pick it up, but stopped when he read the message: 'For Michael. With my love, Rachel.'

'What the … ?'

With an exasperated grunt he swept the card off the sideboard onto the floor and stared at the kettle. The water had started to agitate and protest. Rachel always sent him a card for his birthday, but no anniversary loomed. He had courteously, but firmly, made it plain many years ago that she should not write to him, but still the cards came: a drip-drip torture. He never wrote back. He picked up the envelope to throw it in the bin but felt some hard object inside. He lifted the flap and squeezed the opening so it gaped. A wedding ring. He picked it out and turned it in his fingers.

Three small diamonds. The kettle began to buck and blow.

'Bloody hell!' His mother's ring.

It was cruel, sending him the ring: razor blades would have been more acceptable, certainly more understandable. He cut the kettle's switch and slid the ring onto his little finger. It would not go past the first joint. He rested his hand flat on the kitchen sideboard staring at the three stones. As clear as his own hand he saw his mother's hand as she knelt beside his bed – that time when he was about seven and had wanted to sell one of the diamonds to buy his father a car fast enough to race in the East African Safari Rally. He tried to bring to mind their conversation, but could not even recall the sound of her voice. He did remember pleading with Rachel the next day, something like 'If you don't have a baby girl when you grow up please will you give me Mum's ring, 'cause I'll be your next most special person.'

'Damn her!'

It was not until three weeks later that an event occurred of sufficient consequence to rub out the nagging disturbance of Rachel's gesture. He was in the hall when the postman dropped an air letter through the post-box. It had a brilliant stamp, oversized and colourful, so it looked like a tropical butterfly flapping down onto the mat. The stamp was Tanzanian; the letter from Felice. Michael made himself go and sit down at the dining table before he opened it. He gripped the paper as if it might be snatched from him.

Dear Michael,

I received your letter yesterday. I am so sorry that you've been ill. I pray for your full recovery. Many things have happened since we last met. It has been a great regret to me that I was rude to you when you came to see me in Nairobi – and that I was not able to say what had happened. So now I should have the courage to speak to you. I have a post as a lecturer at the University of Dar es Salaam. Would you be able to come and see me? Circumstances make it impossible for me to come to you. Write soon.

Affectionately,

Felice

He stood up and whooped for joy, as if he had swapped one derangement for another. It was a thin thread of hope, but it was golden.

The man in the smooth black gabardine suit, dark silk shirt and burgundy twill tie in Patel's Precious Stones, Oxford Street, said, 'It's an honour to meet you, Mr Lacey. My cousin in Leicester speaks most highly of you.'

He had a patrician air, and studied Michael imperiously down a sniffy nose, his voice high-pitched, his manner markedly solemn, as if Michael had come to collect a loved one's ashes from a funeral parlour. Michael thought his perfectly swept black hair must be a toupee.

Michael said, 'I first heard of you when I was a schoolboy in Uganda. Your cousin told me about your jewellery business. I thought I'd ring him first to find out if you were still in the same line.'

Mr Patel gave a little cough. 'Mr Lacey, we've come a long way – a very long way, sir – from those Uganda days. Patel's Precious Stones has outlets in New York, Berlin and Paris. None in the colonies now, sir.' His shoulders shuddered. 'Mr Lacey, perhaps you would like to accompany me to a private room.'

His accent was inflected with a dash of French, particularly on his *r*s, which Michael assumed was there to lend weight to his upper-caste deportment. But the effect was more Inspector Clouseau than Hercule Poirot.

'Would you like coffee, some tea?'

'No thanks.'

'Ah, of course; follow me then, sir.'

They passed through two doors, separated by a short dark stub of corridor. The first required number entry, for which Mr Patel brought his nose close to the keypad to block Michael's view, entering the numbers with little stabs of his fingers. The opening of the second was preceded by the flourishing, in a theatrical fashion, of two heavy keys.

'Here we are, sir.'

Subdued lighting, oak panelling, royal-blue carpet thick enough to hush their footsteps as they entered the room, two Queen Anne chairs

– seated with red velvet – either side of a substantial glass-fronted walnut display cabinet. No doubt there were hidden alarms. Michael checked the ceiling for a vent through which a jewel thief would have to squirm if he were to break in, but the room looked as secure as a clenched fist.

'You were seeking a diamond engagement piece, I believe. I hope you'll find what you're looking for in our premier collection. These are too singular to display at the front.'

Mr Patel positioned himself to the side of the cabinet and then bent stiffly at the waist to press a brass switch on the wall. Even allowing for the cunning illumination, Michael found the shower of glancing light and colour dazzling against the black satin backcloth, as if the constellations had been compressed and miniaturised.

His eye settled on a ring with a single round diamond. 'That one,' he said. The diamond was large, although not ostentatious, and was just the sort of breath-taking stone he had hoped to dig up on Crystal Mountain when he was at junior school.

Mr Patel's hand was hovering.

'Yes, that one.' He had had no idea that it would be so easy to make the choice.

'You have an exceedingly good eye, sir. The gem is graded IF – internally flawless. You'll also observe that there's no yellow tint; it's pure, the mark of an exceptionally rare diamond.' He coughed lightly again and arranged his facial muscles to simulate a faint smile. 'For an exceptionally rare lady, sir?'

Michael was sure that he'd said that before.

Mr Patel unlocked the cabinet with a brass key, lifted out the ring with the care and concentration of a bomb disposal expert and placed it on Michael's palm. 'The cut on this diamond, sir, brings out its intrinsic brilliance.'

'I think she'll love it.'

'Would you like to view the other exhibits?'

'No thank you.'

'Of course not. Do you have a ring from the lady, to ensure a perfect fit?'

Michael found himself reaching for the inside pocket of his jacket and taking out Rachel's blue envelope. He had meant to return his mother's ring to his sister, but could not bring himself to do so until he had achieved something: recalled his mother's face and heard her voice. He had lifted out the ring often, to squeeze the stones between his fingers as if he could evoke a genie of remembrance. Nothing came. It was ironic: he could retrieve every memory verse of his childhood, but couldn't call up his mother. Now he felt impelled to pass the ring to Mr Patel, and say, 'This fits her.'

'Ah, excellent, sir.'

'Right, well, I'll take it then.'

The price was the equivalent of a year's earnings from operating at the Bexworth Private Clinic. He did not hesitate.

FOURTEEN

Michael saw Felice looking for him in the wrong direction over the chairs and tables of the hotel's garden café beside the Indian Ocean. He leapt up and hurried over to her, the rest of the world falling away. Ahead of him he saw his oasis, his infinite light, his bejewelled city. She wore a red silk tube-top and the long twists of her hair extensions – a new style – coiled about her bare shoulders as she turned towards him. He vowed in that moment not to leave Dar es Salaam without her.

He stopped a couple of steps away from her. He could not speak, only look at her. She seemed as tongue-tied as he. Stepping forward to close the space between them he raised a hand to cup her shoulder but let it fall back, as if it would be to touch a woman for the first time, as if in trepidation of the emotions it would evoke. He moved to kiss her on the cheek but then thought it inappropriate to her culture. She started to turn her face to accept him but then checked herself and proffered her hand instead, wrist set a little crooked. She looked down, as if overwhelmed and shy, as he took her hand with the lightest of touches.

He spoke her name and for a moment she let the weight of her hand rest in his palm. He said, 'You're more beautiful than ever.'

She looked back at him, a flashing connection between them. Then it was gone. She turned quickly, abashed or confused; he could not judge.

Michael showed her to his table, pulled out her chair, waited for her to adjust it and then sat opposite, folding his sunglasses and placing them down in front of him. She held her own hands in her lap. The waiter had seen them take their seats and hurried over to take their orders.

Felice smiled fleetingly when he said, 'Indulge yourself: I'm a big chief with many cattle.' She ordered water.

As soon as the waiter had gone she spoke quietly, so that Michael had to lean forward a little to hear. 'I've something important to tell you straight away.'

'That's why I'm here – to listen, to talk.' He saw her throat move but she delayed. 'Go on. There's nothing that can matter between us.'

'I'm engaged to be married again.'

He withdrew his hands. He tried to speak, but failed.

'Michael?' she said, timidly.

'I …' he said eventually, and lapsed into a long silence.

'Michael?' she said again. She twisted and squeezed her fingers. He noticed her ring – an elaborate affair stuck with coloured stones. Even in his shock he found himself thinking they didn't look right on her.

He felt a flush of anger. 'Perhaps you could have told me before I left. I didn't pretend to come for a conference this time. It was at your invitation.'

She looked uncomfortable, but said in a soft but resolute voice, 'I wanted to explain to you why I'm unable to return your love.'

The hot air became viscid. Michael could hardly draw breath to say, 'Where's your fiancé?'

'He's had to go to Kampala.'

He sat silent again, before asking, 'Who's the luckiest man in the world?'

She shifted a little in her chair. 'It's our custom to marry a close relative of the deceased husband.'

He knew it. Kabutiiti, the lucky devil. Now a savage wish gripped him: that Zachye had succeeded in eliminating Kabutiiti. If only it was he that had been born Stanley's relative; perhaps blood brotherhood would have been enough. He had got sufficiently spattered with Stanley's blood to claim it as a ceremony.

He asked, 'Haven't you put your incestuous traditions before your religion?'

She flinched, but then said with conviction, 'They're not incompatible.'

'So – you're to marry Kabutiiti?'

'No, Kabutiiti has an American girlfriend. The custom is to marry the husband's brother. I'm to marry Zachye.'

He stared at her. 'Zachye?'

She did not repeat it. His chest felt constricted. He stood up, knocking his chair over behind him, and walked fast to the edge of the paving. He paced to and fro beside the monstrous sisal leaves in the border – their barbarous thorns. He fought to understand what trickery, what cultural bondage, would lead a woman like Felice to agree to shackle herself to a man like Zachye. It was plain now: he understood nothing about her; only that she was unpredictable. The mid-morning sun roasted his scalp. His eyes smarted from the glare off the paving.

A waiter picked up Michael's chair, casting apprehensive glances at him. Felice had not moved. Their table was under a mango tree; he remembered how he had first met her under another tree, and how it had seemed back then that she might be inviting him to enjoy its fruits. Now she was casting him out: the fiery sword of her new marriage would bar his return forever. Her marriage to the devil.

When he sat down again he saw that her eyes welled with tears. He knew it would make no difference.

He put on his sunglasses. 'I thought Zachye was safely in jail.'

Felice said nothing.

'I thought he'd been arrested for the armed robbery of Kabutiiti's house.'

She regained her voice. 'Kabutiiti refused to press charges. After that Zachye came back to us.' Michael gave a sceptical look. 'He who's forgiven much loves much.' Her voice had strengthened, but held no emotion.

'But you're to marry Zachye, of all people, over the man who loves you!'

'Yes ... Zachye's no longer as you remember him.'

He could see that she was ready to come to Zachye's defence. Could Zachye have changed so much? A Damascus-road-type turnaround?

'I find that hard to believe. Do you love him?' he asked.

She did not respond immediately. 'Does that matter to you?'

Michael nodded.

'Love can grow. He's an honourable man now. He's received forgiveness and he's grateful.'

'So he should be.'

The waiter brought their drinks. Michael's Tropical Sundae Surprise looked ludicrous. The celebration had become a wake. He tried to imagine what it was in Zachye that made Felice feel that she might grow to love him. An extraordinary wit? A little boy lost?

She said in a rush, 'You may hear him on the radio; he plays music. Everyone's playing him. The media have discovered him.'

Michael tried to picture Zachye on a stage, but found himself transported back to the noisy bars near the brothel on the night he had returned from Lwesala to Kampala – those blaring radios.

'He's developed his own style of Congolese soukous,' she added, her voice fading at the end.

There was a stifling silence, during which Felice studied her untouched glass of water and Michael bowed his head and closed his eyes. When the waiter returned and asked if they wanted to eat, Michael waved him away. He steeled himself then, siphoned in the humid air and prepared himself to take his leave. A sudden intense tenderness welled. He had to make this easy for her; he had to find it in himself to allow her the dignity of a courteous parting.

'You're happy?'

She had not yet lifted her glass. 'I'm peaceful.'

He thought he should say he was pleased about that and he wished her well, but changed his mind. 'I think that might not be true, Felice. You're upset. I hate to see that. Is there anything else?'

She glanced anxiously at him as if aware their time together was closing down. 'It's … you and me …'

He saw something in her eyes then that he had not seen plainly before: bewilderment, hurt and the weight of a dilemma. And he saw that she loved him, and he was stricken – they shared the same pain, were trying to reach each other over an unbridgeable gulf. And some beast was in the gulf, which Felice could see and he could not.

'What made you change your mind in Nairobi?'

She let out a retained breath. 'If only ... why did you reject the ways of your parents?'

'My parents?'

'Yes. I knew them well – your mother.'

'You knew her?' He scanned his childhood and remembered the Bible classes on the sisal mat in his childhood home. A room full of eager schoolgirls, captivated by his mother.

'Yes, your mother. I loved her, and your grandfather – he was revered. We're not blind to motives, us Africans. Aid workers, expatriates, religious people, business people; they all have their reasons. We can distinguish.'

He tried to recall Felice as a child but he had not taken much notice of his mother's Bible class girls.

'Then why did you never tell me you knew my parents?' he asked, slumping back in his chair.

'Because I only found out the day before you came to Nairobi for your conference. Your sister told me that you'd cut yourself off from her after your parents' death. She said you'd thrown away everything to do with your childhood.'

'This gets worse! You know my sister?'

'Of course. Rachel. From those days when she sat with us in your mother's home – sometimes she sat on my lap. We've corresponded occasionally. But it was only when I wrote and mentioned I was to meet you – a surgeon called Michael that I'd got to know – that she put two and two together.'

Michael wanted to wet his lips on his drink but Felice had pinned him down with a hard eye.

'Your sister!' She shook her head once. 'Your own sister. She grieves for you.' He was taken aback by her anger. 'I found that cruel: that a man could become so hard. For me, Michael, loyalty to family is everything. As an African, I am not alone in believing that. That's why I didn't want to know you any more.'

Michael was sickened by the way Felice presented it. He nodded –

322

to accept her verdict. Then he sighed, liberated, for a burden of secrecy had been lifted. He wanted to tell her everything. To expose his withered soul.

'Perhaps I should try to explain – although it's far too late.' Her face was still set in anger but she indicated with a small nod of her head that he should continue. He took a quick sip of his drink, and made himself remember. 'Both my parents were killed on the road as they returned home from dropping me at the railway station on my way to school. Died in that bloody Anglia. I might add that they would have asked God for protection before their journey: it was their trusting habit.' He paused to take a deep breath. 'This I learnt within twenty-four hours of the death of my best friend, Simon.'

'I didn't know about your friend.'

'Simon and I fell out of the window of the train on that same journey – an accident in retrospect, although I was to some degree culpable: there was a moment when I wished him dead, when I might have saved him. We both went through the window; except that I got a grip on the sill and hung there until rescued, knowing that Simon must be dead beside the tracks. I blamed myself without reservation at the time.'

He looked stony-faced at his Tropical Sundae Surprise.

'After that I had to come to terms with four deaths – my parents, Simon's and God's. The first three bereavements would've been bad enough, but the death of God – well – let's just say that I was a very trusting child. I was a clay pot crushed.'

He cleared his throat, picked the garish paper adornments from his drink, dropped them onto the table and took a large draught. Felice waited for him to go on, looking fully at him now, eyes dry.

'My sister and I went to live with my father's elderly aunt near Birmingham. She tried her best, but she was unable to do much more than provide shelter, food and clothing. She was out of her depth, handling two psychologically stunned children. We were sent to different boarding schools. I was on my own.

He stopped to control himself. Felice sat patiently.

'Since I'd been left on my own I decided to stand on my own; to erase Michael the child. I even considered changing my name.'

Felice nodded slowly.

'I buried the child, left him in the African soil. I disowned everything I'd ever been taught and believed. The fairy tales. I was no longer the missionaries' child. Jesus was no longer a friend, just a swear word. I became someone else. Sounds impossible, but it's not. A man can reinvent himself, make a resolution to forget his past, never talk about it and never think about it except in his bad dreams: look at Holocaust survivors, or Nazis after the war.'

He stared out to sea. The horizon looked like the edge of the world; there was a just-visible agitation of the water at the lip, a line of spume; he could imagine the plunge into an emptiness so great that the falling water soon became foam, and then mist, and then vanished. He could see himself swimming out to the lip.

Felice eventually said, 'But you became successful. A surgeon.'

'I remade myself. I went for achievement, and satisfaction in doing a job well. Maybe I helped a few people along the way.' He signalled with a puckering of his cheeks and an out-turning of his hands that he had told her his story.

'But you returned to Uganda.'

'Yes, to the conference. When I accepted the invitation I was sure the past couldn't reach me – but maybe I was looking for something as well. I'd lost Michael of my own volition, but nevertheless it was a fifth bereavement. Perhaps I thought the child was out here somewhere.' He found himself remembering that claustrophobic aisle in the medical school library where he had browsed for insights into Felice's loss, memorising a paragraph here, a sentence there; how he had become distracted by a chapter on childhood bereavement: 'Our sense of self, our identity, is largely dependent on the internal narrative that we construct about our lives. We are capable of reformulating the story to accommodate unexpected and difficult events, but an overwhelming trauma may remain unstoried. A child may be unable to integrate the event into their narrative, they suffer dissociation, their sense of self becomes dislocated ...'

324

He tried to stab the cherry in his glass with a cocktail stick but it bobbed away from him. 'Here in Africa I started seeing malign spirits. A vacuum in me – call it spiritual if you want – sucked in malevolent ghosts. Deaths, feathers, fetishes took on sinister meanings. Then I met you. I suppose you represented something of my family to me – I must have sensed it in you: the hidden connection. Of course, there's much more: you're a beautiful woman – and the first I truly loved. The first I felt I could tell my story to. Too late.' Felice looked down at her hands. 'Then you rejected me. Other things happened, and I had a breakdown.'

He waited for her to say something but she was burying her ring hand in the other, gripping it tightly. 'I know you believe we have something called a soul, Felice. I did look a little myself for some sort of spirituality in … take-it-or-leave-it vagaries.' He gave a forced laugh. 'While you Africans have gone from animism to Christianity – at least three hundred million of you, I read somewhere – we Europeans have gone from Christianity to animism: reading horoscopes, appeasing demons of poor health, or neurosis, with our shaman-psychoanalysts, worshipping spirits in machines, ascribing to nature magical powers in force lines and energies. Despite our science.'

'But your flesh and blood – your own sister!'

Michael almost smiled, the way she refused to be distracted from the important. She might have added what Simon had said, with unwitting insight, on that fateful railway platform to his mother: It's about *love*.

He said, 'Rachel grew up saintly. She reminded me of all I wished to forget. I couldn't bear it.' He tried not to think of his sister. He might blub, as the child Michael would have said. 'I made the wrong decision. I reacted the wrong way, Felice. But I was overwhelmed by what had happened to me. I was just a child.'

She nodded slowly, sadly, and said, 'I understand better now.'

'I never stood a chance: your customs, your traditional ways.'

She looked pained. 'Maybe you should be like us Africans and listen to your ancestors.'

He sighed. 'There'd be no progress if …'

But Felice talked over him as if she could see it all now. 'You've uprooted yourself from the soil you grew in, Michael. You've cut yourself off from your inheritance.'

'Inheritance?'

She nodded. 'Your inheritance of love. Now you're all dried up.'

The sapping heat seemed to confirm her.

'I was a quirky, unusually pious child, Felice. Too trusting. I wouldn't want to go back.'

'You didn't have to go back to a child's understanding. You could have budded in other ways, out of the soil you found yourself in. You could have taken strength from your ancestors, learnt something from them even if you wished to make a different life, become a different tree.'

He felt a plea in her analysis, but for what purpose? 'If I'm such a detestable man, and I can appreciate why you judged me so, then why did you want to see me again?'

She leant a little towards him, a coil of her hair falling off her shoulder. 'Michael, I …' She hesitated, snatched a breath and said in a rush, 'I wanted to apologise for my behaviour when we last met, and to tell you about me and Zachye.'

'You could've done all that in a letter.' He spoke wearily.

Felice unclasped her hands, lifting them from her lap, and placed them on the table so that her fingertips were not far from his. He saw her new ring again, but she had raised her eyes to his. 'I wanted to see you, Michael. Face to face.' He returned her gaze. She did not look away. 'I just wanted to see you. It's very selfish and … it will damn us both.' The tears came again but this time ran unchecked.

He was swept by currents of pain. 'I thought you considered me to be … just out to flatter you.'

She composed herself. 'Sorry – these indulgent tears. You did flatter me when we first met, but I thirsted for it. You must understand that Stanley was a fine man, I loved him, but he didn't always demonstrate his love for me in ways I needed. So when you showed me such appreciation, made it easy to laugh, and … OK, I wanted to be held,' she cast him a colluding look. 'It was hard to remain faithful. But then when my time with Stanley came to an end … I can't deny it, my heart was drawn, Michael.'

Michael felt his heart quicken.

She spoke softly. 'I would've had to break the tradition of my people, marrying you instead of Stanley's brother, or some other member of his clan. But with Zachye as he was, I had some hopes that my family would give my relationship with you their blessing.'

'And when Zachye sought forgiveness you gave it. I would've liked to have had the same chance.'

'How, Michael? My explaining the problem? How would I have known that you were sincere?' Her voice was now so quiet that he hardly heard her say, 'But now I understand you. If only I had known these things before.'

She looked at him as if waiting for him to respond.

'Can you break your engagement?' he murmured.

She shook her head with finality. 'No, I cannot. I have vowed.' She seemed to be concentrating on controlling her breathing. Of course, she would not be the Felice he loved and admired if she were to break a vow.

'Felice,' he said, his voice uncertain.

'Yes?' She was almost inaudible. Her eyes were searching his again.

'I'm staying at the Baobab Hotel. I'll leave tomorrow and will not contact you again, but …' He paused. She still held him with her eyes; she appeared vulnerable, sweetly so. 'Please come to me this evening.'

She broke away, looking out at the ocean for what seemed to Michael to be an age. Then she moved her hands lightly onto his.

'I'll come, Michael. After that you must promise to leave me to my duties. I've eternity to think of.' He saw that she attempted a smile for him. 'I mean – a greater good.'

He nodded once and smiled back, but when he tried to take her hands she said, 'I must go. I'm expected back at work.' He stood up with her but she motioned him to sit down. 'Let me go. I'll see you this evening at about sundown.'

Back at the beachfront, outside his hotel, Michael walked along the shore, curiously carefree – as if there was no tomorrow – feeling the sand as soft as ground almonds beneath his bare feet, hearing the tender rustling of the palms in the light breeze off the ocean, breathing in the dream-filled air. He thought he caught the scent of cloves from the island of Zanzibar, out to sea. The tide was turning, the sea drawing up its lacy skirt to reveal the bejewelled garter of the coral reef. Paradise on earth. She would be giving herself to him at last. He could not think of afterwards. Carpe diem.

The beach became narrower as a low coral cliff from a past age rose along the shoreline, overhanging the sand. A jumble of dead roots, white as bleached bones, formed an untidy meshwork under the overhang. Something red, like a splash of blood under the roots, startled him, making him stop and bend down to investigate. It was just a bright strawberry-top shell; he laughed at himself, at his vivid imagination.

He returned to sipping at his thoughts of the evening to come, but finding less pleasure – even a trace of sourness – he turned up a path that cut up into the cliff, hoping to get a view along the coast. At the top he found himself entering a remnant of forest. He took off his sunglasses to see into the foliage. Large trees had created a dense canopy, protecting each other from onshore winds and laying down thick humus on the forest floor. The path looked ill-frequented and he was barefoot, and he was about to turn back when he noticed slabs of stone, at angles, in the undergrowth. Behind the stones, almost hidden by a bougainvillea bush long gone native, he saw the remains of a small building and, around its crumbling brick walls, blackened tiles from what must have been its roof: an old cemetery with a chapel in a neglected grove; fallen headstones; the dislocated limbs of crosses. Curious, he pulled aside the vegetation to read a faded inscription, now just a darker staining of mould from that on the rest of the stone, the sea air having corroded away the relief. Ghosts of an inscription: '… loving memory …' Then below: '1898 …', the rest indecipherable. There were more headstones: 'Beloved mother of …', 'With Christ, which is far better', 'Aged 31', 'Loving father'.

It struck him: this was the coast where his great-grandfather Thomas

Price had come ashore. Wading ashore when his boat sank. Buried in this country, he didn't know where. Were his bones here? Unlikely; but somewhere in this land – not far. And his grandparents, his father and his mother in the same African soil. All gone. His ancestors, all forgotten. Cut off. He bent down and touched the stone.

'… loving memory …'

It came to him then – the long suppressed grief, like a wave from the sea, in that broken garden. He sank to his knees and remembered, and wept. Wept for his childhood loss. Shafts of light moved amongst the splintered stones and traced the passage of an hour. He supported himself on the limbs of a cross. Later his breath, hard, hungry at first, grew stilled.

When he was spent, emptied of sorrow, relieved of his burden, the ghosts of his ancestors spoke to him at last and he listened. Sweat formed sticky as blood on his brow. He gripped a headstone as they came to him one by one: Thomas, his great-grandfather; Arthur, his grandfather; Bernard, his father; and lastly, so near now that he could see her face for the first time since her death, his mother.

After the ghosts had finished talking he unbuttoned his shirt pocket and took out two small envelopes, one containing his mother's ring and the other the ring that he had bought for Felice. He returned his mother's ring to his pocket, then scooped away the soft earth at the foot of a gravestone with his hands; he kept going until his fingers were mirey and chafed. Taking Felice's ring from its envelope, he buried it deep in the soil.

He stood, unsteadily, and returned to the beach, struggling to make progress against the hot shifting sand under his feet, staggering like a man concussed towards the water. Near the water's edge the beach became as hard as cement. His ancestors had spoken: he could no longer meet Felice in the hotel. It would be an act of violation against her; against her faith, which required fidelity in all things; an act of neocolonisation. If he loved her he should leave her. Now.

Small waves broke around his ankles but he did not feel them. He saw a break in the thin white line of the reef where a channel led to the ocean beyond. A kind oblivion. The water flowed around his knees with such tender ease. Soon it would bear him out from the same shore that his great-grandfather had waded in on.

It took time for the scream behind him and the shouts that followed to reach him, but when the shouts persisted he turned his head distractedly and saw two children in the shallows nearby. The younger, a girl, was crying loudly, and the other, a boy, was calling to him, waving at him to come. Michael turned back towards the ocean. The boy stopped shouting but the girl continued sobbing. Michael saw a dhow in the gap in the reef, its age-stained sail billowing in the wind. Still the child cried. He heard again his ancestors speak, showing him the letter his grandfather had given him as a child concerning his great-grandfather's death: how he had stayed. With the reluctance of driftwood lumber turned by the tide he faced the shore, and waded towards the children.

The girl was sitting on the sand now, holding her foot, still crying.

'*Amekanyaga kishimb*a,' the boy said.

Michael saw black sea urchin spines in the pink sole of her foot. They had broken off and would dissolve, but he knelt down, rinsed the soil from the graveyard off his hands, gently lifted the child's foot and blew on it. She stopped crying with a final shudder.

'Where's your home?' he asked.

The children stared blankly at him.

'I'll take you to the hotel.'

He held out his hand. The girl looked at the boy, but he nodded to reassure her and Michael helped the child up.

Along the beach two people approached: a woman, her blue shawl and kanga flapping as she hurried towards them, and a long way off, a man, walking with purposeful gait. The woman stopped, breathless, in front of Michael and lifted the child, said '*Asante*' and bowed her head appreciatively. She took her children and returned along the beach, leaving Michael looking out to sea again. He watched the ever-roiling surf on the reef, felt the moon's rhythmic suck and release of the helpless waters; saw his body fall like a slowly revolving black feather into the impassive depths. The ocean did not care. He turned away.

Setting his face, he walked briskly away from the water to go back to his hotel. To pack and leave for London.

He took a line along the beach so that he would give the man coming the other way a wide berth, but the man turned to intersect him. Michael prepared to fend off a hawker, but saw that his hands were empty (no pink-lipped shells or silvery fish hanging from a string through their gills) and that he was well dressed: a flashy blend of bright colour and good fit.

'Greetings, Dr Lacey! Do you remember me? I've been looking for you.'

Michael stopped and stared. Zachye appeared larger, more substantial than the sly and sinuous man whom he remembered, and carried an aura of wealth, from his pointed red-leather shoes to his multicoloured collarless shirt, to the heavy gold chain around his neck, to his wrap-around sunglasses. Even his voice sounded richer – deeper and more resonant.

'You've changed,' Michael said flatly. 'It's a surprise to see you.' And very unwelcome, he thought.

'I should be in Kampala, but came back earlier today.' Zachye spoke in a relaxed manner, as if passing the time of day with a friend.

'So why are you looking for me?'

'When I got back I visited my fiancée and saw she had been weeping. I asked her why. She told me she'd seen you. She asked my forgiveness.'

Michael waited for him to go on but Zachye was nodding at him, knowingly, but without menace.

'And did you give it?' Michael asked.

'Yes, I gave my forgiveness.'

'Then there's no need to say any more. I'm leaving now for London.' He made to move past.

Zachye did not attempt to restrain him, but said, 'Do you love her, Doctor?'

Michael stopped, looked beyond Zachye down the beach and said emphatically, 'Yes, enough to leave her – to let her keep faith with the life she's chosen. I'm going back to Britain.'

331

Zachye nodded again as if this was not a surprise. 'Do you believe a man can be saved, Dr Lacey?'

Michael hesitated. Only that morning he would have considered such a question meaningless. He said, 'Yes. From himself.'

'Now I'm peaceful too, Dr Lacey. My father – my ancestors – I've honoured them.'

Michael met his eye and said, 'It seems neither of us can escape our family heritage, our past.'

'On the matter of my past, Doctor, I have some information for you that is between you and me alone. I've been to Kampala to meet my agent, but I also visited a clinic. I've taken a test for HIV, thinking of the future. You'll not be surprised to hear that I'm positive.'

It should not have surprised him, but Zachye had delivered the news with such calm that it took Michael some time to feel its impact.

'I'm not long for this world. Sometime soon Slim will find me,' Zachye added, as if he needed to make himself plain.

Michael took in Zachye's strong shoulders, full frame and firm stance. It was hard to believe that before long the disease would take hold.

'I had it coming, you could say. But for now I'm still fit.'

'Does your fiancée know?'

'She does not.' A question went unasked, but Zachye answered it. 'She's free of HIV. You see, I have not been with her. I have respected her wishes during our betrothal. Those missionaries were a bad influence, don't you think?' He chuckled. 'I hope you, yourself, are free of HIV, Dr Lacey. Those beautiful ladies at the truck-stops were not too careful in those days.'

Michael found himself saying, 'Can I help in any way?' although his words sounded like a social nicety, rather than a genuine offer.

Zachye threw back his head and laughed. 'Dr Lacey! I'm not looking for your assistance. No – my songs are on the radio. I'm bold. I tell the young people about AIDS. My rhythms are from the old Bahima recitations that I knew as a boy. I never forgot them. They speak to the new generation. While I'm able I'll play.'

'Very laudable,' Michael said, his comment a little barbed, unable to give Zachye credit.

'But I must think of Felice.' Zachye took off his shades and looked intently at Michael, as if he wished to see into his soul. 'I'm going to break my engagement to her.'

For a moment Michael believed he had misunderstood him, Zachye's accent making 'break' sound like 'back'. But the way Zachye was looking at him now, watching for his response, told him he had heard right.

'That's a bit extreme. I thought you'd forgiven her.'

'You're not understanding me. I love her as you do. I loved her before you. I'm breaking because it will free her of her obligation.'

Michael looked down at Zachye's red shoes, unable to speak; giddy from Zachye's words.

Zachye spoke again, but with less self-confidence. 'On the night that Stanley died I entered his room through the window. He was conscious. You may believe, Doctor, that I harmed him, but it is not so. I could not speak for shame, but Stanley had words that our father had spoken to him. Our father said that we must walk a new walk.' He paused. 'At that time I was not ready.'

Michael looked up at Zachye. Although he remained steady in his stance, Zachye was looking beyond Michael, dreamily.

When his attention returned Zachye said quietly, 'Let's shake hands on our deal, Doctor. We're brothers now.'

Zachye stepped forward and extended his hand, gold rings catching the sun. Michael took his hand. They stood there for a long time, each feeling the weight of the other's soul.

Zachye spoke once more before they parted. 'You should go back to London first. Give Felice some time. Let her determine her own heart. No doubt she will consult with Ruhanga and with her ancestors.'

Michael dozed on the aeroplane, breathing easily, remembering; opening a channel for love that had nothing to hide, a channel to receive the love of the dead, that he might find a love for the living. Then he turned to practical matters: he must start that link between his own department and the Ugandan surgical students. He opened his eyes as it struck him that he might help sponsor a surgeon at Lwesala – even visit again to help set up the arrangement. And he must contact Rachel ... get to know his nephew.

He settled back and fell asleep, dreaming of a woman with cowry-shell earrings and perfect white teeth. She had a diamond ring on her finger. It was natural and right that it was his mother's.

Far below him the bones of his ancestors lay in the red earth; lay with the bones of Zachye's ancestors; in the same soil. Their ghosts whispered over the grasslands, lakes, mountains and cities; casting small bright patches, seen by those who cared to look.

ACKNOWLEDGEMENTS

A writer stands on, or at least leans on, the shoulders of others. I will always be grateful to the late Corinne Souza of Picnic Publishing Ltd for publishing the first edition and for her encouragement and kindness. Thanks also to the expert team at Troubador for the second printing. Members of Leicester Writers' Club made insightful suggestions and Rod Duncan and Chris d'Lacey offered invaluable comments on the draft as did Ann Meatyard, Margaret Norton, Stephen Paver, Alison Platts, Suzanne Sharp, Alison Timmins, Jan Tozer, Doug Watt, Liz West and Nigel West. My eternal gratitude to Marietta and my family for their love and support.

For reading group questions and information on Andrew JH Sharp's other novels visit www.andrewjhsharp.co.uk

QUOTATIONS

'What a friend we have in Jesus', Joseph M. Scriven (1855)
'All good gifts around us', Matthias Claudius (1782)
'Jesus bids us shine', Susan B. Warner (1868)
'When he cometh, when he cometh', William Orcutt Cushing (1866)
Ugandan National Anthem, words by George Wilberforce Kakomoa
'To Hope', John Keats (1815)

Extracts from the Authorised Version of the Bible (King James Bible), the rights in which are vested in the Crown, are reproduced by permission of the Crown's Patentee, the Cambridge University Press.

This is a work of fiction. Although I have had first-hand experience of the geographical and historical settings, all characters depicted come from my imagination and any resemblance to real persons, living or dead, is coincidental. Similarly, institutions described are not a real-life portrayal of past or present institutions.